THE EVERGREEN HEIR

ALSO BY A.K. MULFORD

The Five Crowns of Okrith
The High Mountain Court
The Witches' Blade
The Rogue Crown
The Evergreen Heir

The Okrith Novellas
The Witch of Crimson Arrows
The Witch Apothecary
The Witchslayer

THE EVERGREEN HEIR

THE FIVE CROWNS OF OKRITH, BOOK FOUR

A.K. MULFORD

HARPER Voyager

An Imprint of HarperCollins*Publishers*

THE EVERGREEN HEIR. Copyright © 2023 by A.K. Mulford. Excerpt from *A River of Golden Bones* © 2023 by A.K. Mulford. All rights reserved. Printed in the United States of America. No part of this book may be used or reproduced in any manner whatsoever without written permission except in the case of brief quotations embodied in critical articles and reviews. For information, address HarperCollins Publishers, 195 Broadway, New York, NY 10007.

HarperCollins books may be purchased for educational, business, or sales promotional use. For information, please email the Special Markets Department at SPsales@harpercollins.com.

Harper Voyager and design are trademarks of HarperCollins Publishers LLC.

FIRST EDITION

Map © 2022 Kristen Timofeev

Chapter opener tree branches © Golden Shrimp / Shutterstock

Library of Congress Cataloging-in-Publication Data has been applied for.

ISBN 978-0-06-329174-4 (paperback)
ISBN 978-0-06-332020-8 (hardcover library edition)

23 24 25 26 27 LBC 7 6 5 4 3

Dedicated to everyone brave enough to be their true selves in a world that feels like it wasn't made for them. Keep being brave xx

CONTENT WARNING

This book contains themes of violence, death, loss, fire, misgendering, ableism, and addiction, as well as sexually explicit scenes.

Okri

No

Murreneir

Valtene

High Mount

Yexshi

Swifthill

Western Court

Silver Sands Harb

Sea of Callipho

n

rn Court

ourt

Sea of Wetamuir

Rotted Peak

Wynreach

Eastern Court

Crushwold

uthern Court

Saxbridge

N
W E
S

THE EVERGREEN HEIR

CHAPTER ONE

N eelo's fingers trembled as they traced down the spines of the old tomes. They took a slow breath, and then another, letting the old book smell steady them.

They couldn't marry him.

The thought came as fast as the engagement had: their mother inciting another brawl to win the title of Neelo's betrothed, the instant, blundering chaos, and somehow Talhan Catullus getting pulled into the fray. The look on Talhan's face flashed through Neelo's mind again. When it was over, he'd just stared at them—shocked. The cavalier smirk he normally wore was wiped clean and something deeper, something that burned into Neelo, had filled Talhan's gaze instead.

Why did it have to be him?

Of all the people Neelo could've easily dismissed . . . why did it have to be the Golden Eagle himself? He was one of the few people in Neelo's life who didn't make them feel like a thorn amongst the roses, and now their mother had ruined that for them too.

Queen Emberspear's increasingly desperate bids to play matchmaker were growing weary already, but this time, she'd really messed up. She'd chosen Neelo's friend. Their mother had pushed for Neelo's coronation the moment they came of age, citing her waning health from the witching brew that addled her mind, but Neelo knew the Queen simply wanted all of the revelry of a Southern Court royal without any more of the responsibility. Life was already a party to her, the least the Queen could do was deign to rule her people from time to time too.

It was a constant battle to convince the Queen to remain on her throne, one that Neelo felt constantly teetering on the precipice of losing, which meant their head would soon be next to bear the crown. Neelo hated imagining it; standing all alone in front of the masses, feeling the needling scrutiny of a thousand eyes upon them, and the inevitable disappointment that an introverted bookworm was now the ruler of their court of debauchery. No, Neelo refused to allow their mother to give up so easily. It wasn't her time to go.

Neelo paused, fingers lingering on a title they'd never read before: *The Witch of Haastmouth*. A tingle shot through them as they selected the midnight-blue book from the tall shelf and flicked through the pages. It was written in Mhenbic, the witches' language. Most fae didn't learn to read Mhenbic, thought it was beneath them, but Neelo had taught themselves to read all three languages of human, witch, and fae before they could even speak. Well, that wasn't entirely true. Neelo *could* speak, they just chose not to for the first five years of their life . . . and mostly regretted starting ever since. The written word was their first language and stories had always made more sense to them. It was real life—and interacting with real people—that was confusing.

They glanced around the library of Murreneir. The shelves were only half filled and the further Neelo crept into the library, the sparser they became. The grand, circular room still smelled of fresh varnish and wood dust from its hasty construction. Neelo was impressed they'd managed to finish the build before the party at all. The old, worn carpets and dusty leather-bound tomes sat in stark juxtaposition to the fresh candlesticks and perfect blue satin chairs that looked as though they'd never been sat in. The library's future beauty was clear, though, and Neelo planned to return when it was truly completed.

The momentary reprieve disappeared at the sound of the library door creaking open.

Neelo rushed down the stacks, hoping to disappear amongst the scant rows, but as they turned the corner, swift footsteps followed. They climbed up four steps on a rolling ladder before Talhan Catullus turned the corner and they froze.

"I knew I'd find you here." His molten gold eyes landed upon them. Crossing his arms and leaning into the nearest shelf, he asked, "Were you about to hide from me on top of that bookshelf?"

Neelo's voice dripped with sarcasm as they gave him a scornful look. "I was dusting." They fought the urge to mention the fact that this library was too new to have collected dust.

"With your jacket?"

"No!" they said, though they looked down to check if they were covered in soot.

Talhan's smile disappeared into something more contemplative, and Neelo's pulse began to race.

"Neelo," Talhan whispered, making their stomach clench at the sound of their name on his lips. "I—"

"She'll forget in the morning," Neelo cut him off. Bristling, they took a further step down the ladder and met Talhan's eyes. Those eyes . . . like pools of amber—the sun just after dawn . . .

Neelo hated that look on Talhan's face as his lips parted and he said, "Oh?"

"Don't worry. I'm not going to let her tie you to me," Neelo reassured him, gripping the rail of the ladder tighter. Its wheels wobbled, probably newly greased. "I won't let her do that to you."

Talhan took another step closer, his hand perching on the shelf beside Neelo's waist. "And what if I *want* to be tied to you?"

Heart pounding, Neelo shook their head. "What you'd be getting yourself into . . . you don't understand what that means."

"Then show me what it means." His low, gravelly voice made their toes curl in their boots. "What if I come visit Saxbridge? I could stay until the Solstice and—"

"In the heat?" Neelo scoffed. "You Easterners melt into a puddle in the Southern summer. It's the worst time to—"

"Neelo." Talhan said their name again, like a chant, like a prayer even as it chided.

"Okay, yes." They sighed, folding their arms tightly across their chest. "Come visit. In the summer." They rolled their eyes up to the blank ceiling they were certain would soon display beautiful frescoes. "Then you'll understand why this is a bad idea."

Talhan shuffled closer still. He lifted his hand and, for a moment, Neelo thought he might touch their black velvet jacket, but his hand dropped lower and he plucked the book from their hands.

"Have you found one you haven't read yet?" he asked, smoothing his large, calloused hand over the linen-bound tome. Gods, the way he touched that cover, as if that little witch story was worthy of such reverence. It made Neelo's own palms—and other parts—buzz. They could still feel the texture of the fabric rubbing beneath their own fingertips.

"We shall see." Neelo blew out a soft breath. "Sometimes it's a translated title from Ific or Yexshiri, and I've actually read the story before in another language."

Talhan's eyebrows shot up. "You can read in Yexshiri?"

"Of course." Neelo's lip curved to one side, the closest to a grin they seemed to be able to muster. "Can't you?"

"I can barely read Ific," Talhan said ruefully.

He passed the book back to Neelo, and, as they took it, Talhan's long index finger grazed the back of their hand. Neelo's breath hitched as his finger slowly trailed away. It was such a small, intimate gesture, like the tiniest bolt of lightning zinged straight through them, and yet it was almost too much.

Neelo's eyes dropped back to the book and Talhan reached out again, his finger gently touching their chin and lifting their gaze.

"I—"

The door burst open, followed by the sound of heeled boots clicking across the polished wood. Talhan retreated a step as Rish turned the corner. Neelo's personal attendant looked harried. Sweeping her black locks off her face, the green witch adjusted her emerald gossamer shawl around her shoulders like a songbird ruffling her feathers.

Neelo's face morphed back to its normal sharp countenance. "What's she done this time?"

"Forgive me," Rish panted, a sheen of sweat covering her flushed cheeks. "Do you remember that time in Southport?"

"Gods," Neelo cursed, giving Talhan a quick, apologetic look. "I need to go."

Talhan took a step toward Rish. "Where's Rua? She's the host. Why can't she handle this?"

"She's with Bri," Rish said, already turning toward the door.

He quirked his brow. "And where's Bri?"

Neelo stepped off the ladder and pushed past Talhan, the fabric of their sleeve brushing against his muscled torso. "I'm coming. Don't worry."

"Wait," Talhan said, taking Neelo by the hand, his brows pinching together in concern.

Neelo looked down to where their hands touched and swallowed as the sensation made their whole body warm. "I'll see you in Sax-bridge," they whispered, yanking their hand away and thundering off after their green witch, unsure if they were happy or distraught for this new crisis because it meant getting away from Talhan's gaze.

CHAPTER TWO

Neelo dusted the charcoal from the pencil stub onto their sleeve and flipped the letter over, studying each of the sentences as if they might've missed something the first hundred times they'd read it. Their mind whirred as they tried to grasp answers just beyond their reach. What was that violet witch, Adisa Monroe, planning for the Southern Court?

Condensation beaded down the windowpane beside them like droplets of sweat. The hatches to the tunnels below Saxbridge Palace had been opened, emitting cool air to combat the springtime heat. Soon it would be scorching—the season when gowns turned to sundresses, breeches crept shorter, and colorfully dyed veils were needed to protect from biting insects and the blinding summer sun . . .

But Neelo Emberspear remained in their black jacket, swapping only from velvet to satin, and long charcoal-gray trousers of a lighter blend. Practice kept them from overheating . . . that and a general lack of exertion.

Neelo had no idea why they were built like a workhorse, their stout muscular frame hiding under a layer of soft flesh. Along with their ever-present scowl, their size and breadth kept most people from pestering them and Neelo loved their body for it. Still, Neelo preferred loose clothing that didn't hug their broadness—their shape more of an amorphous rectangle than a soldierly triangle or curving hourglass.

Lounging upon the bench seat in the vacant council chamber, Neelo wiped at the wet window and peered out at the vibrant gardens that stretched out to the forest beyond. To the right sat a large oak desk with drawers stuffed with parchment and quills. A tattered centuries-old map of the Southern Court hung on the wall and a beautiful round table was positioned in the center of the room. The table and chairs were constructed of pale wood, tinged in red, built from the *amasa* tree—the evergreen emblazoned on the Southern Court crest. The council chamber had a modest library, mostly filled with dusty old histories and long-winded manuscripts about court politics. Along the far wall by the windows was a gallery of oil paintings and marble statues of the Gods.

This was a stagnant part of the castle, infrequently visited apart from when the Queen bothered to attend a meeting. The servants would spend weeks afterward cleaning and scrubbing the marble statues—many precious pieces of art almost destroyed in the cloud of smoke their mother left in her wake.

She wasn't here, now, though, and that meant Neelo could have some peace. There was one window in particular that Neelo liked to read under. It was originally a flaw in the design, a window in the middle of a neat line of oil paintings. But the designer dressed the window in a matching silver frame to hide the imperfection . . . turning the view of the balcony and lawns into an ever-changing painting.

A fluffy gray tabby cat purred loudly on Neelo's lap, his fur covering the crumpled letter balanced on Neelo's knee. Neelo stroked a hand over Indi's tufted ears as he leaned into their scratches. After finding him as an abandoned kitten covered in dye outside of the weaver's, Indigo—Indi—seemed like the perfect fit. Many people in Saxbridge favored names ending with "O" and, like many others, Neelo shortened it to a nickname. The stray kitten took quite nicely to royal life. Indi haunted the library during the daylight hours, keeping the lizards and mice at bay, and slept at the foot of Neelo's bed at night. But occasionally on mornings such as this one, he would deign to venture beyond the library so long as there was a comfortable lap to cuddle in.

Neelo circled their charcoal pencil around the word "witches" again. The letter from the Northern Queen was stained with Neelo's markings, blurring the ink into barely legible lines.

Neelo had asked Rua to send the letter after a chaotic conversation through the magical fae fires. Rua's frantic voice still seemed to race off the page. Her words about the *sickeningly sweet smoke* and the *cursed witches* were unclear and rushed, warning Neelo of an impending threat to the Southern Court—a promise from the former prince of the Eastern Court, Augustus Norwood, but with little in the way of details. Whatever the Norwood prince had planned for the Southern Court, his intentions were vague, but Rua seemed convinced that those plans were already in motion.

Neelo's mouth tightened as they circled the words in Rua's letter another time, as if this act would divine the future: violet witches, curse, smoke, Adisa Monroe, Augustus Norwood, Cole Doledir. How were these all connected to the Southern Court and, specifically, how were these three players tied together? An ancient immortal violet witch, a bratty fae prince, and a brown witch healer who felt compelled to flee from a dinner table in Murreneir only a few moons ago. Their intentions felt completely out of reach to Neelo, if connected at all.

The hairs on their arm stood on end and they felt that static thread of fear. A faceless storm was coming for their court, and they needed to unmask it before the South befell the same fate as the assassinated Western Court Queen.

Mind whirling once more, they focused on the prince. Had Augustus Norwood perished with his fleet in the Southern storms as rumors would believe or was he still a part of the violet witch's plans? The Eastern Court didn't have enough guidance without a king to direct a full search of their court, maybe he was still hiding there, along with the traitor, Cole Doledir.

Neelo's strained eyes trailed up to the long, white gravel road that wound through the palace gates and into the city of Saxbridge. They imagined an army of violet witches battering down their gates, a storm of violet smoke advancing with them. A few dawdling servants wandered the road, carrying baskets and leading pack mules, and there were no storms on the horizon, nor any fae warriors riding into town either.

But it was easy to see the attack. Too easy.

"He just sent word," Rish said and Neelo jumped, catching the letter midair.

Indi flew off Neelo's lap and landed with a mewling chirp. The tabby cat's tail swished back and forth and he narrowed his eyes at Rish as if being awoken was a grave insult. He sauntered off, presumably back to hunt lizards in the library.

"Rish," Neelo said, scowling as they took a calming breath. "Don't do that."

Neelo scooped the letter off the floor and set it back in their lap. They hadn't reached any conclusions about the impending threat before the green witch snuck up on them, but it was no matter. Rua's letter was a dead end. Neelo wouldn't find the answer to save their court from that one charcoal-stained page.

"He is leaving Swifthill before the Western Court funerals," Rish continued, unworried at Neelo's surprise. The stout little witch adjusted her forest-green apron around her neck, her clothing dusted with corn flour.

She smelled of ginger and cinnamon, and Neelo wondered if she was making her sweet bean cakes. Their stomach grumbled and Neelo had to redirect their thoughts back to the conversation. Rish was still talking, and they hadn't heard a word she'd said . . .

". . . and for whatever reason, he believes it is important to get here with haste." Rish cocked a slender black eyebrow at Neelo as a knowing smirk pulled at her lips.

"He will see this court through fresh eyes during his trip, I'm sure." Neelo rubbed their fingers across the gold inlaid letters of the books on the shelf behind them. "He'll probably turn tail and run when he realizes it's more than drinking and partying."

Placing a plump hand on her hip, Rish snickered. "We shall see."

"Who in their right mind would want this?" Neelo gestured out to the gazebo in the middle of the gardens where five courtiers were taking turns placing pink fruits atop their heads and shooting them off with blunted arrows. One fool already wore an eye patch.

The courtiers of the Southern Court differed from the ones of other royal courts. Though Queen Emberspear called them "courtiers," they served much more *intimate* purposes. Some were in committed relationships with their mother and each other, others were flavors of the week, flitting in and out at their leisure, the group constantly expanding and contracting in size. Neelo saw no point in trying to learn their names or faces, preferring the group to be blurs in their periphery and nothing more. Though some did seem to truly love their mother, most of them seemed like they were simply hiding from lives they didn't want to face, all in the relative comfort of the royal home. The revelry of Saxbridge was the perfect place to hide. Still, Neelo didn't understand why any of them would accept the invitation to live in the palace and serve the Queen that way . . . but then again Neelo didn't understand how to navigate desire at all.

Rish's chuckle interrupted Neelo's swirling thoughts. The green witch clasped her hands together and rested her forearms on her belly. "When has Talhan Catullus ever been in his right mind?"

"Was there another reason you interrupted me?" Neelo asked, trying to change the subject as they selected a book from the shelf and rhythmically rubbed their thumb down the soft cream pages, enjoying the sound like shuffling a deck of cards. "Or was it just to tell me the Golden Eagle is flying south?"

Rish grimaced. "The Queen wishes to speak with you."

"Of course." Neelo sighed. "Where is she?"

Shuffling her weight from foot to foot, Rish said, "In the bathhouses."

"Of course," Neelo echoed with a cringe.

They glanced longingly at their book, but it was too precious to bring into the steam rooms and ruin the pages. Neelo stood and lifted the cushioned bench seat under their favorite window, revealing a selection of stories hidden underneath. They replaced the book in their hands back onto the shelf and picked up a small burgundy title. It wasn't a beautifully poetic story, but it was entertaining and short . . . and Neelo had four copies, so they didn't mind if it accidentally got wet.

The Gods knew they weren't going anywhere without a book, though.

They tucked it into their jacket pocket and pulled down their bunching hem. Straightening their shoulders, they looked halfway to Rish, their eyes not quite meeting hers, and said, "Gods, spare me."

Rish guffawed. "I don't think even the Gods themselves protect the bathhouses of Saxbridge."

Neelo glowered at the map on the wall displaying their homeland in beautiful relief. "Indeed."

The Southern Court hadn't always been synonymous with debauchery. It was a twisted version of their actual history, which prized beautiful gardens, delicious cooking, vibrant colors, and all different kinds of love. Now, the South was known for drinking, gambling, and fucking . . . and not necessarily in that order.

Neelo had barely stepped out into the corridor before a short, elderly fae converged on them. His salt-and-pepper hair circled his head and his bushy eyebrows reached halfway up his forehead. His face was pinched in permanent condescension.

"You didn't attend the council meeting this morning, Your Highness," the councilor's scratchy voice chased them down the hall. "And yet I find you in the chamber now?"

Neelo's hand instinctively reached for the outline of their book in their pocket. They kept their head bowed as they picked up their pace. "Write up a report as usual, Denton, and I'll reply in kind."

Queen Emberspear only really bothered to liaise with one of the seven councilors—Denton—the most disagreeable fae Neelo had ever known, and Neelo knew far too many.

"We hold the meetings in person for a *reason*, Your Highness," he called, scuttling after them. "There is much back-and-forth. Corresponding in written form takes ten times as long and Her Majesty said you were to begin attending in her stead?"

"My mother is still the Queen," Neelo replied tightly. "She is still the one to whom you should be speaking with. I am merely relaying the information to her."

"But aren't you taking over the throne soon?"

Neelo's footsteps faltered for a second and they ground their teeth together. Queen Emberspear really needed to stop telling people she was abdicating. She might have muddled her mind with drink and drugs, but Neelo would fix that. Their mother certainly wasn't beyond saving. And they certainly weren't ready to rule.

"One day, Denton," Neelo said, ducking down another white stone corridor. "But not anytime in the near future. The sooner my mother can get that ridiculous notion out of her head, the better."

Denton stopped in his tracks, stomping his foot with indignation. "The Southern Court doesn't need another Emberspear shirking their duties to their people."

Rage built in Neelo's chest, one that burned them from within, but they didn't dare let it out. How dare he stomp his foot at them? They tamped down on the pressure, knowing that if they exploded at Denton, it would be the talk of the town. Neelo Emberspear was quiet, vacant, and reserved. They were the inverse to their mother in every way and they couldn't just go around shouting at people, regardless of how much that person deserved it.

"You are dismissed, Denton," Neelo gritted out. They opened the nearest door, pausing to let Rish enter before slamming it shut behind them.

Neelo rested their head against the door, hearing Denton's litany of grumbled curses as he stormed off.

"You can't keep avoiding the meetings forever, *mea raga*," Rish said, leaning against the wall beside Neelo.

"Are you a blue witch now?" Neelo taunted. "Have you suddenly developed the gift of Sight?"

"No." Rish breezed toward the lounge seat of the rainbow-hued sitting room. She stared at the high circular window, taking her time before saying, "I think I'll make honey delights for dessert tonight." Rish beckoned for Neelo to sit beside her. "Your favorite."

"You say everything you make is my favorite." Neelo trudged over, shoulders drooping, as they sat beside Rish. "Why do I feel like you're bribing me into sitting for a lecture?"

Rish shrugged. "Because you're smart."

"I already know all the things you're going to say."

"But that doesn't mean it's not worth hearing them again," Rish said with a tsk.

"What is it that I need to hear again?"

Rish reached across the seat and placed her hand over Neelo's own. The green witch was one of the few people Neelo didn't mind touching them. Her gentle hand brought comfort instead of the normal irritation, like the scratch of poorly blended wool. It felt the same holding the gaze of certain people—most people—which was like beetles crawling across their skin. Neelo itched at their arm just thinking about it.

"You can't save your mother from her ways." Rish's voice was so soft Neelo could barely hear it.

"I learned that long ago," Neelo muttered.

"Yes." Rish squeezed their hand again and then pulled it away. "Except you still haven't accepted what that means for you."

"What does it mean?" Neelo grumbled. "Other than further embarrassment?"

"She cannot stay on her throne—you know this," Rish beseeched, but the moment the words left her mouth, Neelo pushed the thought away, the shutters to their mind snapping closed. "You need to take over now."

"Not now."

"Yes, now."

"Rish."

"It is time, *mea raga*." The green witch looked hopefully toward the window. "At least Talhan Catullus will be here soon. At least you won't have to face it alone."

"He's only staying for the Solstice and the Southern Court will give him a million reasons not to stay beyond that," Neelo snapped. Rish raised a knowing eyebrow and Neelo scowled. "I promise you. Talhan Catullus will not want to stay." They stood and smoothed down their bunched jacket, cursing the easily wrinkled material. "Now if you'll excuse me, my mother beckons."

Rish hummed. "I would make a wager with you about Lord Talhan, *mea raga*." Her voice rose, shouting to Neelo as they hastily rushed out of the room. "But I know you are the only Southerner who doesn't make bets!"

CHAPTER THREE

Steam swirled through the thick air, blanketing Neelo's skin. The cloying aroma of floral smoke and oils filled the room along with the sizzle of water being tossed onto hot stones. Neelo could barely make out the shapes of their mother's courtiers. The number always changed, sometimes ten, sometimes fifty, but a handful of them always remained the same. Amongst the group, there were males and females, as well as several fae who, like Neelo, existed between and outside of those blurred lines. Neelo always wondered if their mother had selected those particular courtiers to prove a point to Neelo: it was still possible to be a promiscuous partying Southerner regardless of gender.

Neelo ignored that lesson, as it was irrelevant to them.

Neelo stalked further into the bathhouses, keeping their eyes glued to the floor as naked forms popped into their periphery. There was no such thing as modesty in the Southern Court. Nudity was highly praised and displayed in artwork and sculptures. Still, Neelo bathed in their private chamber, wore loose clothing, and preferred to not draw the eye of any potential suitors, let alone playthings.

"There you are!" The Queen's voice echoed off the low stone ceiling.

Neelo spotted her sitting in a steaming, circular pool. Her black hair was piled atop her head and streaks of kohl ran down her cheeks, but Queen Emberspear still looked regal, even naked in a bath. The only clothes she wore were her dove-gray gloves—an ever-present accessory since the death of the Western Court Queen. Once their mother learned that Queen Thorne had died from touching poisoned cutlery, her gloves never came off. Many of her courtiers took on the fashion as well, without fully understanding why it was so important. Maybe that was what Adisa Monroe had planned for the Southern Court? More poisoned metals?

Two of those closest to the Queen, Farros and Thiago, sat on either side of her in the bath. Thankfully, they weren't naked. Instead they were wrapped in wet green fabric soaked in minty poultices that made Neelo's eyes sting. The witches claimed it was good for clearing the lungs. Whenever Neelo had a cold as a child, Rish would wrap them in warm, wet blankets and make Neelo sit in the steam rooms, breathing in the vapors. It didn't surprise Neelo their mother spent so much time in the place, considering she was constantly wheezing.

Neelo glanced between Thiago's gruff, soldierly face and Farros's soft feminine one. One of these two was certainly Neelo's sire. Though they could never truly confirm, Neelo saw a lot of themself in Thiago's stoicism and Farros's inquisitive nature. They even begrudgingly saw a bit of themself in their mother. The Queen kept people emotionally at a distance by surrounding herself with courtiers, just as Neelo surrounded themself with books. Equally as stubborn.

Neelo hated even acknowledging any such connection.

"What was it that was so urgent it couldn't wait?" Neelo muttered, already knowing it was because if the Queen waited until she was done bathing, she would forget whatever it was she wanted to say.

Queen Emberspear's mind had become a sieve over the past few years, rotting away from excessive drink, drugs, and the potent witching smoke nicknamed *brew*. It was why, in a moment of clarity, the Queen had pushed for Neelo to take the throne. Queen Emberspear didn't think she'd be able to keep herself together for much longer and while Neelo feared their mother was right, they were determined to convince their mother she was wrong.

It didn't help that Neelo wasn't sure *either* of them was right for the throne. Queen Emberspear was the sort of ruler who turned fountain water to wine and flew sparkling lanterns in the sky on a whim. She delighted and mesmerized, giving speeches with her feet dangling over balustrades and throwing hallucinogenic sweets into the crowd. Meanwhile, Neelo would be the sort of ruler to give perfunctory speeches, write decrees with no flowery words, and try to move along any dawdling onlookers as quickly as possible. There would be no more delight in the Southern Court, and their people would hate them for it.

"Talhan Catullus was seen riding past Silver Sands," the Queen said as the lines around her smug eyes deepened. "It seems he is quite hasty to be with you."

"And he'll be just as hasty to leave—he is not staying," Neelo grumbled. "It's only until the Summer Solstice, then he will leave with the others who come to celebrate."

"I thought you had some affection for him?" The Queen snapped her fingers at Farros and he produced her pipe, refilled with more brew. Neelo rolled their eyes. No amount of bathhouse steam would counteract the witching smoke being pulled into her lungs. "Weren't you two friends as children?"

"*Friends,* Mother," Neelo replied. "Nothing more."

Neelo darted a nasty look at Farros for giving the pipe to the Queen, but Farros only gave Neelo a wink back and shrugged his shoulders. There was nothing Farros could do about it. They both knew that. Of all their mother's courtiers, Neelo had grown the closest to Farros over the years. The raven-haired courtier hadn't aged a day since Neelo was young. With deep smile lines, warm hazel eyes, and smooth light brown skin, Farros too eschewed the confines of the rigid fae world—preferring dresses to tunics and makeup to stubble. Neelo had hoped many times that Farros was their other parent, though it was more likely to be Thiago with his darker complexion, thicker brows, and sharp features that matched Neelo's own.

"You need him, Neelo." The Queen's voice pulled them back into the room, abandoning once more their curiosity to uncover the identity of their other parent. It didn't matter. No books or records existed documenting Neelo's parentage, and there were at least a dozen possible candidates—one big, confusing sort of family, Southern Court to the core.

"I don't need anyone," they insisted. Maybe if they denied her a little longer, she'd forget all about her abdication. "You are going to rule for many more years and then I will take over. If you'd only let people help you to—"

"So obstinate." The Queen's cheeks puckered as she puffed on her pipe, the noxious smoke swirling through her dark hair.

"I'm being sensible."

"You're being stubborn. The people don't want a ruler who is smart and *sensible*." Queen Emberspear waved her pipe, whorls of white left in the wake of her gesticulating arms. "They want a ruler who is brave and gallant, like Talhan."

"I'm brave," Neelo muttered under their breath, pulling the book from their jacket pocket and rhythmically thumbing the edges.

"Talhan Catullus is charming, personable, lovable . . ." The Queen eyed them up and down. "All qualities you severely lack." They braced for the sting of her words, but it didn't come. Because it was true. All Neelo was to their mother was *lacking*. "Let him be the face of your court and you can live out your days behind a book just as you have always done." Her pleased smile pulled wider. "You see? I'm only thinking of you."

"How kind, Mother."

"Not everyone is born to be the center of attention. Not everyone can command an army. Let Talhan be that for you and *you* can pull his strings, make the decisions, have time to weigh the pros and cons, as I know you love to do." Neelo looked up into their mother's kohl-lined eyes, a hint of surprise on their face. "I do know a little about you, child."

Neelo snickered. "Yes. You know I'm not charming, not personable, not lovable."

"The love of one's people and the love of a mother are two different things." The Queen rolled her eyes to the ceiling in exasperation. "You know I love you. It hurts that you'd ever doubt it."

This is what Queen Emberspear did so well: she twisted one's words against them, made it seem like it was their mistake and not hers. She always tied the conversations into knots, ones that Neelo couldn't pull apart until hours afterward. It wasn't a fair game; it never was.

"You have many admirable qualities, child, *needed* qualities." The Queen took another drag on her pipe. "But what wins people's affections and what they need are two different things. I have won their love by indulging their every desire . . . and I haven't given them nearly enough of what they need." The glaze in her eyes lifted and her countenance seemed to sharpen. So rarely did she have her wits about her anymore. "That is why you and Talhan are the perfect match, one stoic and logical, one charming and heroic. The perfect pairing of need and desire, if I do say so myself."

"You can't possibly take credit for that brawl you incited in Murreneir."

Puffs of white smoke curled into the steamy air as the Queen arched her brow. "And how many brawls before that one did I so easily forget?"

Neelo's eyes widened. Queen Emberspear was still full of surprises. So absent-minded, it would've been easy enough to convince others she'd forgotten her previous matchmaking attempts, but now it was clear why: she'd been waiting for Talhan Catullus to be pulled into the fray.

"Why him?" Neelo whispered, gripping the edges of their book tighter in their hands.

"Who else *but* him? His alliances speak for themselves." The Queen passed her pipe back to the blond courtier perched behind her. "He is family to the new Western Queens and best friend with the High Mountain King. He spent the winter protecting the Northern Court Queen too . . ." Queen Emberspear shrugged. "Besides, I like him. And I think you do too."

Neelo tucked their book back into their jacket and folded their arms over their chest. "Is that all?"

Their mother nodded, waving her hand and effectively dismissing them. The fog settled back over her hooded eyes as she peeked around the steamy room and waved away more of that sickeningly sweet smoke.

Sickeningly sweet smoke. Neelo had just read that same description in Rua's letter. Their pulse picked up speed as their mind began to race with unanswered questions. Was there some connection between the smoke that clouded the skies of Murreneir the night of Rua's attack and the smoke that Queen Emberspear now pulled into her lungs? Brew was something Neelo had never taken the slightest interest in, but now a lightning strike of inspiration demanded they know more. It was likely another dead end, but Neelo felt the sudden urge to know everything about the making of these potent blends.

Neelo bowed, already forgetting their mother's words as they set their intention to investigate the brew merchants at the docks in the morning. They skirted past Denton who lingered in the doorway, waiting to speak to their mother. Racing down the hall, they tried to get away before they heard another drug-laced laugh or moan from the bathhouses, their mind finally grasping something to research. And if there was one thing Neelo Emberspear was good at, it was research.

It was only halfway down the hall that Neelo remembered a certain Golden Eagle would soon be arriving at the palace. Dread pooled in their stomach. The memory of that moment with Talhan in Murreneir played over and over in their mind. Their mother had picked him for a reason—for a number of reasons, none so easily dismissed . . .

Which would make it that much harder to get rid of him.

NEELO'S SCRATCHY THROAT woke them enough to reach for their glass of water . . . and then the sickening scent hit them.

Smoke.

Their first hazy thought was the violet witches had come for the Southern Court just as they had in Rua's letter, as if they'd manifested the attack by dwelling on it the day before. But this didn't carry the scent of magical smoke. Not the rich smell of candle fires and witching brews.

No, this smelled like an inferno.

Neelo shot up, scanning their darkened bedroom, trying to discern shadow from smoke. Then they heard the screams. Piercing shrieks bounced across the white marble as they leapt out of bed, darting to their wardrobe. They hastily pulled on a double-breasted jacket and tugged their charcoal-gray trousers over their round, muscular thighs.

A guard pounded on the door. "Your Highness!"

"Coming!" Neelo shouted back.

"There's a fire. You must leave at once," the guard called, testing the handle. The golden knob clicked, but the door didn't budge.

Neelo stalked across the room to their personal library. Sea-green shelves stretched all the way up to vaulted ceilings, perfectly cut to fit the sloping roofline. Neelo rolled their bronzed ladder out of the way and opened the gilt-framed glass doors that protected their favorite books—the ones they kept pride of place on the mid-center shelf. They couldn't lose them to the inferno.

Whirling back to their bed, they did up the buttons of their jacket and searched the bed linen for a telltale bump.

"Sorry," Neelo muttered at Indi's indignant mewl as they lifted him up and tucked him inside their jacket.

A towering guard greeted them as they unlocked the door, his body filling the entire doorframe. He frowned down at Indi's little face and then disdainfully at the stack of books in Neelo's hands. Smoke filled the corridor, stinging Neelo's eyes, and they tucked Indi deeper into their jacket to protect his little lungs. They lifted their lapel over their nose and swatted at the impenetrable blanket of stinging smoke.

Hustling after their guard, they bolted down the spiraling stairs, taking them two at a time. The air cleared as they reached the landing to the ground floor and they took a sweet breath of crisp evening air as they stumbled out into the dark gardens.

Circles of servants and courtiers clung to the hedgerow, whispering in shocked, gossiping voices as if this were another one of their many games. Neelo started counting heads. Hundreds of people were already out of the palace, more spilling from the other exits where the smoke didn't seem to reach, but Neelo still couldn't spot the origin of the blaze.

Relief flooded through Neelo as they spotted Rish far across the field, searching undoubtedly for them. Neelo waved to the green witch and watched her shoulders sag as she clutched her totem pouch to her chest.

But someone was still missing . . .

Neelo pulled Indi out of their jacket and set him on a garden bench beside their stack of books. "Guard these for me," Neelo whispered to the cat with a final pat and set a course for the western end of the palace.

"Your Highness," their guard chastised as he hastily followed, "we should stay with the group."

Neelo only picked up the pace, their bare feet stomping along the narrow strip of manicured grass beside the gravel paths.

As they turned the corner, shouts rang out, the castle coming alive as flames licked up from the highest window. Neelo searched for the heart of the blaze . . . and looked straight up to their mother's window.

"The Queen." Neelo twisted toward their guard, scanning the gardens behind him again. "Is she accounted for?"

His eyebrows pinched together in concern, and he didn't respond. Answer enough.

"No," Neelo whispered, staring in horror at the bright orange flames that reached toward the midnight sky.

Without another thought, Neelo bolted toward the smoke-filled archway.

"Your Highness!" the guard screamed, hustling after them.

Neelo's throat constricted as they dove back into the thick cloud of smoke. The shouts of their guard faded away as they raced blindly down the hall. With closed, stinging eyes, they navigated the halls of Saxbridge Palace from memory alone.

Even as the fire raged and their heart thundered, they knew if this was it, people wouldn't be the least bit surprised. If their mother died in an accidental blaze of her own making, Southerners would probably think it was inevitable, only a matter of time before one of the Queen's many stunts finally caught up with her. She'd drank poisons, walked tightropes, thrown axes, played with lions in the menagerie . . . and she had a lit pipe in her hand until the moment she fell asleep. If the stunts didn't catch her, the drinking and drugs would, and the people of Saxbridge would only mourn the party ending.

It was why no one was here now, trying to rescue her. Neelo was certain of it. All of Saxbridge had given up on their Queen . . . all except her heir and only child.

And the last person who should be putting themself in danger as the sovereign-to-be.

The smoke burned into Neelo's eyes and tears streaked down their cheeks. Dropping to their hands and knees, they felt blindly for the top step. In the back of their mind, they already knew, if the Queen was any further ahead, she was gone. But they didn't stop—couldn't— not now, not yet. They weren't ready to be the ruler of the Southern Court.

Neelo wasn't sure they'd ever be ready.

They didn't know if they entered the blaze for some misplaced love for their mother, or for fear of taking her throne, but all they knew for certain was they couldn't let the Queen die.

"Mother!" Neelo screamed, the heat rising as they reached the landing and stormed through the corridor. "Mother!"

They couldn't hear over the sizzle and shriek of splitting wood. They choked and spluttered on the thick smoke as they felt for her door handle—

Only for strong arms to circle around them, hauling them backward, Neelo bellowing a roar. Their bare heels scraped against the stone as the giant, muscled arms of their guard dragged them toward the stairwell. Despite struggling against his mighty grip, they were easily yanked down the steps, somehow both rough and yet careful enough to not harm the heir. Even at Neelo's size, their guard lifted them like they were a waif. They scrambled and clawed, trying desperately to get forward as they screamed their mother's name.

A fresh breeze slammed into them like a crashing wave, their lungs filling with cool air, but they didn't stop. They spun in their guard's grip to shout in his face.

He eased his hold, just enough for them to turn, but when Neelo looked up, it wasn't their guard whose arms encircled them . . .

It was Talhan Catullus.

CHAPTER FOUR

They stared up into his breathless face.

"You," Neelo panted, wiping the tear stains with the back of their hand.

Talhan's wide-eyed face was covered in soot, his hair stained white with ash. Only the crease of his lips and corners of his eyes remained pink.

"I have to go find her." Neelo's voice came out rougher than they intended, as always. It was how everyone thought of them: sharp and unfeeling. But their appearance didn't matter now—only their mother did.

Talhan shook his head, his hands splaying across their back as if fearful Neelo might try to dart from his grasp. As if they could outrun the Golden Eagle. "You can't go back in there."

"No one else is," they gritted out, swallowing the burning knot in their throat. "No one is even trying."

"It's too late," he whispered, eliciting a snarl from Neelo.

"No—"

Talhan's brows dropped heavily over his eyes. "You are the future of this court." His fingers pressed into the black satin of Neelo's jacket as more shouts rang out, calling for red witches to stop the blaze. "You can't go back in there."

"How dare you—"

"You know I'm right. About going back in. About . . . your mother."

"She can't," they rasped. "It's too soon. I . . ."

In the darkness, Talhan's amber eyes glowed like molten gold. "Neelo—"

"No," they growled, pushing out of his hold.

"There you are!" a shrill voice called from beyond the palm trees.

Neelo's body went slack at the sound, relief coursing through them so strongly they thought their legs might give out. They turned to find Queen Emberspear clad in a flowing lilac robe and her ever-present gloves, a gaggle of courtiers rushing behind her. Neelo raced over, embracing their mother. The Queen let out a hoarse guffaw. When was the last time Neelo had hugged her? When was the last time they'd made her laugh?

They couldn't remember.

"I'm here, child. I'm well." She chuckled with her light tittering laugh that ended abruptly on a rough hacking cough.

Once again, Neelo was the only one aware of how close the Queen had come to death. Queen Emberspear laughed it all away as if it was just another stunt. Neelo couldn't remember the first time they realized it was their job to keep their mother alive—that no one else would—that's how far into the past it was.

It was almost certainly the reason they were so exhausted, running into a fire be damned. Neelo released their mother, stepping back to scowl at her. "What have you done this time?"

"Oh please, not another one of your admonishments." The Queen waved her hand, snapping for a courtier to bring her pipe even as she tried to suppress another cough. "The sun hasn't even risen yet."

"There's enough light coming from your bedroom! You nearly burned down the entire palace!" They gestured toward the blackened windows. The fire now eased as three red witches used levitation magic to douse fountain water onto the flames.

It was an incredible sight—watching the crimson magic flicker in the darkness as the witches heaved orbs of water into the Queen's chambers. After the fall of the Northern King, Hennen Vostemur, not all the red witches hidden about the realm wanted to return to the High Mountain Court. Some had been in hiding in the South, started families and secret lives they didn't want to leave. Queen Emberspear was all too keen to have red witches working in the palace for her again. As much as they were awed by the spectacle, though, Neelo had other concerns.

"I will have you know that a candle was knocked over by a maid," the Queen hissed and her courtiers immediately whispered the gossip to one another. "An accident that could've gotten her Queen killed!" she exclaimed loudly for the rest of the congregating crowd to hear. Like a bard summoning an audience, Queen Emberspear effortlessly pulled the group toward her. "Luckily, I was still awake . . ."

Her eyes slid to the half-dressed courtier Thiago, his tunic still unbuttoned down to the navel. He winked at the Queen and Neelo mimed gagging. At the sound of Talhan's chuckle beside them, Neelo stopped. Embarrassment flushed through them knowing that the Golden Eagle was there bearing witness to yet another Southern escapade.

Although maybe this was all he'd need to see to run from there—and them—forever.

"Everyone was out and accounted for before the blaze took hold, Neelo," the Queen continued. "Everyone apart from you. If only you partook in a little of—"

"I was sleeping! And I ran back in to save you, you fool!"

The crowd gasped and their mother's face sharpened. Her eyes narrowed like a wildcat readying to strike. They knew Queen Emberspear wouldn't hit them with her fists, though Gods sometimes they wished she would. Instead, she was as precise as a seasoned archer, shooting insults and jibes like poisoned arrows into Neelo's mind. There, that poison would fester, until Neelo believed her words to be the truth.

"Careful," their mother snarled under her breath. Her eyes snagged on the looming figure over Neelo's shoulder, and Neelo tensed as the Queen took aim. Her practiced mask of pleasantry lifted again as she loudly proclaimed, "How fortunate that Talhan Catullus was here to bravely rescue his wayward betrothed."

The crowd burst into applause and drunken cheers as Neelo's hands clenched into fists. Many still dressed as if it weren't the middle of the night, while others wore only light summer chemises. Witches, humans, and fae alike, gathered around, all gawking at Talhan Catullus, the famous Golden Eagle and now their future sovereign's *betrothed*.

Talhan straightened, ignoring the crowd as he stepped up beside Neelo. He gave a tight half-bow to the Queen.

"I commend the Heir of Saxbridge on their unwavering devotion to you, Your Majesty," he said, matching her airy pitch with a telling smile. Neelo knew that look served as a warning: he could be just as calculated with his words as he could with his sword. He could also sway people with simply his presence. The crowd sighed, swooning at Talhan's every breath. "We should all be so lucky to have someone willing to risk their lives for us."

"Indeed," the Queen said in that same carefree way, but Neelo spotted how her lips twisted downward.

Queen Emberspear turned toward her assembly of whispering courtiers and the group parted for her to walk away. When she had marched far enough down the gravel path, Talhan turned back to Neelo.

"Are you all right?" he asked, lifting his hand into the air as if to touch their cheek before they stepped out of his reach. "Can you take a deep breath?" He took one himself and Neelo begrudgingly followed suit, coughing a little. "Shall we fetch a brown witch?"

"I'm fine," Neelo groused, hugging their arms to their chest. "When did you arrive?"

"Just now." Talhan pointed a thumb over his shoulder toward the main gates. "I saw the smoke as I was riding in and rushed to see what happened. That's when I spotted you running into the palace."

Neelo's jaw ached from clenching their teeth so tightly. "You should've let me go."

Eyes darkening, Talhan took a step forward. "You would've died if I let you go."

"I don't care," they spat.

Talhan rocked backward at their words, a storm brewing in the hair's breadth between them. "Well, then, I shall care enough for the both of us."

"There is no *us*," Neelo countered, waving at the charred palace edifice. "*This*. This is what my life is. This is what you cannot be a part of."

The crowds dispersed, moving around the other side of the palace, but Talhan still kept his voice low. "Why not?"

Neelo's shoulders bunched up around their ears as they snarled, "Because I will not pull you under with me."

Talhan's cheeks dimpled, and the sight of that carefree smirk made Neelo grit their teeth again. "I thought you didn't care?"

"I . . . I don't. My future is already decided."

"You don't care for yourself." Talhan took a step closer, his tunic brushing up against the buttons of their obsidian jacket. "But you worry about me?"

The night breeze tousled Neelo's short hair. "I didn't say that. I only want to spare you from this life."

"Hmm." Talhan rubbed his thumb thoughtfully across his bottom lip. He looked down at Neelo, and the action made their gut clench. Curse him. Why did he have to look at them like that? "So you'd rather suffer this future alone?"

Suffer. That's what it was: suffering the truth of what their life would be.

Neelo glanced up at the crowds spreading out through the manicured gardens. Already the evacuated residents were smoking and passing bottles around, trying to turn their near-death experience into a party.

How could Neelo rule this place? How could they wrangle people who didn't care if they lived or died? What would happen when the drinks stopped flowing and the glaring light of day shined upon the Southern Court? That is when Neelo would be left to pick up the pieces and everyone would hate them for it. That is what they needed to protect Talhan from.

Someone who was joyful and charming and lighthearted? This place would strip him of it all, and they refused to watch that vibrant spirit fade. All the colors had already leached from Neelo's life and Talhan Catullus would never survive it. Neelo knew it would be the worst sort of *suffering* seeing his slow demise.

Neelo cleared their throat, taking a step back.

"You must be tired from your travels." Neelo waved down a lingering maid and called to her. "Help Lord Catullus find his chambers."

"But—"

Talhan reached out to them again, but they were already stepping away, preempting his touch.

"Welcome to Saxbridge," they tossed over their shoulder and disappeared into the night to find Indi.

THERE WAS NO way Neelo could sleep after that fire. Instead, they found Indi chasing moths in the garden, gathered up their rescued tomes, and took him to the library. They lit only a single lantern and stared at it every other page as if the flames might jump out and consume their precious books.

The royal library sat on the eastern side of the palace, untouched by the fire. Neelo was more grateful than they would ever show. They would've mourned the loss of the library like losing a loved one. They still ached to think of the sacked library at Silver Sands and wished they'd traveled to visit it long ago.

The palace's library was an afterthought—an addition to the original structure, built by Neelo's great-grandfather. With dark-stained wood shelves and emerald-green upholstery, the two-story library sat ignored and unappreciated by everyone apart from the Heir of Saxbridge. Hints of their patron evergreen tree hid amongst the decor from the broad-leafed embellishments on the silver curtain rods to the roots carved climbing up the tables and desks. Flecks of silver swirled in the marble floors and complemented the ancient stone architecture of the rest of the palace. For royalty, the library was rather modest compared to the other courts. It still had a glorious domed roof, two stories of floor-to-ceiling books, and a view out to the orchard, but it wasn't so grand to spark envy among bibliophiles.

Neelo had always wished for it to be more.

The library in Wynreach had carved the stories of their court into the wood of their bookshelves. Yexshire's library had giant stained glass windows and rose-gold finishings. The library in Swifthill had living trees shooting up through its center and a curving open roof that turned into a waterfall when it rained. Perhaps the only benefit in Neelo one day becoming sovereign was that they could create a new library . . . if they could ever settle on just one design.

Sitting beneath the lone lantern in their favorite chair, Neelo was tucked in the farthest corner of the library. Neelo's chair had perfectly molded to their body over the years, hugging them from behind.

"What are you reading?" a voice called and Neelo jolted. Indi leapt off Neelo's lap and skittered down into the stacks.

Grimacing at their jump, Neelo leaned back from their reading nook and scowled at the smug face of Talhan Catullus. He swaggered up out of the darkness and took the seat across from them.

"It's about being in one's quarters to rest after a long journey."

"Ah—a fantasy, then."

"It's about dragons," Neelo muttered. They should've known after their spat in the gardens Talhan would track them down and try to settle things. He could never just let things lie, even as a child.

"What about dragons?" Talhan asked. "Fighting them? Riding them? Stealing gold from them?" He kicked up his feet on the low table and looked out toward the orchard. The outline of the nearest trees danced in torchlight. The lemongrass smoke kept the beetles from destroying the fruiting trees, although the fire from their mother's bedroom surely was doing that job at the moment.

Neelo let out a long sigh, noting from their periphery how the muscle in Talhan's cheek twitched as if his face were always on the precipice of a smile.

His voice was lightly taunting, but his deep resonant timbre made every word carry weight. "Am I disturbing you?"

"Yes." Neelo clenched the edges of their book tighter. "And I know you don't actually care about—"

"I do," Talhan countered.

"No," Neelo grumbled. "You don't."

"You don't wish to talk. That's fine." Talhan crossed his arms and smirked. "We can sit in companionable silence."

"Companionable silence." They huffed and shut their book. "I could think of nothing worse. Why don't you pick your own book to read? I have a recommendation for just about anything that might interest you."

"You do? Which one of these is about Neelo Emberspear, then?"

Neelo shook that off as a jest and instead reached up to the lantern hanging above their head and twisted the dial, opening the metal panes and casting more light upon the surrounding shelves.

Talhan's eyes danced with candlelight as he surveyed the books beside him. "Have you read all of these?"

"Yes."

That secret smile flickered across his lips again and Neelo's pulse ratcheted up. "More than once?"

"Some of them." They kept their voice a steely neutral. "Yes."

"Impressive."

Neelo's eyes fixed on the words of the book in their hands, the images of the story still playing in the back of their mind even as they spoke. "Don't pity me."

"Pity you?" Talhan let out a surprised chortle. "Who would pity you? I envy you. Never in my lifetime could I read this many books. So many stories I will never know."

Neelo flipped the page, tracing their finger across the lines to keep them focused on the words and not the affable fae warrior sitting across from them. "You could if you got started right now."

"No." Talhan's voice grew softer—distant. "I couldn't. I . . . I struggle with reading. I mean, I *can* read," he scrambled to add. "It's just . . . The words are like puzzles. It takes a while to decipher their meaning and it seems to take me ten times as long as everyone else, let alone you, who easily reads a book a day."

Neelo felt his eyes upon them, though they didn't look up, only adding a soft, "Oh."

Why had he never told them this before? They could tell from the way he picked at the velvet of the armchair and the way he shifted in his seat: this struggle was a secret. Neelo guessed he shared it now as a peace offering—a way to make amends for his eventful arrival.

"I do like stories," Talhan added, more to himself than to Neelo. "I love songs, poems, plays, hearing stories around the campfire, but books . . . seem lost to me."

A twinge of pain shot through Neelo. They couldn't imagine their life without books. They lived in stories more than they lived in their own body—a retreat, a reprieve, from the discomfort of simply existing. The world made little sense without stories.

One more thing to keep us apart, they thought.

Talhan and Neelo sat in silence for a long time, Neelo flipping four more pages before they spoke. "What's your favorite kind of story?"

Neelo knew from that little breathy sound that Talhan was grinning again. They seemed to know all of Talhan's expressions without even looking. Just a shift of his body weight or a clearing of his throat and they knew exactly what expression would be on his face.

"Adventures, of course," Talhan said, waving a hand down his burgundy tunic and to the dagger strapped to his belt. "Daring quests, obviously. Dashing heroes—"

"Hmph." Yet Neelo peeked up from their book to look down the darkened library path behind them, trying to decide between the red or blue books on the third shelf along.

"Anything with romance too," Talhan added with a waggle of his eyebrows.

Neelo stood up, decision made. "Adventure. Quests. Romance. Got it." They ventured down the row of shelves.

"Where are you going?"

They stopped at the second window and the circular shelf built around the frame. They lifted onto their tiptoes to select a garnet and gold tome.

Proffering the book out like a server with a platter of food, Neelo said, "This one will be your new favorite."

Talhan kept his arms folded, a frown deepening the lines of his face—such a rare expression coming from him. "I . . . I told you I don't read for fun."

A blush stained Talhan's cheeks as Neelo sat. They obviously struck a nerve and Neelo suddenly realized their mistake: they'd embarrassed him. Struggling to read was clearly a topic of discomfort for the normally confident and cavalier Golden Eagle. Neelo thought Talhan might get up, might leave after the slight, but suddenly they didn't want him to go . . . How strange. They wanted him to stay.

"I didn't mean— I . . ." Neelo swallowed. "I mean, I'm reading anyway . . . I could read it aloud?"

Talhan's eyebrows shot up, a quizzical frown still pulling down his lips. "Wouldn't that bore you?"

"Not at all," Neelo said, equally puzzled at such a question, putting the book they were reading to the side and opening the heavy red tome. "I haven't read this one in ages and I want to know if you'll like it as much as I think you will."

Talhan smiled. "You just want to be right, don't you?"

"Maybe." Neelo shrugged and flipped to the first chapter.

"Fine." Talhan leaned back in the chair and looked back out the window. "But if it gets boring for you, stop. Don't continue on my account."

"Agreed." Neelo's stomach flipped, noting the eagerness Talhan was trying to restrain. They didn't think there was anything they could give Talhan Catullus he didn't already have. He was rich, strong, smart, and esteemed. And yet here, now, they could tell him a story they knew he'd love that he otherwise never would've heard. For the first time, they felt like they suddenly had something to offer too.

"This library suits you," Talhan said, looking around where the lantern's light reached. "It's dark but warm, sophisticated but serene. I'm surprised it's not larger though."

"I didn't get to decide the size of the palace library." Neelo looked up to the towering shelves, books crammed onto every shelf. "Why we need *three* ballrooms and one library, I'll never understand."

A chirping meow sounded from under the table and Indi clawed his way up onto the armrest of Talhan's chair.

"And who is this?" Talhan asked with a smile, stroking Indi as the purring tabby cat leaned into his touch.

"Indigo," Neelo said. "Indi."

Talhan lifted his hand and Indi rubbed his face into the warrior's biceps, demanding further pats. "Hello, Indi." Talhan chuckled and continued to scratch Indi's cheek and chin. Once, twice . . . and on the third scratch, Indi turned his head and nipped Talhan's hand.

"Two chin scratches is the maximum," Neelo said. They pressed their lips together, watching Talhan's indignant stare down with Indi. The small fluffy gray cat put the giant warrior in his place. Neelo made a kissing sound and rubbed their fingers on the armrest of their chair. "Indi," they called.

The cat hopped down from Talhan's chair and resettled himself on Neelo's lap, still warm from when he'd leapt off moments before.

Snickering, Talhan looked at Indi and said, "Oh, I see how it is."

"The fact he didn't bite your hand off means he already likes you," Neelo snorted. "You've got to give him some time to warm up to you."

Talhan's golden eyes lifted from Indi to Neelo. "I've got time."

Neelo cleared their throat, their cheeks burning as their thumb brushed across the page. "Chapter one . . ."

CHAPTER FIVE

Dawn was Neelo's favorite time of day. The quiet calm was rarer than any gem in Saxbridge. Neelo wandered down through the sleepy city, only a few stray dogs still out on the cobblestones at this time of day. Colorful birds clustered amongst the palm trees that dotted the street corners, singing their morning songs. The same pinks, oranges, and blues as the birds' wings tinted the early sky.

Neelo turned down the road toward the river, where they knew a few merchants were still awake. Only the seediest people—those who didn't want to be seen by the city guards—were selling their wares at this hour. But those people were the exact ones Neelo needed to speak with. The palace fire hadn't made them forget their mission to unlock the secrets of the witching brew trade.

They passed a little shop with stucco walls painted in bright yellow and closed turquoise shutters. Painted in magenta above the door were the Mhenbic words: *Satsa Berleia*. Sweet shop. Neelo's cheeks dimpled as they thought of one fae warrior who would delight in the confections sold in the green witch shop.

It had been a favorite haunt of Talhan's whenever he visited Saxbridge as a child, them tagging along. Neelo and Talhan had made a habit of drifting off from the group of royal and high-class fae. They must've been a funny sight: Neelo, half the size of Talhan, even as children, with dark features and clothing, next to Talhan with his golden eyes, tan skin, and auburn hair.

Talhan's mother, Helvia Catullus, seemed to delight in her son's closeness with the Heir of Saxbridge—always trying to position her children as close to royalty as possible. But Neelo and Talhan usually snuck off for different purposes: Neelo to find a quiet corner to read, and Talhan to find the best of the Southern Court cuisine. He would sit on the banks of the river with his waxed bundle of confections and Neelo would sit beside him, reading the latest book they could get their hands on. Neelo had always wondered if they were just using the excuse of each other's company, but they'd come to enjoy those little moments together too.

Sighing, Neelo debated hanging back until the store opened at midday to buy some honey cakes and frosted treats for Talhan. But that's not who they were to each other anymore. Their childhood friendship had faded. Talhan had pledged his sword to Hale and he'd been off fighting King Norwood's foolish border wars for the past several years. He was here for the summer, nothing more. There was no time for the high-class fae of Okrith to gather and celebrate.

Neelo too pulled more and more away as they matured—fearful of how they would be treated by posturing courtiers trying to elevate their standing by wooing them. It made Neelo even more closed off and the possibility of engaging in the South's debauchery even less tempting. It was far easier to say they had an interest in no one than to say they had an interest in only one person . . .

They turned onto the last road and the river came into view, when a sob shattered the peaceful morning air.

Neelo whipped their head toward the sound, running before they could even register where the mournful wails were coming from. They darted down the nearest alleyway, where they found the source of the pained sounds: a middle-aged witch knelt in the alley, her skirts wet with the puddles of putrid water. She held aloft a limp body in her arms. His beard was still patchy with youth and he looked similar in age to Neelo. They recognized him from the markets. He was a green witch who used to run a tea stand in the center of the clothier district.

Javen, Neelo recalled. They hadn't seen his tea cart for over a year now. They'd assumed the young witch had moved away to seek his fortune in another town. But this emaciated body being cradled in the older witch's arms was Javen, no doubt.

"My son," the witch, his mother, wailed. "My son." Her voice was a broken cry, cutting like a knife straight into Neelo's soul.

"Wh-what happened?" Neelo asked, stumbling closer.

The witch turned hateful, bleary eyes on Neelo. "What do you think happened?" she hissed.

Neelo took another step and peered into the back alley den from where the witch had pulled her son's body. The walls were lined with corpses—no, not corpses—some were still alive. The sickly sweet scent of witching brew wafted out from the slats, smoke curling into the morning air. But the scent had a slight bitterness to it too, like hay and horse manure, different from the scent that wafted around the Queen's chambers. Even amongst the chaos, the thought gave Neelo pause. How many blends of witching brew were sold around Saxbridge? Ten, twenty? Neelo regretted not investing any interest into the favored recreational drug of the South sooner.

Another sob pulled Neelo back into their body and away from their racing thoughts. Shame swarmed through them that they'd been distracted at a time like this. Neelo's stomach roiled at the sight of those hooded, lifeless eyes, those bone-thin hands that lifted the pipes back to their gaunt, thin-lipped mouths and smoked themselves into oblivion. Neelo shuddered. They'd heard rumors that some people became addicted to the new blends of witching brew, but gossiping about drugs was of no interest to them. Regret mounted within them anew. The Queen had brushed it off as a few wayward people and nothing more. Neelo had always doubted her estimates . . . but neither had they intervened any further. Which galled them now as they looked at the dozens of bodies crammed into the bare room.

"How many places like this are there?"

"Half of Western Row is lined with rooms like this." The witch choked on her tears, gasping for breath. "They crawl into these dens and never come back out. Do you know how long it took me to find him?" She sobbed again. "Too long."

Neelo shook their head in horror. "I didn't know."

"You didn't *care* to know," the witch barked, the pitch of her voice jarring amongst the stillness of the bodies.

Tears pricked Neelo's eyes. The witch could be killed for shouting at the Heir of Saxbridge like that, but she obviously didn't care, not when her child was dead in her hands.

The witch folded back over her son. "It was the whispers that got him."

"Whispers?"

"The voices filling his head put there by this damned brew." She spat onto the ground. "But the more whispers that haunted his mind, the more brew he needed to make them go away." She wiped her nose with her shirtsleeve. "All you see is one big party. Most of the people of Saxbridge love your mother for it, but there is a cost, Heir of Saxbridge, a terrible cost. One I'm sure the Queen will leave for *you* to pay. Now get out of here with your black clothes and your bad luck." She sniffed again and raised her glowing hateful green eyes to Neelo. "I hope you never forget my face."

Words fell out of Neelo's mind at that look. The witch's stare hit Neelo like a curse, and they knew indeed they would never forget that witch's face or the sounds of her suffering. Neelo gave the barest nod and turned away, their body numb.

They needed to get to the bottom of what was in these new blends of witching brew, but instead of steering toward the docks as they'd originally intended, Neelo headed back uphill toward the library. After what they just saw, they needed the comfort of books, research, and more detailed information to better question the brew merchants. What had been a suspicion from piqued interest had suddenly become more urgent than Neelo realized. Southerners had smoked the stuff for centuries and it did little more than give the briefest of buzzes, but over the past few years, the new blends were so potent, so toxic. The witch mother's cries started again and Neelo's gut tightened. They needed to find the source of this new poisoned smoke and stop the Queen's downward spiral before she ended up as another casualty.

NEELO ARRIVED AT the chamber door and waited for the guard to announce their entrance. The guard seemed surprised that Neelo didn't barge right in like every other visitor who flounced around the place, but Neelo knew what happened behind these closed doors—every Southerner did—and they weren't about to intrude on another one of their mother's *parties*.

They waited, folding their arms over their torso so they could feel the outline of the book they kept in their breast pocket.

The guard finally caught Neelo's meaning and rapped on the door of the Queen's bedroom chamber. "Pardon, Your Majesty," he said in his gruff voice. "Are you decent?"

The Queen's squawk of laughter sounded through the door. "Never."

Neelo grimaced. Why did they even bother?

"The Heir of Saxbridge is here to see you, Your Majesty," the guard called.

"Send them in!"

Neelo's shoulders tightened as they opened the door and stepped into the dimly lit room. With the curtains pulled haphazardly shut, splinters of sunlight peeped through the thick fabric. The new chambers appeared to be decorated in homage to the Queen's now ruined wing of the palace. The same silk pillows, plush blankets, and mattresses circled in nests across the floors—lounging spaces for the many courtiers who now dotted the space. Neelo barely glanced in the courtiers' direction, knowing what they might see. Queen Emberspear perched on the edge of her giant four-poster bed. The sheer curtains to protect from insects hugged her back like a cape. Neelo tentatively approached and found she was surveying sketches for the redesign of her quarters.

"Might as well take the opportunity to redecorate," the Queen said, her words ending on a wet cough. She hacked out a rough breath, the sound rattling through her chest. Each drag of air made Neelo's gut tighten and the images of the limp bodies in that awful room flash into their mind.

"Mother," Neelo said with a surprising sharpness that pulled the Queen's attention up. "I need to speak with you about the witching brew. What is the name of the blend you smoke? Where does it come from?"

"This again?" The Queen threw her hands in the air in a dramatic show of frustration. "I told you we're cutting back. There's no need to—"

"It's much more serious than you realize," Neelo protested. "What I just saw . . ." They couldn't bring themself to say it. Giving more life to that horrifying scene felt like they might curse their mother to the same fate. "Augustus Norwood and his violet witch ally could be circling this court as we speak for all we know—a witch whose power is tied to magical smoke."

"Adisa Monroe's curse was upon other witches, ones with tortured minds who were easily preyed upon by her magic, not fae," the Queen reminded them, waving her hand as if Neelo was sharing a harebrained conspiracy. "And the new Northern King was able to break the curse with his Fated's witching stone blade." She shrugged it off as if countless lives hadn't been lost in the Battle of Valtene only two seasons ago. "Are we to gaze suspiciously at every bonfire and flickering candle because of one old witch?" She lifted the candlestick from beside her, circling it in the air like an ominous spirit. The courtiers all tittered as if she had just told a hilarious joke.

"I'm saying, all of this is more serious than you're willing to admit." Neelo pressed on, trying to hold firm to the instinct that something wasn't right. But Neelo listened to evidence, to logic, not to their gut. Instincts alone couldn't be trusted, and they didn't have an answer to the Queen's questions, only a lingering suspicion. Until they could get to the bottom of it, their mother would be much safer if she eschewed the brew entirely, lest she end up like Javen. Neelo took a tight breath, their mother already seeming to know what they were going to say based on her frown. "If you would only—"

"If I would only quit?" the Queen cut in, arching her slender brow. "Then I would stay on the throne and you wouldn't have to ever leave your precious library, hmm?"

Neelo's mouth fell open. The memory of that witch mother's cry echoed in their mind. "I can't do this," they whispered. How were they meant to take on these invisible forces? How were they, of all people, meant to pull Saxbridge through this storm?

The Queen twisted her knife deeper. "Or is this about your betrothed?"

"He is *not* my betrothed," Neelo gritted out.

"Is he not?" The Queen's wicked smirk stretched toward her pointed ears. "I believe I named him as such? I believe too that *he* accepted."

She reached for the candle on her bedside and dipped her fingers into the oil. The candles in the South were made from a special blend of oil that didn't burn as hot. The Southerners used it for all manner of things—*salacious things*—and it was one of the many reasons candles were everywhere at Southern parties.

And, apparently, why the Queen's previous quarters burned.

"Like it or not," the Queen said as she rubbed the perfumed oil up her forearms, "the Golden Eagle is here to stay."

"No," Neelo snarled. "I've already told you: when the Solstice is over, Talhan will be gone and you will still be on your throne. Just give me that time to convince you. Please."

The "please" made the Queen's eyebrows lift. She opened her mouth to speak, but instead took another gasping breath, hacking and coughing. Her cough had turned worse since the fire, and the witch's face once again flashed in their mind.

They darted a look to Thiago who sat beside her and his eyes told Neelo everything. He slicked his short hair back with his hand, his dark eyes falling to his feet. The Queen's oldest lover and friend clearly worried for her too.

Thiago patted Queen Emberspear on her back and she grabbed his forearm to steady herself. Her shoulders sagged and her eyelids fluttered.

"Your Majesty?" Thiago called, grabbing her by the shoulders as she slumped back on the bed. "Vitra? Call for the healer!"

As decadent and indulgent as the room was, two of the younger courtiers immediately shot up from where they perched—half dressed—and raced off into the hallway. Neelo marveled there was anyone here even remotely cognizant, and wondered if those two's sole purpose was to keep aware in case something was needed.

"Is she breathing?" Farros asked, lingering over the Queen. He touched a hand to her clammy cheek.

"Yes," Thiago muttered, groaning as he lifted her torso and placed her head on top of a pillow. "Barely."

Dozens of courtiers swarmed the bed, some gasping, some giggling and whispering, as if this was just another one of the Queen's antics. The crowd buzzed about, clanking gold jewelry and scuffling their sandals across the marble floor. The sounds were too loud, too spirited, for the severity of what was happening. All Neelo could think of was Javen's rail-thin body in the alley. Would they be too late again?

Neelo stood stock-still, watching as if they were underwater while everyone raced around them. The tighter Neelo seemed to hang on to their mother, the more she seemed to slip through their fingers.

"Everybody out!" A booming voice cut above the clamor. "And take your bloody pipes with you."

The group turned, but Neelo didn't move, already knowing the unmistakable voice of Talhan Catullus.

Thiago glared past Neelo to Talhan in the doorway. "You dare give us orders?"

"I am betrothed to your future sovereign," he reminded them with that voice like rolling thunder. "More, I seem to be willing to act when no one else will. Do you wish to cross me?"

"I—"

"Thiago and Farros can stay," Neelo cut in. "The rest of you do as he says."

At Neelo's command, the group hustled out, a trail of smoke lingering in their wake. Neelo fought the urge to cough as the sickly floral scent clung to their clothes and hair. It would take several baths to wash out the stench of this brief visit.

Neelo overheard two of the blond-haired courtiers tittering to each other as they breezed out the door.

"It was only a matter of time before that smoke got her," one said.

"No surprise when she likes the heaviest blends," the other replied.

Talhan swiftly slammed the door behind them and took another measured step into the room. "What is wrong with her?"

"Nothing," Thiago said at the same time Neelo said, "Everything."

A brown witch rushed in—her face dripping with sweat and her chest heaving as if she'd run all the way up the cliffs from the harbor. The elixirs in her satchel clinked together as she rushed to the Queen's side. She put her glowing brown hand on the Queen's clammy face, her magic assessing as the Queen's eyelids twitched. The tight knot in Neelo's chest loosened as their mother opened her eyes and the brown witch helped Thiago prop her up on another pillow.

The Queen's gaze darted around the room, searching for a memory she couldn't seem to grasp. She panted a wet, vexing breath and placed a steadying hand on her chest. When her kohl-smudged eyes landed on Neelo, they guttered.

"I'm going to stop," she rasped. "I'm done. I swear it."

Neelo swallowed, tracing the outline of the book in their pocket. The feeling of the satin lining beneath their fingertips calmed the rage brewing inside them. "I can only hope, Mother."

"Perhaps if you were a little more supportive of my efforts," the Queen hissed. "Perhaps if you cared a little more about your family than your *books*."

Neelo attempted to put on an air of indifference as they found the nearest armchair and collapsed into it. How many times had this conversation played out between them? It always seemed to be Neelo's lack of effort that put the Queen into her constant predicaments, not the pipe that found its way to her lips time and again. Neelo grabbed their book out of their pocket and opened it. Their eyes easily landed on the place they left off, ready for their mind to be battling dragons and not listening to their mother's miserable lies.

As Talhan watched the brown witch work her magic, he ambled over and perched silently on the tufted armrest of their chair. He bounced his knee, his hand finding the hilt of his dagger in the same way Neelo reached for the outline of their book.

Neelo watched from their periphery as the Queen slapped the brown witch's hand away.

"If I had better healers," the Queen snarled, "maybe this wouldn't be such a problem."

The witch's mouth tightened, but she didn't reply.

"Ava is a great healer, Mother, but you are not so easily healed," Neelo said without lifting their eyes from their book. "Not when you are so intent on continuing to harm yourself."

The Queen snickered. "Everyone in the South partakes in the witching brews."

"Not everyone. *I* don't. And the others only do because they follow your example," Neelo shot back. "You set the fashions, not follow them."

"We've been smoking it for centuries," the Queen countered.

"But you keep commissioning more and more potent blends," Neelo gritted out, trying to push down on the fire rising in their chest. "Children used to smoke the old blends, that's how mild they were, for the Gods' sake!"

"Ah, here we go. Another lecture." The Queen sneered and snatched the elixir proffered by Ava. She swigged it down in one go and grimaced as she wiped her painted red lips with the back of her hand. Farros quickly dabbed at the scarlet smudge on her cheek.

"I'm not the one who is going to talk. I need you to tell *me* what's in these new blends before you become a victim of them! Or, if you don't know that, at least tell me where they come from?"

"I couldn't think of a worse person to trust the identity of my suppliers to," the Queen countered with a hiss. She clearly didn't fear for her safety, nor the safety of her people. She only feared what would happen if Neelo took it all away.

Staring daggers at the pages of their book, Neelo took a steeling breath. "I'm simply stating the truth—"

"Perhaps I shall ask Her Majesty, the Queen of the High Mountain Court, to spare *her* healer for me." The Queen shot a nasty glare to the brown witch as she passed back the empty vial.

Talhan's bouncing leg paused. "Fenrin?"

"I hear he is the best brown witch healer alive." The Queen turned her blotchy, wet eyes to Talhan. "Rumor is he saved your life, didn't he?"

"I doubt Remy will let him just come here on a whim," Neelo said, even as their fingers tightened on their book. They'd heard of Talhan's near brush with death during the Battle of Valtene. They'd had the worst nightmares of his bloodied body on the brink of death after that. It made them shift in their seat until their sleeve brushed against his hip.

"The High Mountain Queen will lend me her brown witch if I say my life is at stake." The Queen looked the healer up and down, her lip curling. "Which it very well may be."

Ava scoffed at the slight, pulling her satchel back over her shoulder as she bristled. She gave a nearly imperceptible bow to the Queen and left without another word or instruction. It wasn't the first time Ava was summoned in a panic and then blamed for the emergency. The Queen, for all her power, was lucky Ava was devoted to healing no matter who the patient was, or else she might truly lose the services of a competent witch.

"How was your rest last night, Lord Talhan?" the Queen asked, shifting the conversation with practiced ease. "Are your accommodations to your liking?"

"Yes, Your Majesty," Talhan said with a wide, mocking grin. "Albeit a bit smoky."

Neelo pressed their lips together to keep from smiling as Talhan nudged them with his elbow. They liked the feeling of being brought into his mischief with him. Neelo always felt like they were missing the joke, but Talhan made them feel like a coconspirator.

The Queen narrowed her eyes at them as if to say: *Two can play at this game.* "Perhaps you'd like to get the scent of smoke off of you." Her eyes narrowed as she grabbed Thiago's hand and squeezed it tightly. "Why don't you escort Talhan and Neelo to the bathhouses. See that they have a good wash."

Neelo opened their mouth to protest. "M—"

"I've frequented many of them, thank you, Your Majesty," Talhan cut in. "I will be fine with a basin tonight though."

"In this heat? No, no. Saxbridge is renowned for its bathhouses," she proclaimed, cocking an eyebrow at Neelo. "And I doubt our guest has seen the royal ones. A wash, both of you. It'll be a nice day spent together, you and your betrothed."

"Thiago should stay with you," Neelo insisted. "I'll take Talhan to the bathhouses."

The Queen's wicked eyes gleamed in victory. "Have fun."

Neelo clutched their book tighter, not lifting their eyes from the pages as they rose and walked out of the room with Talhan trailing behind.

CHAPTER SIX

Talhan craned his neck up to the verdant green canopy stretching out above him. "Where are we going?"

"The bathhouses are noisy and overcrowded at this time of day," Neelo groused, climbing up the forest trail. "We're going for a walk for the acceptable amount of time and then returning. There's a waterfall if you still wish to bathe."

"But you're not bathing?" Talhan asked, cocking his head as he fell into step beside them.

"No."

"Why not?"

"I'd rather bathe alone." Neelo mindlessly pinched a sprig of wild parsley and tucked it in their cheek, trying to get the taste of smoke out of their mouth. "Besides, I don't want to wear my vest in the water."

"Why don't you take it off? It's just us." Talhan easily kept pace as they veered off the path and up the steep trail toward the waterfall.

"I'm not as casual as other Southerners when it comes to showing off my body." Neelo took the roughly carved steps two at a time, lunging up the switchback trail. Their large thighs easily carrying them up the steep ascent.

Talhan hummed in understanding, but Neelo didn't think he really comprehended what they were trying to say. How could he? Not wanting to be nude in front of others wasn't as simple as being modest or uncomfortable. Their reasons were much more complicated. No, they liked their body. It served them well: strong, functional, good for carrying massive stacks of books. Besides, they were too logical to care about something as subjective as attractiveness, or wondering if others found them as such. A song could be beloved or hated, depending on the listener. A piece of art found its meaning in the one admiring it. For Neelo, though—they had never wanted to be admired physically by anyone before. But with Talhan . . .

Neelo's pace slowed. They almost opened their mouth a dozen times. How were they meant to explain to Talhan why they couldn't be like every other Southerner and undress in front of him? He'd seemed to have moved on, admiring the birds and the gently swaying trees, but Neelo felt the sudden urge for him, of all people, to understand their reasons, and so they tried to explain again. "The reason I don't undress publicly . . . it's not out of embarrassment and it isn't as simple as shyness . . . it's hard to explain."

"Try me."

Releasing a long breath, Neelo reached the landing and looked from their broad shoulders to their soft belly and down to their thick, corded thighs. "I was born to the Queen of the Southern Court. Every person in Okrith knows what's under these clothes . . ." They gestured to themself up and down. "The truth of who I am cannot be divined from something as simple as my physical form. I am the same person both dressed and undressed. I am confident in exactly who that person is . . . But I just don't want anyone else to mistake me for something I'm not because of it."

Talhan crested the steep hill, surprising Neelo by seeming to ignore their comments as he stood beside them and took in the sight of the turquoise pool. A thick stream of water plunged into the pond, spouting from the middle of the hillside from an underground aquifer. A heavy shroud of mist covered the cavernous space behind the waterfall.

"I'm going to dip my feet in," Neelo said, shucking their boots. They rolled their trousers up to the knee, revealing muscled calves covered in coarse dark hair. They took a single step down toward the water before Talhan put his hand on their elbow and stopped them. Neelo tensed at the fleeting touch and turned to look at him. "What?"

"I could never mistake you for anything else than what you are," he murmured, his golden eyes filling them with warmth. "You are entirely unique, and not because of your name or title." He shook his head and his dark auburn hair fell across his brow. "But because of the way you can speak every language, you know every story that was ever told, you are the wisest person in every room and yet you aren't arrogant about it even though you have every right to be. You're proud of your court even though you don't always agree with or wish to take part in it." Neelo's chest seized at his words and the heated look in his eyes. "You are magnificent, Neelo, and I could never mistake you for anything else."

"I wish you wouldn't say such things," they whispered.

Talhan smirked, arching his brow. "You'd rather I lie?"

Neelo shook their head and Talhan shrugged. He stooped to roll up his trousers.

"You're not going to bathe?"

Talhan's cheeks dimpled with a catlike grin. "Did you want me to?"

Neelo tried to hide their surprise as they quickly replied, "No, I—"

"Liar." He chuckled, but continued before Neelo could protest. "If you're soaking your feet, then I will too."

He looked around the perimeter of the pool and found a smooth rock to sit and soak his feet. Neelo tentatively followed behind, making sure they sat far enough away from Talhan so their shoulders didn't touch.

As Talhan's feet hit the water, a rumbling groan of pleasure escaped his lips. Neelo froze at the sound, every hair on their body standing on end.

Curse that bloody sound. Hearing it made their body react of its own volition. It zinged straight through them like biting into a lemon, but Gods, it felt good too.

Magnificent. He thought they were magnificent.

Talhan cleared his throat and Neelo looked up at his expectant, waiting face. Had he asked something?

"What?" Neelo asked in their normal monotone.

Talhan swirled his feet idly, looking back at the water falling from the belly of the mountain. "I said: Did you bring a book?"

Tapping their pocket, Neelo tried to pretend their mind hadn't wandered off. "I'm surprised you're even asking me that."

"It seems like a good spot for reading a book."

"It is," Neelo murmured, considering the fae warrior leaning back on his elbows to bask in the sunshine. The Southern climate suited him, the boisterous people of the South suited him too . . . but there was one person who didn't suit him at all, one he'd be tied to forever if he stayed.

Talhan closed his eyes and turned toward a beam of sunlight bursting through the canopy. Neelo sighed at the sight of his golden, sun-kissed face. It was as if even the Gods themselves knew he deserved that extra bit of sunlight—even the sky knew Talhan Catullus was special.

Neelo had always seen it in him. Talhan walked around with a golden halo of sunlight and Neelo saw how everyone looked at him that way. He couldn't help but be loved.

Lovable. That's what their mother had called him and at least in that they could agree. Even the Northern Court Queen, Rua, fell under his spell in the end, allowing him to stay as her guard in the North. She had contacted Saxbridge through fae fire many times in the past few weeks to see if he safely arrived, more times than even her sister, Remy. Rua seemed sharp and cutting, not warm and friendly like her sister, but still, she cared, perhaps even more deeply.

Neelo knew that duality of steely exterior combined with a staggering depth of feeling all too well. Rish always told Neelo there was more than one way of existing in the world, but Neelo felt like everyone else was born with a knowledge they themself were lacking. People all seemed to know how to act, how to speak, how to smile and chat about things that were incredibly boring but pretend they were interested in anyway. There was some secret they were all in on—a secret just out of Neelo's grasp. Their whole life they kept reaching for it, thinking just another step and they'd understand what everyone else seemed to know.

But they never got there, never understood the joke, never grasped that secret, and at some point, they stopped trying and decided it wasn't meant for them.

Sighing, Neelo produced a mauve ledger from their pocket.

"I'm shocked that isn't covered in sweat," Talhan said, shaking the wet linen shirt clinging to his muscled chest.

Neelo flipped a third of the way into the book. "You get used to the heat."

"I hope so," he said, and once more they had to look away from all that those words wanted to promise for the future.

"What's your book about?"

"It's a healer's ledger from decades ago," they replied.

Talhan snorted. "You're so desperate for new books that you're reading ledgers now?" He leaned over, his chin grazing their shoulder as he peered down at the paper. "This is Drunehan all over again."

"Ah yes." Neelo peered through the paper and back into time, remembering that day.

"You rescued me from my sword training with that awful Northern tutor." The lines around Talhan's eyes crinkled. "You yanked me into that hidden room so I didn't have to go."

"I ranted at you about conifers for two hours."

Talhan shrugged. "You were so excited about it, that I was too." He leaned his shoulder into them, heat spreading through Neelo from where they touched. "Do you find ledgers riveting too?"

Neelo rolled their eyes and nudged him away. "No—well, a little bit, but that's not why I'm reading it. I'm investigating something, and this information is helpful."

"How so?"

"I'm looking for patterns." They trailed their finger down the rows of notes and numbers. "What townspeople purchase on a day-to-day basis, what potions are common and which are rare, which names pop up over and over, and which ones show up only once."

"And?"

"And what?"

"Okay, maybe 'why' is the better question here."

"Because that information helps me spot anomalies," they said. "If I understand what is normal, I can more easily find the ones that break the pattern."

"I could see why that's enjoyable," Talhan mused. "It's like solving a riddle."

"It is." Neelo glanced up at him, pressing their lips together. Something softened in them at Talhan's acknowledgment. He understood that small part of them—a part most would find ridiculous.

Neelo had to remind themself again that there was a difference between understanding and romantic interest. They'd learned that lesson the hard way a dozen times before. Kindness—affection even—did not equate to love, and Talhan Catullus was nothing if not kind. They needed to stop reading into his every little interaction with them before it left them hurt . . . again. That sort of feeling was just another secret Neelo knew wasn't meant for them to unlock.

"I like solving riddles too," Talhan murmured, refocusing Neelo's drifting mind. "Though not as well as you, obviously, because you're brilliant but . . ." Neelo bit the corner of their lip, tucking that word away to remember later. In less than an hour, he'd called them *magnificent* and *brilliant* as if it were as common knowledge as the sky being blue. "What in particular are you trying to discover?"

"I'm trying to figure out what happened in Valtene," Neelo said. "Ever since I visited Silver Sands library, I've been trying to uncover everything I can about Adisa Monroe, the self-appointed High Priestess of the apparently not-extinct violet witches."

"Is that all?" he said, playfully mocking the scope of such a search. Talhan flicked an iridescent beetle off the back of his hand and began searching the ledge for more insects. "And what have you learned?"

"At some point, Adisa Monroe was buried in Valtene . . . or at least her casket was. Her descendants, the Monroes, had lived nearby but I can't find trace of them in the current records." Neelo licked their finger and flipped another page. "How did Adisa Monroe go from a brown witch's ancestor buried in a grave in the West, to a High Priestess of an extinct coven in the East?"

"Do you have any guesses?" Talhan leaned in again as if Neelo was about to share a secret. His eyes cut down to the paper. "What's that?"

"A spotted *boshtu*?" Neelo asked incredulously. "It's a breed of duck. The witches use their feathers in elixirs."

Talhan blew out a puff of air. "You say it like everyone knows that." Neelo flipped another page and pointed to the third line. They held it up to Talhan, but he closed his eyes and turned his face back into the sunshine, instead saying, "Read it to me."

They snickered at his faux arrogance and found the line again, tracing their finger down the page to find twenty more of the same strange notation. "These odd potions start popping up more and more around the Harvest Moon. A clarity elixir of bonemeal and rosemary to ward off mind control."

That made Talhan peek his eyes open again. "Mind control? Like what happened to the cursed blue witches?"

"Something like that, yes." Neelo nodded. "But not quite. More and more of these ailments are listed as *whispers*." Neelo shuddered, thinking of Javen and his mother, their thoughts coming together with a terrifying click. Why was the town of Valtene plagued with a similar sickness that was now claiming the lives of Southerners?

"Gods," Talhan breathed, swatting away a fly buzzing around his head. "What was happening in that sleepy little witch town in the West?"

"The Harvest Moon is when the witches believe they can speak to their ancestors . . . perhaps proximity to Adisa Monroe's grave gave her access to their minds?"

"Her mind?" Talhan's eyebrows shot up. "As in her conscious mind? As in you think she was awake and alive *in* her grave?"

"Maybe," Neelo hedged. "I don't know." It still didn't explain what voices people like Javen were hearing now . . . unless the High Priestess was powerful enough to reach anyone anywhere. But how? What witch magic could control people's minds? The curse on the blue witches had been cast with their own talisman of power . . . what was happening with the brown witches in this ledger and Javen was different, and yet, eerily similar.

"That can't be good." Talhan let out a weary groan. "Hale said that the red witch Priestess, Baba Morganna, was able to project her whole spirit to him at the base of the Rotted Peak." He bent and cupped a handful of water. Slicking back his auburn hair, Talhan rubbed the cool liquid across his neck. Neelo's eyes followed the trail of droplets as they slid down his neck and beneath his tunic's neckline and had to force themself to focus. "Maybe other witches could project themselves similarly?"

"It's possible," Neelo said. "It was certainly something that happened in the ancient days of the witch covens, but it's an exhaustive magic, like their candles, a onetime sort of thing. Baba Morganna still hasn't regained the mind-speaking magic from where it was before the Rotted Peak."

"How do you know this?"

"Because I'm invisible." Neelo peeked up at him. "And people feel free to speak around me."

Talhan's amber eyes softened. "You're not invisible."

"You're the only one that seems to think so." They held each other's gazes for a brief moment—a moment too long—and Neelo looked back down to the dark blur of their feet below the water. "But I'm not complaining if it helps me learn things others don't feel inclined to tell me. Either way, if Adisa Monroe was using mind magic from the grave, then she wouldn't be able to do it often. Depending on the distance, it might deplete her for years, maybe even decades. That's a lot of pressure to make the right contact, to send the right message. It's also a *lot* of power. More than any witch possesses nowadays, even the witch who topples mountains, Baba Morganna."

"If Adisa Monroe was buried alive," Talhan said with a shudder, "maybe she was trying to find someone to come dig her up?"

"Maybe," Neelo said, an idea popping into their mind.

"What are you thinking?" Talhan asked, surprising Neelo that he seemed to notice their change in expression. It was so subtle, more of a brief pause than a lightning strike of inspiration, and yet, he had noticed it.

"When did Hennen Vostemur start pushing the Northern Court soldiers into Valtene?"

"A little after the Siege of Yexshire . . . Why?"

"That is when I need books about Valtene from," Neelo said with a nod, pulling their feet out of the pond and standing. "You can stay and—"

"No way!" Talhan exclaimed. "I want to know what is going on in your mind right now. Show me. Let's go."

Neelo let out a rough chuckle at his enthusiasm—a puzzle-solver indeed. But they were also grateful to have someone to share this with.

They were also very aware that he wasn't just doing this because they were interested in Adisa Monroe. No, Talhan Catullus was coming because if ever there was a complicated puzzle, it was Neelo Emberspear themself.

CHAPTER SEVEN

Talhan pulled book after book from the farthest stacks until his clothes were gray with dust. He hauled the heavy volumes to a leaning table by the window where Neelo poured over the pages.

"Anything?" he asked as Neelo's finger zipped down the page, scanning the words and flipping to the next.

"Since the Siege of Yexshire, the history is all choppy." Neelo let out a frustrated groan. "It's like Queen Thorne decided to write Valtene out of the Western Court registries entirely."

"She certainly turned a blind eye to the bloodshed along her borders," Talhan muttered. "Content to bury her head in the sand."

"There's more in the Mhenbic journals than the Ific ones," Neelo said, keeping their eyes glued to the page. "The fae didn't bother to keep diligent records of witch towns like Valtene."

Talhan lifted the hem of his tunic to wipe his sweaty brow. Neelo's fingers paused on the page and they peeked up at that hint of muscled stomach before their eyes darted back down.

"Top floor, fourth row." Neelo waved toward the staircase. "Bring me all the books on the seventh shelf."

Talhan gave them a mocking bow. "Right away, Your Highness."

"If you want to go—"

"Did I say I wanted to go?" Talhan arched his brow and winked at them. Indi twisted between his legs and Talhan scooped up the purring cat by the belly and placed a kiss atop his head. "Come on, Indi. You can help me."

He turned with the cat in his arms as he ambled toward the stairs. Neelo gaped at their cat. He let Talhan pick him up? Indi barely let Neelo pick him up!

Neelo shook their head. "Talhan Catullus," they muttered. "Charmer of fae and animals alike." They flipped another page and called up to Talhan. "You'll like Indi well enough until he drops a flying cockroach in your bed as a present."

Talhan's echo of laughter was his only response. It took the fae warrior eight trips to carry all the books because Indi refused to be put down. Neelo's cat would dig his claws into Talhan's shoulder every time the Eagle attempted to let him go. After the eighth trip, Talhan dropped into a green channel back chair so that Indi could settle on his lap.

"Anything?"

"I wish you'd stop asking that," Neelo gritted out.

Talhan scratched Indi's cheek and tried another tack. "Any more about the whispers?"

"Yes and no," Neelo said, flipping another page. "There are lots of notes about whispered words of wisdom around the Harvest Moon. But that is when the witches believe they can commune with their ancestors through candlelight. I don't think it's the same as the 'whispers' the apothecaries were treating."

The library door creaked open. Indi stood with a big stretch and leapt off Talhan's lap.

"Rish!" Talhan called, rising to greet the green witch. He cupped her face and kissed her on either cheek.

Rish carried a tray filled with dishes and dented copper bowls. The smell of spiced rice and sweet chutneys wafted through the air.

"I brought you some food," she said. "I told the Queen's maids that you two were busy and she seemed more than happy to excuse you from dinner."

Neelo's stomach twisted, knowing exactly what kind of *business* the Queen thought they were attending to. Queen Emberspear was probably delighted and it made Neelo clench their teeth so tightly their jaw ached.

"How can you even see in here, *mea raga*?" Rish tutted as she set the tray down on the low table beside Talhan and hastily rushed to light more candles.

Neelo looked up at her, blinking several times before their eyes adjusted to the distance. They were suddenly aware of the soreness in their neck and the rumble of hunger in their stomach. The sun was setting outside. Neelo blinked again as a wave of exhaustion hit them.

"Is it really dinnertime already?"

Talhan cocked his head at them curiously.

"Neelo does this all the time," Rish said, tapping Talhan's shoulder with her tea towel. "Lucky they have a green witch who reminds them to eat."

"I don't think I could ever forget such a thing." Talhan clasped a hand to his chest, pretending to be scandalized.

Rish squeezed his cheek. "And that is one of the many reasons why I love when you're here." She gestured back over to the tray. "I wasn't sure what you felt like tonight, so I made a little bit of everything."

Neelo's race for answers halted, the momentum severed by the smell of food and Rish's warm voice. Rish was one of the few people who could pull Neelo out of focus without summoning their wrath. It probably would've been sunrise before they lifted their head from the Mhenbic books were it not for Rish.

Neelo wandered over to the chair beside Talhan and collapsed into it, their mind in a fog from the hours of reading. With every blink, they saw the Mhenbic words inked upon yellowing pages. There were still too many unanswered questions: What happened in Valtene? What did it have to do with the violet witch resurgence? What did it have to do with the brew that was killing their mother and their people?

"Neelo?" Talhan asked.

Neelo looked down at the cup of coffee that Rish held out to them and they realized the green witch and Talhan had been talking. They hadn't heard a word.

"Thanks," they muttered, taking the tiny cup and sipping the spiced, rich liquid. The bold flavor zipped across their taste buds, filling them with warmth and bringing them back into their body.

Rish had said something else, but she was already walking away, leaving them to eat their dinner.

Neelo sighed, setting the cup down and rubbing their eyes.

"That was . . . impressive," Talhan said. He ripped off a bite of flatbread with his teeth while he heaped a spoonful of rice onto another piece.

"What was?" Neelo grabbed a handful of spiced snap peas, staining their fingertips red.

"Watching you." Talhan's words were muffled through a mouthful of food. "It was like watching a soldier train or a musician play. The dedication. The drive."

Neelo snickered. "I was just reading."

"You were hunting for answers." Talhan used the flatbread to pick up a dollop of bean dip. "The way you switched back and forth between all three languages. From ancient scrolls to modern registers. It was incredible. If anyone could find the answers to a mystery, it would be you."

"I'm surprised you stuck around," Neelo mused.

"I wasn't much help, but I could haul the books over for you."

"That was a huge help," Neelo countered. Indi reappeared from the stacks and jumped up on Neelo's lap. "Oh, now you deign to notice me, hmm?"

Indi let out a soft meow, knowing Neelo was talking to him.

Talhan smacked his lips as he took a sip of the strong Southern coffee. "He just likes me because I'm new."

"That's not why."

"Then why do you think?"

Neelo frowned, searching the floor in front of them. The patterns in the carpet began to look like Mhenbic symbols—they'd been staring at the books for too long without a break. Worse, they couldn't bring themself to tell Talhan why Indi was drawn to him. It was the same reason why everyone was drawn to him. He had this hypnotic power—a current that pulled everyone in its undertow. Talhan was beautiful, warm, and easily lovable, but tough and rugged all at once. He was everything Neelo lacked in themself.

And to tell him all that was too much for them to bear. They took a bite of flatbread themself, then switched subjects. "There was mention of a hand mirror in one of the texts. A poisoned hand mirror. It was said the victim touched the handle and then their veins turned to ash."

Talhan's brow furrowed. "Like the poisoned cutlery that killed Queen Thorne?"

"Possibly." Neelo rubbed their sore neck. "Or it could be something entirely different, but it's worth looking into. It happened two towns south of Valtene six years ago."

"That's pretty random," Talhan said.

"After we eat, I'll pull the records for that town." Neelo yawned and grabbed their cup of coffee again. "You should go. I'm sure there are better ways to spend an evening in Saxbridge."

"You're wrong." Talhan's cheeks dimpled. "After we eat, I'll get more books for you."

"You don't have to sta—"

"I *want* to stay," Talhan insisted with a resolute nod. "Besides, you can't get up now that Indi has fallen asleep on you."

Neelo smiled ruefully. It was true. They could never move the cat once he'd gotten comfortable. It felt like an unspoken rule.

"*Faraa asht ent a valassa,*" Neelo whispered. "*Ashanna an venist.*"

Talhan took another bite of roasted pepper. "What does that mean?"

"It's an old Mhenbic saying." Neelo stroked a hand down Indi's back. "'Don't wake a cat who's blessed you with warmth, or you'll forever feel ice.'"

Talhan blew out a low whistle. "Well, that's grim."

"It means if you don't appreciate what you have, you'll always feel lacking," Neelo said, biting the corner of their lip. "But it works this way too."

61

Talhan hummed. "You see? I need to fetch the books for you or you'll forever feel ice."

Neelo rolled their eyes. "It's just an expression."

"Nope." Talhan's eyes twinkled with mischief. "With ancient magic rising in this world, the last thing we need is bad luck."

"I'm not going to stop wearing black," Neelo muttered. They were the only Southerner who dared to wear the color, considered to be bad luck in the vibrant, colorful South.

Talhan tipped his head to Indi. "All the more reason to improve your luck with the cat thing."

Neelo scrutinized the cheeky look on his face. "You're really going to stay here all night with me, aren't you?"

Talhan only gave them a wink and kept eating.

NEELO PEEKED OPEN their eyes and squinted against the beams of light shining directly in their face . . . They stared out at the orchard covered in morning mist.

The orchard?

Neelo blinked a few more times and searched around them. They were still in the library with a heavy leather book lying across their legs. It wouldn't be the first time they fell asleep in that spot, but something about this time was decidedly different: Talhan Catullus slept in the armchair beside them.

His arms were folded over his chest, his legs propped up on the little table between his chair and the window bench, and his head hung back, resting on a silk pillow. His breathing was rhythmic and slow. How strange to see him without his big smile and bright eyes. So still—this person who existed beneath the exuberance and charm. Neelo had always known this version of him was there, had seen it in the quiet pauses between smiles and the thoughtful stares out toward the horizon. They saw it beyond the laughter and twinkling eyes, and they wondered if they were the only one.

Indi slept, purring furiously on Talhan's lap. The tabby cat seemed even smaller on top of Talhan's massive, muscled leg.

Traitor, Neelo thought even as they smiled to themself. Indi seemed as besotted with Talhan as the rest of Okrith. Neelo slowly shut their book, careful not to wake the sleeping cat and fae. The situation suddenly felt far too intimate, and they needed to get out of there before he woke up.

Ever so slowly, they shifted their weight off the bench seat and rose, grimacing at the loud click of their stiff joints as they stood.

Neelo managed four steps, feeling more confident in their success, until a deep voice murmured, "Where are you off to at this early hour?"

Wincing, they turned to see Tal peeping one eye open. His lips curved into that irrepressible expression of his and he swept his sleep-tousled hair off his face and rubbed his stubbled jawline.

"Trying to sneak away?" he asked, stretching his arms over his head and letting out a gruff breath that made Neelo's stomach flutter. They liked this version of him, the quiet version, where his guard was down and his energy wasn't through the roof.

And they hated that they liked it so much.

"I didn't want to wake you." Neelo shrugged and shifted toward the books on the shelf to their right. They reorganized the novels, needing to busy their hands as those sleepy morning eyes watched them. Indi arched into a long stretch and jumped off Talhan's lap, ambling down the rows of books toward the exit, in search of breakfast, no doubt.

"The question remains: Where are you sneaking off to this fine morning?"

"I'm not sneaking," Neelo reminded him, refusing to be baited by his taunting words. "I'm heading back to my room. I need to change and freshen up before breakfast."

It was a lie. Neelo had someone they needed to speak with, especially after their failed attempt the previous morning when they ran into Javen's mother.

The shing of metal sounded, followed by a heavy thunk. Neelo whirled to the sound, finding a giant teal and pink beetle impaled by a dagger against the bookshelf.

"Did you see the size of that thing?" Talhan said, his eyes already drooping with sleep again as if he didn't just make an incredible shot from several paces away. Neelo's eyes widened—warrior indeed. "Those are the ones that nibble at the paper, aren't they?"

Neelo yanked the blade free, schooling their impressed expression back to a sour neutral. "While your aim is impressive," they said, dropping his dagger onto the table beside him, "if you struck a book, I'd be forced to banish you."

"I won't strike a book, then," he said in that infuriatingly confident way of his. He probably could strike a needle from across the room . . . but the world would crack in two before Neelo let him do it around their books.

"New rule: no dagger throwing in the library."

"Fine," he moped. Talhan's head flopped onto his shoulder, as if its weight was too heavy for him to hold up. His eyes closed as he asked, "I'll see you at breakfast?"

"Yep," Neelo muttered, straightening one last book and turning. "See you, then."

"Neelo?" Talhan called as he folded his arms back over his chest and shrugged down into a sleeping position in his chair. Neelo paused, but didn't respond. "Thank you for letting me help yesterday."

Neelo stared at Talhan's sleeping form for a long moment, their throat constricting with emotions, before they finally whispered, "You're welcome." And crept away.

CHAPTER EIGHT

I didn't expect to see you here, Your Highness." The scraggily merchant dropped into a hasty bow. His green eyes shifted nervously from side to side as if searching for a phalanx of guards ready to arrest him.

"I'm not here to interrupt your . . . business," Neelo said, scanning over the crates covered in thick burlap. "I merely have some questions that need answering."

The merchant's posture relaxed. "I am happy to help however I can."

Neelo tipped their head to his wares. "Where do you pick up your . . . *supplies*? Are they different than the traditional blends?"

"No, Your Highness." He tapped his hand atop the tallest crate. "They come from Arboa, same as the regular blends." His voice lowered as he leaned in again, concern clouding his expression. "I know the royal blends were meant only for the Queen, but if there's people willing to pay to follow her fancy, then why not?"

"That's certainly one way to frame it." Neelo scowled and the merchant lurched backward as if they might strike him. "I'm not going to punish you," they reminded him again. They sniffed the air, catching the waft of bitter brew. Whether the merchant claimed this was the Queen's blend or not, the scent didn't carry the same saccharine notes that clouded the Queen's chamber. "I just need answers. Now, what is in this exclusive blend that makes it so potent?"

The merchant opened his mouth to speak, but when he glanced over Neelo's shoulder, his eyes widened like saucers. Neelo grimaced, knowing exactly who the merchant was staring at.

Talhan Catullus swaggered up behind them.

"Excuse me one moment," Neelo muttered, whirling around and stalking back to Talhan. "Go away," they snapped, low enough that the human ears of the merchant wouldn't be able to hear.

"Not a chance." Talhan huffed, folding his arms pointedly across his broad chest. "Not when you're interrogating a *brew* merchant."

"I'm not interrogating anyone," Neelo gritted out. "I simply have questions, ones that won't be answered with the Golden Eagle hovering over me. You will scare them away. I need answers and I don't need the distraction."

Talhan cocked his head and smirked. "You find me distracting?"

"That is not the point," Neelo snarled. "And yet this conversation also proves that point!"

"Why didn't you tell me you were coming here this morning?"

"Because I don't owe you an explanation of my plans."

He chuckled. "Nor the courtesy of them."

"Indeed." Neelo's frown tightened. "You are here as a guest and visitor of the Southern Court," they reminded him, knowing their words would sting but needing him to back off before their lead disappeared. "But I continue to conduct business that I need to attend to and I have no obligation to involve you in it."

"Well, don't let me stop you."

"You already have stopped me," they growled, wishing they could smack that infuriating smugness off Talhan's face.

They turned back to the merchant just in time to see him pushing off the dock.

"Apologies, Your Highness," he called back to them, using his pole to navigate downriver. "I need to get back to the harbor before the changing tides."

"See what you've done?" Neelo spun toward Talhan, waving out to the river. "This is exactly why I didn't tell you where I was going. How did you find me anyway?" They didn't wait for Talhan to reply before they scowled. "Rish."

"Don't blame her. She was worried about you." Talhan shrugged. "If you told me what it was you're investigating, maybe I could help."

"I don't want your help." Neelo clenched and unclenched their hands, debating smacking the warrior again.

"Oh, come on," Talhan prodded. "Yesterday was fun. Let me help."

"You fit so well in the Southern Court." Neelo frowned, walking off at full speed, uncaring if Talhan followed. "Everything is just fun and games with you all, isn't it?"

"Not everything." Talhan easily fell into stride, his long legs eating up the distance between them. "There are some things I take seriously. My oaths and duties, protecting my friends, keeping my promises."

"Don't make any promises to me, then."

"I already have," Talhan murmured, "you just don't know about them yet."

Silence hung between them as Neelo stormed toward the markets. They noted the way Talhan looked longingly at the sweet shop as the two of them raced by. Neelo tossed Talhan's words around in their mind. What promises could he have made to them without Neelo knowing?

"Where are you going?" Talhan finally asked as he ducked under a low washing line. Neelo intentionally chose the alley with the lowest hanging garments out of spite for their ruined plans, though the brew merchant's information didn't seem to be leading them anywhere either. Whether he claimed he sold the Queen's blend or not, whatever was in his stash was not the same as what the Queen was smoking.

"The green witch temple," Neelo called over their shoulder. They rushed under the washing lines without needing to duck. "I have some questions that I'm hoping the witches can answer . . . as long as you don't chase them away too."

Neelo waved their hand at the rainbow-hued buildings of the witch quarter. Colorfully dyed shade sails flapped over the central square that housed the witches' marketplace. Only faint peeks of white stone could be seen through the myriad of colors. Every resident decorated their dwellings—painting the trim, doors, shutters, and walls, all in bright, contrasting colors. The only monochromatic part of the markets were the white stone pavers that kept the ground cool even in the heat of summer.

"Why don't you go peruse the stalls?" Neelo suggested, swerving around a fountain and back down the main path. They veered off through another narrow alley and the pavers gave way to pale gravel. It crunched beneath their black boots as Neelo took a shortcut through the botanical gardens.

Talhan's boots crunched as well, the Golden Eagle remaining one step behind Neelo, no matter how often they ducked and swerved. "Can't I come to the temple with you?"

"You can, but it will be boring."

"No, it won't," Talhan insisted. "I hear they have a taster kitchen with all sorts of new recipes."

Neelo paused, whirling so fast that Talhan almost collided into them. "Why are you so infuriatingly optimistic?"

"Because I know it irks you."

They ducked under a thorny vine and pushed through the overgrown hedgerow. "It's no fun bickering with you."

"I agree. And yet you keep trying. If you just accept my presence, we wouldn't be arguing."

Neelo paused and shot him a menacing look. Talhan laughed, a low rough laugh that sounded so good to their ears that they had to remind themself that they were angry with him.

"I can't help it," Talhan continued. "This is who I am, this is who I *like* to be. When I was young, I felt like I had to be mean and angry all the time and it just felt wrong, like wearing a belt that was too tight. In the same way you skipping and singing through the markets would feel wrong," he added with a wink.

"At least you have that right."

"We all need a bit of both, though, don't we?" He easily parted the thick foliage and followed Neelo's winding path. Though Talhan's smile was easy, his eyes held more intensity than they were prepared for.

"Yes," they whispered. "I suppose we do."

Most of the time, Neelo felt completely shrouded in shadow, but, with Talhan, they felt that peek of sunlight that broke through the thickest canopy of trees. He had a way of beaming through the deepest darkness without even trying. Of dispelling the shroud around them.

"Fine, you can come," Neelo relented.

"Yes," Talhan hissed, pumping his fist like a gambler winning a bet.

Neelo rolled their eyes, but couldn't help their smile. "But you need to behave." They gave Talhan a look and added quickly, "And not eat all of their food."

He placed his hand on his chest as if affronted and Neelo arched their brow at him. "Okay, fine," Talhan said. "You may have a point."

He gestured his hand forward for Neelo to lead the way, and they dove back into the twisting labyrinth toward the green witch temple.

"HE SEEMS LIKE a good one," Baba Visello murmured with a faux warm smile. Neelo braced for the condescending remark. "Though I'm surprised. Him with," she glanced Neelo up and down, "you."

"There it is," Neelo muttered, pretending the jibes didn't pierce their steely exterior. The High Priestess was only saying what everyone was thinking. Why would Talhan Catullus, a Twin Eagle and famed warrior, want to be with someone like Neelo?

Talhan's laughter echoed through the temple behind them. They'd left him at the tasting kitchens by the front entrance, where locals would pass by throughout the day and sample the latest creations of Southern Court fare. Talhan had looked like a dragon amongst a trove of treasures, the way he lit up when he saw all the decadent food laid out.

The green witch temple was a sprawling open-air complex with tropical plants and gardens interspersed between the different rooms. The scent was sumptuous and sweet, wafting through the arched windows and drifting down the greenstone corridors. Parrots drank water collected in palm fronds, snakes slithered through the twisting vines, and monkeys howled, scrambling across rooftops and stealing ripening fruit from the trees. It was an oasis if ever there was one, teeming with life and beauty. The temple exemplified the powers of the green witches who made gardens grow even in the most barren soil and the most delicious foods, even from the barest ingredients.

Music drifted in and out of the corridor, first a lone horn, then the light strings of a fiddle. Witchlings danced in the atrium, where the sounds reverberated off the walls in a hypnotic echo. The building was a shrine to all things creation: food, flowers, art, music . . .

And insults, apparently.

They stood there patiently, waiting until Baba Visello moved on from her pointed observations to the actual business at hand. As if realizing her faux pas—though clearly unembarrassed by it—the witch asked, "Why do you care to see this painting so badly?" gesturing toward a hallway lined with oil paintings.

Neelo craned their neck up to the frescoed ceilings covered in creeping pink flowers. "I'm trying to remember something."

The High Priestess arched her perfectly shaped eyebrow, and Neelo noted how Baba Visello hid behind a facade of beauty, just like their mother. She adjusted the knot of her woven hair wrap; the fabric matching her robes—a deep forest green embroidered with every color of the rainbow.

"You remember everything," she said.

"Well, I'm confirming it, then."

"Very well," she said and set off. The golden beads of Baba Visello's earrings clinked with every step as Neelo walked beside the Priestess. "How is my sister doing these days?"

Neelo had been waiting for the inevitable question. "Rish is very well."

"Still no lovers?" Baba Visello prodded. "No family?"

"*I* am her family," Neelo countered.

Baba Visello had the same umber skin and straight black hair as her sister, but that's where the likeness ended. Despite her colorful attire, the High Priestess was scholarly and cold, whereas Rish was warm and gentle. Both were beautiful, but Rish—at least to Neelo—was beautiful in the ways that counted the most.

"She never, not once in her life, showed any interest in romantic companionship." Baba Visello pulled aside the woven flax screen bisecting the room and gestured for Neelo to go ahead.

"Meddling is definitely a family trait, I see," Neelo muttered. "Do you find her not having romantic companionship odd?"

The High Priestess balked, her beaded bracelets rattling as she opened the final door toward the gallery. "I find it decidedly un-Southern of her."

"Then does that make me *decidedly un-Southern* as well?"

Baba Visello pulled up short, clutching her hand to her stomach. "My apologies, Your Highness. That is not what I meant." She sketched a quick bow, clearly not sorry, and her sandals scuffed across the floor again. "Besides, you are betrothed."

"By way of a misguided duel and nothing more," Neelo grumbled, their cheeks flaming again at the memory of the brawl in Murreneir. "Though this one of my mother's harebrained schemes seems to have stuck."

"Hmm."

Neelo shot her a sharp look. "Do you have something you wish to say?"

"No," Baba Visello said. "I only wish for my sister to not be lonely."

"Rish has many close friends in the palace, *and* she has me," Neelo countered.

"It was my mistake, Your Highness." The High Priestess said it in a way that made it clear she regretted nothing about any part of this conversation. "Some people never want to marry and others marry even when they don't want to."

Neelo knew she was speaking of Talhan again. A seed of doubt bloomed in the pit of Neelo's stomach. Talhan was too kind, too good, and being shackled to Neelo for the rest of his life was something he might not regret now, but what about in ten years, twenty? When he realized that ruling the Southern Court wasn't one big party and there were more tempting *indulgences* to be had outside of Neelo. Worse, what if he truly came to care for Neelo only to realize Neelo couldn't reciprocate that emotion in the ways he deserved? The thoughts churned over and over.

What if their mother's tricks had doomed Talhan to a lifetime of unhappiness?

Baba Visello was seemingly unaware of the anxious spiral of thoughts she'd sent Neelo down. The High Priestess led Neelo into the art gallery—an airy room crammed with paintings from the wainscoting panels to the high vaulted ceilings. The room was perfectly positioned between the two breezeways to pull moisture from the humid air and protect the artwork, a clever feature Neelo appreciated. Baba Visello stopped at a portrait of ten faces, gathered in what appeared to be a Solstice celebration, judging by the paper lanterns and golden decor. A young Queen Emberspear was depicted in the center of the painting—still just Princess Emberspear then. Courtiers gathered all around her, painted mid-action, laughing and drinking.

"Do you notice anything strange about this painting?" Neelo asked.

Baba Visello considered it for a moment before saying. "I don't think I do."

"This one here." Neelo pointed to one courtier in the corner, holding aloft a goblet. "What is their name?"

"Sava Hashez, Your Highness. The Lady of Arboa."

"Sy's mother." Neelo cocked their head, already knowing the answer. "And is she still alive?"

Baba Visello twisted her head slowly toward Neelo, knowing Neelo already knew the answer, but saying, "No, she passed soon after this portrait, when her youngest was still a babe. Why?"

"How did she die?"

"Some say it was her breathing," the High Priestess said, brows knitting in confusion. "Others say she got lost to the Arboan wine, Your Highness. The family kept her manner of death rather quiet."

"And this one?" Neelo pointed to a fae reveler lounging across the cushions below their mother's feet. "Alive or dead?"

"Dead, Your Highness."

Neelo pointed again.

"Dead," Baba Visello whispered.

Neelo went down the line of all the people in the picture, all confirmed dead apart from their mother . . . and one other. Their fingers lingered just above the oil paint of the last face—a young fae with light brown hair and sage-green eyes. The shape of her face—the high cheekbones and sharp jawline, the nose, the chin, the eyebrows . . . Neelo knew that face well, had seen it in this person's son. "Who is this?"

"Kira Ashby."

"Hale's mom," Neelo murmured, their eyes narrowing to the hilt of a dagger belted to Kira's hip. They squinted and leaned closer until they were practically kissing the paint, but they couldn't make out the color of the stones on the hilt, too shadowed by the artist. Neelo wasn't one to place bets, but they would've wagered all of Saxbridge's gold on the color of those stones.

"She was a fae of average standing, but Queen Emberspear had taken a liking to Kira in her youth. The two were friends before everything went wrong with Gedwin Norwood," Baba Visello said. "I'm surprised Queen Emberspear never fought against Norwood's banishment of Kira . . . though I suppose she had retreated from court politics by then." Neelo knew by *retreated*, the High Priestess meant that their mother was too focused on partying to remember her old friend. Baba Visello stared at the painting for a long time before asking, "What are you thinking about?"

"This vial with the skull and crown." Neelo pointed to the bottle sitting atop a table in the painting. "What is that?"

Baba Visello shrugged. "It was a potion invented by a brown witch healer to aid the dying."

"What was the healer's name?"

"I'm not sure, Your Highness," Baba Visello said. "It was long before my time."

A leaden weight dropped in Neelo's gut. "Do you know what the significance is of this to the brew they are smoking?"

"That was when Lady Hashez started adding the elixir to the Arboan flowers." Baba Visello walked along to a painting depicting the white blooming fields of Arboa. "It was quite the scandal at the time. Adding brown witch elixirs to the traditional recipes? Some said it was an offense to the Gods themselves." She tipped her head, scrutinizing the painting. "Sometimes I think royal fae consider themselves above the Gods. It was the same decade when the green witches started adding more mint and ginger to our foods, to settle the stomachs of those who overindulged. It was originally only for the Queen's personal use at celebrations, but the blend started finding its way into the palace more and more frequently."

"And outside the palace too," Neelo muttered, wondering if the mint tea and gingered flatbread the green witches plied partygoers with was actually a result of this. They followed Baba Visello, scanning the paintings of the different landscapes of the Southern Court. "I need to know the ingredients of this elixir."

"Something to do with hellebore and bonebane by the smell of it. I don't know exactly." Baba Visello glanced at Neelo. "Perhaps a brown witch healer would know the secrets? All I know is that it is very hard to come by outside of the Western Court."

Neelo's hands clenched at their sides and they picked up the pace, their footsteps echoing along the stone hallway. They needed to speak with Fenrin when he arrived and then travel to the blooming fields of

Arboa as soon as possible. Something was stirring in Okrith. Neelo could feel it in their bones, and some of the people closest to them were unwittingly a part of whatever schemes Adisa Monroe was conjuring throughout the realm.

They barely mumbled a thank-you to Baba Visello before dismissing her and racing to the kitchens to find Talhan.

CHAPTER NINE

All their plans to tell Talhan of their suspicions vanished upon seeing him.

Neelo turned the corner back to the kitchens and what they saw made their face split into a smile.

Talhan sat backward on a chair pulled into the middle of the kitchen. Seven older green witches gathered around him, offering him food and laughing. He regaled them with a story that had them wiping tears of laughter from their eyes. He was so entertaining, so easily adored . . . and it made Neelo's chest crack.

He wasn't just brightness; he was the blistering sun, so powerful and all-consuming, so brilliant he burned away everything else. And in that moment, Neelo knew one thing for certain: he needed someone who shone just as brightly as him, someone who didn't dim his light . . . someone other than Neelo. Baba Visello's voice echoed in Neelo's mind: *Him . . . with you?*

Talhan's eyes darted to Neelo, finding them instantly, as if he sensed their presence. Neelo felt the scorching heat of that brilliant smile and the pain of watching it fade as he spotted them. The room sobered as the green witches' attention shifted to the Heir of Saxbridge. This is what

Neelo did: sucked the joy and light out of every room. Taxing. Burden-some. More poisonous than the smoke lining their mother's lungs.

Neelo shook their head. They refused to watch Talhan's smile disappear over the years, and even more so, they refused to be the cause for it. Maybe in the quiet moments when it was just the two of them, maybe then some of it made sense, but in times like this—when Talhan was meant to be in the center of the crowd—they knew it would never work out between them, doomed from the start.

"Stay if you'd like," Neelo called from the door, already turning away. "I'll see you at the palace."

They departed before Talhan could protest and cringed as they heard his hurried apologies to the green witches and the scratch of his chair being pushed back as he stood.

"Seriously, stay." Neelo threw the words over their shoulder as they steered toward the vine-covered entryway.

Talhan's hand gently touched their elbow, barely a tap, but it was enough to make Neelo stop.

"What happened?" he asked, moving around to their front. "What did you find?"

Neelo felt his eyes upon them like a golden summer's day. "I con-firmed my suspicions."

Talhan crouched slightly so his eyes were parallel with Neelo's own. "Which are?"

"It's complicated," they muttered.

"I'm sure of that, with you," Talhan snorted. "So un-complicate it."

"I want to do more research first," Neelo replied, picking at the loose thread on the hem of their jacket. Would it be acceptable to pull out the book in their pocket right then and there?

"I would be surprised if you didn't." Talhan chuckled, looking up to the twisting vines forming an arch above his head. He plucked a coral flower, twirled it, and placed it behind his ear.

Neelo bit the inside of their cheek. Only Talhan Catullus would look ever the warrior with a flower tucked behind his ear.

"So you're really not going to tell me anything until you're finished researching?" Talhan pouted and Neelo became instantly frustrated with themself for the smile that pulled at their lips.

"I . . ." They were about to relent, convinced by Talhan's enthusiasm that he too would be intrigued by their findings: the different scented blends, the brown witch elixir being added to the brew, the mysterious dagger on Kira Ashby's hip . . . but then they remembered the sight of Talhan in that gaggle of witches and Baba Visello's snide remarks. "I just need some time and space to think this over on my own," they grumbled instead of voicing every concern racing through their head, many of them having nothing to do with brew or global politics.

"I understand." Talhan flashed that knightly grin and gestured toward the doorway, but Neelo spotted that hint of hurt and they cursed all the Gods for forcing them to make him feel that way. They cursed the Gods even more for giving them the singular ability to read Talhan Catullus's emotions like an open book. The sooner Talhan left, the sooner this torment would end. Besides, with Talhan around they would be stuck solving the puzzle of the flutter in their stomach instead of the puzzle of the threat to their court.

WEEKS PASSED, WITH Neelo hiding away from Talhan as best they could, and Talhan, to his credit, giving them the space they'd demanded. Talhan had seemed to charm every other person in the court in the interim, calling every palace resident by their first name. Even Indi wanted to sneak off to find him during the day. Little traitor. But Neelo ignored Talhan even when they were forced together for meals, barely deigning him with a cursory glance. The sooner he realized he wasn't staying, the better. Summer was upon them and the Solstice wouldn't be long after. Seeing Talhan with those green witches, so filled with life, had twisted those dark shameful parts in Neelo, made them feel as broken and warped as they were certain everyone else thought they were.

Neelo had barely visited the library—the space tainted by the images of Talhan sleeping across from their favorite chair. Instead, they ventured out to their other haunts—ones even Talhan wouldn't find them in . . . not that he was looking.

They found a spot in the shade where the glaring sun didn't sear their dark tunic. The jungle was a raucous of chirping birdsong and buzzing insects swarming around the creek. Neelo sat perched on a tree branch, surveying the long road that led through the gardens to the palace. This patch of jungle on the western edge of the grounds was one of their many hiding spots as a child.

They reached into the hollowed-out tree trunk and grabbed a parcel wrapped in layers of waxed paper to keep it dry from the rain. Six small books in a rainbow of colors sat inside—a poetry collection. The books always reminded them of this creek and the cool shade of this edge of forest, and so they'd given the collection a home here within the tree itself so that they could read the books whenever they visited.

The sound of horse hooves clomping up the road made them lift their head. They spotted the lanky torso and the mop of blond hair and, for a split second, they thought it was Cole Doledir, the brown witch who had been investigating the Western Queen's murder only to later flee a dinner party in the Northern Court. What was he doing in Saxbridge? They blinked and the heat bending the rider's visage faded until they realized it wasn't Cole at all, but Fenrin.

They hopped from their perch and ambled down the path to where they could cut him off, but just as they moved to turn the corner, Talhan came barreling out of the house, shouting Fenrin's name with a wave.

Neelo was intrigued by the Eagle's eagerness to greet his friend—such strange enthusiasm. The night of the fire was the first time Neelo had shouted in years, the first time they'd had lowered their defenses in the panic and chaos. To see exuberance just for the sake of it didn't quite make sense to them.

They debated not greeting the brown witch since Talhan was present, but they needed Fenrin's help and it couldn't wait. Neelo slowed their steps, watching as Fenrin dismounted and hugged Talhan. The Eagle clapped him on the shoulder. Judging by the way Talhan looked him up and down, Neelo was sure he was complimenting Fenrin on something about his figure. Sure enough, Fenrin had grown a considerable amount of muscle since the wedding in Yexshire. It seemed like he was intent on training as a soldier.

When Talhan spotted Neelo across the field, he waved them over. The action made them pause. Talhan behaved as if weeks hadn't passed, as if Neelo hadn't been intentionally cold toward him. It seemed the Eagle was going to stubbornly wait out this distance and Neelo couldn't help but be a little bit impressed at his persistence even while simultaneously frustrated at their lack of success in driving him away.

"Your Highness," Fenrin said, dropping into a deep bow as Neelo reached him.

"Just Neelo," they corrected, giving Fenrin a bob of their head in return. "Thank you for coming on such short notice."

"Remy said it was urgent." Fenrin glanced between Neelo and Talhan, his voice falling into a hush. "She said it was for the Queen."

"It seems my mother forgot that urgency when she waited so long to send for you," Neelo grumbled. "But she forgets most things these days, even things that could save her life. My mother is as stubborn as the rumors say and has shirked every brown witch healer in the Southern Court." Their eyes dropped to the scuffed leather bag in Fenrin's hand. "But I know you come from a long line of powerful brown witches—"

Fenrin's eyebrows lifted. "Did Remy say that?"

"Renwick did," Neelo said, cocking their head at the surprise that crossed Fenrin's face. "I think you will be more than capable of treating my mother," Neelo continued with a confident nod. "I hope her stubbornness doesn't get the better of you too."

"He grew up with Remy," Talhan said with a laugh. "I think he'll be fine."

"What ails her?" Fenrin asked, ignoring Talhan's jest.

Talhan snorted. "What doesn't?"

"Many things," Neelo interjected, pulling Fenrin's attention back to them. "Though I am primarily concerned about the witching brew she smokes more than the air she breathes."

"Ah, yes," Fenrin said with a knowing frown. "I've heard about your Southern blends. I'd be interested to know what magic is contained within the ingredients to make it so potent."

"As would I," Neelo muttered. "I will be sending scouts to the Arboan blooming fields to find out firsthand." Talhan arched his brow at Neelo, but Neelo ignored it.

"Good," Fenrin said. "Though I think the simplest solution would be she simply stop."

"That's the *best* solution, but not the simplest," Neelo grumbled. "If there is a way to treat her, I trust you to find out."

Fenrin's lips quirked up on one side. "Thank you."

"Don't thank me yet," Neelo warned.

"Right." Fenrin blew out a ragged breath and rolled his shoulders.

"You'll probably want to change your shoes first," Talhan said, nodding down at Fenrin's black boots.

"Why?"

"Wearing black is considered bad luck in Saxbridge," Talhan replied. Fenrin's brow furrowed as he scanned Neelo from their black jacket to their black closed-toed sandals. Talhan hooked his thumb at Neelo. "They have the worst luck."

"Not everyone here is so superstitious." Neelo scowled. "Besides, it serves my purposes well enough." Wearing the dark colors was another layer of protection against unwanted attention. Especially since the courtiers believed bad luck could rub off on other people and so they mostly steered clear of Neelo.

"I guess I should get changed before I see the patient." Fenrin took a tentative step and glanced back at Talhan. "Why do I feel like I should be wearing armor?"

Talhan snickered and clapped him on the back. "Because you probably should."

FENRIN BURST THROUGH the doors, his cheeks a ruddy shade of crimson and his eyes wide with exasperation. "She is the most frustrating person I've ever met," he blustered, waving his hand back at the mahogany doors as they unceremoniously slammed closed behind him.

Neelo tensed as they peeked up from over their book.

Talhan chuckled, folding his arms across his chest and leaning back against the wall, matching Neelo's posture. "Clearly."

Neelo gripped their book tighter until the edges bit into their skin. They couldn't imagine the torment Queen Emberspear probably had just put Fenrin through, but despite his lanky frame and kind face, he seemed tough. There was a resolve there that only came from being forced to summon it. Fenrin had seen darkness, of that Neelo was certain.

"Is she beyond saving?" Neelo bit the inside of their cheek, waiting for that crestfallen look and the feeling of their world dropping out from underneath them. But instead, Fenrin just frowned.

"Not if she quits what she's doing," he groused. "I think I could heal her then . . ." He rubbed his hand across the back of his neck. "But it's much harder to treat someone who says they'd rather die happy."

Neelo cringed. That's what brew equated to in their mother's life now: happiness. Without it, she saw no point in carrying on. She probably thought she'd go up in a glorious inferno of brew like on the night of the fire. The fact she had survived this long was a bloody miracle.

"I will keep trying," Fenrin said, taking a tentative step toward Neelo. "She has a *lot* of fight in her." He chuckled, his cheek dimpling on one side. "If anyone could spit in the face of death, it would be Queen Emberspear."

Neelo offered him a gruff nod in return. "Thank you for being here," they murmured, pushing off the wall.

"Of course," Fenrin said. "I wasn't much use in the High Mountain Court anyway. Not my favorite climate. The air is too thin for my Western skin," he added with a chuckle. "I'm constantly having to cover myself in salve. Cool rainy days and cloudy skies are what I prefer. I was planning on heading north to see—"

"Aneryn?" Talhan interjected, giving Fenrin a wink.

The angry red blush staining Fenrin's cheeks crept down to his neck until his entire face flushed with scarlet. "To help with the blue witch recovery."

"And to see Aneryn," Talhan taunted again.

"Rua's friend?" Neelo asked, cocking their head. "I didn't realize you two were . . . close."

"Not you too," Fenrin moaned. "You've been spending too much time with Talhan."

"Not nearly enough," Talhan said, and Neelo's eyes dropped back to their hands. He said it so lightly, but Neelo heard the barb of his pointed words.

Fenrin shrugged, though his eyes remained fixed straight ahead, seemingly lost in a memory.

Neelo considered him for a moment: the look in his eyes and the sorrowful thread of his words. "With everything that's going on, I think we might need a few powerful blue witches in the South again. I will fae fire Rua and ask if any of her witches are interested in a Southern job. Aneryn could accompany them, of course, and help them settle in for a few weeks."

"You're not just doing this—"

"I'm doing it as the Heir of Saxbridge," they said firmly, but tried to put as much warmth in their eyes as possible.

"Thank you," Fenrin whispered. Neelo was about to turn when he added, "And a green witch named Laris. She would have much to learn from the green witches of Saxbridge . . . could you ask about her too?"

"Look at you having little witch friends." Talhan chuckled and clapped Fenrin on the shoulder. "Are you wooing several lovers? Very Southern of you."

"I'm not . . . ," Fenrin spluttered.

"I'm teasing. Seriously—I'm happy for you, Fen."

At that Fenrin rolled his eyes, playfully shoving Talhan's hand off his shoulder, but it was plain that he was pleased by Talhan's approval. He looked at Neelo, waiting for theirs.

"For saving my mother's life, it's the least I can do," Neelo said with a bob of their head. It was a kind thing to do—to request his friends join him in Saxbridge—but it wasn't entirely selfless either. With the aid of his companions, Fenrin would hopefully feel more compelled to save the Queen, and if he started to flounder, Neelo could threaten to send them away again.

They gritted their teeth, knowing using the witches as leverage was callous, but also knowing they would do it anyway. That being cruel was sometimes a royal's job. Neelo's mother needed help if she were to remain as Queen. Fae lived long lives, double, sometimes triple, the lifespan of humans. Which meant another lifetime should pass before Neelo had to step into their role as sovereign.

Neelo saw what it did to the rest of them: Remy Dammacus, Renwick Vostemur, Lina Thorne—all so young to have crowns placed upon their heads. But that's what happened in times of war. Whole generations were wiped off the slate. The wisdom and guidance of elders disappeared as more and more were lost to the fighting. Of their parents' generation, only Queen Emberspear was still upon her throne and her contemporaries of the houses of Norwood, Vostemur, Dammacus, and Thorne were all dead.

Neelo's mother had feared it for many years—Queen Emberspear knew the Fates were coming for her next. When Queen Thorne was assassinated, it was the final straw, and their mother drowned herself in drink and the most potent brew, wearing those fucking gloves, all the while waiting for death to claim her at long last. How did one fight someone convinced that their time had come? How could Neelo battle the invisible hand of Fate?

Heading off down the corridor, Neelo glanced back over their shoulder, finding the Eagle's golden eyes trained upon them, as if Talhan could hear their swirling thoughts as readily as if Neelo spoke them aloud. They picked up their pace even though Talhan's telltale bootsteps didn't trail behind.

"How am I going to save her this time?" they whispered, and veered off toward the gardens, leaving Talhan in their wake once more. That Fenrin wasn't able to swoop in and save their mother was both inevitable and yet frustrating. But not quite as frustrating as the fact that another concern floated to the front of their mind:

Would it be another several weeks before they locked eyes with Talhan Catullus again?

CHAPTER TEN

The room was so thick with white smoke that Neelo had to wave their hand vigorously just to see an inch in front of them. Soft breaths and moans carried from distant corners, making Neelo's cheeks burn.

They'd gotten used to it over the years . . . mostly. Their mother used to call upon them outside of these times before they were of age, but orgies were so common in Saxbridge that they'd stumbled past—and through—a few before. There was always at least one couple tucked into a corner of a party or a little garden alcove. Pleasure was what the Southern Court was all about. But the Southerners had binged on every mortal pleasure to the point where it no longer even seemed enjoyable anymore, always chasing a bigger high, a stronger rush.

Neelo thought of their mother and of how she began to fade. Queen Emberspear was once lauded as a celebrant of life and now her dwindling suite of courtiers seemed rather sad. Those who once cheered her as a goddess of carnal desires now spoke with false praise, their faces pinched and pitying.

After all, debauchery is well and good until it becomes debasement. And Queen Emberspear was right on the verge of the latter.

Venturing through the cloud of smoke, Neelo finally found the

Queen sitting on a makeshift throne in the corner. She wore a bright yellow dress that highlighted her curves against her dark skin. Kohl smudges trailed down to her cheekbones and her eyes were half hooded with wine and lust. The room stunk of sex and brew and it made Neelo's stomach roil.

"What do you want?" Neelo growled.

"So prickly," the Queen tittered. "You need more fun in your life."

"I think you have enough for the both of us," Neelo quipped, not permitting their gaze to wander. They knew exactly what was happening in the shadows.

Queen Emberspear took a long sip from her goblet. "I wanted to talk to you about that brown witch, Henrin."

"Fenrin."

"Whatever," the Queen hissed, waving away Neelo's remark. "I thought he'd be helpful, but he's not right for the South. Send him home."

Neelo bristled, their shoulders bunching up around their ears. "He is here to help you."

"He wants to change me." The Queen's eyes barely opened a slit. "He wants to change our way of life."

"He wants to *save* your life," Neelo snarled. "The only change he wants is to make you healthy."

Queen Emberspear considered Neelo for a moment, her expression sobering. "Sometimes I think I'm only one step from madness. If I don't stop thinking about it, stop worrying about it, it'll finally catch me." She snapped at the young blond courtier to her right to bring her more wine and when she looked back at Neelo, their stomach dropped to their feet. "If I stare straight in its face, it'll sink its talons in me and never let me go. It'll whisper into my mind until I can't stop it."

The word "whisper" made Neelo pause. "Whispers? What whispers do you hear?"

"The only thing I hear is 'more,'" the Queen said, looking at Neelo as if they were the one on the verge of lunacy. "Do not ask me to give up the only thing that is keeping me here."

"Maybe there are other things to keep you here," they murmured, their chest cracking open. Their mother might love Neelo in her own twisted way, but that love wasn't enough, *they* weren't enough, to make her want to try.

Queen Emberspear threw her head back and cackled. Neelo already knew what their mother was going to say as her lip curled and she hissed, "I'd rather die than find out."

The door slammed open behind Neelo and a few courtiers gasped as the room filled with the sound of stomping boots. Neelo's stomach sank further, their flush ratcheting up as Talhan barged past them and straight up to Queen Emberspear.

"Talhan Catullus, what a pleasant—"

"What is the meaning of this?" Talhan growled, interrupting the Queen's cheerful greeting. "This is *no place* to be summoning anyone, let alone discussing important affairs."

The Queen arched her slender brow, snatching a pipe from a nearby courtier's hand. The courtier scuttled off, her bare feet slapping across the tiles. Neelo narrowed their eyes at the smoke, wondering where their mother's stash was located and fantasizing about setting the whole thing ablaze.

Queen Emberspear's words slurred as she said, "You better get used to it if you still plan on marrying my child and being on the Southern throne one day."

Talhan seemed to grow another inch taller, his countenance darkening as he rumbled, "Is that a threat?"

"It is a warning to respect the ways of the South," Queen Emberspear insisted, taking a long drag on her pipe and letting the smoke swirl through her hair.

Talhan inclined his head. "The ways of the South or the ways of its Queen?"

"I don't like your tone." The Queen's lip curled as her eyes landed on Neelo. They braced for what they knew she was about to say. "Perhaps if you were getting your *needs* met—"

"Enough!" Talhan shouted and the entire room froze. "If you want to speak to Neelo, you will do so in the council chamber or at meals, with their councilors present, and no one else."

"You do not give me orders," the Queen balked. "I—"

"You won't be around long enough to threaten me if you don't accept Fenrin's aid." Talhan's eyes were filled with fire as the Queen's mouth dropped open.

No one spoke to Queen Emberspear that way. No one. Neelo suppressed the laugh that stirred in their chest at that shocked look on their mother's face. Gods, it felt good to see Talhan cut her down like that.

Talhan turned his golden gaze at Neelo. "Do you agree?"

Neelo's voice was breathless as they said, "Yes."

"Good." Talhan nodded. "Let's go."

Neelo's heart thundered in their ears as they followed Talhan into the quiet hall. The heady smoke cleared and they clasped their hands in front of them, forcing themself not to take out the book from their pocket as Talhan stepped up beside them.

"Did Rish tell you I was in there?" Neelo muttered, suddenly feeling small in the stillness of the hallway.

Talhan looked like he wanted to punch his fist into the wall. "She did." His hands formed and released fists as if he had no control over them. "And something in me just snapped and I couldn't take it anymore. She shouldn't be treating herself like that. And she *definitely* shouldn't be treating you like that."

"I'm sorry about her," Neelo said, even though they had no idea why. They'd grown too accustomed to apologizing for their mother's behavior.

"It wasn't your fault."

Neelo sighed. "I should've just told her that myself, but . . ."

"It's easier to stick up for the people we care about than it is to stick up for ourselves," Talhan said, rolling his shoulders. "It can be your turn next time."

"That means I'd have to care about you." The words came spilling out of Neelo's mouth before they could stop them.

"It does. But that's okay." Talhan grinned. "Because you already do."

Neelo clenched their jaw and muttered, "How do you know?"

"You grip your book tighter when you're nervous," Talhan said.

Neelo scowled at him. "I'm not holding a book."

"And the muscle in your jaw pops out," Talhan added.

Neelo immediately relaxed their jaw. "Maybe you just make me nervous," they muttered.

"Maybe." Laughter tinged Talhan's voice. "Maybe being nervous in this case is a good thing. Maybe you make me nervous too."

"There is no way that Talhan Catullus, the Golden Eagle himself, gets nervous around me."

"Have you met yourself?" Talhan huffed, waving a hand from the top of their dark hair to their shined leather sandals. "You are the most intimidating person I know."

Neelo's shoulders shook with laughter. They looked Talhan up and down, their eyes lingering on the weapons strapped to his belt.

Talhan started to chuckle too, his eyes lighting up. "Why are we laughing?"

"It's just ridiculous," Neelo said, biting their lip to try to stop the absurd laughter escaping from them. How funny the two of them must've looked—Neelo with their baggy black clothes, short stature, and *fuck off* glare, walking beside Talhan tall and muscled, smiling like he was the hero of his own parade.

"I'm being serious." Talhan laughed harder, his bemused chuckle only encouraging Neelo further and they wondered if the brew had gone to their head. "You see everything. You're the smartest person in Okrith, always one step ahead. To be your enemy would be truly terrifying."

Neelo laughed even harder, their stomach muscles aching as their whole body shook. Talhan Catullus, one of the greatest warriors in the realm, thought *they* were terrifying.

THE RECEPTION IN the dining room was cold after the royal telling-off that Talhan gave Queen Emberspear, but Neelo's iciness toward Talhan had softened a bit since their laughing fit in the corridor. By dinnertime, the entire palace had heard of the way Talhan had spoken to the Queen and Neelo was already dreading whatever her form of retaliation would be.

The Queen perched on the head chair, glowering at the lineup of ten performers. Standing on pedestals were acrobats, jugglers, and contortionists, all vying for a prime spot in the Summer Solstice celebrations—ideally one closest to the dais. The Queen frowned at them each in turn, clearly unimpressed. Rolling her eyes, she selected a square of flatbread and dipped it into the spiced bean sauce and chewed morosely.

The Queen glanced at Denton, who dined to her right. His mustache twitched as she asked, "Do you have any more?"

"Yes, of course, Your Majesty," he spluttered. He blotted the corners of his mouth with a napkin and clapped his hands. The performers jolted and then scattered, their shoulders drooping and winning smiles fading. "Bring in the next lot!"

Another ten performers entered, taking the spots on the pedestals. With their shoulders thrown back and unsettlingly enormous smiles upon their faces, the troupe began their acts.

"Perhaps if we knew what kind of entertainment you're looking for?" Denton beseeched Queen Emberspear.

The Queen swiveled toward the councilor, eyes filled with venom. "Performers worthy of the renowned Summer Solstice festivities," she barked.

Neelo took a sip of their juice, the sweet acidic flavor cutting the spiciness of the food. They kept their eyes fixed on the book in their hands. Talhan ate beside them, seemingly enjoying the entertainment and ignoring the Queen's hateful glances. Fenrin sat on Neelo's other side, also carefully focused on his plate.

Neelo knew why their mother was in a foul mood—a reason worse than even Talhan's snarky comments. It was easy to discern without the telltale halo of white smoke that normally circled her at all times. The Queen knew she needed to quit, knew her mind wouldn't survive much more abuse, but Neelo had seen these brief respites before, and didn't have high hopes that she'd survive this agitation for much longer. Soon she'd relent as she always did, and a few hours later she'd be quitting again and seeking an equal amount of praise as the previous time . . . and the time before that.

A plate of curried rice drifted into Neelo's line of sight as Talhan silently offered the bowl. Neelo knew it was his way of saying he'd noted their change in mood. They wondered if he counted the seconds it normally took them before they flipped a page. It seemed preposterous that he would be paying that close attention . . . but somehow he knew.

"Thank you," Neelo murmured, accepting the bowl and serving a heaped spoonful onto their plate.

Talhan leaned in and asked, "What do you think of the performers?"

Neelo shrugged. "I don't care much for this sort of entertainment."

"None of them?" Fenrin's voice was incredulous as he leaned into the table and helped himself to another serving of summer berries dressed in mint and lime. He ate eagerly, as if he'd never tasted green witch cooking before. "Not even that fire spinner?"

"I suppose it's enjoyable if you haven't seen it a thousand times before." Neelo flipped another page and peeked up at Talhan. "Which are your favorites?"

Talhan's eyebrows lifted in surprise. "I like the fire spinners, the contortionists—"

"And the plate jugglers," Fenrin added through a mouthful of food.

"Excellent," Neelo said, raising their voice to call down the table, their eyes never leaving their book. "I've made my selections, Mother."

The Queen didn't hide her shock. "*You* have picked performers for the Solstice?"

"Your Majesty!" a voice called. A messenger burst into the dining hall and hastened over to the Queen. Seeming to debate with himself whether to run or walk, the messenger moved in an awkward scamper.

The entertainers gasped, whirling toward the harried human. He stumbled over one of the pedestals, knocking into the fire spinners.

Queen Emberspear swayed to her feet. "What news?" She held her hand out, waiting for the letter to be placed in her outstretched fingers, while around her, a flaming baton whirled to the floor, setting the pant leg of the juggler on fire. Shouts and curses were exchanged as two other performers erupted into fisticuffs.

Talhan nudged Neelo with his elbow. "Neelo." Neelo ignored him. He nudged them again. "*Neelo.*"

They flipped the page of their book. "What?"

"Are you going to do something about this?" Talhan murmured, taking a long drink from his goblet and nodding to the chaos across the table.

"Oh," Neelo muttered. "Right."

This pandemonium was fairly commonplace, but Talhan and Fenrin weren't as desensitized to the constant havoc of Saxbridge Palace. Neelo carefully put their bookmark back on the selected page and slowly set the book on the table. Unhurried even as a contortionist and acrobat pummeled each other, they rose from their chair and ambled around the table. They grabbed the nearest water jug and chucked it on the juggler, who was trying to pat down her smoking pant leg. The room paused as the water splashed onto the juggler and across the floor.

"Everybody out," Neelo said in a quiet voice, but the performers listened and hastened away. Neelo turned back to Talhan and Fenrin, both watching them with curious expressions.

Talhan laughed and took another long drink from his goblet. "That is one way to get someone's attention."

"You don't need to wield a dagger to get someone to listen," Neelo grumbled, rolling their eyes.

"Ah, but it helps sometimes," Talhan replied with a wink. His smile faltered as he glanced down the table to the Queen.

Neelo followed his stare and saw their mother frowning at a piece of paper. "What does it say?"

The Queen looked up, her eyes cold and sharp. "It's from Lord Ersan of Arboa. He says the wreckage of a ship has washed ashore and he thinks it might have something to do with Augustus Norwood."

"Ersan?" Talhan growled, his muscles tightening as if readying to fight an invisible foe. "Not Carys's Ersan?"

Neelo bobbed their head, their only acknowledgment. The falling-out between Carys and Ersan—Sy as his friends called him—was still a tender subject all these many years later.

Fenrin cocked his head, glancing between Talhan and the Queen. "I thought Norwood's fleet was sunk by the Southern storms in Silver Sands Harbor." He took another mouthful of roasted squash, eating the green witch fare as if he'd never been fed before. "That's a long way

93

for wreckage to drift. Could it be pulled out to sea and pushed inland again like that?"

"I think this is a different ship," Queen Emberspear said, staring intently at the letter like it had some hidden code. "We—"

Neelo cleared their throat, glancing at Denton. "We should have a full council meeting to discuss this."

The Queen arched her brow at Neelo. "Look at you picking performers and calling for council meetings."

"If it pleases you, yes," Neelo muttered, their tone cutting through the pleasantness of their words.

The heavy cloud that hung over the Queen's features seemed to ease slightly, her expression brightening as she assessed Neelo. "It does. Greatly," she said, her voice fading into a whisper. "It is my greatest delight to see you stepping into your role as sovereign."

Neelo readied their protest, hating that the Queen was so certain she needed to be replaced, but the words didn't come as the Queen nodded to Denton, who wore an equally perplexed expression. "Go tell the others. The Heir of Saxbridge will represent me in the meeting."

Neelo pushed back from their seat, the meal forgotten. "I'll meet you in the council chamber in half an hour." They didn't say it to anyone in particular, just stepped over the charred spot the fire spinner's baton made on the stone floor, and left. They wondered if Talhan would rise to follow them and they were both grateful and disheartened when he didn't.

Whatever laid amongst the debris of this shipwreck might be the missing piece to the puzzle they'd struggled in vain to solve. Adisa Monroe and Augustus Norwood were allies after all—their goals one and the same. Neelo's mind flashed back to Rua's letter and the plans that Augustus Norwood threatened were already in action in the Southern Court. Was the violet witch planning another poisoning like she had in the West? Another mind-controlling curse like she had in the North? Perhaps their hunt into the origins of the Queen's brew was only one of their many problems and not Adisa Monroe's point of attack at all. Was a violet grip already tightening around the South's neck without Neelo even realizing?

Too many questions, but at least now there was a potential place to get answers. So, as they walked down toward the chamber, they knew they needed to go to Arboa and see this wreckage themself . . . and they also knew that it would be a disaster if the Golden Eagle came with them.

CHAPTER ELEVEN

The half-drunk, befuddled councilors stumbled into the chamber, frowning as if they'd been interrupted from much more important business. Neelo stood by the wall of oil paintings, staring out their favorite framed window. Candlelight twinkled through the gardens and the shadows of moths danced in their glow. The sky was not fully bleached of color with the sun setting so late into the evenings. It was a beautiful living painting this evening, a contrast to the dread they felt inside.

Neelo had the urge to open the door to their right and step out onto the balcony. They knew the air would smell of evening jasmine and the lemongrass oil from the torches. Queen Emberspear used to give her yearly addresses on that balcony, though she'd stopped her public speeches since the Siege of Yexshire. All of Neelo's ancestors were coronated just inches from where they now stood, and they prayed it would be many decades more before they were crowned upon the same balcony.

Seeing how much their prayers had been answered in the past, they weren't sure the Gods were listening.

The clamor behind Neelo made them turn and wander over to a chair on the far side of the *amasa* wood table. As they pulled out a book from their jacket, the final stragglers wandered in. Neelo peeked up expectantly, wondering if a certain fae warrior would join them.

"What is going on?" one councilor asked, buttoning up his tunic as he dropped into an upholstered bench along the far wall.

"We've had word from the Lord of Arboa," Denton said again, repeating the same speech for each of the six councilors who entered the chamber. He held up the crinkled letter. "Ersan Almah contacted us. The wreckage of three ships has washed up on the shores of Arboa."

"Three?" Neelo looked up from their book, knowing they should probably put it away. They did, after all, call for this council meeting, and now they were acting like their normal disinterested self.

"I spoke to Lord Ersan through the fae fire after dinner, Your Highness," Denton said. "He had no other information for us. Just that wreckage washed ashore, and that he suspects three ships from the miscellany of debris."

Three ships was new information. That was a lot of wreckage and, hopefully, a lot of clues as to what Augustus Norwood's fleet was planning.

"What did Lord Ersan find?" Talhan asked, pushing past the gathering crowd of grumpy councilors and finding a chair beside Neelo. The sight of him made Neelo press their lips together, not granting themself permission to smile.

Talhan's hair was wet and he smelled fresh, like bay leaves and spiced coffee. He casually leaned back on the carved wood chair and Neelo thought he looked more like a king than Neelo would ever look like a ruler.

"He said nothing more of note." Denton sighed dramatically at having to repeat himself once again, and this time placed the letter on the table's center and tapped it pointedly. "Only that there looked to be multiple ships in the wreckage."

Another councilor rolled out a map of Arboa—a more detailed version of the tapestry of the Southern Court hanging on the wall.

"He has pulled the wreckage further to shore in case we wished to send someone to inspect it," Denton said to the room.

Talhan eagerly turned to Neelo, his face full of excitement, and said, "We should—"

"No," Neelo cut him off before he had a chance to get out the final word. Talhan couldn't go to Arboa, and if he knew Neelo was planning on going, he would surely follow. Their head was swimming with their mother's collapse and the memory of that dead boy. Talhan's current closeness was distracting them from the one thing they needed to achieve: restoring order to their court by stopping whatever threat Adisa Monroe and Augustus Norwood were planning for the South.

"We should go see it for ourselves," Talhan pushed, swiveling in his chair to face Neelo. "There might be clues as to what happened or where the rest of the fleet is. You trust a guard to discern and deliver that information to you?"

Neelo bit the inside of their cheek. He knew them too well. Of course Neelo wouldn't trust anyone else to do it, but Talhan didn't need to know that. A week away in Arboa, getting the smell of their mother's brew—and Talhan's scent—out of their brain would be just what they needed.

"The rest of the fleet is probably at the bottom of the ocean," Neelo countered. "As Fenrin said, most of Augustus's ships sank in the storms off Silver Sands. Local villagers said they spotted the fleet being claimed by the waves."

"Or so they thought." Talhan surveyed the tapestry of the Southern Court on the wall, his eyes trailing from Silver Sands Harbor in the easternmost part of the region to Arboa located at the mouth of the Crushwold River. "At least three ships, probably battered from the storms, made it around the Southern coastline . . . probably heading to the Eastern Court." He shook his head as he scrutinized the distance a ship would have to travel to wash ashore in Arboa. "It's worth looking into."

Neelo had to press their lips together to keep from agreeing. The fact that a suspicious ship—*ships*—washed ashore so close to the river mouth was worrying. Had *any* of Augustus's fleet returned to the Eastern Court capital of Wynreach? Was he lobbying for power there again? If there were any allies to the Norwood throne in the Eastern capital, it would be a problem for whoever competed in the autumn games for the throne. So far, Carys and Talhan were the favored competitors, though

Talhan's participation was thrown into question what with his sudden betrothal to Neelo. All the more reason Neelo needed to get away from him and make it clear that they weren't interested. Then Talhan could go East and become a real King . . . and find someone who knew how to love him the way he deserved.

"Do you think he intends to reclaim his father's throne?" Denton asked, giving voice to Neelo's concerns.

The eldest councilor guffawed. "Of course he does," she said.

The councilors murmured to one another in hushed conversations as Neelo's chest tightened.

Talhan leaned over so his breath was hot in their ear. "Not to mention a particular purple flower that only blooms on the eastern shores of the Crushwold River . . . ," he whispered. "One used in violet witch magic."

The hair on Neelo's arm stood on end as they tried to ignore the heat blossoming low in their belly at the feel of Talhan's breath . . . and the intrigue he stirred with his words.

"More and more we're realizing the potency of the blooming amethyst flower," Neelo whispered back, trying to keep from gripping the corners of their book in the way Talhan noted earlier. "And the important role it plays in violet witch magic. Something about this isn't right."

"If only we knew what," Talhan agreed. "Which is why we should go to Arboa and investigate."

Neelo contemplated the timbre of his voice, how it was smooth and robust and warm, flavored like the coffee scent that wafted off his freshly washed skin. They glanced up, finding Talhan watching them, a smirk on his face, and Neelo realized he was waiting for their reply.

"I will send three of my best guards," they said, praying that Talhan didn't guess the direction of their wayward thoughts.

"You are the future ruler," Talhan groused, clearly disappointed at missing a potential new adventure. "It is you who should go."

"You are exactly right. *I* am the future ruler." Neelo closed their book and rested it on their lap, trying to look convincing. "It is my job to lead, not to be every type of person on my staff." They watched as Talhan's eyes widened at their sharper than normal tone. "Should I master the art of cooking, fighting, horse taming . . . simply because those skills are needed in my court? No, I am wise enough to know I am not the best person for every job. I will find the most suitable person to go." They picked their book back up, dismissing him. "You can go if you like, but I'm staying."

Talhan's shoulders drooped, and Neelo knew the exact deflated look they'd find if they glanced back up. Talhan wasn't afraid to wear every emotion on his face. It made him easy to be around, steady, reassuring. There was no subtext that Neelo was missing when it came to Talhan, nothing they should infer but didn't. Most people spoke in riddles. They spoke with looks and winks and arched brows, as if a subtle flicker of a dimple was enough for Neelo to understand the words that they weren't saying.

But Talhan was one of the most honest people they'd ever met. It shouldn't have surprised them so much when Talhan whispered, "I don't want to go without you."

"We will send some guards, then. It's decided," Neelo said with a nod. They made a mental note to tell Denton to call off the envoy once Talhan left for the evening.

Talhan pouted, but pushed off his knees with a groan and shrugged. "A little adventure would've been fun, I promise."

Neelo's lips tightened. Everything felt jumbled when Talhan was around. He was—their mind flashed with the image of him wiping his sweaty brow with his tunic—distracting. But also, perhaps, a bit frivolous. This wasn't about fun. This was about their mother, and their court, and Okrith as a whole.

Right now, with all that in the balance, they couldn't be distracted, and they certainly couldn't have fun.

"I prefer my adventures to be between the pages of a book, thank you."

AS THEY PACED down the hall to their chambers, they passed an open doorway. Laughter and music echoed from the room as a group of ten courtiers danced and drank. One sat in the corner hitting cloth-covered mallets across the wooden plates of a *sembasta*—a witch's drum. The room filled with the warm, robust notes of the instrument as the courtiers gyrated to the sound. Some of the courtiers were already half naked while others were fully clothed and wearing their colorful veils to keep away the biting insects that swarmed in the evenings. One courtier was completely naked apart from the veil and Neelo snorted at the ridiculous sight. The group size seemed to have swelled over the past few weeks, probably with newcomers eager to get a front-row seat to the Summer Solstice festivities. Neelo did their very best not to learn the names or faces of these fair-weathered courtiers. Some would be in the palace over a year before they made awkward eye contact with them. They wished the Queen would cloister the group away so they wouldn't have to see them at all.

The ever-present white smoke filled the room, swirling through the dancers as they passed pipes around. Something about the sight filled Neelo's veins with fire. They couldn't leave their mother like this while they ventured to Arboa, trading finding answers about her waning health for answers of an impending Southern Court attack. The lifeless body of the boy in the alley flashed in their mind. The Queen might not hang on long enough for Neelo to save her . . .

Neelo stalked into the room and grabbed the nearest courtier—a blond-haired fae named Gara. She wore a sheer vermillion dress that was barely a panel of fabric covering between her legs with two thigh slits that rose above her hip bones.

Gara's eyes widened when she saw who had yanked her from the group. "Your Highness," she whispered, dropping into a quick bow. That lazy, drugged smile disappeared from her face.

"Where does my mother keep her witching brew?" Neelo asked with a bored yawn. "A whole crate of the bloody stuff ended up in my chambers by accident."

"Ooh." Gara seemed to perk up at that. Her brew-addled mind didn't think to ask any more questions. She swayed to the music of the *sembasta* and her eyes rolled back.

Neelo poked her again with their book, not wanting to touch her oil-slick skin with their hands again.

"Oh, um," Gara continued. "Well, most of it she keeps in her room, but she hides the restock in her sitting room. You know the one with the ugly furniture? She keeps it there so that we don't steal it." The words came spilling out of her in a rush of slurred words. Gara shifted her eyes down the hall. "Although we all know it's there and sometimes we— Oh Gods, you're not going to tell her, are you?" Gara swallowed.

Neelo realized they were scowling at Gara, but they were always scowling at the courtiers on the rare occasions they were forced to converse with one. They tried to force a half smile and Gara reared back. No. That had only made it worse.

"I won't tell her," Neelo replied. "Thank you," they added stiffly. "Now go drink some water."

Gara chuckled as if Neelo had just made an excellent joke and twirled back to the party. The other courtiers barely noticed them, too lost in their revels to care who watched.

Neelo marched toward the sitting room on the second floor. Apparently, Gara considered the refined decor *ugly*, but Neelo rather liked it. The room was straightforward, functional, not filled with pillows and candles and tables covered in casks of wine. The room was stoic and still, so very unused that Neelo wondered if the maids even bothered to dust in there.

The formal sitting room was once used for entertaining foreign dignitaries in the times of Neelo's ancestors. Now, when the royals of other courts visited the South, they were entertained by gambling games and orgies.

Neelo tiptoed into the room and shut the door. There was no reason for their stealth. No one ever came here, so close to the sleepy library wing, except to pinch more hidden brew—which the footprints in the dust led them right to. Neelo's eyes scanned along that path and landed on the paneling against the far wall. The trim stuck out slightly farther than the rest. Neelo spotted the break in the pattern almost instantly. They walked over and pushed on the panel and it clicked open. Pulling it back, Neelo found three shallow shelves built into the wall, crammed full of paper bags. A miniature posy of dried snowflowers hung from the top shelf, as if the floral scent was enough to combat the stench of brew . . . or perhaps it was left behind by one of the pilfering courtiers?

The smell hit them like a slap to the face.

"For fuck's sake," Neelo gritted out, grabbing up the armfuls of brew and bringing them to the empty fireplace.

How could their mother possibly go through this much brew, even with her swell of new courtiers? Only a pinch of the stuff would make anyone higher than the clouds. Once all the bags were on the blackened stone floor, Neelo grabbed the flint from the mantel and struck a spark. The dried bags immediately ignited, thick white smoke wafting into the room . . . and not up the chimney.

"Shit," Neelo growled, grabbing a poker and trying to open the hatch. The rusted iron wouldn't budge. The bags combusted and the flames grew higher as Neelo grabbed the neckline of their tunic and pulled it over their nose and mouth against the cloying fumes filling their nostrils. They blinked back the stinging smoke from their eyes.

"Shit. Shit. Shit." They gagged on the perfumed brew and muttered a long string of curses as they stabbed at the hatch. The air thickened so much they could barely breathe.

Their fingers tingled until they lost their grip on the poker and it clattered to the floor. Neelo vibrated like a purring cat, their whole body drifting higher, weightless, until it felt like they were hovering an inch above the ground.

"Gods," they whispered, pulling their tunic off their face as they took another deep breath. The room was so thick with smoke they couldn't see their hands in front of them . . . and they realized they didn't seem to care.

Their body trembled with ecstasy and they wondered if this was the feeling those books on pleasure were referencing. Neelo could have stopped after reading one little book on sex, but they'd read the whole shelf. They had wanted to feel those sensations the books spoke of, just not with anyone else . . . Gods, they lied even to themself. Why couldn't they be like Rish or like their mother? Why couldn't they want all the pleasure or none? Wanting it with only one person seemed like the worst sort of punishment.

Neelo felt like they were navigating this constant tightrope between forces pulling them in and pushing them away . . . but this—this moment felt like lightning shooting through their veins. Whatever feeling buzzed in them now made them drop to their knees, their body trembling with desire.

In the very back of their mind, they were shouting at themself to get up, get out of this room, but another voice, a louder voice, warm and smooth and confident said, "No." They cracked a smile and laughed. "Maybe it is my turn to be the irresponsible one for once."

CHAPTER TWELVE

They closed their eyes, listening to the rhythm of the music echoing up from the gardens, the beat of the drums seeming to pulse through them until they were aching with desire. Neelo understood it now, that rush, that thrumming vibration, getting out of their head and into their body until every inch of them tingled.

"Neelo, open your eyes," a voice commanded, shaking them by their shoulders.

Neelo licked their lips, peeking their eyes open and finding Talhan's wide amber eyes staring daggers into them. Their fingers instinctively lifted and roved his chiseled jawline and up into his auburn hair with delight.

"Neelo." Talhan panted, his voice laced with concern. Had he been running?

Neelo turned to the fireplace. It was dark now, only blackened ashes and soot staining all the way up to the mantel. The windows had been thrown wide open, swallowing the gossamer curtains into the evening breeze. Neelo tried to focus their eyes, but couldn't. The filigree wallpaper undulated in chorus with the drums and the entire room thrummed with rolling thunder. Strange, perhaps, but Neelo realized they didn't care, not as that spiced coffee scent filled their senses and made them swiftly ache with lust.

They were vaguely aware of Talhan calling their name, shaking them, but it felt so far away with the brilliant burning torchlight that filled their veins. Strong hands cupped their cheeks, forcing their head back to meet those fiery eyes, and Neelo knew they wanted him—needed him—right then and there.

Neelo's voice wasn't their own as they rasped, "Take your clothes off." Their hand traced down Talhan's tunic and dipped a finger under his belt before he snatched their hand away.

"Neelo," Talhan warned.

"Such a tease." Neelo pouted. "I thought you were always game for a party, Eagle. I thought you fit right in with the Southern ways."

"If you still want me to take my clothes off in the morning," Talhan said, easily immobilizing Neelo with his light grip on their wrists, "I'll gladly oblige."

Neelo laughed, the sound strange to their own ears. "Aren't you having fun?"

"No."

"Isn't this what you wanted?" Neelo threw their head back and cackled, sounding just like the courtiers, the old witches, and everyone else who mocked Neelo their whole life. "Isn't this what you signed up for when you agreed to my mother's proposal?"

"No," Talhan growled. "It's not,"

"Come on, future husband. Ravish me." Neelo taunted, leaning forward until their chest crashed into Talhan's own. Talhan took a step away.

"Neelo." Their name felt like a reprimand and the scolding tone of his voice made Neelo snap.

"What?" Neelo's temper swung from lustful to furious in the blink of an eye. They ripped their wrists from Talhan's grip and stumbled back another step. "This." They waved themself up and down, realizing at some point their jacket and shoes had come off and they were just in their buckled leather vest and trousers. "This is who they've always wanted me to be. *The Heir of Saxbridge.* The heir to revels and orgies and drunken escapades." They were screaming at him now, that raging voice sounding strange even to their own ears. "Don't you dare chastise me for finally being the successor my mother always wished to have! This is who everyone wished for me to be!"

Talhan's brows pinched together and they hated the sadness in his eyes. "And who do you wish to be, Neelo Emberspear?"

"I wish to be no one," they seethed. "I wish for my mother to reign forever and I wish to be left alone. Ignored. Unimportant. Just me and my books and silence."

Talhan shook his head slowly. "You're so used to telling lies, you wouldn't even whisper the truth, would you?"

Neelo curled their lip in a snarl, their eyes hooded with an odd mixture of yearning and rage. "Did you expect me to say I wanted you?" They chuckled and Talhan scowled as they paced over to him, their hands roving his muscled body again and this time Talhan didn't stop them. "Do you think that's who I wish to be? The one who breaks you? Bores you? *Ruins you?* I'll tell you what, Golden Eagle, fuck me and then I'll tell you what I truly want."

Fast as an asp, Talhan grabbed Neelo's wrists with one hand and spun them, pinning their back to the wall and their wrists above their head. His lips were a hair's breadth from Neelo's own as he whispered, "Like this?"

"Yes." Neelo's words hissed out of their teeth.

Talhan pressed his chest against theirs, anchoring them to the wall. A devious smirk pulled up the corner of his lips. "Tell me how badly you want me."

"You know I do," Neelo panted.

Talhan cocked his head, his features sharp and searching. "Tell me you'll stop pushing me away."

"No." Neelo pulled at Talhan's grip and his fingers squeezed even tighter, making their whole body throb with a deep-seated need.

"*That* is the line you draw?" Talhan guffawed, leaning harder against them. "While I love hearing your unbridled demands, Your Highness"—Talhan's lips skimmed up Neelo's jaw to their ear—"when I touch you, you will have all of your senses about you. Each and every nerve in your body will be perfectly attuned to my hands, my mouth." Neelo shuddered against him. "The only thing you'll be high on is your yearning for *me*."

They were feeling that deep yearning now, so when he suddenly released Neelo's wrists and stepped away, the feeling of his absence left Neelo cold and bereft. They ground their teeth so tight they were sure one chipped. Neelo's head was still spinning, their need to be pleasured an infuriating itch they couldn't scratch. They unbuckled their belt and let their trousers fall to the floor. Kicking the heavy gray fabric across the room, Neelo enjoyed the feeling of being only in their undershorts and vest, the evening air soothing the burning inside them.

Yes. Go on, that foreign voice inside their head chanted.

"Stop. It," Talhan snarled, though his eyes roved every inch of their exposed skin.

Standing half naked before Talhan, Neelo gave him one last angry look and turned to the door.

"What are you doing?"

"What any good Southerner would do," Neelo said, glancing over their shoulder. "I'm finding someone to indulge my desires."

They threw open the door and pulled it behind them, stepping out into the fresh air of the hall. They hadn't realized how smoky the sitting room was until they left. Talhan threw open the door and chased after them as Neelo began sprinting down the shadowed palace. Not a single person darkened the halls and Neelo was acutely disappointed that no one was watching their undressed run.

Burning euphoria filled their veins as they bolted faster down the hall.

"Neelo!" Talhan called after them. His heavy footsteps caught up with ease as curses rolled off his tongue. His hand snaked around Neelo's waist, halting them as they battled against his grip. "Stop."

"Let me go," Neelo shouted, thrashing against him.

"Not even the Goddess of Death herself would convince me to let you go right now," he growled in their ear.

Neelo's hand scrambled for the dagger on Talhan's hip, but he twisted out of their reach. They stomped on his foot and he barked out a curse but didn't release them. His arms caged them in as he dragged them flailing back down the hall.

"Release me, you son of a bitch," Neelo raged.

Talhan snickered. "Well, at least on that we can agree."

A gust of wind blew in from the window and the shock of it felt like being dropped in a barrel of ice. Neelo sucked in a sharp breath, pins and needles covering their skin, as they let out a pained cry. Their knees buckled. Suddenly, they were burning and not with desire.

"Shit," Talhan hissed as he quickly scooped up Neelo's legs and ran, carrying them toward their bedroom.

Ice and fire flayed Neelo's flesh and they screamed an unearthly cry.

"Hang on," Talhan shouted, unceremoniously dropping them onto their bed. They were vaguely aware of other voices and Talhan barking commands to fetch Fenrin.

Neelo screamed, the sheets feeling like barnacles grating across their back, before the pain overwhelmed them and they succumbed to the black storm clouds pulling them into the shadows.

PAIN LANCED THROUGH them—such earth-shaking pain. Their stomach churned with acid and every muscle tensed until they were trembling. Neelo drifted in and out of consciousness, unsure if the whispers across their cheek were real or imagined. Maybe they were going mad like the others.

They felt scorching heat and then were plunged into frigid cold, only to swing back again. All they wanted was for it to stop, to feel that euphoria that had ripped through their bones and made them feel like they were flying again.

They heard frantic voices. Rish. And then Talhan issuing orders as they writhed in pain. More voices and Neelo strained to open their eyes, but they couldn't. Pain. Only miserable pain.

They didn't know how much time had passed between their brief sips of consciousness—minutes, hours?

"Leave us," Talhan growled finally and Neelo shivered at the venom in his voice before slipping below the waves of consciousness once more.

Their throat was dry and rough. Had they been screaming? Strong arms caged them in, holding them against a bare, solid chest.

Neelo groaned and the arms constricted. Lips dropped to their ear. "Easy," the voice cautioned in a sweet lover's whisper.

"Tal?"

"Yes," he murmured softly.

Neelo leaned forward, but Talhan wouldn't let them pull away. "Stay still."

"It hurts," Neelo groaned as a new wave of sharp stinging pain shot through their body.

His hand constricted on the soft flesh of Neelo's belly. "I know, love."

"I . . ." A sudden realization shot through them. "Where are my clothes?"

"You took them off," Talhan said, not a single ounce of amusement in his voice.

Neelo's stomach dropped. "In front of people?"

"No," Talhan assured, his thumb sweeping a circle around Neelo's navel. "We were in private."

Neelo cleared their throat. "Did we . . . ?"

"I don't fuck people higher than the clouds," Talhan murmured. "No matter how badly they seem to want it."

Neelo's hand slid up to their forehead and rubbed across their throbbing temples. "Then why are you only in your trousers?"

"Because you were sick all over my tunic."

Neelo groaned and clenched their eyes shut. "I wasn't trying to—I just wanted to get rid of the—and—"

"Shh," Talhan soothed. "I know."

"My mother is going to kill me," they grumbled, turning their face further into their pillow. Most parents would throw a fit for their child getting high, but the Queen would only rage that Neelo destroyed her stash. At least it would buy them some time while they traveled to Arboa to investigate the shipwreck. That had been the plan, hadn't it? To keep their mother from the brew while Neelo was gone? Gods, just the thought of standing up and getting dressed felt impossible, let alone traveling a day's ride on horseback.

"I won't let your mother hurt you." Talhan hummed, that thumb circling their belly again in that same distracting way. "You were trying to help her."

"Yes," Neelo whispered. "I'm always trying. Always failing."

Talhan smiled against their neck. "Just remember to open the hatch next time."

Neelo cringed. "Right." They opened their mouth to say something more when another sharp wave of pain rocked into them. They hissed through their teeth.

"Sleep," Talhan whispered. "It should be out of your system by sunrise. The fact you didn't kill yourself is a miracle. Thank the Gods Fenrin was here."

Thank the Gods you were here, they thought, but couldn't quite say aloud.

A long pause stretched between them. The sound of nighttime insects and the flap of curtains in the breeze accompanied the sound of Talhan's slow steady breaths.

"Why are you taking care of me?" Neelo asked. "I'm sure Rish would—"

"She wasn't strong enough to keep you from hurting yourself," Talhan said, his voice strained as if reliving a memory that Neelo couldn't recall.

Neelo feebly pulled away again and didn't budge an inch. "You are taking this whole betrothed thing too seriously."

"I'm not doing it because I'm your betrothed," Talhan said. "I'm doing it because I'm your friend."

Neelo flinched at another stab of pain and Talhan's fingers splayed wider across their soft middle. Neelo's hand drifted over Talhan's and held it in place, anchoring into him as the storm swirled. Their mind was a fog, barely able to grasp flashes of information before they drifted out of reach. Their feet vibrated and they realized it was the purring thrum of Indi's body, healing Neelo in his own little way.

"I know the past few years we haven't been around each other as much," Talhan continued. "War has a way of doing that." He nestled his face closer to the back of Neelo's head. "But because of this whole betrothal thing, it feels like you forgot."

Exhaustion tugged at Neelo and the only question they could summon was a single hum.

"You forgot that we were friends, that we *are* friends," Talhan whispered and Neelo wasn't sure if they imagined it but something like pain strained his voice. "We've always been friends. Except now you treat me with suspicion like we had no past at all, like I'm your mother's puppet."

"Are you not?" Neelo's voice drifted so far they weren't sure it was even them speaking aloud until Talhan snarled. "Isn't she the reason you're here?"

"You know why I'm here," he whispered.

His soft voice tugged Neelo deeper until they were certain this was all a dream, another hallucination conjured by the witching brew. But if it was all a fantasy, at least it was one they'd had dreamt of before. They let Talhan's voice pull them under as his chest rumbled against their back.

"You know I'm not here for a crown or a title," he whispered. "Nor am I here for the food and wine. And I'm certainly not here for the unending summer heat and the biting insects and the prying eyes of a gossiping court . . . but I like being here, Neelo, and deep down in your soul, you know why."

And as they fell deep down into slumber, they *did* know why. They just didn't know how to say it.

CHAPTER THIRTEEN

I just don't understand you sometimes, *mea raga*," Rish whispered, tiptoeing down the hall behind Neelo. "Why are we leaving him behind?"

"Will you be quiet?" Neelo's words were barely audible, but they knew Rish got the message from the glare they gave her.

Neelo crept down the long, tiled hallway toward the stables, shuffling their riding boots so as not to make a sound. This was the most treacherous stretch of hallway before the stables. The ceilings stretched up four stories high and on every floor were trellised openings in the stone to allow air to circulate through the bedrooms. It also meant a sneeze could be heard echoing up to the guest wing. It was why the stables were off-limits for most of the morning, so that the night-owl guests of the palace—of which there were usually many—could sleep.

When Neelo had awoken to the first slivers of dawn light, Talhan was gone. The sheets were damp from sweat, Neelo's stomach still ached, and their throat felt raw. They should've probably taken another day to rest, but they wanted to get away while Talhan didn't suspect . . . and definitely before their mother discovered Neelo burned a mountain of gold's worth of her witching brew.

Neelo had tasked the kitchen witches with feeding Indi and, though they knew their aloof little cat would be fine, they debated turning back for him again. No. He would probably get eaten by a snake or get lost on the trail. He was safer here, pampered and adored. Talhan would probably dote on him too.

"And why do *we* have to go?" Rish asked.

Rolling their eyes, Neelo shot Rish a look. "Because," they whispered, "I don't trust anyone else to do it. Sy could miss a clue, and with Rua's foreboding prediction of a violet witch attack, there is too much at stake to miss a clue. I need to see it with my own eyes. Now, *be quiet.*" Rish's lips puckered and Neelo quickly added, "Please."

Taking another tentative step, Neelo prayed the back of their throat didn't tickle or a songbird suddenly swooped into the atrium. If they could reach the stables without waking anyone, they'd be able to sneak off without notice. It would be many hours until the rest of the palace woke up and by then they'd be halfway to Arboa.

Rish tsked. "I just—"

Neelo whirled on her and drew their finger across their lips. The green witch rolled her eyes but continued creeping along a pace behind Neelo.

Neelo wasn't going to explain to her why they were leaving Talhan behind, only that they knew he shouldn't come. If they said it aloud, Rish would see it for what it truly was: hiding.

Maybe it made them a coward—to hide in the shadows, to whisper when they should shout, to let their excitement be stymied by fear. But there would be time to regret their mistakes when their court was protected from violet witches and their mother wasn't talking about abdicating her throne anymore. Talhan Catullus would have to wait. Let him toil away in the Saxbridge heat and decide a relationship with Neelo was no longer worth pursuing.

He was a warrior. He could handle it.

Neelo wiped the sweat beading on their brow. The sun rose so early this close to the Solstice; it felt like there was barely a night. Thank the Gods they'd be in the shade of the forest before midmorning. The further east they rode toward Arboa, the cooler it would be—still hot, but with less humidity and a robust ocean breeze. It would be a nice reprieve from the stagnant heat and reek of spilled wine and body odor. Many Southerners left the capital in the summer to seaside homes that clustered around the Southern shoreline, but Queen Emberspear would never leave the heart of the party in Saxbridge nowadays. Teetering at the very edge of debauchery seemed to be the only thing the Queen lived for anymore, which also meant Neelo didn't feel as confident to leave her side for long stretches as they did when they were young.

Neelo had spent many summers in Arboa as a child. They could still remember each book they brought on those trips, as if the location and the stories now coalesced into one. Neelo read a book about snow pirates while sitting under a palm tree at the beach, and a story about water dragons whilst laying under the stars amongst the blooming fields with Carys and Ersan . . . that was back when they were young, before Neelo started to feel like a third wheel, and *long* before Carys and Ersan's relationship imploded.

Still, with their mother's meddlesome ways far off in Saxbridge, Neelo had always loved the reprieve when Carys's father, Lord Hilgaard, would invite Neelo out to visit their castle halfway between Arboa and Saxbridge.

Neelo had always wondered if Lord Hilgaard was trying to form royal alliances for better standing, or if he truly thought his daughter needed a friend. Neelo never knew, but they seized every opportunity to visit Carys when they were young. The Heir of Saxbridge thought for a time that they might even be falling in love with her, before they understood they fell in love with anyone who was kind to them. It wasn't actually love—they realized as they grew older—it was gratitude, a yearning to be heard, to be liked, that pulled them so close to those who really saw them. The emotions used to get mixed up in their mind . . . now they were clear. Friendship didn't equate to love, and after that time with Carys, Neelo started to think they didn't possess the parts of themself to love someone at all, let alone allow someone to love them in return.

Neelo knew Carys was a good friend, family even, but they'd never wanted a romance with her or with anyone . . . or at least so they'd thought. They'd never understood what the fuss was about before—

before a strange sensation pulled low in their belly around one person. His eyes, his smell, his voice . . . and for the first time, they'd wondered what if—

Crash!

The loud clang on the floor made Neelo jump out of their skin. They spun to find Rish's hands hovering midair as if she just missed catching the lantern that clattered across the tiles, ringing like a fucking temple bell for the entire city to hear.

Neelo balled their fists at their sides. "You did that on purpose," they snapped.

"I'm getting older and clumsier," Rish said, but her casual shrug confirmed she knew exactly what she was doing.

"You're just as meddlesome as my mother." Neelo cursed, scanning the windows above them to see if anyone had rushed toward the sound.

Rish adjusted the heavy pack on her shoulders. "At least when I meddle, I do it for your own good."

"My mother thinks that too," Neelo muttered, hustling faster toward the stables now that the entire palace was alerted to the fact they were on the move.

"Yes, but *I* am actually right." Rish squared her shoulders. Her pack was probably laden with enough food to circle Okrith twice. It was two days' journey to Arboa—one if they were swift—and Neelo wouldn't be surprised if Rish had brought the entire kitchens with her.

Neelo craned their neck down the far passageway, but saw not a single stirring. "I'm not sure if we should be thankful or concerned that no guards have come running."

"They probably think it's the last straggler wandering home from a party," Rish said, though she also looked expectantly down the hall as if hoping someone would see them.

Neelo's shoulders drooped. They didn't want Talhan to come with them . . . so there was no reason for this disappointment churning in their chest. They took the last steps toward the stable door, their hand hovering on the handle for a moment as if wanting to give Talhan just one more second to find them. Finally, they cleared their throat and turned the copper handle, internally scolding themself for their childish feelings.

But as the door swung open, they found, leaning against the doorframe, none other than Talhan Catullus. His eyes twinkled with mischief as his lips curled up. He was dressed in full riding clothes with his dagger and sword belted to his hips and a packed saddlebag at his feet.

He gave Neelo a wink. "Going somewhere?"

NEELO CURSED EVERY God as they set off on their journey with the Golden Eagle in tow. They felt Talhan's eyes boring into their back like leaden weights pushing down on their shoulders. Neelo's posture drooped with his presence behind them, as if they could shrink out of sight.

Talhan waited until the cavalcade rode into the depths of the forest before asking the question Neelo had been bracing for: "I thought you were going to send scouts to Arboa on your behalf?"

"I changed my mind," they muttered, keeping their eyes fixed on the trail ahead.

Talhan feigned shock. "So quickly you couldn't inform me?"

They watched Rish's shoulders shake from her horse up ahead and Neelo scowled. "I invited you to summer in Saxbridge. I said nothing about *me* needing to be there." Talhan's deep accompanying chuckle made Neelo grip the reins in their hands tighter.

"I see," he said simply. "So you've gone from avoiding me to outright leaving me behind? Well, I'm glad I had the good sense to suspect you nonetheless."

Neelo ducked under a low-hanging vine, swinging it out of the way. They half-hoped it would smack into Talhan on the rebound. "Not a very good actor, am I?"

"I think you could fool most, but not me." Talhan's voice was slow and warm. "I know you."

I know you. Neelo felt every syllable dance across their skin.

"For instance, when you said that you'd rather send someone else, I

117

knew you were lying," Talhan continued. "You wouldn't trust anyone else to report back to you. You'd want to see the wreckage yourself, come up with your own conclusions, make sure you had every piece of the puzzle. You forget I just spent a day in the library with you, watching how intently you track down leads."

Rish's silent laughter shook her whole body faster as Talhan echoed Neelo's exact sentiments from earlier. It was true. A scout could overlook something important, and Neelo couldn't risk it. Which meant they weren't lying—not completely—about not wanting Talhan around, potentially distracting them, possibly making them miss something key. But it was more than that. They also had other answers they needed, ones that Lord Ersan would have for them.

Ones they didn't want Talhan to hear them asking about.

"How far is today's ride?" Talhan called.

Neelo looked up to the thick canopy, dappled with tiny rays of sunlight, and they were grateful they had gotten deeper into the shade before the sun rose so high.

"We'll stay at Hilgaard Castle tonight," Rish shouted from up ahead, her lively voice scaring the bright red and blue parrots from the trees. "We should arrive before dinner."

"Hilgaard?" Talhan asked. "Carys's home?"

"It's not her home anymore," Neelo cut in. "It's no more than a ruin."

"Right," Talhan replied. "Will she be okay with us staying there?"

Neelo smiled to themself at the gentleness of that sentiment and they were grateful Talhan couldn't see their face. "I doubt she'll be paying a visit anytime soon," Neelo said. "But she doesn't mind when we use the place for shelter. Of course, we could ride into the evening and get to Arboa in a day—"

"No," Rish protested. "I brought all the ingredients for campfire stew *and* sweet fruit rolls for breakfast. You'll ruin all my fun."

"We certainly can't say no to that," Talhan said with a hearty laugh.

"Thank you, sweet Eagle," Rish cooed in her motherly way. "I knew *you* would appreciate my efforts."

Neelo rolled their eyes. "You two are insufferable."

Which wasn't *exactly* what they wanted to say, but they practiced restraint here. Were it not for their love of Rish, Neelo would've protested harder. They were reminded again that Talhan's nature that charmed and delighted could also be short-sighted. His desire for *fun* superseded all sense of urgency. And, while it made him just like any other Southerner, it was the last thing the South needed more of—a ruler who put fun above their people.

"It's nice to be appreciated for once," Rish added in her taunting tone she used whenever she was scolding Neelo.

"And I'd appreciate having my wishes respected, but look where we are."

"Yes—look where we are: together, having a nice ride, and protected by a strong warrior, rather than risking the heir of the Southern Court in their stubborn—"

"Fine." Neelo relented. "We'll stay in Hilgaard tonight, but we leave for Arboa at first light."

"I can't believe I'm going to finally meet the scum who broke Carys's heart." Talhan's voice filled with menace.

"You're not allowed to kill him," Neelo interjected.

"But—"

"You're not allowed to maim him either." They knew Talhan would be pouting behind them. "And before you even suggest it, that counts for indirect harm too. No scorpions in his boots, no snakes in his bed."

The memory of Talhan doing both such things to a young Belenus Norwood flashed in their mind. Belenus had made some snide remark about Neelo's appearance at a wedding in Wynreach when they were younger and that night he ended up with all manner of venomous creatures in his bedchamber. Still, no one knew who had done it . . . no one except Neelo.

"Ugh, you're no fun," Talhan grumbled.

There he went with his "fun" again, but Neelo couldn't resist saying, "You promised me adventures with you would be fun." Talhan let out a rough laugh and Neelo wished Talhan hadn't so easily goaded them into this conversation—charming indeed.

"Who says beating up Carys's ex wouldn't be a fun adventure?"

119

"Hear, hear," Rish called from up ahead.

"Not you too," Neelo groaned. The two of them were already in cahoots and they were barely halfway through the day's ride. "Don't encourage him."

"I can't help it," Rish said, swiping at a cobweb that stretched across the path. "Everything the Golden Eagle suggests sounds like fun."

"We'll make a warrior out of you yet, Rish," Talhan shouted to her up ahead.

Neelo rolled their eyes for what felt like the hundredth time in the span of two minutes. "This is exactly why I wanted to leave you behind," they muttered, more to themself, but Talhan heard nonetheless.

"If you haven't figured this out yet," Talhan called to them, "I'm not so easily dissuaded."

"No," Neelo grumbled. "You're fucking relentless."

"Indeed," Talhan said with pride.

Neelo leaned back to rummage in their horse's saddlebag. "That wasn't a compliment."

"I'm taking it as one anyway." Talhan's chuckling paused. "What are you doing?"

Neelo's fingers finally clasped around the soft edges of their book and they pulled it from the saddlebag. The texture instantly soothed them, along with the comfort of knowing they'd now be able to distance themself from the conversation. Maybe they couldn't so easily leave Talhan behind, but they could ignore him.

"You can't be serious," Talhan said, incredulous and laughing at the same time. Why did that sound make their stomach flip every time they heard it? "How exactly do you read on horseback?"

Neelo shrugged, taking the reins in one hand and resting the spine of their book along their horse's mane. "Practice."

"How many books did you bring with you?"

"Twelve."

"*Twelve?*"

Rish cackled her loud witch's laugh and the chirping insects quieted at the sound. "That should maybe last them to Arboa."

Neelo acknowledged that with a nod, but kept reading.

Talhan cleared his throat, fumbling for his words and saying, "But—"

"I'm trying to read," Neelo cut him off.

Talhan's laugh deepened and the sound made Neelo grip the pages of their book tighter. "And you call *me* relentless."

I call you a lot of things, they thought, feeling the slight flush even as they buried their nose deeper into their book.

CHAPTER FOURTEEN

The sun dipped below the canopy as they arrived at the ruins of Hilgaard. The once glorious castle had been reclaimed by the jungle. It was amazing and horrifying how quickly the place seemed to disappear beneath roots and vines—a lifetime of memories erased in a matter of years. Somewhere in this dense jungle were the graves of Carys's parents. Beyond the crumbling gray stone foundations, a stable and paddocks should have been, but now it was mostly rubble apart from the entryway that still towered up as high as the tallest trees. A patch in the far eastern corner was reduced to ash. Most would've probably assumed it was from a lightning strike, but Neelo suspected a certain heartbroken Arboan lord as the instigator of the blaze that claimed the eastern wing.

"They should've never built this place in the Northern style." Rish's voice was surprisingly soft, as if the ruins demanded it. "Only the grand hall remains because they built it in Southern white stone." She gestured to the templelike structure covered in vines. The white stone arches held up the roof like the rib cage of a giant beast. "The wood rotted so quickly that they needed to replace it every couple of years. Pride." Rish shook her finger as if she could scold the spirits that still dwelled there. "That was always the problem with the Northern fae.

They were too confident in their own beliefs to build things the sensible way, too precious about their traditions."

"If Carys had taken over," Neelo said, dismounting their horse with a groan and stretching their weary legs, "she would've rebuilt it in the Southern style. Carys is a Southerner, after all. She favors our architecture."

"It would take a miracle to rebuild this place now," Talhan murmured as he tied up a grazing line for the horses. "Not that she'd ever want to return here anyway."

Neelo didn't disagree. They unbuckled the saddlebags and propped them atop a crumbling slab of gray stone.

"Wait," Talhan said, rushing over to help Rish with her heavy bags. "Allow me."

"I can handle it," Rish said. Talhan hefted the other bag onto the ground before Rish could bat him away. "Why don't you go wash up for dinner? There's a stream just beyond that tree."

Neelo knew it was a charade—they were smart enough to get that he was helping her so that they would notice—and yet . . . they did notice, and it bothered them that they noticed.

Too many things about this trip bothered them.

Talhan was moving toward the giant *amasa* tree that stretched up toward the sky. The Emberspears not only chose the tree that graced the Southern Court crest for its strength and beauty, but also its importance to everyday Southern life. The paths through the jungles of the South were designed to follow the trail of giant evergreens, sentinels that rose above the canopy and led travelers to the next lookout and life-giving spring. Neelo glanced at the rough bark of the centuries-old tree. This particular *amasa* once marked the castle of Hilgaard, but now was only useful to travelers in marking the river that ran alongside it.

"Ah, look," Talhan said, craning his neck up toward the broad-leafed evergreen. "It's your tree."

Neelo didn't know why Talhan's words irked them the way they did. Maybe it was another reminder that Neelo was meant to take the throne, another symbol of the yoke around their neck, of the burden they'd soon have to take on: the patron heir to debauchery, gambling, and tricks, instead of art, feasts, and evergreen gardens.

Neelo's fingers curled into their palm, their heart pounding in their ears, even as they said, "It's not *my* anything. It's just a tree." They stomped off into the forest, aiming toward the stream and hoping that Talhan wouldn't follow.

Of course they had no such luck.

"What's wrong?" Talhan asked, easily keeping up with their quickened pace.

"Nothing."

"Neelo." Talhan's tone awakened a memory from the night Neelo had burned their mother's brew . . . of Talhan's chest pinned against their own, of his breath in their hair . . .

Neelo's shoulders bunched around their ears. "I just don't like when you talk about these things," they snarled. "I don't like thinking about being a ruler. Or about you and me."

Talhan kept right on Neelo's trail. "Why not?"

They pulled another branch out of their way and let it snap back, knowing it would lash Talhan straight in the chest. "Many reasons."

Talhan grunted as the branch hit him. "Name one."

"I never want children, for one." Neelo picked up their speed, ducking and weaving through the forest, desperate to set distance between them. "I'll name an heir based on my confidence that they'll be able to do the job."

"But maybe you will in the future?"

"I won't, but it doesn't matter. A brown witch healer helped me many moons ago. I don't drink the teas anymore. I don't bleed. The palace isn't a place for a child and neither is my body." Another branch snapped back behind them with a thunk. "That doesn't bother you?"

In the blink of an eye, Talhan shot in front of Neelo and they walked smack into his chest, bouncing off his hard muscle. Talhan steadied Neelo with a hand on each of their arms and Neelo scowled up at him.

"Nothing about you *bothers* me, except how much you push me away." Talhan's breath was shaky as he searched Neelo's eyes. "Besides,

I never really pictured myself as a father. Don't I strike you as more of the fun uncle type anyway? Remy and Hale, Rua and Renwick. They all want children. Bri and Lina will probably have a dozen by my wager. There will be plenty of family to dote upon. Who knows, one might even become your successor one day. They don't need to be mine. It's never been the thing I've wanted."

Neelo stepped out of his grip, their throat tightening as they asked, "And what is the thing you've wanted, Tal?"

Neelo's cheeks burned as they realized what they'd just asked. They started walking away before Talhan could reply, instantly regretting the question, and afraid they already knew the answer.

Talhan fell into stride beside them. "I like when you call me Tal."

He reached out to Neelo again, his hand sliding into Neelo's grip and holding their hand with such gentleness that Neelo's fingertips lit up with a thousand pins and needles. It was too much. They yanked their hand away.

Talhan nodded up to the tree above them and Neelo rolled their eyes as they stared at another *amasa* evergreen.

Neelo studied the waxy broad leaves and stroked an idle hand along the rough bark. "It doesn't look like the pine forests of the North, but it is evergreen," Neelo said, needing something to talk about other than whatever it was they had been discussing, their mind wandering back to the drawings in their tree specimen identification book. "That dark green never fades or wanes. These trees—the ones tall enough to touch the clouds—are older than the words we have to name them."

"They remind me of you," Talhan murmured, craning his neck up to the towering canopy.

"Old?"

Talhan snorted. "No, evergreen, timeless. You are steady and strong and wise, a quality that will always be powerful and humbling to me," he whispered. "Beautiful yet deceptively wild."

Neelo gave him a sideways look. "You've been listening to too many of our Southern songs."

"Perhaps, but it's true." Talhan grinned. "That's what you are, Neelo. It's the best way I know how to describe you."

Neelo circled the giant trunk, listening to the lively hum of jungle insects. "If I am evergreen, what are you?"

Talhan stooped and picked up a fallen leaf, twirling it in his fingers as he seemed to toss the question around in his mind. "I don't know what I am."

"And yet you are so certain about me?" Their fingers danced along the bark, their voice soft amongst the chorus of jungle sounds, and when Neelo circled back round, they found Talhan staring at them.

"Yes."

"Why?"

He took a breath, his eyes scorching into Neelo until they had to keep moving, and trailed around the tree again. "Because sometimes it's easier to see the qualities of others," Talhan said, "than to see them in ourselves."

"Fine." Neelo lifted their fingers from the tree when they spotted a frog camouflaged against the bark and grinned. "I am certain about you too, then."

"Oh really?" Talhan's voice filled with intrigue from the other side of the tree. "How so?"

"I need to search through some poetry. Something better to describe you than what I would say." They could feel Talhan's amber eyes tracking them as they turned around the trunk.

"I don't want to know what a poet would say. I want to hear what *you* would say," Talhan insisted.

Neelo paused, looking back to where Talhan watched them and feeling the force of his stare wash over them like being toppled by an ocean wave. "You wear a constant smirk, even in the face of danger," Neelo said, cautiously, mulling over each word before speaking it. "You lift people up when they are low. You balance the weight of sorrow with all of your light. You are the most brilliant star, the brightest sun. But despite your lighthearted exterior, I know your well runs deep. There is more to you than the joke-telling warrior. You care so deeply about your friends and family . . . and you care deeply about this world too."

"As do you," Talhan whispered, taking another step toward them.

"Yes, but you're not afraid to take charge." Neelo took a step back. "To do what's right. To fight."

"I don't know about that," Talhan said with a chuckle. "I've done an awful lot of wrong things."

Neelo gave him a quizzical look. "Like what?"

A flock of noisy parrots swooped through the trees and Talhan tilted his head back to watch them. "Like fight."

"What do you mean?"

"Another time."

Neelo nodded, clutching their hands together. "I know what you're going to say anyway."

Talhan lowered his chin and cocked his brow. "You're so certain about that too?"

"We've known each other our whole lives."

"*Your* whole life," Talhan corrected. "I'm older."

"Not by that much." Neelo folded their arms. "But I've seen you. The way you are with your sister . . . and the rest of your family. I don't know everything that happened, but I see it."

Talhan bobbed his head, dropping his gaze down to his boots. The action told Neelo they had suspected correctly and it hurt to know that Talhan still blamed himself for the events of his childhood.

"The actions of your family are not your fault," Neelo whispered, taking a tentative step forward.

Talhan's amber eyes lifted to theirs and Neelo forced themself to hold his gaze. "Neither are yours."

Neelo sighed. They should've known they were walking right into that trap. "It is different when you are an heir to a throne."

"No, it's not," Talhan countered, shuffling closer still. "You said your family's actions are not your fault. That is true no matter who you are."

"But I can't just walk away." Neelo's voice raised an octave and they hated how desperate and young it made them sound. Clearing their throat, they said, "You distanced yourself from your parents. You made your own way in the world as a member of Hale's crew . . . I have to stay here and live with the endless string of bad choices my mother makes."

127

"It's a good thing she's stepping down, then." Talhan reached out to take Neelo's hand and they snatched it away one more time.

"Is it?" Neelo asked, fire beginning to rise within them, and another memory from that night flashed through their mind. They'd had this argument before . . . or something akin to it, at least. And they hated how everyone was so happy to see Queen Emberspear step down. "Is it a good thing that she's giving up?" Talhan's eyes widened as Neelo took another angry step toward him, wondering if enough heat flowed through their veins to shout in Talhan Catullus's face. "Is it a good thing that she would rather lose herself to drinks and drugs than to rule her kingdom? Is it a *good thing* that she wants to leave me to pick up the pieces while I watch her wither away? A good thing that she doesn't care at all if I'm ready or not? My life is not one of those Southern songs, Tal," they seethed. "There is no riding off into the sunset and living happily forever."

"No," Talhan whispered, though not backing down an inch. "But I will *earn* that happiness each and every day. I can think of nothing I'd rather spend my life doing than fighting for the future I see when I close my eyes."

Neelo's chest rose and fell in sharp breaths, the sudden weight of everything crashing down upon them. They balled their fists, finally snapping the magical spell that tethered them so tightly to Talhan.

"Wait," Talhan said, reaching for them in one stride.

Neelo ripped their elbow from his gentle grip. They wished he'd stop doing that. Such infuriatingly casual touches as if they were already his. It was an unfair game he played, one that dizzied Neelo's mind and distracted them from all the fears they were trying to contain.

Talhan took another two strides, sidestepping in front of them and halting their path. Neelo moved to walk around him and he stepped in front of them again, holding up his hands like a stablehand calming a skittish horse.

"Talk to me. What do you need?" he pleaded. "What do you need from *me*?"

"There's nothing more to say," Neelo said in a tight, controlled tone, waiting for Talhan to back down so they could pass.

"Bullshit," Talhan growled. "You're hiding from me again. This might work on your councilors, but not me. You can't just say your world is falling apart and then walk away."

"Yes, Talhan, I can," Neelo snarled, shoving Talhan out of the way with their shoulder and storming back through the forest. They knew it would hurt him to have his nickname revoked, to put that wall up between them again, but they couldn't think, couldn't breathe. Everything hurt. And the worst of it was, they weren't quite sure whose fault that was.

Their chest swelled as tears pinpricked their eyes. They listened for Talhan to stomp up behind them and try again, but he didn't follow.

CHAPTER FIFTEEN

Rish's even, rolling snores filled the vast space of the grand hall. Vines grew through the windows and bold seedlings sprung from the cracks in the floor. Rish had found an alcove that wasn't covered in dirt and dried leaves to serve them dinner. Neelo's stomach was still in knots and their head aching from the night prior, but the bowl of Rish's famous stew helped considerably. The taste was equally warming and nostalgic—a recipe Rish had made for Neelo many times over the years. The green witch especially loved cooking the giant pot of hearty stew over a campfire.

Talhan had refused to let Rish wash the dishes and had taken them from her protesting hands. Shame had filled Neelo upon seeing his gesture. It was clear Rish was exhausted and ready to sleep, but Neelo had never offered to wash up for Rish . . . not because they didn't love her, but because they didn't know how to do that thing where someone rejects an offer of help and the other person pushes to do it anyway. They didn't know how to *insist*, how to make their insistence not seem strange or awkward. Most people would probably think it was lazy or uncaring or privileged of Neelo, but they knew Talhan didn't. He had a practiced chivalry, an ease with which he did these things, whereas Rish would've told Neelo "no" and Neelo wouldn't have known the right way to nudge her until she relented.

It was just another way Neelo felt like a stranger within their own life, as if there was a world of meaning that they never quite learned to comprehend. Neelo could speak all three languages of Okrith, but they never grasped the language that flashed between quick glances and quirked eyebrows. That language they didn't know at all . . . except for one face they could read like a book.

Rish was already asleep when Talhan returned from washing pots. Neelo had placed their bedroll against the wall and tucked under a broken bench seat. With their back turned, they read their book, grateful the sun stayed in the sky so late into the evening.

When Talhan entered the ruins of the grand hall, he lit a small fire in the copper bracer underneath the giant front window. Neelo was certain the flames were for them to have enough light to read. They thought he'd find his own corner, far from Neelo after their brutal shutdown, but instead, he shuffled his bedroll up right beside them and fell straight asleep.

Neelo turned the page quietly, listening to the steady rhythmic breaths of Talhan accompanied by the staccato snores of Rish across the space. Neelo read until the sky darkened and firelight was low, lost in a realm of monsters and magic, where humans turned into wolves and prayed to strange gods. And it felt so good to be somewhere else—somewhere other than in their body and their constantly churning mind, that when the book ended a bittersweet sorrow bloomed in their chest. They'd read this book a dozen times before, but even then, they were sad the story had ended like being pulled from a beautiful dream. Reaching for their pack, Neelo tried to ruffle through the front pocket quietly. Their fingers closed around the small leather book and they slowly extracted it and opened to the first page.

Talhan's sleepy breath faltered and he peeked open one eye. "You're still awake?" His voice was rough with sleep.

Neelo glanced up from their new book and then quickly back down to the page. Why did he need to look like that? His hair stuck up at odd angles, his normal enthusiasm tempered by a slowness that made Neelo want to bridge the distance, rest their cheek on his chest, and listen to the steady thump of his heart.

They licked their thumb and flipped the page. "I can't sleep in places like this."

Talhan let out a sleepy grunt as he rolled onto his side. "Why not?"

"It's too big and open," Neelo murmured.

"Then why did we stop here?"

"Because both you and Rish were very excited about *stew*," they grumbled. "I didn't want to ruin your fun."

From the corner of their eye, Neelo saw Talhan's face soften. "That was very kind of you."

Shrugging, they kept their eyes fixed on the page. "I can sleep in Arboa."

Talhan's fingers hooked over the edge of Neelo's book, pulling it down until they were forced to look at him. Gods, his eyes glowed like a swordsmith's forge. How were they filled with such light, like a night cat reflecting in the darkness?

Neelo stared at his finger hooked over the page. "What?"

Talhan smirked, shadows dancing across his face. "Have you ever heard the one about the Silver Sands mermaid?"

"If it's in a book, then I've heard of it."

"It's a story Bri used to love when we were kids," Talhan said. "I don't know where it came from, but I used to tell it to her during the stormy seasons when she couldn't fall asleep."

"That was kind of you," Neelo echoed. It didn't surprise Neelo at all that Talhan would tell his twin sister stories to help her fall asleep. That was the person he was—thoughtful, kind, loyal.

"It was the least I could do . . ." Talhan's voice faded and Neelo knew the exact direction of his thoughts. Helvia Catullus had tortured Bri into the puppet of the daughter she'd wanted. Neelo could see the mantle of guilt upon Talhan's shoulders, as if he had held the switch himself. No wonder he was so fiercely loyal now that he was a towering warrior—now that he had the power to protect his loved ones.

Neelo knew better than to say their thoughts out loud. People didn't like having their truths laid so bare . . . they'd learned that the hard way . . . several times. Instead, they asked quizzically, "You're going to tell me a bedtime story?"

Talhan shrugged. "If you're not sleepy by the end of the story, I'll feed the fire and you can keep reading your book."

"Does that mean it's a very boring story?" Neelo marked the page in their book and set it down beside them.

"Just close your eyes."

Lifting their head, Neelo strained to search the dark shadows of the large room.

Talhan followed their line of sight. "I'm one of the best warriors in all of Okrith." His hand landed on their shoulder and he gently urged them back down. "The fact you think you need to be on guard is rather insulting."

Neelo scowled at him. "I don't do it to insult you."

"Do you trust that I could take on any attacker?" Talhan's palm drifted to the hilt of his dagger resting beside him, reaching for it without even looking as if it were an appendage of his own body. "You know that I'd always protect you, right?"

There it was, that fierce loyalty again. Neelo's frown deepened as they begrudgingly said, "Yes."

"Then close your eyes."

They let out a long sigh but relented, closing their eyes with a frown that elicited a soft laugh from Talhan. They settled their cheek onto their pack and wrapped their arms tightly around themself. Neelo heard Talhan shuffling and they peeked their eyes open to see him pulling his jacket out of his pack, too hot for him to wear on the ride.

"I don't—"

"Shh." Talhan silenced Neelo's protest as he draped his jacket over Neelo's torso. Few things made Neelo feel small, but the jacket of the giant warrior blanketed them with ease.

"Thank you," they muttered, pulling the collar up to tuck under their chin. Talhan's scent circled around them and they had the urge to breathe it in more deeply—bay leaves, citrus, and dark roasted coffee—rich, powerful, but energizing too, playful even, and so very Talhan.

Neelo squinted an eye open again and saw Talhan staring at them. "Don't watch me sleep. That's creepy."

Talhan's light chuckle echoed off the stone, accompanying Rish's heavy snoring. He rolled onto his back, slinging his forearm under his head like a pillow and staring up at the vaulted ceiling.

His voice was a deep, slow timbre. "I promise I won't watch you sleep if you promise to keep your eyes closed for the whole story."

"Why do I feel like I'm five years old again?" Neelo asked.

Even with their eyes closed, they knew from that soft little breath that Talhan was grinning. "Because everyone loves being told a story."

Neelo huffed, nuzzling their face deeper into Talhan's jacket. "Well, at least on that we can agree."

"We can agree on a lot of things," Talhan mumbled to himself.

Silence hung between them for a moment, and they knew it was true. Neelo and Talhan had always gotten along. During all the parties and weddings and celebrations of their childhood, the unlikely friends always seemed to end up in a corner somewhere. The Golden Eagle would bring Neelo a tray of food he'd stolen from the banquet and Neelo would sit beside him, reading their book while he ate. Then he'd go gallivanting off again, dancing and reveling. The life of every party.

But there would always be that moment between them. Always. Where it was just the two of them tucked in a corner, sitting quietly, enjoying each other's company. Neelo could never admit how much they cherished those quiet moments together, nor admit how they regretted how often they'd push him away.

He was just a friendly person. Just pitied them. He was just that nice to everyone.

Just.

They had a million reasons for it, excuses they could use to deny what they felt, but there was a little spark, a little question that lit within Neelo every time Talhan sat beside them: *Maybe he likes me. Maybe he really does just want to be here. With me.*

Finally, Talhan let out a long breath and began his story. "Once upon a time . . ."

But before he could even finish his first sentence, Neelo was fading away from that room and into the memories of the two of them and those secret little moments that seemed to string together into a friendship.

CHAPTER SIXTEEN

They wound through the twisting valley road, crossing over a trickling riverbed, and up the last hill toward Arboa. When the monsoon season came, the whole valley would be a roaring river, but now they didn't even need to cross at the bridge. The salty breeze of the ocean cut through the thick cloud of humidity lingering in the dense jungle. Just a few more turns and they'd be in the tropical seaside town of Arboa—an oasis to any traveler who managed to venture so far south.

"What is that?" Talhan called from up ahead.

Taking up the rear, Neelo leaned to the side to spot a large wagon wheel jutting up from the thick undergrowth. It's color had bleached to a faded gray and the spokes splintered from decades exposed to the elements—a skeleton of what the wagon used to be.

"There's a few of them along this trail," Rish said from the front. "We call it the wagon graveyard." She twisted around enough that Neelo knew she was talking to them and said, "Shall we break here for lunch?"

"But we're so close to Arboa," Talhan grumbled to himself, "and the refreshments that are bound to be there."

"We always stop at the midnight-blue wagon," Neelo said. "It's the best view in the South."

Talhan was about to say something when Rish added, "And I have packed plenty of treats to eat while we rest."

Talhan perked up at that. The Southern heat was clearly starting to wear on him. "As long as it's in the shade," he murmured, wiping a palm across his sweaty forehead.

"There." Neelo tipped their head to the wagon on the crest of the hill. Even though Talhan faced the other direction, Neelo was certain he was smiling.

The dark blue paint had mostly chipped off the wagon. Neelo remembered when the golden swirling sun was still visible on its side. It had faded to an echo of memory now. Their mind still filled in the blanks and made the sun appear even though all the golden paint had washed away.

Rish dismounted her horse first, tying it to a tree and then searching through the saddlebags for the carefully wrapped parcels she'd packed inside. Talhan dismounted second, and before Neelo could stop him, he came around to the side of their horse and offered his hand.

Neelo's frown deepened at his chivalry. They started at his paling complexion, the sweat that beaded across his lip and brow, his parted lips . . .

"You look like you're about to pass out," Neelo admonished him with a disapproving look. "Go sit and drink the rest of your water. Now. There'll be more in Arboa soon."

Talhan guffawed. "You seriously won't take my hand, will you?"

"No."

He wiped his forehead again. "Why not?"

"Because I don't need a charming knight," Neelo snapped. "Besides, you offered to be a guard and right now, I'm pretty sure I could blow you over with a single breath." Talhan pressed his lips together, hiding a smirk, and Neelo quickly added, "Don't," cutting him off before the inevitable lewd comment about *blowing* escaped his mouth.

"You know me too well." Talhan chuckled, holding up his hands in mock defense. "Okay, okay, I'm going."

He wandered off up the hillside, leaving Neelo to dismount and gather their things. Neelo's heart thundered as they watched him go.

Neelo moved to the back of the wagon, tossing around Talhan's words and feeling like a door was opened in their mind they finally might step through. The view opened out to a vast stretch of sapphire ocean. The jungle yielded to long stretches of white sand beaches and foam-topped ocean waves. There, at the mouth of the Crushwold River, where the brackish water met the rolling sea, was the town of Arboa.

A castle sat on the center hill, the village clinging to it from all sides, and beyond, like a halo circling the city, were fields of white flowers. The blooming fields. The white flower—*tussago filatra*—commonly called summer's snowflower, was the main ingredient in witching brews and its leaves were a staple of green witch cooking. Built long ago by the snowflower traders, the town of Arboa was now presided over by the Almah family—one of the most prestigious fae families in all of Okrith.

Neelo could just make out the white bricks and clay tiled roofs of the palatial home. Built like a flat-topped pyramid, the shadow of the waving Arboan flag acted like a sundial to the city below. Neelo could tell it was midafternoon based on the flag's shadow over the market district.

The wind rustled through the blooming fields, rippling the flowers like waves radiating out from every angle. It had been years since Neelo had visited the perfumed coastal town that smelled of fresh flowers, even in the seediest alleyways. Neelo and Carys had grown up so close to Arboa that they used to visit Ersan all the time . . . before everything fell apart.

Rish's hand pulled Neelo's focus back to the wagon. She passed out savory pastry rolls filled with goat's cheese, tomato, red pepper, and egg.

Talhan moaned indecently at the first bite and Neelo quickly picked up the book they'd brought from their saddlebag.

"You are an absolute goddess, Rish." Talhan licked his fingers. "I'm certain you sprouted straight from the earth divine."

"Goddess of Death, strike me down," Neelo muttered, keeping their eyes fixed on the heavy book on their lap.

"He is appreciating my cooking," Rish protested as she puffed out her chest with pride. "The highest compliment you can pay a green witch." The swarming bugs clung to her light dress and she fanned her linen napkin, swatting them away. "My little Eagles were always such charmers. I love cooking for you and your sister." Rish smacked a bug on her arm. "The one problem with this lookout; it's rife with biters."

"They seem to only be picking on you." Talhan waved at the cloud of insects as Rish let out a frustrated groan.

Rish hopped off the back of the wagon and smoothed down her dress. "I'm going to ride ahead. I'll see you in town."

Neelo peeked up from their book. "What?"

Rish smiled at them sweetly—too sweetly—and Neelo saw straight through the facade. What mischief was she up to?

"There are too many bugs," Rish said with a shrug. "I'm going to head off and I'll meet you in Arboa."

"You were the one who insisted on—" Neelo sniffed the air. "Why do you smell like perfume?"

Rish grinned even as she asked, "What do you mean?"

"You never wear perfume. How odd that you'd pick a fragrance that you know mosquitoes love . . ."

"Must've been something in my bag; got on my clothes." Rish waved through the cloud of bugs and began walking away. "Have a nice lunch."

Oh, she was truly wicked, that mischievous, meddling witch. Neelo gritted their teeth, giving Rish a knowing look and squeezing the edges of their book until Talhan nudged them with his elbow.

"It's going to bother you the whole trip if you bend the cover," he whispered.

Neelo loosened their grip. He was right. It would annoy them every time they opened the book. Rish called a final farewell as she guided her horse back down the trail, taking the swarm of mosquitoes with her.

Talhan pulled one of Neelo's hands away from their book and their gut clenched until he placed a roll in their hands and said, "Eat. Food."

Neelo rolled their eyes and took a bite. Rish had perfectly blended the spice and cheese flavors, one of the best ones she'd ever made, and it took a huge force of will to not make a moaning sound that mirrored Talhan's own. Whoever thought green witches didn't possess powerful magic had never tasted Rish's cooking. It wasn't as exciting as gleaning the future, but it was endlessly comforting and healing in its own way.

"Only Rish would willingly be attacked by bugs to meddle in my life," Neelo said through a mouthful of food. "Bloody busybody."

Talhan chuckled. "I noticed her spraying it on about ten minutes back."

Neelo took another bite, the cloud of insects now gone, leaving them to enjoy the view. They shot Talhan a look. "You knew what she was up to?"

"I had no idea." He grinned and picked up the second roll Rish had left for him. The moment stretched on before he added more quietly, "She loves you a lot."

"She's constantly doting and nagging," Neelo countered. "She must've been a mother hen in a past life."

Talhan looked out toward the strip of ocean on the horizon. "I wish my own mother was more hen and less fox."

Neelo knew his words were meant to sound as light and easy as he always did, but Neelo heard the hollowness. Neelo saw it in his eyes the night of the ball in Murreneir: the looks between his parents and his sister across a crowded ballroom seemed hard to miss, but perhaps that was because Neelo knew what to look for—the crease in the corner of Talhan's eyes when he was trying to hide his sadness, the way his cheeks didn't dimple when he smiled . . .

"That's really unfair." Neelo waited to feel Talhan's gaze upon them before adding, "Foxes aren't that bad."

Talhan snorted, his broad shoulders shaking with laughter, and Neelo had to press their lips together to keep from laughing with him.

"Very true." He clutched his belly. "I apologize to all foxes for the offense."

His laughter abruptly cut off and he froze. Neelo followed his line of sight through the forest, but saw nothing, and whispered, "What is it?"

"Four, maybe five of them," Talhan whispered back. "Green clothing, no weapons."

"Ah. I was wondering when they'd show up," Neelo said, lifting their book and leaning back against the wagon frame. "Arboan bandits."

Talhan quirked his brow. "Huh?"

"They're Arboan bandits," Neelo said, setting aside their bookmark and finding the place they left off. "They don't have weapons and have an oath not to kill, but they'll steal from anyone, royalty or no. Just let them have what they want."

"Let them have it? I can't do that—we need to protect our things." Talhan jumped off the wagon and then turned back to Neelo.

"I didn't bring anything that couldn't be replaced," Neelo said with a shrug, unworried about the five figures doing a terrible job of sneaking up the hillside.

"Well I did," Talhan gritted out.

That peaked Neelo's interest. "What did you bring?"

Talhan folded his arms. "It's a secret." Now Neelo was really intrigued.

"Okay, well, don't let them take whatever that secret thing is." Neelo chuckled at the way Talhan's mouth fell open. "Let them have the rest."

"You're serious?"

"This is practically an Arboan welcome." Neelo waved to the shaking trees. The easily spotted band of dastardly humans drew closer. "It's tradition."

"I don't want any part of this tradition," Talhan growled, digging through the saddlebags for something. "Are you coming?"

"I want to finish this chapter first," Neelo said. "You distracted me with the food."

"You're going to make me fight off five bandits by myself?" Talhan's hand drifted to the hilt of his dagger.

"No—I told you not to fight them."

"Neelo," he hissed.

"They're harmless. But if you feel like you need to fight, you can handle it on your own," they chastised, flipping the page again. "Just"—they glanced over the pages of their book at Talhan's hand and he sheathed his dagger again—"don't kill anyone. It's against their code."

"You're seriously—"

A barked order cut off Talhan's words as five green-clad bandits rushed out from the forest.

CHAPTER SEVENTEEN

Neelo kept their eyes fixed on their book as the five humans burst through the jungle. If Talhan wouldn't tell them what his secret belonging was, then Neelo wouldn't help him protect it. The ragtag crew wasn't going to harm Talhan anyway, part of the group's unscrupulous oath. Half of the time, the stolen objects would find a way back to their owner through merchants at the markets or turn up in foreign trading posts. The only thing the Arboan bandits never looted was Neelo's books, as if Neelo's black clothes and surly demeanor would curse the thieves to bad luck as well.

Neelo already knew what the looters looked like from many run-ins with them in the past. They wore mottled dark green fabric, dyed to blend with the jungle surrounds—fat lot of good it did them considering they bumbled around with all the stealth of half-drunk tapirs. The Arboan bandits stuck to the highways on the northeastern side of Arboan territory and it was pretty much a guarantee that they'd be encountered this close to the city. As a child, Neelo would steal a few objects from the palace to give to the bandits—just another item on their packing list. Southerners treated it like an involuntary tithe, paying them so that they'd be left alone as they passed through. But occasionally those brash enough from other courts would try to fight them, and the bandits always won.

They were curious if Talhan would prove an exception.

"Neelo!" Talhan hissed, ducking under the swipe of a bandit's fist. The group whooped and cheered with all the joy of a flock of gulls descending on a fish cart. "A little help here!"

Guess not.

"They're harmless," Neelo said, licking their thumb and flipping another page. "They don't have any weapons."

"But there are *five* of them. And they're still trying to *steal* from us," Talhan shouted. One human reached for Neelo's saddlebag and Talhan yanked the thief by the back of the collar, practically throwing him across the clearing with the force of his strength.

"You're doing fine," Neelo said, noting from their periphery how Talhan easily took on three of them at once. Dodging each flailing arm and wayward strike, he lured away the ones trying to get to the horses. "Where's that Catullus mastery I've heard so much about?" Neelo pointed the toe of their black boot toward one bandit at the edge of the group. "That one hasn't even put out his cigarette yet."

"You said I can't kill them." Talhan elbowed one behind him in the nose. "That's why."

The bloody-nosed bandit stumbled backward toward the wagon, his back smacking into the wheel beside Neelo. Sighing, Neelo closed their heavy book and smacked the Arboan bandit over the head with their large tome.

"There," they said, smirking as the bandit's knees folded and he dropped to the ground. "I'm helping."

Talhan let out an exasperated grunt as he tried to lift two bandits in one arm. Each of the thieves seemed miniature compared with Talhan's large, powerful frame. The fae warrior looked more like a harried parent wrestling small children. Talhan booted another away, clearly turning back to implore Neelo for aid again when a figure on horseback came galloping up the trail. At first, he was partially obscured through the thick forest, but Neelo knew who he was instantly. The bandits seemed to know too and instantly scattered back into the forest . . . well, the few who were still conscious did at least.

Neelo opened their book and leaned back against the wagon again. "I'm surprised it took you so long, Sy," they called to the figure emerging through the trees. "I wondered if you'd come out to greet us at all."

Ersan Almah patted the neck of his golden brown horse, plucking a fallen leaf from its braided blond mane. He wore a wide-brimmed slate-gray hat, shielding his eyes from the bright midday sun. His high-collared white shirt was unlaced to the center of his chest, revealing dark hair and tawny brown skin. With his high cheekbones, strong stubbled jawline, and muscled physique, it was no wonder Carys had fallen in love with the Arboan lord many moons ago. But she was young then . . . young enough that an attractive and confident fae Lord was all she needed him to be.

Talhan folded his arms, pushing up his biceps in a way that made Neelo roll their eyes. "You must be Sy."

The Lord of Arboa shifted in his saddle, placing a gloved fist on his hip and lifting his chin so he stared down his nose at Talhan. "Only friends call me Sy."

"And I only care what my friends want to be called." Talhan's eyes darkened. "You broke *my* friend's heart."

"She had plenty to do with it." Ersan huffed, his thick dark lashes shifting to Neelo. "Your puppy is loyal, I'll give you that."

"My *puppy* is about to decapitate you if you call him that again." Neelo moved toward one of the unconscious bandits, stooped, and gingerly picked up their discarded cigarette. "Why does this smell different from the brew back in Saxbridge?"

Talhan finally broke his stare with Ersan and shifted to Neelo's side.

"Because we only smoke real witching brew here in Arboa." Ersan inclined his head. "Not that swill you all smoke in Saxbridge, tainted by those many Eastern flowers, changing flavors year to year. We like tradition in Arboa. We stick to pure Arboan smoke flavors."

Neelo's jaw tightened. "But you're happy to sell the *swill* to Saxbridge?"

Ersan's lips curled up in a wicked grin. "Of course." He spoke with a confidence that bordered on arrogance, but Neelo knew it was all for show. That personality was put in place the day Carys left, and whenever Neelo saw his puffed-out chest and lifted chin, all they saw was how broken he was. No one else seemed to read the current of sorrow that flowed beneath his sharp exterior, but perhaps that was because Neelo saw themself in Ersan's mask of indifference.

"That's why we've come," Neelo said, standing from their crouch.

Ersan cocked his thick eyebrow. "I thought you came to survey the wreckage of Augustus Norwood's fleet?"

"That too," Neelo added, dusting off their trousers and glancing at the two stubborn fae Lords. "Now, if you two are done peacocking, let's get on with it."

Ersan grinned at Neelo. "I've missed you, Heir of Saxbridge. It's been too long."

Neelo noted Talhan's shift in demeanor at Ersan's familiarity. He stiffened, his hands in fists and leaning in front of Neelo until he was practically blocking them with his body. Peacocking indeed.

"Come," Ersan said, watching shrewdly as Talhan inched closer to Neelo still. "I'll accompany you back to the Almah manor."

Neelo brushed past Talhan toward their horse, muttering to Talhan under their breath, "Why don't you piss on my leg to mark me with your scent while you're at it?"

"Do you think that would help?" Talhan replied.

Neelo curled their lip and shoved their book back in their horse's saddlebag. "I don't belong to you."

"You've certainly made that clear." Talhan mounted his horse, as Neelo did the same. He nudged his mare up beside Neelo's, until he could see Neelo's face, though they kept their eyes fixed on their hands. "You don't belong *to* anyone, Neelo," Talhan whispered, and Neelo could see him gauge how far ahead Ersan was from the corner of their eyes. "But you belong. Always."

Neelo softened a little at his words. "Then don't let Sy get under your skin," they muttered, spotting Ersan's horse on the crest of the hill, waiting for them to follow. "He is an arrogant, rich lord, to be sure, but he's not a bad person."

"If Carys hates him, I hate him."

Neelo huffed. "Carys doesn't hate him nearly as much as she thinks she does."

"It sure seems like it." Talhan clicked his tongue and his horse fell in to step behind Neelo's mare.

"Many things are not what they seem."

Talhan chuckled. "Of that, I have no doubt."

"I'll have my tailor pull some fresh clothes for you, Lord Catullus," Ersan called from up ahead. "I think we are roughly the same size."

"I'm twice your size," Talhan gritted out and Neelo shot him a pointed look. "I mean, thank you for the hospitality," Talhan called louder. "But I have brought my own attire."

Ersan twisted on his mount to look back at Talhan's sweat-soaked tunic. The dark navy shade was probably radiating heat into Talhan. "If your attire is anything like what you're wearing now, you will be a puddle by the time you leave this place." Talhan sized up Ersan's wide hat, lightweight shirt, and tan linen trousers that hugged his muscled thighs. "You aren't prepared for the Southern heat."

"The Southern heat perhaps will take some adjusting to," Talhan said, waving out his sweaty tunic. "But I am suited to the Southern food and drink just fine."

"Ah. I have refreshments waiting on the veranda for you," Ersan said, spurring his horse into a trot. He shouted to be heard as he took off through the jungle. "Arboan wine and cinnamon cakes."

"Okay, fine," Talhan muttered from the corner of his mouth as Neelo watched Ersan ride down into the valley and out onto the blooming fields of white flowers. "He's not that bad."

"So easily won over with cinnamon cakes," Neelo teased. "Come on."

They tapped their horse with their calves and sped down into the valley below. The trees dwindled to golden earth and neat rows of white flowers radiating out in lines like a bursting sun. The saccharine scent hit Neelo all at once, their arms tingling with goose bumps at the aroma. Neelo glanced back to see Talhan, his smile widening at the look on Neelo's face, and Neelo realized they were smiling too.

"I'VE PROVIDED YOUR guest with some more appropriate attire, Heir of Saxbridge," Ersan's deep voice called from the top of the staircase. Despite its similarly low register, Ersan's voice was clipped and cold compared to Talhan's warmth. The Lord of Arboa leaned on the railing with each step, his face falling into a neutral look that edged in a frown. "He should be with us shortly."

Neelo could only imagine what Talhan had said to Ersan to put that tension in his voice. They were surprised Ersan wasn't sporting a black eye, but it seemed like Talhan had actually listened to Neelo and accepted the new clothes begrudgingly . . . probably because he was seconds from heat sickness.

Ersan slowly made his way down the stairs, giving a brief glance to each of the oil paintings lining the wall.

"Where's Collam?" Neelo asked, admiring the beautiful artwork painted by Ersan's younger brother.

"In his studio." Ersan's dark eyes flitted to Neelo. "I think he spends more time in there than you spend in your library."

Neelo let out a little hum. "That's certainly saying something."

"Indeed." Ersan's tone didn't carry any of the admiration it used to for his little brother. Well, not so little anymore. Collam was the same age as Neelo, after all, but Ersan used to love his little brother's passion for art. The younger Almah brother painted in the Arboan style: more muted palettes than in Saxbridge, beautiful creamy landscapes and detailed portraits that lacked the chaotic brushstrokes of the capital's artists. That no longer seemed the case.

That wasn't the only thing that had changed. Ersan didn't look anything like his exuberant younger brother anymore either. From all they could tell, the Lord of Arboa wasn't the carefree fae that Neelo had once known. His clothes were more structured now, his demeanor strained. His hat hung from a string around his neck, bouncing off his shoulder blades with each step he walked. Gold buttons decorated his fitted trousers, matching the golden embroidery on his pointed brown leather boots. The outline of his wooden leg beneath his trousers was more noticeable standing than on horseback. Ersan used to keep the left trouser leg rolled up but now wore it down, befitting his more stoic attire. A hooked sword hung on his hip, a dagger on the other, and he leaned on a golden-topped cane that Neelo knew had a hidden knife in it as well. He was a formidable fighter and, though his weapons were beautiful, Neelo knew they weren't purely decorative.

Ersan Almah now looked equal parts warrior and nobleman: the Lord of a wealthy province and a skilled fighter. But he also looked like a person with a shadow looming over his head, and Neelo knew its twin shadow still hung over a blond-haired fae in another court.

"Thank you," Neelo said, reigniting their conversation. "For lending him some appropriate attire."

"You sound surprised." Ersan's face split into a bitter grin as he walked, his cane clicking on the floor with every other step. "It's not so long ago that we were friends."

"We're still friends, Sy," Neelo corrected him. "Though time and circumstance have kept us from being closer."

Ersan's expression flickered with a hint of pain before he inclined his head. "Of course."

Talhan appeared at the top of the stairs and Neelo's heart leapt into their throat. He wore the traditional Arboan garb: fitted linen trousers and a loose white shirt laced up from the navel. Neelo's eyes trailed down the open neckline, roving over the peaks of his defined shoulders.

"Sy," Neelo said, clearing their throat. "You've met Tal, but I haven't formally introduced you." They waved a hand up at Talhan, hating the formality but doing it anyway. "Talhan Catullus—the Golden Eagle, son of the Eastern Lord and Lady Catullus, and twin brother to the Queen Consort of the Western Court." Neelo gestured to Ersan. "Ersan Almah, son of the late Lord and Lady Almah, and Lord of the blooming fields and the city of Arboa."

"I'm fairly certain we've met a few times before in our youth," Talhan said, giving Ersan a hasty nod. "All the weddings and solstices have jumbled together in my mind over the years."

"For me, as well." Ersan huffed. "Though I haven't managed to travel much since my father's passing." He paused and shook his head, as if remembering his manners. Ersan gestured down the long hallway. "Welcome to Arboa."

The Lord of Arboa waited at the bottom step for Talhan before leading them through the entryway and along the first-floor hallway. The palace was designed in warm red and brown earth tones, high-lighted in accents of cream and gold paint, and sprinkled through-out were the vibrant rainbow colors of the South. Neelo loved the bright hues so abundantly displayed, from the curtain tassels to the flamboyant flower beds. Whenever Neelo visited the other courts, it felt like they all lived in perpetual winter, the homes and houses dark and devoid of color and life. The other palaces' decor was beautiful, no doubt, but cold, unfeeling. Neelo stared down at their tunic and trousers, knowing they were a black, dead rose in a bed of spring flowers. But still, they liked to be around it, see it, even if they did not embrace the vibrancy in their own attire.

Talhan sniffed the air as he fell into stride beside Neelo. "Something smells delicious."

Neelo shot him a look to behave and he gave them an innocent *Who, me?* look in return.

"When Queen Emberspear's councilor said that you were sending scouts in your stead, I knew that you were coming yourself," Ersan said, leading them out onto a veranda that overlooked the city. "There's no way you'd allow it."

They couldn't deny it, but didn't say anything to confirm—not with Talhan so close. Ersan simply nodded at their silence and stepped through two sets of sheer curtains, Talhan and Neelo following. As they walked back out into the midafternoon heat, a sweeping view of the city appeared. Narrow cobblestone pathways twisted through a landscape of russet rooftops and tapered sandstone buildings. Creeping red flowers clung to windowsills and curved over cream-colored doorways.

As Neelo stepped further out onto the red stone, a rush of cool air wafted over them. A gushing stream bisected the veranda, spilling over the steps of the manor and down into an aqueduct that sped toward the city below.

Talhan sighed, glorying in the breeze's sensation, and fanning his light shirt out from where it clung to his chest with sweat.

"Clever," Neelo said, inspecting the wicker paddles woven to look like palm fronds. They rotated on a wheel, driven by the rushing stream much the same as a watermill might. But instead of using the power of the water to grind wheat into flour, this contraption created a steady breeze.

"An invention of mine," Ersan said proudly, flourishing a hand as he stared up at the fan. "I can send the designs to the palace if you like."

"Please," Talhan moaned before Neelo could open their mouth. He gave Neelo a sheepish look. "It would help with all the biting insects at twilight too."

"You have the Eastern blood in you," Ersan said tightly. "They'll leave us alone entirely with you around." He gestured to the cushioned wicker chairs. A platter of food and pitcher of punch sat on a low table between them with a fine layer of netting covering it.

Ersan sat with a groan and Neelo noted the way Talhan still sized him up. An idea sparked in their mind.

"You two should train together while we're here," Neelo suggested.

"Mm." Talhan shoved the rest of the cinnamon cake into his cheek and dusted the sugar off his hands. "I need to get back to training. I can feel my sister's judging eyes upon me all the way from the West. *A soldier is only as sharp as his dullest day,* she'd say."

151

"Wise indeed." Ersan arched his thick black eyebrow. "Tomorrow morning. We can train at dawn?"

"Must it be dawn?"

Ersan chuckled. "Trust me. You don't want to be sparring when the sun is high in these parts."

Talhan glanced at Neelo. "And what will you be doing?"

Ersan cut in before Neelo could reply. "I've had some new books shipped in specifically for your arrival, plus, of course, the papers collected from the shipwreck." He passed Neelo a goblet of punch and they accepted it with a nod, trying to hide their excitement at some new books to read. "Some of the parchment we found at the bottom of a trunk still has legible writing, though it seems nothing more than inventory notes. I figured you'd want to see it nevertheless. We'll go visit the site after you settle in." Ersan took a letter out of his pocket and passed it to Neelo. "Here."

Neelo took the paper and, without opening it, looked at the Lord of Arboa. "Is it true?"

Ersan's brow furrowed and his chin dipped in a curt nod. Neelo grumbled a curse to the Fates.

Talhan leaned forward, staring at the unopened letter in Neelo's hands. "What?"

"Gods," Neelo said, ignoring Talhan and pocketing the letter. "We'll go inspect the wreckage now. Ready your horses."

Talhan muttered something under his breath and hastily chucked three more miniature cakes into his mouth before standing.

Ersan's cane tapped Neelo's elbow and they paused. "You're wearing that to the beaches?"

Talhan growled, but Ersan merely shrugged off Talhan's sudden menace. "I am not insulting their clothing," he said flatly. "But the Arboan heat is different than other parts of the Southern Court. That thick, dark clothing could get them killed."

Talhan's voice dropped an octave. "They wear what they like."

Neelo took a step closer to Talhan. "Easy, Tal. Three sullen fae is one too many."

Talhan's steely expression cracked at that. "Fine."

Neelo looked at Ersan, the knowing look in his smug eyes making Neelo scowl even more.

"I'll go change while you prepare to depart," they said with a frown, leaving the two brooding warriors to stare each other down. "Don't kill each other while I'm gone."

"No promises," Talhan muttered.

CHAPTER EIGHTEEN

Neelo and Talhan trudged across the white sand beaches with
Ersan leading the way. The powder was so fine it was like
walking on flour. It took twice as long to cross the stretch of
beach as the grittier golden beaches of Saxbridge.

Here, every footstep sunk deep into the sand, but at least it didn't
burn their bare feet. The lightness of the grains didn't seem to hold
the heat the same way as the golden sand, for which they were grateful. Neelo rolled their tan trousers up to the knee. Their arms were
on full display in their sleeveless gray tunic, with a wide, open collar that flapped in the breeze. They wore the elegant, wide-brimmed
Arboan hat that shaded their eyes from the sun and accentuated their
sharp features. Without the many layers of black clothing, Neelo
looked debonair, *approachable* even, and that felt incredibly strange.
They preferred clothes that would disincline people from interrupting their reading, but they could see the benefit of the softness of the
fabric and the lightness with which it caught the wind. If only they
made it in black . . .

Neelo caught Talhan stealing glances at them for the hundredth
time in a matter of minutes.

"Do I really look that bad?" Neelo scowled, feeling Talhan's eyes on them like a horde of spiders scuttling across their skin. Of all things, would this be the thing that finally pushed him away?

"Bad?" Talhan guffawed, his eyes widening with amusement. "You think you look *bad*?"

Neelo tugged the brim of their hat to shade from the glaring sun. "Then why do you keep staring at me?"

Talhan brushed his hair off his forehead, his dimples deepening. "Because you look . . . quite the opposite." He cleared his throat. "Of bad."

Cheeks burning, Neelo muttered, "Oh." And quickly kept walking. It hadn't even crossed their mind that Talhan would *like* the way they looked.

"I mean, I like your normal attire too, I . . ." Talhan rubbed his hand down his stubbled jawline. "But right now, in *that* tunic and with that look on your face, you look dashing, powerful, like a pirate who takes what they want and I—I should stop talking."

"It's the hat, isn't it?" Emboldened to take a step closer, Neelo arched their brow. "So you have a thing for pirates?"

"Who doesn't?" Talhan feigned a laugh as he anxiously rubbed the back of his neck. "I just meant, you look good, and, um . . ." He cleared his throat and quickly hustled ahead, leaving Neelo open-mouthed as they watched him go.

Did their outfit make Talhan Catullus, *the Golden Eagle himself,* nervous? Neelo had never seen him so flustered. It made an odd sort of pride bloom in their chest to know that, for a brief moment, they were the one on balance and him off kilter.

Neelo used their clothes and name and demeanor to remind people that what's beneath their clothing had nothing to do with who they were. People shouldn't decide how to treat one another based on a sliver of flesh, and so Neelo dressed the way they did, not because they were confused about their own body, but because everyone else was. They glanced at Talhan, speed-walking ahead. He certainly didn't seem confused. Flustered, maybe. Lustful, even. But not confused in the slightest.

With that, their confidence and pride turned to confusion itself.

"Here!" Ersan called from far ahead, moving swiftly across the compacted sand closer to the water's edge. He'd attached a netted circle to the bottom of his cane so that it flared out from the base and didn't pierce into the sand as he walked. Neelo wondered if it was another one of his many inventions.

Ersan led them out to the furthest point and when they turned the corner, dipping back into the next bay, they spotted the shipwreck. Waves crashed into the splintering hull, sails and ropes still swaying in the surf. Debris littered the beach, wading along the tidal lines with the seaweed and shells.

"We brought a trunk of the most important finds back to the manor for safekeeping," he said, turning toward Neelo. His eyes were hidden in the shade of his wide hat. "But this is where we found them."

"Were there any bodies?" Talhan asked, pausing at the point, and Neelo knew he was waiting for them to catch up.

"Three bodies made it over the reef," Ersan replied. "There were more out past the breakers." He motioned to where the turquoise waters turned to deep ocean blue. "We paddled out to retrieve them, but they were gone. The sharks probably got to them first."

Neelo clenched their jaw. "And no survivors?"

"A local boy was the first to spot the wreck." Ersan shook his head. "He didn't see any survivors and we didn't find any footsteps . . . but it's always possible they washed ashore closer to the mouth of the river."

Talhan swallowed, surveying the splintered boards, rusted pieces of metal, and debris caked in sand. "How do we know this was part of Augustus's fleet?"

"Besides the fact that no one else has claimed this vessel?" Ersan countered. "Not a single report of missing ships? Where are the people out searching for their loved ones? Where are the mourners for those who never returned home?" He stooped and picked up a piece of metal. Part of a scabbard or armor? "I'll tell you why, because whoever died on that ship was there in secret." He held the piece of metal out to Neelo.

They scrutinized the etchings of a lion head above two crashing waves. "The Eastern Court crest. But this could be an Eastern merchant vessel—"

"In the trunk we collected for you is armor engraved in the old Northern Court crest," Ersan said. "What sort of merchant vessel is carrying soldiers loyal to Hennen Vostemur *and* Gedwin Norwood?"

Neelo shrugged. "Maybe they were pirates, trafficking stolen goods."

"Then why didn't they have any stolen goods from the other three courts?"

Talhan loomed over Neelo, his shadow casting a welcome shade upon them. "Have there been any other sightings of Augustus's fleet?"

"No. The last we heard, it sank just past Silver Sands Harbor." Ersan shook his head. "There's been no other wreckage along the shoreline either."

"Great," Talhan muttered. "That violet witch wasn't with Norwood during the storms, anyway." Talhan's voice grew vacant. "She nearly staged a coup for the Western Court throne. If we hadn't arrived when we did . . ." He cleared his throat. "The violet witch Priestess was there that stormy night in Swifthill and she left right after the battle, so she's alive, and out there somewhere, even if Augustus perished with his fleet."

Ersan snorted as if Talhan had said something funny and then paused, darting glances between the two of them. "Wait . . . a *violet witch*? You can't be serious."

"We have a lot to catch him up on," Talhan jeered, elbowing Neelo.

"I wouldn't be surprised if that witch conjured the storms to get rid of Norwood, now that she has enough power to claim the Eastern crown for herself," Neelo mused. "Her notes were all about violet witch sovereignty and taking their own throne and so many bloody seed metaphors it was nearly impossible to decipher. *To sow the seeds of rebellion* and *The smallest seed will be king*. She wrote them over and over in her notebook. Gods, I wish Cole hadn't stolen that journal away," Neelo growled, thinking of the tall witch who had disappeared from Rua's dinner table in Murreneir.

Neelo had scouts searching the South for the brown witch they'd met in Silver Sands, but so far he was no more than a shadow. Curse him for letting Neelo peek at that fascinating and terrifying journal and then vanishing with it.

Talhan toed the sand with his boot. "I still don't understand why she would align herself with a petty brat like Augustus Norwood."

"For his armies and his money," Neelo muttered. "And probably because he was so easily manipulated."

Talhan shuddered. "Gods, she was so creepy."

"Sounds delightful," Ersan said drolly and then turned to Neelo. "So you're telling me there's a violet witch still alive? One powerful enough to be vying for the Eastern throne?"

"She's not just an impressive witch," Neelo said, meandering down the line of debris. "She very well may be an immortal one." Ersan's mouth fell open for a split second before he schooled his expression again. "She comes from a time when witches whispered powerful spells into the world and the dominion of fae was uncertain."

Ersan pulled his wide-brimmed hat lower over his eyes. "Then where has she been all these many years?"

"I have my suspicions." Neelo stooped and picked up another rusted piece of scrap metal. They glanced at Talhan. "You remember that amethyst dagger Lina had in Silver Sands? The one you said Baba Monroe needed to save Lina's life?"

Talhan frowned. "Yes?"

"I requested a copy of the Valtene death registry to be written out and sent to me," Neelo said. Talhan's eyebrows shot up. "Chalked it up to royal curiosity."

"So that's why you were reading that witch's ledger about Valtene," Talhan whispered, the locks seeming to click into place in his mind.

"It's never good when you say these things, Neelo," Ersan grumbled. "And what did you find?"

"Adisa Monroe was buried in Valtene hundreds of years ago, with her totem pouch and spell book."

Ersan cursed the witches' moon. "Who did they bury if not her?"

"That's the thing—I think they *did* bury her," Neelo said, with a frustrated sigh.

"What? How?"

"Cole let me look at her journals in Silver Sands," Neelo said. "Toward the end, it was clear she was losing her grip on reality. She was playing with sleeping curses and trying to control other's minds . . ." The muscle in Talhan's jaw popped out from his cheek. "I think she accidentally cursed herself and it appeared like she was dead."

"Dear Gods," he whispered. "They buried her alive?"

"She'd already spelled herself into immortality, I think." Neelo picked at their fingernails. "Not so easily killed, but unable to get out of her earthly prison either. There are reports from long ago of the graves of Valtene, how they whisper and trick people's minds."

"The whispers from the ledger," Talhan murmured. "You think she was trying to get someone to dig her up?"

"It worked in the end." Neelo nodded. "When the battles in Valtene began, the Northern soldiers looted the gravesites."

"Shit," Talhan growled. "They dug her up?"

Neelo took the letter Ersan had passed them earlier out of their pocket and bobbed their chin. "And violet witch magic has been growing ever since."

"But how would you know she's not in her grave unless . . ." Talhan glanced between Neelo and Ersan. "You asked Ersan to dig up a *grave*?"

"I had my contacts in the West do it for me." Ersan crossed his arm and smirked at Talhan's gaping face. "Pretty squeamish for a warrior, aren't you?"

"There's a difference between creating the dead and desecrating them, you cretin," Talhan snarled and Ersan stepped forward as if ready to throw a punch at the insult.

"Gods, you two." Neelo stepped in between them. "I didn't trust anyone at the palace to be quiet about it." They shot the Lord of Arboa a look and Ersan took a step backward. "Sy is good at keeping secrets."

"That's low for someone who's just asked me for their help," Ersan growled and Neelo realized too late they'd struck a raw nerve.

"I'm not saying that it's a bad thing," Neelo countered, quickly trying to fix their mistake. They hadn't meant to bring up what he'd done to Carys. "It makes you trustworthy . . . most of the time. I—" They scrambled to balance their loyalties between the two. Shit. They had to say it. "Except when you're too good at keeping secrets from the only people who truly matter."

Ersan's head dropped to gaze at his boots, the shade of his hat dipping all the way down to his neck.

"There's more," Neelo said, staring out at the ocean. Ersan didn't move, seemingly lost in his own thoughts and Neelo grimaced, knowing they sent him down that spiral. It wasn't intentional . . . they just always had a way of saying the wrong thing. Unfortunately, they didn't know how to make it right, and wasn't sure they had time to figure it out, their mind whirling aggressively at all this information . . . and lack of it. "But I'll have to tell you that later. Right now, I have suspicions I'm unable to confirm."

"Such as?" Ersan asked.

"I think more people are tied to this Baba Monroe than we first realized."

Talhan shuffled a step closer to Neelo, fully covering them with his shade. "How many?"

"There may be more people alive with violet witch blood." Neelo watched the white-capped waves tumble over the breakers in the distance.

"Cole and?" Talhan whispered, keeping a wary glance at Ersan, but Neelo knew Ersan could be trusted. "More?"

"Yes," Neelo replied.

"Who?"

Neelo craned their head up to Talhan, squinting to see his features sharpened by the midday sun. "I want to confirm it first."

Talhan frowned, clearly put out at not being included. "Planning on digging up more bodies?"

"Not if I can help it," Neelo muttered. They turned to Ersan. "I want to see this trunk of shipwrecked items."

Talhan fanned out his tunic soaked with sweat. "Thank the Gods."

"Good," Ersan added. "It'll give me more time to prepare for the party."

Neelo groaned. "Must there be a party?"

"You are the Heir of our court," Ersan said with a mischievous look. "It would be a dishonor not to celebrate your visit."

"Even if I pardon you?" they asked hopefully.

Ersan grinned. "I'll try to limit the guest list."

"Thank you," Neelo grumbled.

Talhan turned and headed back for the break in the beach grasses. "Can we please have this conversation in the shade?"

"He seems like a handful," Ersan said out of the corner of his mouth as they followed after the giant warrior. "You two seem like an odd pair, if you don't mind me saying."

"We're not a pair," Neelo protested, even as his observation struck them like an arrow. "You have no idea," they said quietly to themself.

CHAPTER NINETEEN

Cobwebs clung between the palm trees, gossamer threads floating on the breeze as Neelo sat in the atrium. They pulled apart the trunk of salvaged items that Ersan had left there. Papers lay strewn about on either side of Neelo as they dug deeper. The trunk contained mostly lists of inventory and letters for restock. A shriveled-up posy of snowflowers sat in the corner of the trunk, the petals all having fallen off, but the small, scalloped leaves were easily identifiable. They found one small corner of a map but couldn't identify the bare stretch of coastline without names or trail markers. The single stamp from the Port of Wynreach made Neelo suspect the Eastern capital was either where the ships were headed or leaving from . . . but it wasn't enough to formulate any sort of bigger theory.

Frustration mounted as Neelo grabbed another sheet of useless paper. The only legible letter was an "A" on the bottom right corner—too overly flourished to be the writing of a common sailor. Neelo scrutinized the blurred letters. Maybe it was for Augustus or maybe it was just wishful thinking. If it was Augustus's signature, the evidence only lent itself further to the fact that Augustus perished in a shipwreck, if not in Silver Sands, then here in Arboa. There had to be something more. They stared at the letter again, but it did nothing to confirm their suspicions nor inspire new ones.

Neelo scoured through the box for several hours, and there was nothing else that showed who these people were. The frustration was mounting and, although stationed in the atrium where the breeze filtered in, they were still dripping sweat onto the taupe tiles by the time they grabbed the last object . . . a packet of seeds.

The salt water had washed off the writing on the label and the packet was a mushy mess in their hands. A sailor carrying seeds wasn't suspicious in its own right . . . but Neelo cataloged that item in the notebook beside them, just in case. They carefully opened the packet, which fell apart in their hands as they lifted the sodden top. Five swollen seeds plopped into their palm and Neelo pushed them around with their thumb: banded stripes, shaped almost like a miniature pumpkin, it seemed like a seed of the Eastern variety judging by its markings. But even with their plant identification book, the seeds might be too warped from the salt water to identify accurately. It was the right size to be an eastern thorn violet or . . .

Could these be blooming amethyst seeds? Like the ones used to poison the Western Queen? Waterlogged seeds weren't enough to confirm it, but Neelo's pulse quickened anyway, along with a growing agitation. They didn't have a single answer, only more questions.

Which meant that this trunk had been a waste of time, and they were no closer to knowing where Adisa Monroe was, what magic was she raising in Okrith, and what—if anything—it had to do with the witching brew that was killing people in Saxbridge.

Maybe I should have just sent someone to review this mess after all, they thought.

As the sun began to set, green witches had come to tend the potted plants in the atrium, silently working around Neelo, which they appreciated. The witches swept away all the newly built cobwebs, making a perfect floral display for those touring the gardens once more. It felt criminal to destroy the beautiful tapestries those spiders wove and to let more mosquitoes go uncaught. Neelo knew what it felt like to be considered a nuisance, even when they were trying to be helpful. Spiders spun their webs. Neelo read their books. And on many days, Neelo felt like there was no place for either of them in the lives of the fae.

Neelo stood, dusting the sand from the wrecked items off their knees. They needed to let their mind wander, to ponder the trunk's contents and see if there was any connection or pattern they'd been missing. To see if this trip wasn't truly the wild goose chase it was appearing to be.

Passing through a domed room, Neelo peered up at the glass spotted with dew. The sky was lit up in pink and purple hues as the sun sank below the trees. Through the glass, they could see servants lighting small lanterns throughout the gardens. Others carried trays of glassware and platters of table linen to the finely netted tents erected throughout the botanical gardens for people to mingle without being attacked by evening insects until, once the sun set, the smoke of the torches would shoo the pests away.

The servants hurried to finish setting up for the dinner so that they could turn in for what Arboans called "first sleep." The entire province would go to bed in the late afternoon and rise in the middle of the night to feast. Dinner would stretch for several hours and then they would return to bed until dawn. Ersan extended Neelo an invitation to dine with him that evening, but Neelo refused, claiming they looked forward to sleeping in a bed straight through the night. Neelo always struggled to get into the Arboan routine. They couldn't fall asleep with the sun still in the sky and then rise from bed when it was pitch dark, let alone eat and converse.

Knowing they'd have to attend the ball Ersan was throwing in their honor the following night made tonight all the more precious. They groaned, trying to think of a believable lie to excuse themself from attending . . . but they knew if Talhan didn't prod them into going, then Rish certainly would. The green witch had disappeared into the Arboan kitchens to meet with old friends and had been busy testing out the new workspace ever since—Rish had a way of taking over every kitchen they traveled to—but she'd pop up if it was inconvenient for Neelo, of that they were assured.

Too, even if they could ignore Rish and Talhan saying how this banquet would be fun, they were aware enough that it was also their duty as heir.

Sweeping a finger across the pane, Neelo turned from the gardens and ventured toward the patio. What they saw made them halt mid-step, their black boot hovering an inch above the tile. There, perfectly framed by the setting sun, was Talhan Catullus.

He had his back turned to the building, a sword in one hand and a dagger in the other. His tunic lay crumpled and discarded beside his two scabbards as he faced the sunset. Heat burned up Neelo's neck to their cheeks as they watched his magnificent, sweat-slicked form illuminated in the shades of gold as he stood beneath a giant *amasa* tree.

They watched silently as Talhan fought an invisible foe, each swipe and stab confident and smooth. He was so perfectly in his element. It was a dance—poetry—life and death, blood and glory, in one precise movement.

And Gods, it was glorious movement.

They didn't want to simply watch this moment from afar, something about it called to them, and for the first time in a long time, Neelo didn't wish to be alone . . . or at least, maybe they could be alone together.

Neelo's fingers twitched at their side and they pressed their lips tightly together, digging their teeth into the seam as they contemplated interrupting Talhan. They knew he wouldn't mind, but . . . Neelo was someone who observed the world, assessed. They didn't partake in it. But now, with the way Talhan had looked at them today still fresh in their mind, Neelo imagined the buzz of standing next to that gorgeous warrior and it felt more thrilling than terrifying.

Maybe they just wanted to prove Ersan wrong, that this pairing wasn't that odd at all. Neelo wasn't entirely sure what compelled them, but they took a steadying breath, marched to the end of the hall, and opened the bronze-framed door to the gardens. The door clanked and creaked as they opened it, the glass rattling in the frames as they stepped out onto the red stone terrace.

Talhan spun toward the sound, his eyes searching for a brief moment before landing on Neelo. When he spotted them, he paused, his face unreadable for one tantalizingly heated moment before his expression cracked into his usual charming grin. But that one split second made Neelo's heart flutter. Their hands clasped together in front of them as they held Talhan's stare. Something about those amber eyes, the same shade as the golden sunset, were easy to stare into, that gaze feeling more satisfying than the smell of old books or the taste of freshly baked bread. Those eyes—*his* eyes—fed Neelo's soul in a way they'd seldom known.

Neelo drifted mindlessly across the terrace and perched their forearms on the balustrade.

"Sorry to interrupt," they said.

"I was nearly done." Talhan shrugged. "Do you want to train with me?"

Neelo blinked at the offer. No one had asked them that before. They'd been forced to learn basic fighting skills by their mother: dagger, sword, archery, even a few ill-fated attempts with a battle-axe, but no one had ever *invited* them to train before. "I doubt I'd be very good at it."

Talhan's cheeks dimpled. "No one is when they're starting out."

Neelo tracked the beads of sweat dripping down Talhan's neck. "I trust the guards to protect me."

"Wouldn't you also like to know how to protect yourself?"

It was the same thing their mother had told them, but Neelo suddenly felt unwilling to admit they knew how to defend themself. Not when Talhan was pulling a dagger from the belt around his thigh, flipping it over, and offering out the hilt. He bridged the distance to the balustrade in three short strides.

With each step closer, Neelo's shoulders caved further inward as if they were a night-blooming flower closing against the brightness of the sun. "I don't know."

"Can I show you a few things?" Talhan waggled his eyebrows.

A rock formed in Neelo's throat. There were a great many things they wouldn't mind Talhan showing them.

"You'd look pretty intimidating with a dagger," Talhan goaded, holding the hilt up.

Neelo rolled their eyes. "Fine."

"Yes," Talhan whispered like a giddy child who'd been allowed an extra dessert.

It was utterly endearing—this fearsome warrior, built of thick corded muscle, delighting in such small things, so easily joyful. He could be happy and silly and vulnerable without appearing weak. No one would bully Talhan for his personality, not when his body and fighting prowess showed he could cut their head off in one fell swoop.

Neelo took the dagger and held it out in front of them like a snake that might bite, feigning ignorance, though Neelo knew more about the weapon than they'd let on. In a lifetime of always being the teacher, this time, they wanted to be the student.

Talhan chuckled, taking Neelo's hand so that their fingers wrapped around the width and off the point guard. "There," he murmured, his fingers lingering on Neelo's skin for a moment longer than necessary.

Neelo inwardly thrilled at the touch, surprising even themself that they didn't pull their hand away. In one swift move, Talhan vaulted over the balustrade to stand beside them. His ever-present scent mixed with the salty tang of his sweat and Neelo had the sudden urge to sweep away the moisture clinging to Talhan's biceps like the dew on a fogged windowpane.

Talhan placed his hand over Neelo's own, guiding their hand back, around, and up in curving arches. "Yes?"

Neelo nodded and Talhan stepped away, his presence clinging to Neelo's tunic. Talhan watched as Neelo kept doing the fluid motions as instructed and it took a great amount of effort for Neelo to not do it perfectly on the first try.

"Widen your stance." Talhan hummed, rubbing his thumb contemplatively across his bottom lip in a way that was entirely distracting. "Bend your knees." Neelo scowled at Talhan and he quickly added, "Please?"

Neelo repeated the motion a few more times before they peeked up at Talhan. They weren't ready for this moment to end. Magic hovered over the two of them—a buzz filled the air—and they wanted to cling to it for a little bit longer. Neelo flipped the dagger over in their hands.

"So how does one defend themselves against an opponent with a longer weapon?"

Talhan's smile stretched, flashing his white teeth in a wolflike grin. "I am so glad you asked."

RISH SEEMED TO have no problem shifting to the Arboans' evening routine. When Neelo had come searching for dinner, they found the green witch fast asleep in her chambers. What would have been dinner was finger food drudged up by a maid about to turn in for the evening, and by the time Neelo was ready for an actual dinner, the kitchens were closed down for the "first sleep." When Neelo went to go hunting for a proper meal, they found a coconspirator digging through the kitchen shelves in the shape of a fae warrior.

Talhan gave Neelo a quick wink and kept searching, like a hound on the scent, and he quickly found Rish's leftover campfire stew. The cooked food was kept in a pantry cut into the ground where the cool air kept the food from spoiling. Green witch magic tended to make food keep longer too—another one of their many underrated gifts. The South was underestimated in many ways like that, with witches who made food and gardens grow and a court crest of an evergreen tree instead of a lion like the East or a battle-axe like the West.

"How Rish managed to keep this from spilling everywhere is a miracle," Talhan said from the bottom of the ladder. He passed up the covered pot from the earthen pantry and Neelo twisted the interlocking lid. "Ah." Talhan nodded. "Clever."

"Green witches make delicious food and Southern fae find ways to keep it from spilling."

"Like I said: clever."

They lit the fire in the hearth beside them and hung the pot on the blackened hook while Talhan searched for drinks. The light of the fire and the lone candle on the wooden table cast heavy shadows into the quiet room. The sun was just falling below the horizon and the entire manor was fast asleep. Neelo was certain they would be drooling onto a pillow before the manor woke for "dinner."

"What is this red drink?" Talhan's hand appeared, holding aloft a ceramic pitcher.

"Arboan punch," Neelo said. "A mix of fresh tropical fruits from the orchards and spices."

"Perfect." He clambered up the ladder with one arm and set the pitcher on the table between them.

Neelo scooted their stool closer to the fire and slowly stirred the stew. Talhan poured them both glasses of punch and set to work slicing a loaf of day-old bread.

"Rish would explode if she knew." Neelo chuckled at the rock-hard loaf. "I wouldn't be surprised if she senses it all the way from her bed-chamber and comes running."

Talhan bounced his leg under the table, practically salivating at the stew. "Is it warm yet?"

"I just put it on," Neelo scolded, even as a fond smile pulled at their lips. "Go fetch some bowls and spoons."

"And where would those be?"

Shrugging, Neelo said, "I'm sure you can hunt them down."

Talhan huffed. "Fear not." He put his hand on his chest and foot on the stool in the pose of a gallant knight. "For I am used to rifling through stranger's kitchens."

Neelo bit the corner of their lip, stirring faster and Talhan disappeared. Their hands felt jittery, their throat dry, filled with the same nerves that often plagued them before royal events. But this was just Talhan . . . only Talhan . . . Talhan alone *with them.*

Something about being in the darkness while the residents of Arboa were asleep felt secret, intimate even, like just the two of them existed—like it had in the gardens earlier, like it had so many times over the years when the two of them secreted away to their own corner of the world. But this . . . something about this felt like a crescendo to all those other times, and Neelo knew whatever this moment was, it was the kind they'd turn over in their mind for days afterward.

Talhan returned and proffered out two ceramic bowls. "Is it hot now?"

Neelo chuckled. "Probably tepid at best."

"I don't mind," he said, nudging his bowl closer. "I'm hungry enough to eat whatever temperature it is."

"Fine." Neelo ladled a hearty helping of stew for him and a smaller portion for themself, scooting their stool backward while Talhan took the seat across the narrow worktable, so close their plates touched.

Talhan hummed as he took his first bite. "It's excellent at room temperature as well," he said through a mouthful of food.

"Just don't tell Rish that," Neelo said. "It's one of my favorite meals. Simple. Hearty." They glanced up at Talhan. "Reliably delicious, particularly when Rish makes it, and she'd be mortified with how we're treating it."

"Does Rish make this for you often?" Talhan asked through a mouthful of food.

"Whenever we travel to other provinces and courts." Neelo's face softened at the memories. "She has a way of taking over the kitchens wherever we travel. She brought a whole cart of kitchen supplies on our trip to Silver Sands."

"I wish I could've been there." Talhan brought another heaping spoonful to his mouth. "I think it might be my new favorite too."

"You don't always have to agree with me, you know," Neelo said, their voice coming out sharper than they intended.

"Oh, I know," Talhan said, then laughed. "We might both like the same stories and food, but there are plenty of things I like that you don't."

For some reason, even though it contradicted what they just said, those words chilled Neelo. Their spoon hovered over their bowl. "Like what?"

"Conversation."

"I like convers—"

"With strangers?"

"No one likes that," Neelo said, rolling their eyes. "How many times can one have a conversation about the weather?"

"It doesn't just have to be about the weather, Neelo."

"Fine, so you like innocuous small talk."

He sighed. "I like dancing." Talhan dipped the corner of his hard bread into the stew, staining it golden red with the spiced mixture of herbs and sauce.

"I could like dancing," Neelo hedged. "If people weren't watching me, maybe."

"We need to find a dark corner some time to test out that theory," Talhan said with a grin. He swirled his bread in his stew again, before adding more quietly, "I like being touched."

Neelo frowned, staring straight down at their bowl and they knew Talhan's statement was, in fact, a question. A thought popped into their mind and before they could think better of it, the words came spilling out. "I don't like being touched . . . by most people." Neelo's hands stilled and they whispered, "But . . . I think I'd like it if you touched me."

Talhan paused for so long that Neelo's stomach sank and embarrassment burned through them. But Talhan finally flashed a shy smirk and bit into his bread. "I think so too."

Neelo's toes curled in their boots. They thought their words might unleash him, that he might leap across the table and ruin everything building between them . . . but he hadn't. He'd simply smiled that mischievous grin and kept eating. It made Neelo feel steadier. There would be no surprises, no ambush kisses, not unless Neelo initiated them. But *would* Neelo ever initiate them? They'd never considered themself as the sort of person who would want to, much less know how.

Let alone find someone who would want *them* to in the first place.

It had always been a fear of Neelo's since they were a child. The slightest wrong look or advance would be taken as an invitation in Saxbridge. In a court that relished carnal desires, everyone seemed teetering on the edge of it, and Neelo felt they needed to make it abundantly clear that they did not want that kind of attention from anyone . . . well, not anyone, not anymore. There was one person in the entire realm that made them understand it. One person that made them feel just as much like a giddy fool as the rest of them, and it was terrifying.

Neelo scowled at Talhan. "Stop smiling."

His smile broadened. "I like smiling too."

Neelo rolled their eyes. "I know you do."

"Just another way you and I are different," he taunted. "You see? I don't feel like I need to agree with you on everything. I just like that we share a love of certain things."

Neelo's eyes held his a moment too long, that honeyed amber filling them with such warmth that it made their muscles coil. They cut off the shared gaze, eyes dropping to the table. "Like stew."

"Yeah." Talhan blew out a soft breath, the whisper of a laugh in his voice. "Like stew."

CHAPTER TWENTY

The blast of heady aroma made Neelo rock back on their heels as they entered the giant barn. There were twelve of these buildings circling the perimeter of the city, each wedged between the old stone houses and the city walls. From the ceiling hung thousands of bouquets of dried white snowflowers and down the center of the barn sat worktables covered in buckets, jars, mortars and pestles—a production line halted for the day. At the far wall were stacks of barrels of what Neelo assumed was the final brew to be shipped out around the continent.

They'd waited until late afternoon to venture to the drying barns, the palace sleeping in and the heat of midday too strong to venture out in the city. For once, Neelo hadn't minded the delay, enjoying exploring the Arboan library in the quiet morning hours while everyone else slept. They already had plans to return to the library that night and rifle through the stacks again.

Talhan walked a pace behind them and Neelo tried to dutifully ignore him after their intimate moment eating dinner together the night before. Neelo hauled up that layer of cool indifference, hoping their armor would hold, even though they already knew Talhan could break through all of their defenses with a single smile.

"Those." Neelo pointed to the farthest barrels marked with the letter "A."

Rish wandered down the line, inspecting each workstation with a curious eye. "What are those?"

"'A' for Arboa," Ersan said. "Those blends are set aside for my people. They aren't tainted with all the ingredients that get shipped to Saxbridge and the like." His voice once again insinuated that he was insulted the people of Saxbridge would dare tamper with the traditional Arboan brews.

"So you said before. Show me."

Ersan led the way down to a table covered in sifting trays and small bowls of dried herbs and flowers. "These are the ingredients to the traditional blend," he said, waving his hand over the table. "We add some of these different dried herbs and fruits depending on the flavors requested. I'm partial to the spiced blood orange."

Neelo scrutinized each ingredient—all commonly used by green witches and brown witches alike for their magical foods and healing elixirs.

"And this," Ersan said, carrying on down the table. "Is the Saxbridge blend. What you locals call *brew*."

Neelo froze, staring at the giant vat of dark purple flowers. "Blooming amethyst," they whispered.

Ersan nodded. "It grows on the eastern banks of the Crushwold River. They dry and cure it there and send it downriver for us to add."

Neelo pointed to bowls of black powder and dark brown leaves. "And this?"

"Hellebore and bonebane," Ersan said.

"Shit," Neelo gritted out.

Rish clutched her totem pouch to her chest, the only acknowledgment that she too knew the potency of those ingredients.

Talhan stepped up beside them. "What's wrong?"

"Adisa Monroe," Neelo muttered. "She was the one who invented this pain elixir to aid the dying centuries ago. It was made of hellebore and bonebane amongst other ingredients as yet unknown." Neelo glanced back at the purple tub of flowers. "But we know that violet witch magic is closely tethered to the blooming amethyst flower."

"We used to put that brown witch elixir in the blends directly," Ersan said. "We'd soak the snowflowers in them . . ."

Neelo cocked their head. "What changed, Sy?"

"My mother died," Ersan said with an icy indifference that made Neelo shudder. "When she passed, my father decided to stop, to add the elixir's base ingredients directly, along with the blooming amethyst."

"Shit," Neelo cursed again.

Ersan's eyes flickered. "What are you thinking right now?"

"I can't say for certain," Neelo muttered.

"Say something uncertainly, then," Ersan implored, his grip on his cane tightening.

Neelo looked around the barn. "How long ago did your family start sending this variety to Saxbridge?"

"I was still a cheeky teenager." Ersan chuckled. "Too consumed with chasing after a certain blond-haired beauty."

"Don't talk about Carys like that," Talhan growled, puffing up to twice his size like a dog with his hackles raised. "You lied to her."

Ersan snorted in derision, his wicked grin still in place. "If you think she was some wounded innocent in that situation, then we must be talking about two different people." Talhan blinked as Ersan's eyes narrowed. "I would never underestimate her ferocity like that."

"I am no brown witch," Rish interjected, resting her hand on the tub of violet flowers. "But I can imagine what a lungful of this stuff would do to a person." She lifted her sorrowful eyes to meet Neelo's. "Especially over several years."

Neelo held their fists tightly at their sides as they bent and sniffed the flowers. "How easy would it be for a violet witch to imbue these petals with magic?"

Rish hovered her hand over the flowers, screwing her eyes shut until the crinkled edges glowed a magical green. Emerald flames licked up from her fingertips and Rish yanked her hand away. She gave Neelo a sobering nod.

"That easy, huh?" Talhan asked.

"What a perfect plan," Neelo whispered. "To have every Southerner's mouth filled with her ensorcelled violet smoke. With one muttered spell, and a witching stone like the one atop her dagger, she could curse them all."

Which meant the blue witch army in the North would be nothing compared to the carnage Baba Monroe could reap with another mind control curse. Rua's warning echoed in Neelo's head. Augustus Norwood had promised that the Southern Court would crumble from within . . . that it already was.

This was how.

Neelo thought of the mess in the Western Court, of the spies and traitors Lina had only just conquered with the help of Bri, of the amethyst dagger in her possession. How long had this violet witch been "sowing seeds of rebellion," as she put it? Was this why they were sending blooming amethyst seeds to the Western Court? While all of Okrith watched in horror at the wrath of Hennen Vostemur, Baba Monroe had been in the shadows, devising her own plans and laying her own traps, biding her time until, with one whisper, she could rule the entire continent.

Fear coursed through Neelo's veins, their voice barely a whisper as they murmured aloud, "What if the cursed blue witches was just a practice run?"

"How did you get to that conclusion?" Ersan asked and Neelo realized, as always, they'd jumped ahead of the conversation and hadn't brought any of the rest along for the ride.

They quickly caught the others up on their racing thoughts and the enormity of the threat they faced: the blooming amethyst, the conduit to violet witch power, when combined with a witching stone like Adisa's dagger, could create another mind control curse. And they wouldn't need tortured blue witches with weakened minds this time. No, this time the brew itself would weaken their minds and then Adisa Monroe would slip right in.

Neelo waved a hand down the table of ingredients. "What is the name of the merchant who sells you these flowers? The ones you put in the blend that's delivered to the palace."

176

Ersan frowned. "We don't supply brew to the palace, only the ports."

"The brew in the palace smells different from this," Neelo insisted, rubbing two petals between their thumb and forefinger. "What is in it?"

"There is no special royal blend." Ersan glanced between Neelo, Rish, and Talhan as if he was missing out on a joke. "Or if there is . . . it wasn't supplied to Her Majesty from Arboa."

Neelo's eyes flared. "Then who?"

Talhan nudged them with his elbow. "Good thing you burned it all."

"Mother Moon," Rish whispered, clasping her totem pouch.

Neelo shook their head. They'd have to trace the source when they returned home, hopefully before any more arrived. "The blooming amethyst," they said, turning back to Ersan. "Who sells it to you?"

"I don't know his name." Ersan scoffed as if it was an insult to know the name of all his traders. "He docks his ship down at the markets. Red beard, blue eyes, Eastern complexion. You can't miss him."

Neelo untied the pouch of gold coins on their hip and tossed it to Ersan. He caught the bag in one hand and gave Neelo a questioning look.

"That was your first payment. Whatever brew meant for Saxbridge that you have left over, burn it or dump it into the sea, I don't care." Neelo narrowed their eyes at Ersan. "Only the Arboan blends reach Saxbridge from now on, understood?"

Ersan stared at the coins in his hand. "Are you trying to get me killed?"

"I'm trying to save us," Neelo gritted out. The urgency of their situation dawned on them more with each breath. "An entire city with blooming amethyst in their lungs means an entire city prey to Adisa's mind control. She wouldn't need a single soldier." Horror filled Neelo's voice. "She'd make them as she went with her purple flower already seeded in every person in my city."

Ersan's voice filled with venom. "But the Queen—"

"The Queen's opinion is now secondary to my own." Neelo forced themself to lift their chin. Ersan needed to know they were serious.

"This entire province is built on the brew trade," Ersan spat. "You think Saxbridge will buy as much of our blends as it would the new ones?"

"You think I'm going to let more bodies pile up in the back alleys of Saxbridge for your *profits*?" Neelo pushed back.

"Those *profits* feed people's families." Ersan's eyes flared. "I'm thinking about my people."

"*I* am thinking about *all* of our people," Neelo countered.

"The Queen won't let you."

"I am to be the new sovereign of Saxbridge." Neelo stared daggers into him, forcing power into their voice. "You will do as I command, Lord Ersan."

At the sound of his formal name, Ersan finally relented and bowed. "Yes, Your Highness," he said begrudgingly and Neelo knew this wouldn't be their last battle over this.

Neelo spotted the look of admiration in Talhan's eyes as they glanced out toward the low afternoon sun. "The markets are probably already closed for the day," they said. "We'll go meet this merchant tomorrow morning."

"Yes, Your Highness," Ersan echoed bitterly, stepping back to clear the path for Neelo to leave.

Talhan fell into stride beside them and whispered, "That was hot."

"Shut up," Neelo snapped, even as their shoulders bunched around their ears.

"What are you up to, little troublemaker?" Talhan asked, shuffling after them as they strode toward the doorway.

"Like I told Ersan: I'm saving my people's lives," they said, throwing their shoulders back. "I'm stopping Baba Monroe's plot before it begins."

THE SUN BAKED down on the gardens as Neelo took the shadiest route around the manor, pacing beneath the trellises and shade of the large palms. Talhan trailed after Neelo on their walk, remaining stalwart behind them even as Neelo twisted and twined through the labyrinth of box hedges and rows of bright pink flowers.

Finally, Neelo stopped, gravel flying beneath their shoes as they whirled on Talhan and shot him a look. "What are you doing?"

The sight of Talhan made Neelo bark out a laugh. He was covered in a thick sheen of sweat, his tunic drenched in a deep V shape, and his wet auburn hair clinging to his forehead.

"I'm following you."

"Yes, I can see that. What I want to know is *why* are you following me?"

"Do you know what's going to happen to Arboa if Ersan does as you command?" Talhan asked.

"Nothing he can't handle," Neelo shot back. "Did you seriously follow me around the gardens for the last half hour waiting for me to prompt you to ask this question?"

Talhan shrugged. "Maybe."

"Gods, and I thought my mother was stubborn." Neelo lifted their hand in the air in frustration and snarled, "Stop following me around like a sweaty fucking shadow."

Talhan huffed. "I thought you'd want some time to think first." He lifted the hem of his tunic and mopped his sweaty brow. The peak of his golden tan torso made Neelo pause, their eyes dropping to that trail of hair that led below his belt. When Talhan dropped his tunic, Neelo's eyes shot back to the hedgerow. "I figured you were going to sit and read and I could ask you then."

"*How* am I supposed to save my court, *my family,* if I don't stop the shipments of brew?" Neelo leveled Talhan with a look. "What exactly should I have done? Told him to double the supply and let Adisa Monroe dig her violet claws even deeper into my court?"

Talhan threw his head back and laughed, his whole chest rumbling with the sound. "Well, maybe not like that but"—his smile faded—"but you know your mother won't allow this."

"Apparently her brew doesn't even come from Arboa." Neelo flipped their book between their hands. "Yet another one of her problems I must solve. Right now, we need to neutralize this threat the blooming amethyst poses. I'll have to deal with the mystery of my mother's blend when I return. I only pray to the Gods that her special brew doesn't contain the same flower." Neelo stared, unseeing, at the pages. Anger rising in them at the position their mother had left them in. "Besides, she can't have it both ways. Either I am taking her place and therefore I make the decisions, or she needs to get well enough to stay on her throne."

Talhan gave Neelo a quizzical look. "Really?"

"The blame should be squarely placed on my mother's shoulders for buying the stuff, especially if it's from a foreign trader." Neelo arched their brow. "Seriously, Tal—what else would you have me do?"

"You could sign some sort of trade agreement," Talhan offered, as if Ersan could hide behind a piece of paper if the Queen sent her soldiers to strong-arm Arboa back into making the tainted blends. "Offer to buy an equal amount of brew for the next ten years, but only of the Arboan variety."

"What would the other regions say to that? They'd think the crown was playing favorites."

"Perhaps a few grumbling old lords would be worth it? Ersan's people would be protected financially, and you'd have your brew without the amethyst flowers." Talhan bounced on his heels. "You could announce it at the ball tonight."

"Oh Gods," Neelo groaned. "I forgot about that."

Talhan reached down and rubbed a sprig of lemon balm between his thumb and forefinger. "I'm sure we can find a way to sneak off."

"Like we always do." Neelo wandered over to a stone pedestal between the archways of rambling apricot flowers. They perched on the stone and opened their book, remembering from the first word what had been happening in their story, their mind already beginning to conjure the images again.

"Exactly," Talhan said, hovering over them. "I'll grab the platter of food. You bring an entertaining story, and we'll find a corner to sit in together and you can give people that *piss off* look of yours." Neelo glared up at him. "Yep, that one."

Neelo specifically chose a seat that was large enough only for themself, hoping the message would be clear and Talhan would leave them alone. Neelo licked their thumb and flipped the page. Half of their mind was already trudging through the winter snowstorm in their story. "Why are you still out here, Tal?"

Talhan took a step closer, his shadow landing over the pages of Neelo's book. "I just, I—Gods, how can you be out here?" Talhan muttered, seizing the hem of his tunic and whipping it off over his head.

Droplets of sweat flew onto the pages of Neelo's book, but their growl was silenced as their eyes lifted off the page of their own volition. They had no control as they ogled Talhan's form: broad shoulders, muscled chest, and dark chest hair. He was gorgeous and fearsome and . . . staring straight at them.

"I . . ." Neelo had lost all words. Gods, had he been saying something? Shit. "What were you saying?"

"I was saying that you and I make a good pair." Talhan mopped his tunic down his face and across the back of his neck. "You make the hard decisions like changing the brew shipments, and I find ways to allay the fears of your Arboan allies."

"Right," Neelo muttered, forcing their eyes back down to their sweat-stained book even as their mind screamed at them to look back up at Talhan's half naked form.

"I'm going for a swim down at that watering hole Ersan mentioned," Talhan said. "Want to join me?"

"You go," Neelo said. "I'm in the middle of a good book."

"You can read your good book by the watering hole," Talhan suggested.

Neelo swallowed and shook their head, keeping their eyes glued to the page though they hadn't read a single word. "No, thanks," they murmured. "I like the trade agreement idea—more official that way. It grants Ersan assurances that Saxbridge will continue to patronize his brew industry and will elevate Arboa's status within the court as a bonus to make him willing to comply. Besides, one more hurdle in the way of my mother's inevitable tantrum might be a good thing regardless." Neelo closed their eyes and tried to breath away the stress building inside them. When they opened them again, Talhan was watching them curiously. "I'll think about it at least," they said, dismissing him as they lifted their book high enough to break their line of sight.

"Thank you for considering it," Talhan said with a bow. He got three paces and then said over his shoulder, "I'm sorry about your book."

Neelo didn't reply. They waited until Talhan was far enough away that they were certain he wouldn't turn back around and then lifted their gaze from their book again. They watched that golden torso wandering off toward the orchard and the trail to the waterfall beyond. Gods, he even walked like a warrior. How could someone so kind look so lethal? That duality made him all the more endearing.

Neelo cleared their throat, pressing their lips together, and mindlessly flipping the damp page. They tried to summon the fury at the sweat-spotted book, but for some reason, all they could think about was hoping he'd do it again.

CHAPTER TWENTY-ONE

Neelo frowned down at the silver brocade across their black tunic. Here they were, getting ready for a fucking ball. Again. One of the worst things about traveling to a lord's castle was the inevitable ball. It was custom to welcome a court royal with a party of the most esteemed families in the city, and, even though Ersan knew how much Neelo hated it, he wouldn't go against tradition.

Neelo rubbed their fingers across the delicate embroidery. "Did you seriously bring this in your saddlebag?"

"Of course I did." Rish rubbed her minty moisturizing balm into her hands. For a witch who spent so much time cooking, she swore by the balm for keeping her skin supple and applied it constantly.

"This was meant to be a quiet visit," Neelo muttered, staring at themself in the mirror.

"But it's still a *royal* visit. And that means a ball. So I made sure to be prepared."

And she had been. Neelo's eyes were lined black with kohl and their shoulders looked strong with the black epaulettes that capped their tunic, giving them a roguish silhouette. Maybe Talhan would think they looked like a pirate again . . . but then their stomach twisted in knots at the thought of being in the midst of a crowded ballroom. "Can't I be unwell for this one?"

Rish tsked and carried on rubbing her balm up her arms. "When you were a child, everyone thought you were dying for how often you used that excuse."

"I *was* dying to stay away."

"No, you were dying to read your books."

Same thing. "You used to lie for me," Neelo grumbled, adjusting the hem of their tunic.

Rish shrugged. "If it was just you visiting Lord Ersan, I would lie for you still, but you have a guest accompanying you this time."

"Talhan can more than fend for himself at a party without me," Neelo muttered. "I'd only slow him down anyway."

"Perhaps he needs to be slowed down," Rish said with a grin. "Just as much as you need to be sped up."

Neelo groaned and turned from the mirror, finding the black leather boots and ceremonial dagger left out for them. The dagger had an emerald-green hilt, decorated in the sprawling leaves of the Southern Court evergreen tree. Whenever they were reminded of the *amasa* tree now, they would forever think of Talhan half naked, practicing his sword skills in its shade.

Neelo sat on their bed and pulled on their boots, their heart racing. "I don't want to be sped up."

"I didn't say *want*, did I?" Rish teased. "I said *need*. And you need a lot more out of this life than the weight of responsibility that your mother has given to you."

Neelo could feel it, always, that pressure that pushed them into the ground. It mounded atop them more every day. Every Southerner's expectation—every hope—to turn around Saxbridge and make it a better place. They thought back to Javen's weeping mother, and Neelo knew only they had the power and wits to fix their court.

Just—not yet, at least—the will.

"When Sy stops sending the amethyst-tainted shipments, things will get better," Neelo said, lacing their boots.

Rish shook her head. "It will get a lot worse before it gets better, *mea raga*. You need to prepare for that." She capped the lid to her balm and tucked it into her pocket. "Not everyone will be overjoyed that you're taking their favorite brew away."

"Not you too," Neelo groaned. "I know that. I remember the torture of the night after smoking it. Granted, that was apparently a much stronger blend." They rose from their bed and paced across their chamber to the small bookshelf on the far wall. Neelo had already read every book on the shelf, but their fingers twitched to hold one. "I'm used to people hating me anyways."

Rish cursed in Mhenbic. "When will you realize, *mea raga*, that the person who doubts you the most is yourself?" Neelo paused at their friend's words.

They debated the question for a long time, before finally asking, "How did you know you never wanted a lover?"

If Rish was surprised by the question, she didn't show it. "There was nothing about it that intrigued or excited me." She leaned back in her chair. "There was never any feelings of want. I have a lot of love, people who light me up and give my life meaning. I have you. But the way you are around . . ." Rish didn't say his name but they both knew who she was speaking of. "That was never my path."

"I always thought I'd be like you," Neelo murmured. "It seemed to make more sense."

Rish chuckled. "You are like me in all the ways that matter, *mea raga*."

They'd convinced themself over the years they'd be just like Rish, except for one traitorous spark. With one person, they wanted, they yearned. Neelo did love libraries over ballrooms and solitude over a crowd but . . . the rest was a convenient lie. That they didn't want any kind of romantic love—it wasn't honest like it was with Rish.

That didn't make it any easier to accept.

Rish rose and Neelo could hear her footsteps drift to the door. "I often wonder what you would allow yourself to feel if you knew you were worthy of it."

With that, Rish opened the door and let herself out. Neelo didn't move, staring at the books along the shelf. They read the spines over and over, trying to calm themself and hating the way Rish's words grated against them.

Worthy.

Rish was wrong. Worthiness couldn't be assumed. It was earned, and Neelo had done nothing to earn their worthiness in the eyes of their people. They'd hidden from every problem, tucked away in the corner of every confrontation, never raised their voice or advocated for their people. They'd sat by while their mother drove their court into such chaos that Neelo feared they'd never be able to pull the South out of it. Their inaction spoke volumes. They were not *worthy* of anything until they rectified that.

A soft knock sounded. Neelo didn't reply, but the door opened anyway and they knew by the lumbering footsteps that Talhan had entered.

"I was just about to..." His voice faded as Neelo turned to find Talhan staring at them, lips slightly parted. The Golden Eagle looked like the Sun God personified. He wore a white tunic with golden embroidery that matched the gold painted across his eyelids and the flecks of gold that sparkled in his hair. His attention slowly roamed up Neelo's body until his eyes met their own. "You look . . ."

"So do you," Neelo whispered. They cleared their throat, snapping the spell that hooked their gazes. "Why are you here?"

Talhan tossed a book onto Neelo's desk beside them and climbed onto their bed.

Neelo's eyes dropped to the tome and grinned. It was the story they'd started reading him in Saxbridge. "Looks like I wasn't the only one traveling to Arboa with a book."

"We never finished it." Talhan propped his head in his hand. "I got dressed early, so I wondered if there was time for another chapter before we needed to arrive?"

Neelo's face split into a surprised smile. "Well." They chuckled and turned to their unpacked belongings laid out across the desk and Talhan's book beside them. "I suppose there's always time for one more chapter."

Talhan rolled onto his back and tucked his arms behind his head. "Excellent."

"Ugh," Neelo scolded. "You're going to get gold dust all over my pillows."

Talhan grinned. "Then you'll think of me whenever you see it."

Neelo rolled their eyes, grabbing the garnet and gold book and sitting along the window bench seat. The heavy awnings that covered the windows kept the sun from beating through the curtains and baking the room. Neelo crossed their ankle at the knee and opened the book to where they'd left off. "One chapter, then we have to go."

Talhan gave them a sideways look. "Who'd have ever thought it would be *you* telling *me* that?"

Neelo looked up at Talhan, his golden eyes filling with mischief. Did they really just tell Talhan that they couldn't keep reading? And in that moment, they decided they'd keep reading until Rish came in to scold them for being late.

RISH HAD FINALLY found them after three more chapters and herded them down the sweeping staircase to the ball. Neelo had immediately broken off from Talhan, letting the Eagle enjoy the revels. The event was like every other: clanging, loud music; a throng of exquisitely dressed, simpering fae; the burning stench of alcohol; and plumes of brew smoke that hung over the room like storm clouds.

Neelo tucked into the dark alcove and pulled out a book of brown witch spells. At least they could use this time for something productive. If Neelo were a witch, their magical power would've been finding quiet corners and balancing the line of what being "in attendance" meant. They stood in the shadows, the cool air from the balcony behind them greeting their back. Close enough to the party to be seen and far enough to not be disturbed—the perfect spot. The book they held aloft in their hand at least shooed most of the people away, especially when they saw the Mhenbic writing on the cover. Only one person wasn't dissuaded from approaching them . . . one overly confident fae warrior.

"Aren't you coming in?" Talhan asked. His cheeks were flushed, his face covered in a sheen of sweat, and his breath smelled of honey wine.

"I can hear it all from here," Neelo replied, lifting their book slightly higher.

Talhan pulled the book down with his pointer finger until Neelo looked up at him with a scowl. "But isn't it your job as honored guest to mingle?"

The word "mingle" made them want to retch. "I don't like small talk."

"We've already had this conversation. *I* do," Talhan countered, bouncing up on the balls of his feet.

"Good for you."

"What I'm saying is that I can be the one doing the talking." He took a step closer—that Talhan scent of bay leaves and spiced coffee cutting through the smell of wine on his breath. "I don't want to speak over you, or, um, speak for you on important issues, but what if you told me how you feel about them and I can be your mouthpiece and relay them?" He waggled his eyebrows. "In my own way."

Neelo considered him for a moment. "That doesn't seem appropriate."

"Neither is sitting in a corner at a party thrown in your honor." He held his hand up to stave off their protest. "Never minding that people will think I'm being a cavalier courtier. The charming Eagle who can't stop talking," he said with a laugh. "And you will be spared."

"My own secret herald." Neelo's lips twisted into a smirk. "Okay, fine."

"What do people usually say to you?" Talhan asked.

"They ask me about my mother and make jokes about her, but they're truly fearful that she is going mad. Many worry I can't lead. They're worried the South is walking a fine line between debauchery and ruin. I know they want me to pull my people out of it, but they're also afraid of their joy being taken away." Neelo sighed. "I'm good at that."

"No," Talhan said, taking a step closer. "You're not."

"They mostly want to make sure they are in my plans for the future—that I remember them and they keep their high standing," Neelo muttered. "They're chief concern is themselves."

"Typical," Talhan jeered. "Well, I think I can come up with a dip-lomatic way to walk that line. Flatter them enough to be on your side, give noncommittal answers, but let them know change is coming for the better."

"You've already said it better than I could." Neelo toyed with the edges of their book. "I don't know how you do that."

"You have plans to help an entire court." Talhan gestured to the crowd. "You have ideas. I'm just telling everyone about them."

"Both skills are needed to rule a court," Neelo murmured, instantly wishing they could take it back.

"I'm glad you see it that way." Talhan's smile was so bright it burned them. "This is why you and I make such a good match."

Neelo considered Talhan's offer for a moment. It would be a lot easier, making decrees and passing out sentences, if Talhan was the one delivering them. One look at his handsome face, and the people would submit to the decision. If Neelo was the one meting out judgments, people would riot, curse, and spit at them for taking away their brew and ruining their fun. They'd never do that to Talhan Catullus.

No, they couldn't do that to him. Talhan was too joyful to be the constant bearer of bad news. It would destroy him to always have to be delivering it. Once again, the dream of the two of them being together was dashed, for what would it mean if they let Talhan carry the entire burden?

It would mean they weren't partners. That he was doing too much, and them too little.

That had always been the hardest part. Neelo knew how to help their court, knew all the policies and decisions that would improve the lives of their people, but had no idea how to convey them. Whenever Neelo had a conversation, the words came out strained and clumsy unless they were with close friends. They could talk for hours to Carys or Rish, but talking to the highborn families of the South was another matter entirely. They supposed they spoke with Talhan for hours too, reading books to him, though it wasn't their own thoughts necessarily.

The song changed and Talhan twisted toward the sound, perking up at the jolly notes.

"Go on," Neelo said with a huff. "Dance. We can enact this plan later."

Talhan bounced faster on the balls of his feet. "I don't have to."

"I know you love this song." Neelo smirked, remembering all the times they'd watched Talhan from over the pages of their book as he danced to this tune at one event or another. It was the one song he never seemed to miss. The joy radiated off him when he moved to the music. "It'll be like old times. Go on."

"One song." Talhan grinned. "Then the plan."

"You don't need to hover next to me," Neelo said. "I've been doing this my whole life."

"So have I," he replied with a look that made their whole body feel warm.

They watched as Talhan entered the merry fray, jumping and locking arms with the other dancers. Though his laughter was muffled by the music, Neelo could feel each laugh as if it echoed in their own mind.

A charcoal-gray hat waved across their vision and Neelo had the urge to lift on their tiptoes to keep watching Talhan above it. Instead, they whipped their head to the person beside them.

Neelo eyed the Lord of Arboa as he flourished his wide-brimmed hat. "What are you doing, Sy?" They braced for another verbal attack about his discontentment, but, judging by the sway in his step and wine on his breath, he'd already had enough drinks to seem less concerned.

"Why don't you wear this?" he offered, his dark eyes crinkling at the sides. At least the drinks had seemed to temporarily eclipse the anger he'd surely be harboring against Neelo for canceling his most popular— and potent—brew shipments. "You'd look as good in Arboan garb as your betrothed . . ." He glanced at Talhan on the dance floor. "And it shades out all the watching eyes."

Neelo closed their book with a loud clap and frowned at their friend, knowing he was aware of how uncomfortable Neelo was in this setting. "A hat? I shouldn't need to do that."

Ersan tapped his cane on the red tiles below his feet, the sound clicking across the terrace. "Do I *need* this cane? No. I could walk without it and I could pretend my leg isn't sore after an hour." He leaned in closer. "But I like my life better when I use it." Ersan leveled Neelo with a look. "So I use it. Besides," he said, pulling the handle of his cane, revealing a thin, needlelike dagger, "it comes in handy sometimes."

Neelo huffed. "You want me to hide a dagger in your hat?"

Ersan chuckled, the sound so different from the uninhibited laughter of his youth. "I want you to use all the tools you have to enjoy your life." He glanced up at Talhan again. "And enjoy the people in it."

"Talhan won't be in it for long," Neelo countered. "He should go East, become the ruler there."

Ersan stiffened. "I would love nothing more than for him to win the Eastern crown, but I don't think that's what either of you would truly want."

Neelo cocked their head. "Then why do you want him to win?"

"For starters, because I'd like you to be happy. But also, if Talhan wins," Ersan said, "then there's still hope that Carys might one day come home." His hollow words filled the night air, lingering between them.

"I'm sorry you're still hurting so much," Neelo murmured.

"No, I'm the one who owes *you* an apology," Ersan said, his long lashes shifting to them. "When I said you two were an odd pairing—"

"There's no need to apologize for what is clearly the truth," Neelo cut in.

"You sell yourself too short, Neelo. 'Surprising' was probably a better word for it. I misjudged him as a lumbering oaf, not *good enough* for you. I figured you'd be happier alone." Ersan thoughtfully turned his hat in his hands. "But now, seeing the way he looks at you, and the way you look at him, I think he just might be worthy of you."

Neelo folded their arms. "One younger sibling wasn't enough. You need to play big brother to me too?"

"Always," Ersan said, his cheeks dimpling.

"I'm sorry too," Neelo said. "For my brashness about the brew earlier. I can't let any more of the blooming amethyst make it to Saxbridge, but I will find a way to protect you from my mother."

"She's as unruly as she is unpredictable. I don't think even the Heir of Saxbridge can stop the Queen from plying her people with drugs."

"You're wise to be wary of her, but I promise you, I won't let my mother pull the whole court under with her," Neelo muttered. "Until I can find her special supplier, let her be the only one. No more of the new blends, only the traditional ones. I'll make sure you're compensated."

"And protected," Ersan reminded, glancing back to the crowd. "Perhaps I need my own fae warrior."

They stared out at the dancing crowd, eyes landing on the mop of auburn hair a head taller than the fae surrounding him and remembering Ersan's words. "How does he look at me?"

Ersan sighed and put his hat back on his head. He didn't quite answer their question, though, saying instead, "Don't be a fool like me, Heir of Saxbridge. Don't wait a lifetime to fight for the people you love."

Before Neelo could open their mouth to refute his statement, Ersan walked away, disappearing into the crowd as the jaunty music played its final refrain.

CHAPTER TWENTY-TWO

After another bout of dancing, Talhan came to collect Neelo, and before they could protest, he dragged them into the ballroom to begin their dreaded *mingling*. Neelo stuck close to Talhan's side, their brown witch book held tightly in their grip.

It felt like Talhan was guiding them blindfolded across a tightrope. Talhan glided from conversation to conversation, making small talk and chatting about inane things like the Solstice and Bri's engagement. Neelo didn't know how he did it. He adapted to every new discussion, changing masks for each person he spoke with, always ready with a witty rejoinder in his back pocket.

Never had they seen him so in his element—at least not up close—and it reminded Neelo of the thrill they felt when they were hunting for answers in the library. It was the same skill and precision Talhan demonstrated now. Neelo hung back in Talhan's shadow, delighting that they could listen in without being the focus of attention. In turn, they collected little pieces of information: which households were fighting, which families were politicking the hardest, the pointed questions certain people would ask . . . Neelo stored it all away in their memory for later, for when they might need it one day as sovereign. Canceling the brew shipments would be just the start of things Neelo would be forced to do one day as ruler, and they needed to keep a running tally of potential allies . . . and future enemies.

A terrible, anxious thought flashed into their mind: Would any of these old houses of the Southern Court rather support a powerful witch than a bookish introvert like Neelo? Even if they bore the name of Emberspear, what if they not only had to deal with their people's disdain, but, worse, a rebellion like Lina Thorne had to in the West?

Neelo lacked the stamina for the high energy of conversing, paired with their undercurrent of anxiety at each look and comment. It zapped their energy faster than running up a mountainside in the summer heat. By the time they'd done the rounds, the clamor was attacking Neelo's senses. How did anyone focus on one conversation when hundreds were happening all at once? The heat, the sound, the brightness of the lights, it all escalated as each one assaulted them, scorching and roaring and blinding until their vision was spotted with stars and they swayed on their feet.

A warm hand found the small of their back to steady them and Neelo jolted out of the touch. The handprint left a thousand prickling needles against their flesh. It was all too much. Neelo waited until Talhan turned to speak to another preening matron and slipped away, grateful for their penchant of going unnoticed. They raced into the darkened hallway, sucking in lungfuls of cool evening air. Sweat beaded on their brow and their pulse pounded in their ears. An invisible weight crushed the center of their chest, stealing the air from their lungs.

Breathe. Breathe.

They reached the furthest marble column before they heard the door open behind them and cursed all the Gods they couldn't have this moment of reprieve. The click of dress shoes echoed down the hall and Neelo's breath steadied as the scent of spiced coffee hit them. It wasn't a stranger. It was just Tal.

Talhan found Neelo resting their forehead against the cool stone column. He leaned on the twin column holding up the mosaic tile archway. From their periphery, Neelo saw Talhan looking out at the starry night sky. He didn't say a word. Neelo leaned there for a moment longer, catching their breath and feeling the brand of Talhan's eyes as shame swirled in their gut. They shouldn't have let him see them like this, but they were too exhausted to hide it.

Neelo bit back the groan rising from their throat. How were they meant to do this for the rest of their life?

As if hearing their unspoken thoughts, Talhan took them by the arm and tugged them back down the darkened corridor.

"What—"

"Trust me," Talhan murmured, leading Neelo onto the back terrace and down into the gardens. They followed the steep dusty trail down through the silent row of jeweler and cobbler shops and out to the blooming fields.

The palace was a racket of noise in the distance, but the further they walked, the deeper in shadow and silence they delved. Neelo sighed, enjoying the darkness that wrapped around them like a blanket. Talhan kept going until they were in the center of the blooming fields. The city and palace glowed with life to the right, the nighttime jungle teemed with nocturnal creatures to the left, and all around them white flowers danced in the soft ocean breeze.

Neelo glanced up to the stars, so bright from the fields that new milky constellations appeared before their eyes. Neelo studied the stars one by one, their heartbeat finally slowing to its normal rhythm.

"Better?" Talhan asked, craning his neck up to the stars.

"Everyone was staring," Neelo murmured.

Talhan's huff silenced the chirping crickets around them. "Everyone was too busy trying to count their own dance steps and make sure there was no food in their teeth."

"I felt all of their eyes on me," Neelo whispered, praying Talhan wouldn't judge them for what they were about to say. "Scratching across my skin. Even from a distance, I can feel it somehow."

Neelo had always been keenly aware of people's attention on them. They were the child of a Queen after all, and an oddity to boot. A shy, black-wearing bookworm in the palace of Saxbridge? People leered and studied them as if examining an exotic bird. That's what these parties had always made them feel like: a spectacle.

"People watching you will be commonplace when you become

sovereign," Talhan said, and Neelo knew he didn't realize how much his words twisted that dread in their stomach. "They—"

"I can't," Neelo cut in, clenching their hands in frustration and taking another several strides down the aisle of flowers. "It's too much. It's . . . I want to help my people, but not to rule. I don't want their attention, their scrutiny, their shaming gazes."

"You've put a lot into a single glance. Maybe you just need one of those wide-brimmed Arboan hats," Talhan said with a grin and Neelo rolled their eyes as he echoed Ersan's own sentiments. "Then you can block out their looks entirely, though I doubt they mean what you think. What if their attention actually means respect, trust, admiration?"

"I don't think so."

"Why not?"

"Because I hear everything." Neelo folded their arms over their chest. "I worked most of my life to be the invisible child. I heard all the things my people say about me . . . and my mother. I know my people's spite and fear."

Talhan cocked his head. "And you think if they feel it for your mother, they must for you too?"

"Of course!" How could he not see it? "They will," Neelo said firmly. "If not now, they will someday. They'll all be talking about me. A thousand conversations happening just beyond earshot—rumors and lies I can't defend myself against, buzzing all around me. And I can't bear it."

"The noise?"

"Yes—partially. But also the pressure." They looked up at him. "What if I let them all down?"

Talhan carefully ambled closer, taking his time as he inspected the flower bushes. "Why do you think you'll disappoint them?"

"Some think our court needs change, needs better rulership and more order. I agree." Neelo took a tentative breath. "Others will think I'll ruin our traditions and put unnecessary restrictions upon them." They shook their head. "My mother doesn't see the brown witch healers with patients lined up from drunken brawls and reckless stunts. She doesn't see those sick and dying from excess. She doesn't see the drug

196

dens lined with bodies, nor does she know of the suffering of so many families lost to the ever-increasing potency of her brew. What was once for fun and merriment is now a plague in our city, and I seem to be the only one around when dawn breaks and the light reveals the scars upon my court."

"I can be there too." Talhan took a step closer, filling the space between them easily with his broad shoulders and towering figure. "How can I help?"

Neelo glanced up at him, just a flash of those amber eyes, before looking away again. His gaze seemed to be the only one that didn't grate against Neelo's skin. It felt like a wave rolling from his eyes to theirs—powerful and thrilling and important somehow.

Neelo let that look in his eyes flow through them as they said, "You seem to have your fair share of indulgence." Talhan only smiled, not even pretending to refute the claim. "But you're also levelheaded, kind, smart. You're a skilled warrior. You haven't let the revelry overtake you like Southerners have. Perhaps you can show my people that it can be done. That I won't take away their joy. That there is a way to have it all." Neelo tilted their head to the sky, listening as the strings and lute lifted out the windows of the palace, echoing down the valley and circling them in the shadows. "I love this song." It was a simple melody, slower than the other lively tunes.

"Me too." Talhan extended his hand out to them. "Dance with me?" Neelo quirked their eyebrow at his hand and he grinned. "You don't want to be seen, so we'll dance in the shadows. You said yourself you wanted to show your people there was a way to have it all."

Neelo let out a soft laugh and placed their hand in Talhan's. The feeling sent lightning bolts across their skin, not painful pinpricks, but something exhilarating in even the softest of touches. Talhan's other hand swept around their side, landing in the center of their back. "I should've never told you I would like to dance."

He chuckled. "You said as long as no one was watching."

"*You're* watching."

His grin widened. "I don't count."

Their eyes dropped to their clasped hands. "I think you count more than anybody." They swallowed. "One dance. And be warned, I will step on your toes."

"Do you want to lead or follow?" he asked with a tilt of his head.

"I don't usually participate in these dances. You lead."

"It's an Eastern Court song," Talhan said softly. "Funny that it should be your favorite."

The feeling of his hand closing around Neelo's made them shudder. He pulled them in closer to his muscled body, his other hand placed between their shoulder blades. Normally, this proximity would make Neelo's skin crawl . . . but this, this felt good. Right. A surprised smile pulled on their lips, joy and confusion warring with each other. They didn't want to pull away?

Why not?

Talhan considered them for a long moment before speaking. "You're a good dancer."

They hadn't even noticed they'd started moving, and immediately stepped on his foot as if to disprove his words. They simply laughed and, flustered, asked, "What does that have to do with anything?"

He shrugged. "Just in case you didn't know and that's what was stopping you. But I like dancing better this way. Alone. With you," he said, his breath tickling through Neelo's hair as he smiled.

"Me too."

"We'll find a way forward." Talhan gave a reassuring nod.

"There will be no *we*," Neelo said, even as they shuffled closer to him, bridging the distance between their torsos, their words sounding more and more like lies.

Talhan let out a hum, and Neelo wasn't sure what that meant, but somehow knew it *wasn't* frustration. "Don't ruin this dance." He chuckled. "We have plenty of time to argue about *us* later."

"Fine," Neelo muttered, making Talhan laugh again.

The insects buzzed through the flower fields in the distance and the sound of boisterous laughter and music echoed out from the windows.

"It is strange to hear the sounds of a party without my mother's laughter," Neelo mused.

The distinctly sharp tones of Queen Emberspear cut above the din like a sharpened knife. She was the loudest, brightest flame, a constant burning inferno that Neelo had always known would one day combust into ashes.

Talhan seemed to notice their sudden wooden movements. "Living with her must be like living with a rain cloud above your head."

Neelo peeked up at him. "Most people think it would be fun to have her as a mother. Fire jugglers. Pet lions. Sweets for dinner every night."

"Most people are fools."

Neelo smirked and stepped in closer to him. His other hand dropped theirs and he circled it around their other side, holding them to his chest as they gently swayed.

"My mother," he whispered, dropping his head to the side of theirs, "used to order Bri's tutors to do awful things to her when she wouldn't behave." Neelo's fingers pressed in tighter on his back, the only acknowledgment of his words. "It took me far too long to realize it was happening, and even longer to realize I could stop it, that I could even question my mother for doing it." His voice thickened as if the shame choked the words from him. Neelo leaned into him more, needing Talhan to feel the anchor of their body in that moment. "It's not until we are older, looking back, that we understand what we really needed from our parents."

"What did we really need?"

"Love," Talhan whispered, his head dropping lower with every word until Neelo could feel his breath on their lips. "Respect for being our own person. The strong, slow, and steady kind of love, the endless, unconditional kind, not easily broken by mistakes or flaws. We needed to feel safe, assured, confident in the people who were meant to love us more than anything."

Neelo swallowed and nodded, fighting the urge to lift onto their tiptoes and brush their lips to Talhan's. "Well, it's too late for that now."

"No," Talhan said, so vehement it shocked Neelo even as he swept a hand down their back. "No, it's not. We were just looking for it in the wrong people."

Heat rose in Neelo's cheeks and they wanted to ask who the right person was, but they already knew his answer. It was true. There was nothing erratic or surprising about Talhan. They felt confident in him, in who he was, in the quality of his character. They knew whoever he loved it would be slow and steady and endless . . . and for the hundredth time, knew it couldn't be them. He deserved the greatest kind of love, the heroic, earth-shattering kind, from someone fierce enough to threaten any person who ever darkened his light. And they wouldn't let him waste that kind of once-in-a-generation love on them.

Neelo took a step out of Talhan's grip. His muscles tightened for a second before letting them go, as if he had to command his arms to release Neelo.

What a fool they were. Anyone else would be throwing themself at someone like Talhan, and here Neelo was, running. It was just another way they were too broken, too unworthy.

"It's too much," Neelo said softly. "*I'm* too much."

They turned to walk away, but Talhan darted in front of them and Neelo kept their eyes fixed to their feet as he said, "You will *never* be too much to me."

He kept saying that. Kept meaning it too. And that's what made this unbearable. That he couldn't see what they knew to be true: that being with them would ruin him, ruin what made him such a natural leader, a glowing presence, a true friend.

Tears pricked Neelo's eyes as they sidestepped around him. "I'm sorry," they muttered and stormed off before Talhan could say another word.

CHAPTER TWENTY-THREE

The excitement of finding new books in the Arboan library faded after the encounter in the blooming fields, but Neelo couldn't return to the party, not after that moment with Talhan, and so they steered in the direction of the closest thing they had to a sanctuary here. The library of Arboa was an octagonal room, three stories high, with giant windows that allowed the moonlight to beam in. It was a labyrinth of balconies, anterooms, and alcoves, every archway decorated in detailed mosaic tiles that gave the space the echoing acoustics of a temple.

Neelo's fingers trembled as they wiped under their eyes. A singular thought kept tears from spilling: How could people openly show hurt in front of others? Neelo had no idea how they were supposed to act when they were in pain. Alone, it made sense, but in front of other people they got stuck, their mind whirling with questions instead of giving them the space to feel. What were their eyes meant to be doing? Was their nose supposed to run? Were they sniffing too much? Where did their hands go—what did they touch?

Neelo wended through the maze of shelves, their eyes not searching for books like they had earlier in the day. Rather they picked a book at random, not even bothering to read the title, and wandered to a sitting area tucked nicely away in the far corner. Their thumb rhythmically stroked across the closed pages eliciting the sound of a shuffling deck of cards. Over and over they thumbed the pages as they tried to calm down.

Despite his drunkenness, Ersan had been quieter than usual at the ball, and Neelo knew it was because of what they had ordered him to do. Stopping the supply of brew to Saxbridge might as well be a personal declaration of war against the capital's debauchery. What would their mother attempt to do to Arboa when she learned no more brew was arriving? They'd need to draft up an official document exempting him from responsibility when they returned to their room. What could Queen Emberspear do then?

A lot. She could do a lot to keep the fun flowing and every single one of her citizens supporting her bad habits by encouraging them to do the same. An image of their mother riding to Arboa on lion back flashed into Neelo's mind. She'd done crazier things for smaller offenses. Queen Emberspear seemed determined to make everyone as high—and as sick—as she was, but that was all the more reason Neelo needed to put their foot down.

To speak nothing of the connection of this brew to the violet witch magic.

They plopped into the upholstered armchair and kicked their feet up on the low table, twisting the lantern to cast more light on their book.

Neelo wouldn't be surprised if their mother sent armies to Arboa and demanded they continue making their brew . . . but then, of course, her brew didn't actually come from Arboa. Maybe she wouldn't care at all if she was high enough. And she certainly wasn't about to share her own stash. Neelo needed to find whatever witch or courtier was supplying the palace brew. So many new faces popped in and out of the palace each day. It would be a nightmare.

Their stomach sank with the realization. They couldn't have it both ways. They couldn't save their mother and stay out of public life—one would force the hand of the other. Even if Queen Emberspear came back healthy and strong, it would still take time, time when Neelo would be in charge. Even that, though, was surely a dream—that they'd be thrust into the role for only a short time. Neelo's hope to stay tucked in the shadows and let their mother rule was quickly fading. To save her, they'd have to use their power and title to stop their mother from getting the smoke she so desperately craved.

Once they did that, there was no going back. It would cause too much confusion if councilors heeded the orders of two rulers. No, they would have to step into the light, and the thought—

"I had a feeling I'd find you here."

Neelo jolted, twisting toward the sound of Talhan's voice. The Eagle leaned against the bookshelf, taking in Neelo's startled expression. Their mouth dropped open and then they closed it again. What were they supposed to say? Hi? Gods, they were supposed to be the smartest person in Okrith, but when it came to other people, they had no clue.

"How long have you been there?" Neelo grumbled, settling back in their chair.

"Long enough to realize you weren't reading that book in your hands."

Neelo finally looked down at the book they selected: *Arboan Fish Identification Guide*. They frowned and opened the book anyway, staring at the picture of a spiny, bug-eyed fish.

"What do you want?" Their cheeks burned with their last interaction in the blooming fields. They should've known Talhan wouldn't let them say such a weighted thing and walk away. Neelo hadn't done a very good job in hiding either, going to the library, of all places. Foolish.

"We never finished that story from earlier," Talhan said, dancing around the tense moment from before. "I figured that's what you'd be reading."

"I left it in my room." Neelo glanced halfway toward him, unable to meet his eyes. "I didn't want to read it without you."

Talhan shrugged. "You could've invited me."

"I figured you'd go back to the party." Neelo's frown deepened. "Besides, I wouldn't want you to get any wrong ideas."

His cheeks dimpled as he asked, "Such as?"

"Such as thinking you will be staying in the Southern Court past the Summer Solstice," Neelo muttered. "Such as thinking I'm going to pull you any more into this mess with me."

"I've been in messes before." Talhan slowly paced over to the sitting area and lowered into the chair beside Neelo, his knee pressing into the fabric of Neelo's leg. "What mess are you in?"

Neelo's senses swarmed with his closeness. He smelled like dark corners and whispered confessions, so delicious that Neelo wanted to press closer. Warmth vibrated off his skin where their knees joined.

"I just . . ." All the reasons seemed to fall out of Neelo's mind as Talhan inched to the edge of his seat, so close his fingertips almost grazed Neelo's own.

Neelo shuffled backward, putting distance between them. They licked their thumb and flipped the page.

Talhan cleared his throat.

"What?" Neelo growled.

"Nothing," Talhan said with a wicked grin. "Just admiring you. I like the way you turn a page."

"Please." Neelo rolled their eyes. "You admire my mind and the stories I tell. You tolerate my appearance."

Talhan's mouth dropped open. "Are you serious?"

Neelo scowled back at him. "Yes."

"I don't know what I've done to make you think that, but clearly I need to rectify it." A rough chuckle escaped Talhan's lips. "We must not be looking at the same person."

Neelo leaned back in their chair, their brow furrowing. "Who are you looking at?"

"You." Talhan inched forward further, placing his hands on the armrests of Neelo's chair, caging them in. "Your eyes, your lips, your *scent*. Those shoulders and arms and thighs and . . ." He lifted slightly from his chair, hovering over Neelo so he could whisper in their ear. "I wouldn't tolerate you. I would *worship* you, if given half the chance." He pulled back, his amber eyes glowing with intensity as he scanned Neelo's face and down to their lips.

Desire shot through Neelo at his words, zinging around their body at the feel of Talhan's breath on their lips.

Talhan glanced them over for one more second before he began to pull away and Neelo didn't know what came over them, but they weren't ready for that distance.

Their hand shot out, grabbing Talhan by the back of the neck and pulling his mouth to theirs. At the first touch of his lips, Neelo's whole body ignited, a coursing, burning passion rising to the surface like they had never in their life felt before and for a moment they wondered if they'd been drugged.

Talhan's hum of approval vibrated across their lips as he rested his knee between their spread legs and leaned in to deepen their kiss. Neelo's other hand slid up Talhan's chest, cupping his sharp jaw as his lips worked over their own.

All at once, Neelo's brain caught up to their body, and they pushed on Talhan's chest, breaking their kiss. It wasn't a hard enough shove to actually push the giant fae warrior away, and yet, he instantly pulled back. His warm eyes were filled with lust, his hair tousled, and his lips swollen. Had they done that? Neelo fought the urge to pull him back into a kiss as they skirted up and out of their chair, careful to avoid brushing up against the Eagle again.

"We've got to be in the markets in the morning," Neelo said, sheepishly straightening their tunic. Their cheeks burned with embarrassment, and they couldn't meet Talhan's eyes as they desperately grabbed for an excuse. "I should go draft up that treaty before bed."

"Sleep well," Talhan said, slowly lowering back into his chair, not disappointment on his face but rather that smug grin staring back at them. "I'll see you in the morning."

Neelo wrung their hands. "Okay." They turned and speedily raced away, playing that kiss over and over in their mind.

They had just kissed Talhan Catullus and it had been amazing and now they wanted to go throw up from all the nerves and cry and scream and laugh and jump. Neelo pressed a trembling hand to their lips as they raced down the hall, feeling like a key had just turned a lock inside them.

Shit. What had they done?

NEELO KEPT THEIR gaze fixed on everything but Talhan as they walked along the river. The shadows of the tall buildings granted a reprieve from the hot midmorning sun. Saxbridge was rarely quiet, but Arboa seemed serene. The sun had banished the nighttime revelers, driving the stallholders to the tented marketplaces along the banks of the Crushwold River.

Distant boats sailed upriver and the marketplace bustled with morning shoppers, but on the wide footpath, they were alone. Neelo swept their hand through the tall grasses budding in aromatic orange flowers. In just a few weeks the Arboan sky would be alight with floating paper lanterns, the river crowded with boats, as the Summer Solstice celebrations commenced. The lanterns would be laden with sweets and glittering, rainbow-hued sand. Children would throw rocks at them, trying to knock the sweets back to the ground and painting rainbow dust clouds in the sky. It would be a teeming press of bodies as they celebrated the longest day . . . but right now it was quiet, intimate, even in the vast city.

"This is my favorite part of Arboa." Neelo plucked one of the flowers and passed it to Talhan. He gave it a sniff and placed it behind his ear. "The nature, the waterways, the sound of birdsong."

"It's beautiful," Talhan said, clasping his hands behind his back as he strode beside them.

"People are loud, confusing, erratic, but nature . . ."

"Nature is calming," Talhan finished. "Before every battle, I place my palms on the soil of the battlefield and pray to the Earth Gods for calm, focus, and speed."

Neelo eyed his glinting sword and dagger hanging from his hips. "It seems they've always answered your prayers."

"Mostly," Talhan said, a frank stare at Neelo that made them turn away.

Neelo waited for Talhan to make some mention of their kiss the night before, but he acted as if it had never happened. What had been in the wine at the ball last night? Or maybe Talhan just knew that any mention of the kiss would send Neelo running off like a bolting stag. They cringed, remembering how they fled from the library the night before—just as they had fled the field before that . . . and the party before *that*.

How can he want someone as broken as me?

"People may be too loud, too overwhelming, but sometimes, one person . . ." Neelo didn't know how to describe it. Sometimes being alone with Talhan made their heart race like being dropped into a lion's den, and other times, his presence felt like the slow, warm comfort of reading a good book in a hot bath. How could one person elicit such disparate emotions?

They ambled across the old stone bridge that arched over a bed of purple, cream, and yellow flowers.

"Arboa is beautiful," Talhan said, making easy conversation. "I can see why you and Carys used to come here so often."

"It was her happy place, once," Neelo said softly. "Carys used to say the afterlife must look like Arboa." Neelo ran their fingers across the stone wall, leading them toward the markets. "I'm sure she would've happily chosen Arboa as her home were it not for a certain lord."

"All of this because Ersan didn't tell her about Morgan?" Talhan blew out a slow breath.

Neelo hummed. "Sy made a promise to Carys's father to keep her half sister a secret."

"Secrets don't count amongst those you love," Talhan growled. "Everyone knows that. I could never keep a secret from Bri . . . or Hale, or Carys, or Rua, or Remy, or you."

"It's not really a secret by then." Neelo snickered. "Sy takes his oaths seriously."

Talhan's frown deepened, but he didn't add any more.

They reached the marketplace and meandered past the stalls, searching for the red-bearded human who sold amethyst flowers to the brew merchants. Wearing a wide-brimmed Arboan hat, Neelo glamoured themself so as to not draw as much attention, morphing into their human likeness. Of course, "attention" was the middle name of the giant golden-eyed fae warrior who followed their every step.

"Can't you go look somewhere else?" Neelo scowled at Talhan. "You're going to scare all the merchants away before they answer any of my questions."

Talhan's fingers grazed across the bronze hilt of his sword. "They will answer your questions regardless if they don't have anything to hide."

"Ugh." Neelo rolled their eyes. "Just be nice."

"I'm always nice," Talhan countered. He straightened his posture and added, "To those who deserve it."

Neelo spotted a stall at the end of the last row. A tattered tan shade provided the seller with some reprieve from the morning sun. Already, the earth of Arboa radiated with waves of heat, warping the view of the blooming fields on the horizon.

"There." Neelo pointed, spotting the merchant with the red beard and large blue eyes. Despite the white balm that slathered his freckled skin, his cheeks and nose were bright red with sunburn.

The merchant's stall table wasn't covered with blooming amethyst at all but rather decorative weaponry—ceremonial swords and daggers to be worn during special occasions.

Neelo casually wandered up to the table. "Good morning."

The merchant bowed deeply, the leather gloves on his hands groaning as he clasped them together. "Good morning, Your Highness." Neelo cringed at how quickly the merchant identified them. So much for a glamour. They let out a slow breath and their glamour faded back to their fae form. No point in hiding, then. "Lord Catullus," the merchant added with a smaller dip of his chin. "What brings you to my stall?"

Neelo cocked their head. The brim of their hat lifted on one side and the tropical sun burned up their neck. "We've heard you trade in all sorts."

The merchant's icy blue eyes widened. "I do."

"I have an interest in a particular flower," Neelo hedged. "Is that something you bring southward?"

"Perhaps." The merchant pursed his lips. "How much do you need?"

"Who supplies it to you?"

"An Eastern contact of mine. The flowers, I presume you're speaking of, grow all along the banks of the Crushwold. Many make a business of drying them."

"I'm looking for a name."

The merchant clasped his hands behind his back. "If I give you a name, what's to stop you from working with him directly and cutting me out of future trades with Arboa?"

Talhan's eyes roved over the weapons on the table.

"If you don't give me a name, I will find my own supplier and cut you out regardless," Neelo said. "So you can work with me, or we can go somewhere else."

The merchant's nostrils flared but he only replied, "I see."

Talhan sidled closer. "Their name?" he asked casually, not a hint of menace in his voice, and yet, his size and stature alone were enough to make the merchant relent.

The merchant leaned in and whispered, "Connal Betier. He lives in the west end of Wynreach."

Neelo placed a pouch of coins on the table. "Thank you."

The merchant's wary expression shifted into one of greed at the sight of the coins. "You are most welcome, Your Highness." They turned to leave when the merchant called out, "Lord Catullus! I know your sister is a dagger collector of sorts. I think I have one for her that would make the perfect wedding gift."

Talhan perked up at the offer and turned back to the table. The merchant produced a dulled golden scabbard with a bronzed handle, the cross guard flaring out like the wings of an eagle.

"It's in need of a shine," the merchant added, proffering it out to Talhan. "But it's quite the beauty."

Talhan reached for the hilt when Neelo's hand shot out and gripped him by the elbow. Talhan dropped his hand, his brow furrowing. Something struck in the back of Neelo's mind . . . something about how Queen Thorne had died.

Neelo tried to keep their face neutral, unimpressed. "We'd like to see the blade first." They threaded their hand with Talhan's elbow as if their arms were locked for a stroll, but the way their fingers squeezed into Talhan they knew would put him on alert too.

"You are right, of course." Talhan winked at Neelo, but his eyes were filled with caution.

The merchant reached for the hilt, but Neelo cut him off. "Remove your gloves first, please."

"Your Highness?"

"Remove your gloves first," Neelo added, their muscles coiling as the merchant's eyes darted between them.

In a split second, he knew the jig was up, dropping the dagger and bolting back through the markets. Talhan released Neelo's arm and raced after the merchant, kicking up a dust trail in his wake. Neelo rushed after the two of them, barely keeping sight as the merchant ducked and weaved through the market stalls. Screams rang out as a mushroom cloud of dust erupted from the center stall and the shade posts caved in. People began shrieking and running in the other direction as Neelo neared the broken-down stall.

"Tal!" Neelo shouted, racing forward into the labyrinth of splintering tents.

A hand shot out, fast and greedy, grabbing Neelo around the throat and hauling them backward. A foul-smelling breath whispered across their face. "Hold still."

It wasn't the voice of the red-bearded merchant, but someone else, gruffer. A coconspirator? Neelo didn't dare turn to look when a cloudy metal blade came into view. Neelo clenched their jaw at the sight, knowing one touch of this blade would curse them to the same fate.

CHAPTER TWENTY-FOUR

Talhan flew around the corner, brandishing his sword and dagger. A fresh bruise bloomed over his eyebrow and blood splattered his face. How many attackers were there? Horror filled Talhan's eyes at the sight of the blade hovering over Neelo's neck.

"No closer, Eagle," the voice growled, yanking Neelo tighter against a lean body. Neelo's heartbeat hammered in their ears. They were easily strong enough to fight this human, but the poisoned blade gave him the upper hand. One touch and the blood in their veins would turn to ash.

Talhan's chest rose and fell in angry, heaving breaths. "Hear me now, merchant, or whoever you truly are." Talhan's voice was low and vicious. Gone was the charming young lord, and in his place was the promise of pure wrath and violence. "If that blade so much as whispers across their skin, I promise you, you'll be begging for death by the time I'm finished with you."

"Killing the Heir of Saxbridge will make me a hero." The attacker's pulse pounded in the hand that held Neelo's throat, squeezing tighter as Neelo sucked in a scant breath. "The witches will remember my name forever."

"That ledger you showed me," Talhan snarled, his menacing eyes darting from the merchant to Neelo. "Do you remember that spotted *boshtu*?"

The name of the Southern duck? Neelo's brow furrowed before realization dawned on them.

Shit. He wanted them to duck. Talhan gave them a grave nod. They wanted to protest his harebrained plan, but with that poisoned knife drifting a little further away while the attacker was distracted, now was their chance.

With a strained breath, Neelo held Talhan's gaze for one last second, hoping their eyes said all the things they were feeling—the sorrow they felt if this was goodbye, the regret for not telling him sooner all the ways he made Neelo feel . . . but they didn't say anything. Instead, they just lifted their feet and dropped.

It happened so fast, the shing of metal, the wet splat, the thud. Blood rained down on Neelo and they gasped. They tasted the coppery tang as they looked up at the beam above them. A dagger protruded through the attacker's eye, nailing his lifeless body to the wooden pole behind him. He didn't writhe, didn't move, the perfectly thrown blade cutting his voiceless scream before it escaped his twitching lips.

More shrieks rang out at the sight of him and the last stragglers from the market broke out in a run to escape the gore. The arid ground absorbed the blood as soon as it fell, leaving only a metallic scent and a shadow of crimson sand.

Neelo crawled forward, their stomach churning with acid. Talhan dropped into a crouch in front of them, scanning them for injuries. His hands held Neelo's shoulders as he searched their face.

"Are you okay?" His eyes frantically examined Neelo, but apart from being drenched in someone else's blood, they were unharmed. "Talk to me." Talhan cupped their cheek with his hand. "Did that blade touch you?"

"I'm fine."

At their reassuring words, Talhan's face scrunched and he collapsed backward. The tables turned as Neelo searched him for injuries. "Just a pain in my leg." His eyes opened and he panted a few belabored breaths, rubbing his hand down his leg a few more times before leaning his head back against the beam. "I guess my injuries from Valtene are not quite as healed as I'd hoped."

"Gods." Neelo muttered a string of curses. If Talhan didn't have the quick-healing magic of the fae, his injuries would've surely killed him. Even so, fae magic still needed time to fully recover. "You shouldn't be running like that after such a recent injury."

"I should be able to chase down a few humans," Talhan growled.

"And you will in a few more months if you don't keep mindlessly charging into danger," Neelo snapped back.

"I thought I had them all," Talhan grumbled. "But one got away when he doubled back and my thigh seized right where . . ."

"Right where you were stabbed only so many weeks ago?" Neelo countered with a frown.

"Well, when you say it like that." Talhan rose, rubbing his hand down his aching leg and hobbling toward the body still weeping blood onto the dusty ground.

Neelo brushed their bloodied hair back off their face. "What are you doing?"

"Looking for information about who this man was," Talhan said. He searched through the merchant's jacket pockets, pulling out scraps of paper, copper coins, and a crusty handkerchief. "What in the Gods . . .?" Talhan patted the jacket again. "I can feel something in the lining." He searched for more pockets before finally pulling out another knife from the belt around his thigh and tearing open the lining.

A wrinkled piece of paper fluttered down onto his lap. Neelo's mouth fell open at the ink markings. It was a detailed drawing of the bays and caves along the Crushwold River. Neelo carefully picked up the piece of paper, their eyes roving over the intricate depiction of the riverbanks, scribbled with Mhenbic notes.

"Did we just find a treasure map?" Talhan's eyebrows shot up.

"It's just a map," Neelo corrected, surveying the yellowing paper. They tried to remember the maps of their court, searching for discrepancies between this map and the ones mounted on the walls of the palace.

Talhan's finger dropped to the top left corner. "Look at these caves."

"Large enough to hide a ship in?" Neelo asked, tracing the undulating markings above Westdale.

"Perhaps." Talhan trailed his fingers across the letters. "What does this say?"

"*Varaash ast en tzafarranik,*" Neelo whispered. "It's Mhenbic. It means, 'The smallest seed will be king.'" They glanced sideways at Talhan. "Adisa Monroe had the same phrase written over and over in her journal. Cole was still speculating about what it meant when . . ."

"When he fled that dinner in Murreneir?" Talhan snarled.

"Yes," Neelo whispered. "Shit."

Talhan's eyes widened. "Could they be hiding their supplies in these caves? Could this be where Adisa Monroe is hiding?"

"I don't know." Neelo rolled up the map and looked at Talhan. "But if one of those attackers got away, we need to get out of here. Now. We're getting on the first ship northward before that human has a chance to warn any others."

"I can't believe we found a treasure map."

"Stop calling it a treasure map," Neelo muttered, dusting their clothes off and shooting a wary glance at the merchants who'd returned to tidy up their stalls. "There's not any treasure on it."

"You think there's a hidden ship or storage somewhere on it though," Talhan countered, wiping the blood from his knife and sheathing it. "Yes?"

He grinned. "So it's a map to find the location of a hidden valuable thing?"

"Possibly," Neelo gritted out.

Talhan rubbed his hands together. "Then it's a treasure map."

"If the thought makes you walk any faster, then yes, fine, it's a treasure map," Neelo muttered.

"Yes," he whisper-cheered. "Bri's going to be so jealous."

"You can fae fire her once we're on the road. I don't want to know how long it will be before someone realizes this map is missing." Neelo looked Talhan up and down. "Your leg—"

"My leg is fine," Talhan grumbled. "I just pulled a muscle or something. Stop doting. Speaking of"—he looked around the markets—"are you going to tell Rish and Ersan that we're leaving?"

"I will send a messenger once we reach Westdale." Neelo picked up their pace, watching for any sudden movements from their periphery. What if more than one human got away? What if they were going to return with reinforcements? "The caves are just north of Westdale and we can stop to resupply there."

"You're seriously not going to go back to the manor first? You're covered in blood!" Neelo turned to walk away, but Talhan grabbed them by the crook of the arm. "Rish will be panicked if you don't return for lunch."

Neelo's frown deepened. Finally. *Finally,* they'd found a lead—something promising that might help save their court and they didn't want to wait a single breath to discover what it was. Their mind was so focused on unraveling this mystery . . . but Talhan was right. Rish would be in a frenzy, probably alerting all of the Southern Court that the Heir had gone missing.

Neelo flagged down one of the green witchlings they'd noticed in the palace before. Her name evaded them. Something starting with "A"? She was no more than eight years old and had short, curly brown hair and kind brown eyes that widened to saucers when she saw the two blood-soaked fae approaching her.

Neelo crouched in front of the little girl. "Do you know who I am?" The witchling nodded. "Can you keep a secret?" The witchling nodded again, her eyebrows lifting as a spark of delight flickered in her eyes. "Do you know of the green witch named Rish?"

"The one visiting from the royal palace?"

"Yes." Neelo pulled three coins from the pouch on their belt: a gold coin for the girl to keep and two silver *druni* to give to Rish. "Run to the manor. Tell Rish we're safe and that she can send word to Westdale," Neelo whispered.

"Yes, Your Highness." The green witchling attempted a quick curtsy before running off.

Neelo rose, watching the child scamper up the trail toward the manor, before doing another sweep of the area, searching for any suspicious faces. "Now can we go? People are staring."

Talhan grinned. "As much as I enjoyed Lord Ersan's hospitality, I can't say I'm disappointed to get out of here."

Neelo snickered as they steered through the growing crowds gawking at the carnage and wended their way toward the docks. Maybe it was shock that brought a grin to their lips and a speed to their step. They'd almost just been killed and yet, all they could think about was finally getting answers—so close to finding the source of the South's witching brew problems, saving their mother, and securing her reign. Their heart sank a little as Talhan's shadow fell over them, shading them from the brilliant burning sun. It should've brought Neelo joy to think of going back to their quiet corner of the library in peace. But it didn't.

TALHAN PASSED A waterskin to Neelo and they accepted it gratefully. The scorching sun was beating down on the deck and they prayed they'd set sail soon. Neelo had managed to scrub most of the gore off them in the waters of the Crushwold while they waited for the first vessel to depart Arboa. The ragged ship they found was only stopping in Westdale on its journey to Wynreach. Despite their attire, the captain agreed to give them a ride, apparently knowing of the infamous Golden Eagle but not recognizing the Heir of the very court he was docked in.

Neelo's legs wobbled underneath them. Bloody boats.

It was the fastest way north, hopefully faster than word of their arrival. If the wrong people heard about the death of those merchants, the caves might be cleared out and abandoned by the time they arrived. The sooner they could reach that spot on the map, the better.

"Glamour or no, I'd know that face anywhere," one sailor called, clapping his hand on his leg. Talhan cringed and turned to face the man. "It is! Talhan Catullus, the Eagle of the East, returning home at last?"

"Just up to Westdale," Talhan said, giving the man a friendly pat on the arm. How quickly he morphed back into that charming veneer, so easily at home, even amongst human sailors. "Got some business matters to settle up there."

"Aye," the man said with a laugh. "Knowing you, I'm sure you do." He turned to Neelo, giving them barely a passing glance before turning back to Talhan. "And who's this?" The man tipped his head at them. "Your latest boyfriend?"

Neelo nearly spat out their water. Talhan snorted, but before he could open his mouth, Neelo said, "He wishes."

The sailors crowed with laughter. It felt good, being unknown. Neelo's glamour wasn't particularly camouflaging, but these were Eastern humans, ones who had no reason nor opportunity to see the Heir of Saxbridge before.

Talhan let out a surprised chuckle at Neelo's rueful grin. "I guess I need to up my charms, then."

The sailors laughed harder, animating at the slightest joke from the famous Eagle.

"You sure you can't keep us company the whole way back to Wynreach?" the front sailor asked. "It's been a while since we've had any entertainment around here. Having the Eagle aboard will be a golden bit of story."

Talhan chuckled and just as Neelo tried to retreat, he slung his arm around their shoulders. "Lucky for you, this one is full of stories."

A metal whistle sang out across the ship. The men craned their necks up to their captain, realizing they should be readying to depart and scattered under his scrutinizing gaze.

"Well, you better find a place to sit where we can all hear you, because we're about to set sail," one man called as he rushed toward the bow.

Talhan unbelted a pouch of coins and chucked it up to the captain. Neelo touched the rim of their hat and the captain did the same.

"Welcome aboard the *Wave Skimmer*." He had a brusque Eastern accent, the kind of the seafaring villages in the coastal parts of the Eastern Court. "We'll be docking in Westdale by midafternoon if these bloody fools hurry up!" He shouted the last bit of warning and the crew doubled their pace.

Neelo and Talhan wandered toward the stern and tucked into the side where they wouldn't be in the way of the rope lines.

Neelo folded their arms, grasping the edges of their tunic with a white-knuckle grip as they bounced their leg.

"Not a fan of boats?" Talhan asked.

"You know I'm not."

"Then why are we on one?"

"Because you found a map and I need answers," Neelo said. "And because there was a gang of humans trying to murder us and one of them got away." They pointed in the direction of the market district, out of sight from the docks. "This was the fastest way to get to our answers and away from them. We'll stay at the tavern in Westdale tonight and trek the rest of the way at first light."

The boat rocked and Neelo's hands shot out, gripping the railing.

"I remember trying to goad you onto that boat in Wynreach as children," Talhan said with a laugh. "If only I knew I needed an unsolved puzzle to lure you."

Neelo glowered at him. "You wanted to *steal* that boat, need I remind you? One from King Gedwin Norwood's fleet, no less."

"Oh, come on." Talhan chuckled. "That wasn't your objection to getting aboard and you know it."

Neelo rolled their eyes. "At least Bri had the good sense to stop you."

"I would've returned it." Talhan shrugged. "Eventually."

"Pirate," Neelo muttered. "You've been goading me into harebrained schemes ever since."

"And you've been rejecting them ever since," Talhan added with a waggle of his eyebrows. He paused. "I've never seen your glamour before. You seem almost more confident with it on."

They were surprised by the observation—and the astuteness of it. "I am," Neelo said, pulling a short lock of hair behind their rounded ear.

"Why?"

"Because there is no expectation of who I should be." They stared at their hands gripping the railing. "There is no title. No pressure. I'm just an ordinary human like this."

"Nothing about you is ordinary."

"Exactly."

"No—that's not how I meant it," Talhan said, warmth in his already warm eyes. "But I can see why that would be appealing."

"Your glamour apparently doesn't work so well," Neelo added with a huff. "Why am I not surprised you're well known amongst sailors?"

Talhan's shoulders shook with laughter as he leaned his forearms on the polished wood railing. "Because I be a pirate, arrrr," he said in a gravelly voice, and Neelo couldn't help but giggle at the absurd affectation. In his regular voice he said, "Seriously, I fear I've made myself well known in every corner of Okrith, especially the East." He winked at them. "One of Hale Norwood's dastardly crew."

Neelo stared out at the dark river waves that stretched so far that they could barely make out the sliver of Eastern Court on the other side. "You'll make a good King in the East. The people there already love you."

Talhan's shoulders tensed for a split second before they lowered again. "I'd make a good consort in the South too."

"But the East is your home," Neelo protested.

"Because my childhood was there?" Talhan snorted. "My mother's people are from the High Mountains and we were born in the Western Court. Yes, I spent much of my youth in the East, but most of the childhood that I remember, I wish I could forget." Neelo swallowed. "There's only one court that's ever felt like home to me." He glanced at Neelo. "The tastes, the smells, the music, even the heat. I don't know why my soul has chosen the South, but it has." His hand slid across the balustrade and gently landed on top of Neelo's. Their skin tingled where his hand rested. "Actually, that's not true. I'm certain why my soul has chosen the South. Because I *want* to be here.

"With you."

Neelo's heart leapt into their throat as Talhan's fingers pressed on theirs. "I can't stop thinking about last night," he said quietly and their cheeks flushed and blood roared in their ears. "I can't help but think that you want me to be here too."

They didn't know what to say and were saved from the mortification of trying to process their reaction when another whistle wailed, jarring Neelo upright. They snatched their hand away and whirled to watch as the ship pulled away from the shoreline. Gripping the railing tight with one hand, they stumbled precariously toward the bow.

"Where are you going?"

"You promised them a story from me." Neelo tapped the book in their breast pocket and then the ones in each hip pocket as if trying to decide which one to read. They'd hoped Talhan would stay at the stern but, as always, he was right behind them, and they knew, eventually, they'd have to confront him about what he'd just said. But not now. Now they could distract themself in a good book for a little bit longer.

NEELO NEARLY READ the crew an entire book during the time spent sailing up to Westdale. It was all they could do to keep from looking at Talhan. They'd pulled away from him—again—after grabbing him and kissing him the night before. Gods, every moment with him their restraint seemed to slip a little further, their grasp on their reasons for denying him loosening with his every beautiful breath.

Neelo's voice grew hoarse, their tone even and dull, as if lulling children to sleep. They knew that Talhan would have regaled the crew with a better story. His versions were always livelier, but the only thing between Neelo and the truths they feared was the book in their hands, the stoutest shield they'd ever known, so they kept reading.

When they docked in Westdale, a messenger was already waiting on the wharf for them. A pigeon sat on the messenger's shoulder and Neelo knew instantly who'd sent them. They accepted the outstretched piece of paper from the messenger with a nod, paying him three coppers and unfurling the scroll to find a transcribed note from Rish:

I would be mad, mea raga, if I wasn't so impressed. You boarding a boat on a whim is quite spectacular. I am guessing it had something to do with the incident in the markets that Sy is currently trying to clean up? You certainly are making a mess here in Arboa, but I trust that you know what you're doing. I hope you're being careful. I'm taking care too and will be heading back to Saxbridge by the time you read this. Please assure Talhan that I am returning with all of your belongings. Indi and I will meet you there upon your return. Try not to kill the Eagle, he's a good one, and remember to eat something.

—*Rish*

PS—Out of all the stories you live in your head, mea raga, *I hope you remember to live your own story too*

Neelo swallowed and rolled the miniature scroll back up. How did Rish always manage to do that? Even from a distance, she could cut straight to the core of Neelo. They passed the note to Talhan and he let out a heavy sigh.

"What belongings is she referring to?" Neelo asked. "And why do you need reassurance about them?"

Talhan cleared his throat. "No idea."

"You're a terrible liar." Neelo scrutinized the way he shifted on his feet and the way his brow pinched into a triangle above his nose. "You're so bad at it that you don't even try. You just switch the subject."

"I'll go find us some rooms." Talhan steered around Neelo and toward the tavern across the busy road.

Neelo released a long sigh. "You're seriously not going to tell me?"

"First round is on me," Talhan called over his shoulder.

"So much for not keeping secrets," Neelo growled, but they didn't raise their voice loud enough for Talhan to hear, knowing it made them a terrible hypocrite for even grumbling about it. Besides, there were too many people milling about and the last thing they needed right then was unwanted attention.

Neelo pondered what the *belongings* could be. Presumably, the same one that Talhan was so concerned about the Arboan bandits stealing. What could Rish know that Neelo couldn't? They would need to pull the answers out of the green witch when they returned home. She would probably be more likely to let something slip than Talhan himself— although the way Rish had been acting lately in regard to Talhan, they wondered if their friend was more loyal to the Golden Eagle now, and it left them with a strange feeling.

Is that . . . jealousy?

They shook their head and watched as Talhan sped ahead into Westdale tavern. Alone and yet surrounded by a crowd, all of their bravado had disappeared as the sun went down and the streets filled with people. They'd just found a map and boarded the ship without a second thought. They led with their gut first and left their mind to follow, like pulling Talhan into that kiss and canceling the shipment of brew. It made them feel off-balance, out of control, and yet strangely pleased—whatever their next actions would be a surprise even to themself.

They tucked Rish's note into their pocket, wondering what they would do if they stopped planning the story of their life and started living it instead.

CHAPTER TWENTY-FIVE

When Talhan had knocked on Neelo's door and announced he was going to the bathhouses across the street, Neelo had replied with barely a grunt. It wasn't until the sound of the warrior's bootsteps faded away that they let out a breath. They clutched the book in their hand tighter, wondering if there'd be other people in the bathhouses at this time of night . . . wondering if they'd all be ogling Talhan's naked form . . . and wondering if Talhan would be interested in admiring any of them back.

Thinking of the pointed note they'd just received, Neelo muttered, "Damn it, Rish," even as they tossed their book on the bed and grabbed their room key, making a beeline for the bathhouses.

The building was set up in the same style as most of the Southern Court with a large sauna room with in-ground tubs and then cold rooms shooting off from the main building like branches on a tree. Many people would steam, then dip into a cool tub, then steam again. In the heat of summer, the unheated rooms got busier, but most Southerners didn't like to go more than a few days without a steam. Even Neelo, who preferred bathing by themself instead of the communal setup, would put a towel over their head and sit over a bowl of boiling water to clear out their lungs if nothing else.

With their glamour still on, the bathhouse maids barely gave Neelo a passing glance, and it felt odd to be ignored. Normally they tucked away, feeling the pain of people's stares, the pressure of a crowded room pushing in on them, but now, they were someone else entirely, wearing a mask that didn't require hiding. There was a benefit to normally being a recluse. This far from Saxbridge, no one seemed to recognize them. They tried their glamour before in the capital, but even for a shadow, they were too known there . . . but in Westdale, a town they rarely visited, they were just another human ready for a soak.

They wandered through the steam-filled room, the cloying scent of oils circling through the thick air. They passed people in various stages of undress, hanging their clothing on hooks along the main room. Even the clothing benefited from a trip to the bathhouses—the steam refreshed the clothes and pressed out the creases. They spotted a few totem pouches hanging from hooks, so at least a few witches were in Westdale that night.

Neelo had bribed a tavern courtesan to fetch them fresh clothing and was pleased when she returned with a fresh charcoal-gray tunic, navy trousers, and fitted white undershorts.

They wound through the baths, mostly empty this late in the evening, when people were out partying instead of washing. Searching for one person in particular, their eyes finally landed on a peak of auburn hair, pulled high in a knot atop his head. They forced confidence into their posture, throwing their shoulders back and walking forward through the steam, making it to the edge of the final bath before Talhan's eyes lifted.

A pleased surprise curved his lips and lifted his eyebrows as his eyes trailed up Neelo's fresh clothes to meet their eyes. "Hi."

Neelo's heart thumped and their stomach tightened. How could one syllable make their body react like that?

"Can I join you?" they asked, the words feeling rough and stilted coming out of their throat.

Talhan grinned even wider. "Be my guest."

"Turn around," Neelo said, kicking off their freshly shined shoes toward the slat board wall. They found a hook with a folded towel still above, indicating it was unused.

Talhan dutifully turned as Neelo hauled their tunic over their head and hung it on the hook. Their hands stilled on the buckles of their vest, hesitating for a moment. Biting the inside of their cheek, they left the vest and took off their trousers and undershorts instead. They were about to turn back to the pool when a burst of defiance flooded through them, and they quickly unbuckled their vest, stripping themself bare. They hung the sweat-crusted garment up to dry with a definitive nod and hastily stepped into the bath.

Neelo knew many people were more *comfortable* with the mystery, pretending that nothing existed beneath their clothes at all. The real beauty was in being seen and known and accepted exactly as they were. And they knew that's who they sat across from: the person who didn't need the mystery to still only and perfectly see *them*.

Warm water enveloped their body, a soothing balm against their nerves. Their sore muscles finally relaxed as their shoulders dropped below the frothing lavender-scented surface.

"You can turn around now."

Talhan twisted, his eyebrows rising as he spotted their bare shoulders. "No vest?"

Neelo shrugged and their peek of shoulder made Talhan's mouth go slack. "You said you wouldn't mistake me for anything else, and I believe you."

"Good," he said, idly swirling his hands.

The oiled fragrances billowed up in clouds of steam. Neelo slicked their short black hair off their face. A cackling laugh echoed from a far-off room and they both smiled—it was clearly a witch's laughter.

The Southern Court was one of the few places where humans, witches, and fae would all gather. While no court had rules against such things, the Eastern and Northern Courts had separate facilities for the three types of being that inhabited Okrith: different city quarters, different taverns, different everything. Though now, with Rua and Renwick Vostemur's reign, that was bound to change. Still, it would take time, and while different races might start to find less discriminatory practices, there were also the biases that people, regardless of their background, were going to have to endure as the populace dealt with one massive social change at a time.

And Neelo felt on the precipice of that changing world, like being perched between two crashing waves. They felt the undertow of the next great shift, both flowing through the world and pulling through them, both grand in scale and incredibly minute all at once. The world would either topple them onto the ground or they would ride above it. And Neelo was starting to realize they had a say in which outcome.

Maybe they could harness that power, help other courts see people beyond witch or fae, Northern or Southern, male or female. Maybe so much of life existed between and beyond such distinctions. And maybe they were the one to help the rest of Okrith see that as clearly as the South.

But in the Southern Court, smelly people had always been smelly people, and they all needed a wash. For the first time in a long time, Neelo felt grateful that they were born to a crown where a person's name and appearance held less weight. Despite their mother's disappointment that Neelo wasn't a devotee of her hedonistic lifestyle, Queen Emberspear had never once questioned Neelo's choice of name, title, or gender. If they'd been born in the North or the East . . . They shuddered. Their life would've been inevitably harder. They thought about Bri and the way her mother made her dress and act as a child, as if she could beat the femininity into her.

"What?" Talhan asked and Neelo realized they were staring blankly at him.

"Nothing," they said, dropping their gaze. "I'm just thinking."

"I would expect nothing else," he said fondly. "About what?"

"Bri."

"You're thinking about my sister?" Talhan's shoulders shook with laughter. "Figures. Everyone does."

"About your childhood," Neelo added and Talhan's expression sobered. They knew they needed to walk delicately around the subject. "How hard it must be to not be accepted for who you are."

"I'm sure you can relate," Talhan said softly.

"I can. But I also had others around," Neelo said. "I had my mother's support."

"No." Talhan slowly shook his head as his hands swirled. "You had her support to change your name and title, but I'm talking about *you*, who you really are."

"And who am I?"

"You're Neelo," he said, and the way their name came out of his mouth made it sound like the most special word in the world. "Someone who'd rather read books than throw parties. Someone who'd rather have a handful of meaningful friends than a hundred simpering courtiers." Talhan cocked his head. "Someone who'd rather have real conversations than shouted words over gambling and games and indulgences."

Neelo gripped their hands together under the water, feeling more naked in that breath than they had the previous one.

"*That* is what your mother doesn't accept about you," Talhan murmured, his eyes flitting up from the chalky water to search Neelo's face.

How could he see so clearly things that they were only just beginning to accept?

"Then I suppose we both had parents who wished we'd be something else," Neelo said and Talhan nodded, his chin dipping into the water. Normally Talhan would keep talking, filling the awkward silence with warmth and words, but instead he just kept looking at Neelo until they felt compelled to speak again. "I can't believe we just took off on that ship today."

"It was certainly unexpected." Talhan chuckled. "But I'm as eager to find more answers as you. I feel something stirring in this world. Something dark. Hennen Vostemur wasn't the end of it. Ancient magic is waking."

"And it feels like they're taking aim at the South now," Neelo mused.

"Yes," Talhan agreed.

"If you wanted to eliminate the Southern Court . . . the easiest way would be through the drugs and partying," Neelo said. "It would be more a nudge than a push, and so difficult to point to a perpetrator."

"Is that what you're hoping you'll find in these caves?" Talhan asked. "The source of the violet witch's plans for Saxbridge?"

Neelo held his steely gaze. "I want to save my mother and my people." Their eyes guttered. "And go back to the life I had before all of this began."

Talhan's eyes drifted over Neelo's face. "All of it?" Neelo didn't answer, their mind swirling with the events of the last few days. "And you say *I'm* a bad liar."

"What?"

"You didn't ride off to Arboa in secret to save your mother. You didn't cancel the shipments of brew to save your mother." Talhan leaned back, studying Neelo's face. "And despite what you say, you didn't rush up to Westdale following a treasure map to save your mother either." Neelo opened their mouth to speak but Talhan pushed further. "You can say it's purely selfish," he said, which were the exact words Neelo was about to speak, "that you want your mother to rule so that you don't have to, but every step you're taking right now is for the good of your court, your people, and for the version of yourself I know you want to become."

How perfectly his blow landed. Neelo hated how easily he could lay them so bare. Talhan took a breath, reining himself in, and Neelo was surprised that even naked in a bath he commanded the space like a king on his throne.

"Now," Talhan said. "The caves. What do you hope to find there?"

"Best case?" Neelo said. "We find a detailed account for all of Adisa Monroe's plans for Okrith and what other magic she's waiting to enact in her quest for a violet witch supremacy. Either that, or someone is still in those caves that you could *inspire* answers out of." Talhan's eyebrows shot up. "Are you horrified or impressed?"

He drifted a little closer. "Both." Neelo's gaze dipped down to that spellbinding smile. "What are you thinking about?"

"You," they said, that wave within themself rising as they once again wanted to be the person who led with their body and let their mind follow. "Last night. Today."

Talhan hummed, the sound rumbling through his chest, and Neelo had the sudden urge to place their hand on it to feel the sound vibrating beneath their fingertips.

"Today on the boat, I thought you might kiss me . . . and I kind of panicked." They bit the corner of their lip.

"Ah." Talhan's eyes darkened as his cheeks dimpled. "I assumed that was the reason you read for five hours straight." The slap of bare footsteps faded away as more patrons left the bathhouses for the night. "So why did you come here now?"

"I don't know," Neelo whispered. "Maybe I regretted not kissing you."

Talhan's hands stilled and dropped to his sides. "And do you want to now?"

"Maybe."

"Maybe," he echoed, watching them with a look that would normally make Neelo feel awkward and embarrassed, but now . . . this feeling was entirely different. The way Talhan looked at them made them feel revered, attractive, important. It made them burn, not with shame, but with lust.

Talhan shifted to the middle of the pool, hovering in the water just beyond arm's reach. "Tell me what you want," he said, his voice a raspy whisper.

"Just . . . let me," Neelo said, heat stirring in their core.

Talhan blinked but didn't move, as they lifted off the submerged bench and tiptoed over to him. Talhan leaned forward and Neelo put their hand on his chest.

"Keep still," they commanded and Talhan obeyed.

His chest rose and fell in heavy pants as Neelo's hand swept up his chest and to his neck. Their thumb brushed along his jaw as they looked up into those burning amber eyes. Neelo swept their thumb across his lips and his eyes shuttered. Their thumb lingered on his bottom lip, pulling it slightly in a way they wanted to mirror with their own mouth. They stepped another inch closer, their chest and belly touching Talhan's beneath the water and he groaned against their fingers.

Neelo felt his hardening length against their thigh and it made a bolt of desire shoot through their body. The shock of it made their lips part. They wanted this. They wanted him. And he wanted them back.

"Is this torturing you?" Neelo breathed.

"Yes," Talhan moaned, squeezing shut his eyes as he leaned into Neelo's touch. "The sweetest kind of torture."

Neelo smirked. Talhan peeked down at them and they ordered, "Keep your eyes closed."

He shut them again upon their command. His cheeks flashed a dimple before his lips parted breathlessly again. Gods, those lips. That jaw. The smell of spiced coffee cutting through the lavender steam. Would he taste the same way he smelled?

The urge to find out overwhelmed Neelo and they lifted up onto their toes, their belly brushing against him as their lips reached his. Talhan remained still, eyes shut, hands by his side as Neelo brushed a kiss against his soft, full lips. His only reaction was the moan that caught in his throat at the contact and a stirring lower even they knew he had no way of controlling. Neelo's lips lingered against his, their tongue skimming across his bottom lip, tasting his mouth. Talhan's lips betrayed his stillness, matching Neelo's next kiss with his own, and the feeling made a hot wave rush through them. They wanted his lips and hands. They wanted every part of him. For the first time, they *wanted* it all.

Talhan must have felt the same because he groaned, "Can I move now?"

Neelo smiled against his mouth and whispered, "Yes."

The word barely left Neelo's lips before Talhan's hands were snaking around Neelo's torso, pulling them flush against his body. His mouth landed hot over Neelo's and he hummed his sweet pleasure against their lips. The feeling sent a thrill straight down Neelo's spine, their whole body buzzing, their legs simultaneously losing sensation, the feeling so overwhelming they nearly forgot who they were.

Talhan's lips trailed up Neelo's jaw and he murmured across the shell of their ear, "Say I can stay in the South."

"You can't stay," Neelo panted, their hands gripping Talhan's muscled back to keep from slipping over.

"Why not?" he rumbled into their ear, making them throb with desire.

Every reason seemed to vanish from Neelo's mind at his touch.

Why did they keep fighting this deep-seated yearning that was driving them mad?

"You just can't," they whispered.

Talhan's hand drifted up to cup their neck. "I want you, Neelo. I've *always* wanted you."

Neelo opened their mouth to plead for him to touch them and stop talking, when two tittering voices echoed from beyond the clouds of steam. Neelo shot backward as two naked courtesans appeared. The courtesans paused, darting looks between Talhan and Neelo.

Talhan's eyes stared straight down at the water, not lifting to even glance at the naked bodies beyond and Neelo couldn't help the bizarre chortle that escaped their lips. Talhan looked so sincere, as if even observing another naked body would be a betrayal. Good luck to him. In the Southern Court, there'd be nowhere he could avoid it.

"Lord Catullus," the redheaded courtesan said. "What a pleasant surprise." She stepped into the tub and her friend followed.

"I was actually just leaving," Talhan said, turning and climbing out.

Neelo's eyes trailed over his powerful body, heat rising in them again at his gloriously chiseled form. Their eyes that had trailed down the dusting of hair below his navel for the last several weeks finally got their reward as they eyed the considerable size of him before he snatched a towel and wrapped it around his waist. His hand hovered over the second towel folded above Neelo's clothes and he looked at them from over his shoulder, his body still turned away to hide his arousal.

"Are you getting out too?" The way he asked it made Neelo wonder if it was an invitation to carry on where they left off in private. If Neelo left with him, would that be it? Would they sleep together? *Be* together?

They swallowed, suddenly unsure of what they'd done.

Neelo cleared their throat. "I think I'll stay for a while longer."

Their eyes drifted back down to their hands. They didn't want to look up and see the crestfallen expression that would surely be on Talhan's face.

"Very well," he said with a friendly casualness that made Neelo clench their jaw. Even Talhan didn't sound that breezy normally. "Have a good night."

Neelo gritted their teeth. Gods, they were a coward.

"Did you see it?" one courtesan pressed, tying up her strawberry-blond hair as the other gave a knowing look. "We clearly turned him on. I knew the Golden Eagle would be big."

"He's not that big." The raven-haired courtesan chuckled as she took off her beaded earrings and placed them on the side of the tub. "Have you seen Samser?"

"Yeah, but he's ridiculous. That doesn't even look fun." The other courtesan snickered. "But Talhan Catullus, *he* looks like a lot of fun."

"Yeah, I'm done," Neelo muttered to everyone and no one, shooting up and scuttling over to fetch their towel.

Their cheeks burned as they wrapped the towel around themself. They'd find a cool room to wait in for a while and then run back to their room with their tail between their legs. Gods, what had they done? How were they meant to rule a court when they couldn't even do this? They warred between hunting down Talhan in his room to finish what they started, and banishing him from the Southern Court right then and there. Maybe banishment was a bit of an overreaction. Neelo raked a frustrated hand through their hair. They'd have to face him in the morning and there wasn't a single book in all of Okrith that would help them do that.

CHAPTER TWENTY-SIX

The horses fell into an easy side-by-side gait as they headed upriver. Neelo hired the mares at the Westdale stables, selecting the white and tan dappled horses for their speed and calm countenance—a stark contrast to the anxious pulse in Neelo's ears. After the bathhouse, each infuriating bounce and rock of their hips in the saddle only tormented Neelo's overstimulated imagination—and body—further. What had happened the night before . . . What Neelo had almost allowed themself to do . . .

"This road is so much better than the one we took last autumn," Talhan said, breaking the silence for the first time since sunrise.

Despite the comfortable tavern bed, Neelo had barely slept, thinking instead about the fae warrior one room over and their shared moment in the bathhouse. Neelo studied Talhan's face as he gazed off toward the river. They wondered in that moment if Talhan was truly so laid back or simply a really good actor. For once, they couldn't read him at all. How could he not be thinking about the same things they were?

"We couldn't even ride our horses. The jungle was so thick," Talhan continued.

"The inland road would've been better to not be spotted by passing ships but"—Neelo looked to the dense forest to their left—"that would've been—"

"Misery," Talhan groused. "It was utter misery. Those bitey fucking yellow flies that make your whole body swell up?"

"Oh yes." Neelo chuckled, grateful for the long sleeves of the light-weight gray tunic they now wore. "Did you use the white clay?"

Talhan's whole torso twisted toward them and his horse snorted. "What?"

Neelo gave him a quizzical look in return. "The ground in those parts has patches of white clay in the cracked earth?"

His eyes flared. "And?"

Snickering, Neelo knew exactly what had happened. "And if you rub the white clay on your exposed skin, it deters the yellow flies."

"*What?*" Talhan shouted. He instinctively bent over to give a reassuring pat to his horse, though the mare didn't seem startled by his outburst.

"I'm surprised Carys didn't tell you."

"I'm not. Gods, *that's* why she had that stuff all over her," Talhan growled as Neelo held in a laugh. "I thought it was to protect her fair skin. As soon as we reach the next inn, I am calling her through the fae fires about this."

"No inns this way." Neelo shook their head. "I don't think we'll make it to the caves by nightfall either. They're farther north than it seemed on the map. We might have to set up camp for the night and venture the final way in the morning."

"Great, more camping," Talhan grumbled.

"Camping closer to the river won't be as bad as in the jungle," Neelo assured.

"I don't believe you." Talhan slapped at a mosquito that landed on his arm. "I'm surprised you're so calm about all this. You don't strike me as the camping type either."

"I'm not," Neelo said. "But if these caves hold the answer to Adisa Monroe's plans, and better yet, her stores of power-imbued blooming amethyst that is being used to poison my people, then it is worth a night sleeping under the stars to save our court, don't you think?"

"Our court?" Talhan asked.

Neelo shot him a look. "My mother's and mine."

"Oh."

Neelo bit the inside of their lip and fished a midnight-blue book out of their saddlebag. "Do you want to hear a story to pass the time?"

"What story?"

"The one we started in Saxbridge," Neelo said. "With the knight and her princess?" They flourished the blue book in their hand. "I found a copy on that traveler's shelf in Westdale."

"You were blessed by all the Gods, Neelo Emberspear." Talhan's smile reappeared.

They cleared their throat and flipped the book open with one hand. "Where did we leave off?"

"The knight was about to ride into battle to save her beloved when a dragon appeared." Talhan waggled his fingers and deepened his voice as if telling a spooky tale.

Neelo smiled at Talhan's theatrics. "Oh yes." They flipped to the right page from muscle memory, knowing in a few more chapters the story was about to get really good. Their cheeks heated thinking about that part. Maybe they'd be back in Saxbridge by then and never have to read it out loud.

As they opened their mouth to begin reading, they decided to speak at a slower clip, just to be sure they didn't get to the part when the knight actually found her princess . . . and what happened next.

The breeze from the Crushwold River wafted torrents of cool air, easing the humidity that clung to them. The horses carried on their steady pace, not too fast to overheat as they twined up and around the undulating inlets along the river.

Neelo's words came out in a steady hypnotic hum that seemed to slow the world around them and make time speed up all at once. It felt like only moments had passed before the sun was setting.

Talhan cleared his throat at the end of the chapter and said, "Shall we set up camp?"

Lifting their head, Neelo realized the stars were already starting to twinkle to life and their eyes strained to see the page. They chuckled at how quickly the day seemed to slip through their fingertips. With a good story, and the right person, time seemed to disappear entirely.

TALHAN FOUND SHELTER under a rock ledge, tucked amongst the undulating black rocks that lined the riverside. It was too dark to go any further, but, when the sun rose, they planned to venture through the network of deep caves and hopefully find the answers they'd been seeking.

The size of the flame Talhan conjured was small enough to hold in one hand. Even though it was too hot for a large fire, the little puffs of smoke kept the mosquitoes at bay. Neelo had thought the caves were less than a day's journey and hadn't considered bringing overnight gear. They were grateful for their freshly washed jacket now. It was wildly inappropriate for such tropical weather, but at least they could lay upon it.

"Comfy?" Talhan jeered as Neelo propped their arm under their head and stared at the sloping rock ceiling above them.

"Very funny," they groused. "This is exactly why I don't like adventure."

Talhan chuckled and snapped a stick into pieces to add to the kindling pile beside him. "You're the one who got on a ship with no plans or forethought." He tossed another dry leaf into the fire. "Who knew you'd be the exploring type?"

"I've done more in a week than in my entire life," Neelo said, producing a tiny book from their coat pocket. "And I think my wanderlust has been sated forever."

"Did you get that from the traveler's shelf too?" Talhan asked, nodding to the book.

"I stole it from the room in Westdale," Neelo replied, then added quickly, "I left a book in the drawer in its place."

Talhan let out a low whistle. "But you've got that other book you were reading on the horse too?"

"Yes."

His cheeks dimpled. "How many books did you bring with you to the markets that morning?"

"Three."

"Three books?" Talhan's mouth split into a full grin. "For a walk to the markets?"

Neelo nudged the heavy pack further behind their back, feeling the weight of several more books outlining the stretched leather. "I may have grabbed a few more in Westdale." They glanced at him over the edge of their book. "It proved useful."

"A dagger and rations and a tent would've proved more useful," Talhan countered.

"Says you." Neelo shrugged. "My belly will be hungry, but my mind will be fed."

"So will the mosquitoes," he said, slapping his neck. "Also: never let Rish hear you say that," Talhan teased and Neelo let out a surprised laugh.

Groaning, Talhan lowered himself down beside Neelo, laying with his back to the cave mouth as if guarding the entrance. "You haven't finished the other book without me, have you?"

Neelo shook their head.

"Good, I think they were just about to kiss." Talhan nodded, tucking his arm under his head in mirror to Neelo and looking up to the rock above him. "Can we read that one?"

Neelo set down the booklet and fished out the larger novel they'd been reading with Talhan. They opened to the chapter where they'd left off, their fingers tightening on the cover as they cleared their throat. One page, two, three—the knight had found her princess and the story was finally taking a happy turn when . . .

Opening their mouth to read the next sentence, their throat went dry and their heart thundered as Talhan lifted on an elbow to look at them, eyes hidden in the shadows of the firelight.

"You can't stop it there," he protested.

"I . . ." Neelo swallowed and looked down at the paper. "I don't know if this is, um, appropriate to read out loud."

Talhan's white teeth flashed in the flickering light. "Appropriate?"

"They kiss, and things, and—"

"I definitely want to hear it, then. Especially the 'and things'. . ."

He chuckled. The sound of his deep voice made Neelo fumble with the edges of the book, nearly dropping it. "What's wrong?"

Neelo set the book flat on their chest and dug their fingernails into their palms, wishing they didn't have to say it, but knowing at some point it had to be addressed. The moment had been plaguing them the whole ride up the coast. They struggled to summon the will to say it until the dam finally broke: "I'm sorry about what happened at the bathhouses."

Talhan's eyes finally lifted and the weight of them pierced into Neelo. "I'm not," he murmured. "Are you sorry that you kissed me, or—"

"I'm not sorry I kissed you," Neelo blurted out, making Talhan smile. "Good."

Neelo picked at their fingers. "I just . . . don't know how to do any of this. I mean, I *know* in theory. I've read every book on the subject—"

"Of course." Talhan snorted and chucked another stick on the fire.

"But I don't know anything about initiating. Or . . . participating. All I know is how to avoid it." They nibbled at their lip as shame lowered their voice to a whisper. "How to pull away." Talhan's fingers swept a lock of Neelo's hair off their forehead. "I'm just thinking."

He smiled softly. "What are you thinking about?"

"That if I kiss you," they said and Talhan's smile widened, "it's going to break my heart when you go."

They dropped their eyes and Talhan reached out to bracket their cheek with his hand. His thumb slid under Neelo's jaw and tipped their chin up to look him in the eyes. "I'm not going anywhere," he said. "Not even if you tell me to leave. That's just one more thing we'd have to disagree about. If I have to chain myself to a bookshelf to prove that, I will." He lifted Neelo's chin higher and they smirked. "That's how much I belong with you." Neelo shuddered and Talhan hummed. "Keep reading."

"What?"

"Keep reading," Talhan murmured, a mischievous smirk on his face. "And when you want me to stop, stop reading."

Neelo gulped, picking up the book with shaking hands and read aloud the words. "'Her lips traced up the knight's neck.'"

Talhan rolled onto his side and leaned in until his lips skimmed across Neelo's neck. Neelo trembled at the sensation, their skin tingling in the echoes of his touch. Talhan's mouth trailed up to their lips, hovering a hair's breadth away. "Do you want to keep reading?"

Neelo panted a shallow breath. Their voice was barely a rasp as they read: "'She placed a kiss on the shell of the knight's ear and whispered her promises of pleasure.'"

Talhan smiled, waiting so close that Neelo could taste his breath on their tongue. His mouth roved over the shell of their pointed ear as he planted a soft kiss to it and whispered, "I want to worship every inch of your body until you are moaning my name."

Neelo's lips parted as their gaze lifted to Talhan's mouth.

In response, he skimmed his lips against theirs in a taunting featherlight kiss. "Keep reading." It was no longer a request.

"'Her hand slid down the knight's body and unbuckled her belt.'" Neelo sucked in a sharp breath as Talhan repeated the action. "'Dipping her hand between the knight's legs.'"

Talhan's hand slid under Neelo's belly and into the waistband of Neelo's trousers, cupping them with their palm as Neelo arched into his touch. They panted, looking from the book to Talhan.

His eyes were filled with molten heat, his voice a wanton growl. "Keep. Reading."

Neelo tossed the book aside and threw their arms around Talhan's neck. "Fuck the book."

Talhan laughed in surprise as Neelo pulled their mouth to his. A low groan rumbled from Talhan's lips as he kissed Neelo, his chest coming down upon theirs, pinning them to the earth.

"Touch me," Neelo whispered and Talhan groaned in response as his fingers cupping them pressed into Neelo's flesh.

A strange sort of pride burned in Neelo, that they had commanded this fae warrior and he'd been all too keen to oblige. They'd decided they wanted something and took it. But their pride morphed quickly to pleasure as Talhan slid his fingers over them, swirling in their wet heat in long, slow strokes.

Neelo moaned, arching into his touch. His fingers deftly worked over them, pulling sweet flickers of euphoria out with each circle and glide.

Neelo's hand drifted to Talhan's belt and they rasped out the words, "Do you want me to touch you?"

"Gods, yes," Talhan hissed, burying his head in their neck as they freed him from his belt. Nerves coursed through Neelo again at the size of him. They stroked him tentatively at first and Talhan pushed into their hand in a steady rhythm until they understood.

His fingers circled them faster as Neelo's hand matched his pace. Each touch ratcheted their pulse higher until they were tingling from the crown of their head to the tips of their toes. Nothing had ever felt like this. Nothing in the world had ever felt this good. And they realized that the act itself was only the smallest part of the thrill. It was the person doing it that made their core flood with heat. Books had made them warm.

This was actual flame.

Talhan Catullus. The Golden Eagle. The most handsome and skilled fae warrior in all of Okrith had his hands between their legs and was moaning in their ear and seemed just as desperate for this moment as Neelo was themself. And right then, Neelo knew, knew deep down in their bones what this was, could feel it etched into their very soul even if they feared saying it aloud.

They dug the fingers of their free hand into Talhan's shoulder, grabbing tighter as the world spun out from under them. The pleasure shooting through them lifted them higher and higher . . . except now they battled the sensation building through their body. Panic began to set in, the feeling too strong, like being dragged out to sea by a mighty riptide. All of their boldness yielded to that building feeling.

Gods, what were they doing? They were suddenly acutely aware of the croak of the frogs and the wind on their skin, as if they could crawl their mind away from this moment and the fae warrior touching them. And . . . shit, this was not what they should be thinking about right now and now they were mad at themself for not thinking about Talhan again and—

"I'm here," Talhan whispered, his hot breath in their ear, somehow knowing exactly what Neelo needed to pull them back into their body. "We're here, together. No one else." His fingers circled them faster, making Neelo's swirling thoughts evaporate. Their senses homed back toward that mounting desire building in them, this time with even more intensity. Again, though, they fought it, writhing beneath him, their breathing growing frantic as they clawed a hand down Talhan's back.

"I've got you." Talhan groaned against their neck. "You can let go. I've got you."

With his words, Neelo shattered. The waves they thought would crash into them roared through them instead, filling them with a powerful ecstasy they'd never felt before. Talhan pumped into their hand faster and faster before barking out a matching cry. Starlight flickered behind Neelo's eyes, their core clenching in flutters as bolt after bolt of lightning flashed beneath their skin. Talhan finally removed his hand and collapsed beside them, pulling Neelo into his solid chest.

Neelo's lips pressed into Talhan's shoulder where the neck of his tunic was pulled askew and Talhan placed his chin on their head. Emotions squeezed their throat, that moment, everything between them, suddenly feeling so raw, so big; it was terrifying and thrilling all at once. They tucked their forehead down into Talhan's chest and his fingers squeezed them tighter, as if he also felt the shift between them.

"You know I'm yours, right?" Talhan murmured as Neelo listened to his slowing heart.

Neelo didn't nod, didn't respond, afraid to do anything, afraid that doing anything would change this feeling, and just let the soft rhythm of Talhan's heart and his slow, steady breaths lull them to sleep.

CHAPTER TWENTY-SEVEN

The northern shoreline dipped in and out in erratic patterns
that made Neelo's head swim with a touch of vertigo. The
coastal path became narrower and narrower until they had to
abandon their horses in the nearest village to keep heading forward.

The confused looks the locals gave them made it clear they didn't
have many visitors in this remote region. Everything from the forest
to the birdsong was slightly strange and warped. It was the Southern
Court Neelo knew well, but this close to the High Mountain foothills,
the terrain was steeper, the snakes and insects smaller, and the paths
unmaintained, consumed by tall grasses.

"Any minute now, we're going to reach a dead end," Talhan groused.

Neelo held the map aloft, pointing at the circled area. "It's just
north of here."

"You've been saying that all morning." Talhan slashed at the grasses
with his sword, revealing little beige lizards, who leapt for cover. "And
what if it is only accessible by sea?"

"Then we'll double back and hire a boat."

"But we could have just hired a boat when we were back in—"

"Don't start with me again," Neelo grumbled, making Talhan
chuckle. "I don't like ships. Those dark hulls feel like a tomb, completely

at the mercy of the sea. Not a single ship's captain can outmaneuver the Goddess of Monsoon Winds." They stepped over a lazy python, basking across the stones on the path. The snake didn't even raise its head, and, until Neelo saw its flicking forked tongue, they wondered if it was dead. "You should be grateful I managed the first day's voyage and didn't make you trek through the thickest part of the jungle. If we can go by foot from here, we will."

"A boat would be quicker, though. And we're not going out to sea. There's no mighty ocean waves." Talhan waved out toward the Crushwold. "We're on a river."

Neelo scowled at the choppy, white-capped peaks kicked up by a wind coming from the High Mountains. "A turbulent and unpredictable river. We walk."

"Gods, you're stubborn," Talhan said, sighing. "I'm regretting not taking the inland road now. I'm going to burn to a crisp."

He dropped his heavy pack to the ground with a thud, finally making the python slither off into the grasses. Neelo wondered how much more wildlife hid just an arm's reach away, and they prayed there was nothing stalking them.

Talhan grasped the hemline of his sweat-stained tunic.

"What are you doing?" Neelo bit the inside of their cheek as Talhan whipped his tunic over his head, revealing his golden tan skin and muscled torso.

"I'm protecting my face from burning off," he said, twisting his tunic around his head until his face was shaded like from the brim of a hat.

Neelo's eyes dipped down to the trail of dark hair heading straight below his waistband. Neelo instantly regretted not tracking down more Arboan hats in Westdale. They'd brought clothes appropriate for town living—where shade was only ever a few paces away. The map made it seem like they could get to the caves and back in one day, but whoever had drawn the map had a terrible sense of scale. Neelo had half a mind to track the mapmaker down just to tell them about their flawed designs.

"What are you thinking about?" Talhan's voice dropped an octave and Neelo realized they were still staring at that trail of hair that led below his belt, all the while contemplating map design.

Neelo folded their arms and arched their brow. "Mapmaking."

"Naturally."

They probably should've been thinking about his glorious form. Well, now they *were* thinking about him, and about the previous night, which had been replaying in their mind incessantly all day. Never did they think that story they'd read so many times would play out in real life, but Gods, it made them want to fish every salacious book off their shelves to see if they could act those out too.

Talhan groaned as he hefted the pack back onto his shoulders. "You've definitely put rocks in here, haven't you?"

Neelo snickered. "Just some books."

"I thought you said you brought three to the markets?" Talhan frowned. "How many books did you *acquire* in Westdale?"

They looked to the bright, cloudless sky, counting in their head. "Five."

"Five?"

Neelo's cheeks dimpled. "Impressed I could narrow it down that much?"

"You needed *five* more books for this trip that you thought would take less than a day?"

"Some aren't that long. Besides, I might not be in the mood for one. I wanted to have options."

"Well, your *options* are breaking my spine," Talhan growled.

"Please," Neelo said, waving their hand up and down his muscular physique. "You used to carry cast-iron cookware halfway across the realm as Hale's soldier. You look fine."

Talhan straightened his shoulders and kept walking, letting Neelo trail behind him down the narrow path. "*Fine,* the Heir says," Talhan grumbled. "*Fine.*"

They kept walking until one side of the path dropped off into the wild waters of the Crushwold River, the other dense, impenetrable jungle. The thin strip of earth pushed them right to the brink of the river's edge.

"Are you offended I called you 'fine'?" Neelo asked as Talhan continued to mutter to himself.

"No," he said too quickly, making Neelo scoff.

"You look more than fine, Tal. You know I don't have to tell you that." That made the muttering stop.

"What do I look like?"

"A warrior. A Sun God," Neelo said, more to themself than to him. "Like something out of a book."

"Ah, so you *were* thinking about last night," he said wickedly.

Neelo's pulse sped up. "Maybe a little."

"Maybe I was too . . . a little," Talhan added. "Maybe I'm hoping that one of these books I'm carrying has another story in it like that."

Neelo's cheeks burned. "They do."

"You are mischief, Neelo Emberspear, and I love it. No one else gets to see it: the boat-commandeering, book-stealing mischief-maker you are. But that's who you've always been around me and you never have to change."

His footsteps didn't pause as if he was just casually chatting, but his words made Neelo feel like they were free-falling. They were mischief . . . and he loved it. There was something about them that Talhan Catullus *loved*.

Their first instinct was that he meant it in jest—in that light, playful way of his—but Neelo couldn't deny the sincerity of his words no more than they could accept them. How many times would they need to hear his truth before they allowed themself to believe it? Were they even capable of every believing it, let alone embracing it? They didn't know, but Neelo savored that sentence in their mind, pressing it into their memory like pressing a dried flower between the pages of a book.

There are a lot of things I love about you too, they wanted to say, but held it in.

Talhan turned the corner up ahead and stopped. "I don't think anyone is hiding a fleet around here," he muttered.

Neelo inched up behind him and leaned past to see the three bays curving into the riverside. Deep inlets cut into the land like the bite marks of a giant beast. From the waterline, the forest shot straight up into thick jungle. Vines and shrubbery with needlelike leaves covered the mountainous hills of black rock.

"Please tell me we don't have to climb up and over those," Talhan grumbled.

Neelo surveyed the sharp volcanic rock and the eddies of dark swirling river water. Tropical birds sang in the trees, flying from hill to hill. They scanned along the shoreline to where the path disappeared amongst the blackened stone.

Talhan started, "We should turn b—"

"Shh," Neelo commanded. The strange echoes of the bird's song made them pause and narrow their eyes. "There." They pointed to a spot in the rock where bright green parrots flew between the vines and back past them again. "That's the cave. Can you hear the echo of their song?"

"You think they sailed a ship into there?" Talhan asked incredulously.

"They could've pulled the vines and foliage back down like a curtain to hide the entrance," Neelo said. "We'll have to climb up to the top there and then scale down to the rocks that lead in."

Neelo pushed past him to take the lead and Talhan grabbed their elbow, making them whirl back.

"For someone who doesn't like adventure, you're awfully ready to jump into danger. Why don't you let me—you know, the trained warrior—go and check it out first?"

"I'm not letting you go in there alone," Neelo said resolutely.

The lines around Talhan's eyes crinkled and he pulled Neelo closer, his other hand wrapping around the back of their neck as he dropped his lips to theirs. His mouth lingered against Neelo's, the kiss fervent but soft, as if he was desperate to kiss them again.

"Just as I said," Talhan murmured against their mouth. "Pure mischief."

"They might've left a few guards behind," Neelo whispered across his lips. "Nothing the Golden Eagle can't handle, but I'm not letting you go in there without me."

Talhan smirked and kissed them again, his tongue dipping into their mouth and making them groan. He released Neelo with a snarl of frustration. "To be continued," he said.

Neelo nodded, a secret grin pulling at their lips. "Let's get you into the shade," they said with a chuckle. "Though if you'd like to leave your shirt off, I wouldn't protest."

Talhan planted one more kiss atop Neelo's head and pushed past them to take the lead again. "Come on, troublemaker, let's go find us some treasure."

NEELO'S VISION SPOTTED with flashes of light as their fae vision adjusted to the darkness. The cave was eerily still. Waves gently lapped upon the black rocks and a chorus of twittering birds flew through the cave mouth, but, as they crept deeper, there wasn't a single movement. At first Neelo thought the cave was empty, then they spotted the towering outline against the far wall.

The charred hull of a giant ship.

Neelo's eyes widened at the sight. The ship looked one windy day away from sinking, wrecked up against the far side of the rock wall. Splinters and debris bobbed in the water and Neelo's stomach turned sour as they searched the darkness for bodies. Were it not for the vines covering the entrance, Neelo would've guessed the ship wrecked there in a storm.

"What in the Gods' names," Talhan whispered, pausing every few steps to assess the ship again as if it might jolt to life and attack them. "How did it end up here?"

"Do you think it's one of Augustus's ships?" Neelo's eyes strained to make out the details in the darkness. "The rest of the fleet was washed ashore in Arboa. Maybe this was the only one that made it up the Crushwold?"

"Only to overshoot Wynreach, burnt to a crisp, and be wrecked in the northernmost caves of the Southern Court?" Talhan's hand gripped the hilt of his dagger.

Was this decaying ship the clue they'd been hoping for? One filled with Adisa Monroe's secrets? Or was it just random wreckage with no connection to the violet witch or Augustus's fleet? They'd expected something more—battle-ready ships with a crew still guarding them, or at least a ship that didn't look charred beyond recognition. What evidence could possibly remain intact on a boat so badly damaged?

"Maybe the boat was stolen by thieves and abandoned here once they realized whose vessel they stole?" Neelo pondered, looking over the blackened hull and singed sails. "Maybe they tried to burn it down after all and it drifted in here instead of sinking and they tried to hide the remnants?"

"Remind me to hire whoever built this thing when I need a ship." Talhan's voice rose above a whisper, seemingly growing more confident with each step that they were alone. "It seems damn near indestructible."

"So the merchant in the marketplace had this map not because he was part of Augustus's crew but because he stole this ship?" Neelo crept closer, the scent of burnt wood and wet timber filling their senses. Would they even be able to board the vessel without falling through the deck? "But then why did he have the poison dagger? And why did the map have the Mhenbic words found in Adisa Monroe's journal?"

Talhan shrugged. "Maybe he found it on board?"

Neelo stared up at the ship that loomed like the charred corpse of a once glorious beast. "And *why* did he want to poison you?"

"Believe it or not, a lot of Easterners wish I was dead." Talhan shook his head. "The Catullus family has many enemies, mostly made by my mother."

"Now that, I understand," Neelo said with a huff as they folded their arms and tried to hide their disappointment. There had to be more here. This couldn't be it. "What do we do now?"

Talhan pointed to the fraying rope leading to the top deck. "We climb aboard and investigate."

Neelo hugged their arms tighter around their chest. "That doesn't seem like a good idea."

"We didn't come all this way to gawk at the hull of a burnt ship," Talhan goaded. "You said you wanted answers."

"I'd hoped, though it seemed unlikely, that the stores of blooming amethyst killing my mother and poisoning my people had been left aboard an abandoned ship." Neelo's shoulders drooped at the thought that this might be a dead end. "But that doesn't seem possible, and I doubt Adisa Monroe would just leave another journal lying around for us to decipher."

They needed to find out Adisa Monroe's plans for the Southern Court. It would be much harder to protect their people without knowing. Harder too if the amethyst suppliers were all in the East. Even while the Eastern throne remained unclaimed, the Heir of Saxbridge stepping foot into a foreign kingdom, destroying businesses, and interrogating its people was still tantamount to a declaration of war. Yet another reason the Eastern Court needed to elect a new sovereign sooner rather than later. Until then, they'd have to deal with this matter from the Southern Court side.

"Come on, be a pirate with me," Talhan teased.

Neelo let out a long breath and glanced up at the threadbare rope. "Fine," they grumped. "Hopefully, there will be something left behind."

"Either way, it will make an excellent story to tell at parties."

"So long as you're the one telling it," Neelo snarked.

Talhan's grin widened. "I'd be delighted."

Neelo took the rope and began hauling themself up toward the deck of the ship, and they realized they'd just implied that Talhan would be in their future. Were they finally ready to admit it? Now? In the dark cave beside a ghost ship? Perfect timing. But the thrill still raced through them. Maybe they were done pushing Talhan away. Maybe they could save their mother and let the fae warrior stay in the South with them too. Maybe they could have it all. But as they swung their feet over the ship's side and onto the charred deck, all the excitement in them swiftly shifted to dread.

CHAPTER TWENTY-EIGHT

Bones scattered across the darkened wood. Some were distinctly human, others . . . not. Neelo's stomach clenched as they surveyed the intricate patterns of the bones. They weren't just dumped on the deck, they were *placed*, decorated as if making a Mhenbic rune for a spell.

"Shit," Talhan hissed as he landed beside Neelo.

This was witchcraft—ancient, dark witchcraft—but Neelo couldn't understand the markings.

"I've never seen these symbols before," they whispered. The hair at the back of their neck prickled and they had the distinctive feeling of being watched. "Has Adisa Monroe created a new spell?"

"Where did those teeth come from?" Talhan toed at a giant canine with his boot. It was easily the size of his foot, a long triangle, curved at the end like the teeth of a giant wildcat and unlike the fangs of a snake.

"An Eastern mountain lion, maybe?" Neelo dropped to a crouch and inspected the bones. "The biggest one I've ever seen."

Talhan tentatively paced across the deck to the other side, stepping over a line of thick, rusted chain. "Bri said they encountered a beast in the forests outside Swifthill. It looked like part lion, part goat, part boar—a creature *made* by someone."

"I remember." Neelo stood and circled the puzzle work of bones. "Adisa Monroe's journal had a sketch of just such a beast."

"It looks like she's been experimenting on making more creatures." Talhan frowned as he lifted a crate lid and inspected the inside. "Empty."

"Bri said the beast was commanded by that amethyst dagger," Neelo whispered. "If that's true. Adisa Monroe has no need for a human army anymore."

"An army of monsters?" Talhan shuddered. "Perfect."

Neelo's eyes scanned the perimeter. The deck was empty save for a few overturned buckets and shattered crates. What had happened here? A ritual? A sacrifice?

Talhan found some tattered scraps of sail and a broken lantern to dip the fabric in. He stomped on a protruding piece of balustrade and snapped it clean off. Neelo cocked their head, watching as Talhan wrapped the fabric around the wooden handle and produced a piece of flint from his belt. Neelo's brow furrowed in confusion as Talhan set the torch alight. They could see fine with their fae vision now that their eyes had adjusted to the dim light and there was no need for a fire.

Talhan nodded to the ladder that led down into the belly of the ship. Neelo followed his line of sight to the dark pit below. They gave him a hard shake of their head, mouthing the words, "Fuck no."

"You want answers?" Talhan arched his brow.

"Stop saying that." Neelo gritted their teeth and pushed in front of him, unwilling to admit that the Eagle's presence gave them newfound confidence. They climbed down the steep ladder, gripping the fraying rope in one hand and the creaking chains hanging from the ceiling with the other. The boat shifted so gently that Neelo had to remind themself once more that they were, in fact, on the water.

A musty stench filled the air as Neelo drifted deeper into the hull of the ship. Talhan passed them the torch and they held it aloft. They surveyed the room filled with broken-down crates and coils of thick rope. Opening the crates one by one, Neelo searched inside for clues but found nothing but more buckets, scrub brushes, and tatters of stained fabric. All the useful things seemed to have been taken when the ship was abandoned.

And certainly no amethyst blossoms.

Neelo swallowed the bile rising in their throat and went down another level, finding only a lone crate in the empty room. They cracked the lid and instantly shut it.

"Gods." Neelo coughed and gagged as the stench smacked into them. A bucket of rotted fish guts lay at the bottom of the crate, along with several rats that scurried off as the lid slammed closed.

Neelo lifted their tunic over their nose as the reek clung to them, burning their lungs. Rats squeaked and skittered across the floorboards, the sounds of their scratching filling the tiny cabin.

"Anything?" Talhan called from the floor above.

Neelo looked up to the thin slivers of light peeking through the floorboards, finding the darkened circles of Talhan's boots.

"Just some fish," Neelo snarled, fighting the urge to gag again. "Which I'll never be eating again."

As Talhan's weight shifted, trails of dust fell like dancing autumn leaves, catching the dim light. "Whoever was here picked this place pretty clean."

"There must be something," Neelo grumbled. "There has to be. Why keep that map sewed into your clothes?" they said, thinking of the human from the market. "I'll keep looking."

"Me too," Talhan said, adding hastily, "Be safe."

Neelo ventured through a hatch to the adjoining room and Talhan's footsteps faded away. The air was thicker in this room, damp and cold. The light from Talhan's torch filtered in through the cracks above them as Neelo's eyes adjusted to the darkness. Neelo scanned over the room of bunks built four high on either side of the narrow room. The fabric holding together the straw mattresses was brown with water stains—at least, they hoped they were water stains—and bits of straw poked from the fraying fabric.

It was a bare room apart from the bunks and the black trunk that sat against the far wall. Tracing their fingers along the wet wood, Neelo searched for a notch or carving, initials, anything that would reveal who owned this ship and where they were going. They took another careful step across the slippery film that had grown on the wood floor.

They glanced at the trunk, hearing the scratching of more rats inside. Groaning, they tiptoed over to the trunk and prepared for more scurrying creatures to jump out at them. But as they lifted their hand out to the latch, the whole trunk jolted.

"Curse the Gods," Neelo gritted out, snatching their hand back. The trunk rocked violently, the muffled sound of a voice coming from inside. Whoever was in there was still alive. "Shit. Talhan!" Neelo shouted.

"Yeah?" Talhan's faint voice echoed down to them.

"Come look at this." They tried to keep the panic from their voice as they added, "Now!"

The trunk danced and wobbled across the floor. Muffled grunts and groans escaping from the shaking confines—a human? A pig? A miniature monster for all they knew. Whatever was inside seemed to be making a sudden desperate bid to break free.

"What did you f . . ." Talhan's words fell away as he climbed down the hatch into the bunk room. "Gods." He paused, staring at the wobbling trunk. "Well, open it."

"*You* open it," Neelo shot back.

"You found it," Talhan hissed.

"You're the warrior."

"You're the Heir of Saxbridge."

"And as the Heir of Saxbridge, I command *you* to open the trunk."

"Fine." Talhan touched his fingers to his forehead in silent prayer and walked over to the rocking trunk. "Stop smirking."

Neelo bit the inside of their cheek. "I wasn't." They definitely were.

Talhan pounded his fist onto the trunk lid. "Hold still," he commanded to whatever was inside. "We're going to get you out."

"Why are you talking to it? We don't even know it's a person!"

"Never hurts to be polite."

They gaped at him as he flipped the latch, immediately stepping back and covering his mouth from the acrid burning stench of urine and bile. Neelo's nostrils flared as they buried their face further into their tunic. Their eyes stung as they took a step closer.

A figure, bound and gagged, sat up from the trunk. If it was a person, they weren't far from turning into something else, either through starvation or madness. They wore nothing but a flimsy undershirt and baggy linen breaches stained with filth. Their eyes were bloodshot from screaming, blond hair brown with dirt, but those hollow blue eyes . . . those Neelo recognized.

Cole.

The brown witch Neelo had first met in Silver Sands Harbor was almost unrecognizable. The last they had heard of him was his hasty retreat from a dinner party in the Northern Court. How a brown witch managed to evade Renwick Vostemur's guards, they'd never know . . . unless they could get him to spill his secrets now. Maybe that was witch magic too.

"What in the fucking Gods' names . . ." Talhan gaped at him. "All this time the other courts were hunting for you and you were in the South? What are you doing here?"

"He can't answer you," Neelo muttered. "Get his gag."

"I'm not touching him," Talhan growled. "Whatever he did to end up in this place, I'm sure he deserved it."

"Probably." Neelo stiffened. "But he also has more answers for us when his mouth isn't stuffed with cloth." They tiptoed over to Cole, who sat collapsed against the lid of the trunk, his eyes half hooded from exhaustion. He gave Neelo a wary look. "I'm going to untie the gag," Neelo carefully said to him. "Don't fucking bite me, witch."

Cole nodded as Neelo untied the tight knot at the back of his matted head. When the gag dropped from his mouth, he spluttered panting breaths, folding over the rim of the trunk as thick trails of saliva dripped from his mouth.

"Water," he rasped.

"This isn't a bloody tavern," Talhan jeered, but Neelo shot him a look and he untied his waterskin and tossed it to Neelo.

"So much for being polite," they muttered, and Talhan had the presence of mind to look a little ashamed.

As Neelo held it up to Cole's mouth, the brown witch closed his eyes and drank, savoring each sip and licking his cracked lips. Neelo pulled the waterskin away and Cole leaned forward for more.

"Slowly," Neelo said. "Or you'll throw it all back up."

Talhan folded his arms. "Besides, we haven't decided if you're worth keeping alive yet. Why waste the water on a traitor?" They shot him another look, but this time he didn't back down, his warrior training superseding his normal disposition, and they were reminded once again that for all his lighthearted jokes, Talhan was a trained killer. "What? That's what he is, polite or no."

Cole leaned his exhausted head back against the trunk lid. "Thank you, anyway." His voice was scratchy, breaking at every other word as if he'd been strangled or screaming for days.

"What happened?" Neelo whispered, looking over the mottled bruises covering his pale skin.

"Where to begin." Cole blew out a mirthless laugh. "I was born in the foothills of the High Mountains to a brown witch apothecary. I had two older sisters, both powerful brown witches in their own right, and a younger sister and brother too, putting me smack in the middle, the most unforgettable of the lot."

"Screw it, put the gag back and leave him," Talhan said, pushing off the beam and stalking across the room. "He's clearly delirious."

"I'm sorry." Cole's eyes widened, his smile disturbingly giddy. "This is the first time I can't feel her claws in my mind in days."

Talhan paused. "Who's claws?"

"You know who," Cole snarled. "The witch who calls herself Baba."

"Adisa Monroe?" Neelo asked. "How? Why?"

"Because I tried to warn the others." Cole sneered and then laughed, his emotions swinging from one extreme to the next. "Her shadow has covered my homeland for my entire life, and I've never been able to rid myself of her. She found me once long ago and the second I stepped foot out of the West, she found me again."

"*Found* you?"

"Found my mind," Cole said.

"What in the Gods' names does that mean?" Talhan's hand fell to the hilt of his dagger as he leaned against the bunk ladder.

"It means that she can whisper into the minds of those controlled by her violet witch magic." Cole's words were slow and slurred.

"Whispers," Neelo said, looking at Talhan as recognition lit across his face.

"Like from that ledger in Valtene," he replied.

Neelo nodded. "The people were afflicted with *whispers*. That must've been from Adisa Monroe. She was practicing her mind control, growing stronger even before she was unearthed."

"But how did she go from whispering in her grave"—Talhan gestured around the room—"to all of this?"

"The dagger," Cole said, his eyes darting between them. "The amethyst dagger. Once she was reunited with it, her power became unparalleled." His face puckered in pain as if even the act of breathing was painful. "The red witches weren't the only coven to make talismans of incredible power. The Immortal Blade is nothing compared to what Adisa Monroe can do with that dagger."

"And who had the amethyst dagger all this time?"

Cole blinked at them as if afraid to speak the words. "Kira Ashby."

Talhan sucked in a sharp breath. "Hale's mother?"

"She's my relative, of sorts. Our mothers were cousins. Making her another of Adisa's descendants," Cole said. "Though I doubt how much Kira knew about the dagger. A family heirloom, perhaps, but certainly didn't know its power."

Talhan's eyes widened. "You left that dinner right after Hale mentioned his mother's middle name was Monroe. Is that why?"

Cole nodded.

Talhan's brow creased in confusion. "But she's fae?"

"She's *part* fae," Cole added callously. "Adisa had two lines: fae and witch. My line, the witch line, in the West, and the fae line in the East. The violet witch bloodline is small indeed. But Adisa has magic now that will breed powerful violet witches from her bloodlines again."

Talhan froze. "What does that mean?"

"It means with the help of her magic, whosoever has violet witch blood will be able to sire a child with all the violet witches' ancient powers again."

"If Kira is her descendant, then so is Hale," Neelo whispered. "Would she do that to him?"

"Judging from her journal, I suspect she has a plan already in the works," Cole panted and spat over the edge of the trunk. "I hear her whispering about him over and over again: the smallest seed. The youngest in her bloodline. She's determined to find him. All her plans seem to hedge around him."

"All these fucking plans," Talhan growled. "We need to warn Hale."

"Warn *him*? You need to warn *everyone*. You have no idea." Cole barked out a laugh that made Neelo shudder. "She plans on getting her claws into the rest of Okrith, pulling her true heir back to the East, and using him to take the throne."

"But aren't you her descendant too?" Neelo scanned his hollow face. "Why would she abandon you here?"

"When I heard Kira's name at that dinner in Murreneir, I remembered a note from my sister Rose." Cole sighed, his eyes rolling back as if remembering the heady pull of the drug. "She said she needed to find a fae named Kira. She said Kira was a distant cousin of ours and that our family might be a bigger part of something than she realized. It was the words of madness. Rose was so far gone by then, I didn't believe her. She told me that I needed to stay in Swifthill, stay hidden. I didn't believe her warning, but I was so busy with my work, trying to become the royal brown witch, that I stayed in Swifthill anyways." His voice faded to a whisper. "She took her own life not long after that and the life of my nephew too."

Neelo picked at their fingers as they turned Cole's haunting words over in their mind.

"That still doesn't explain why you ran from that dinner in Murreneir," Talhan said. He shifted the torch to his other hand, making the shadows twist and stretch. "Or how you ended up here."

"That letter has always haunted me," Cole said. "It was only in Murreneir that I finally believed the truth in it. What do you think would happen to me if I accused the *King* of the High Mountain Court that his mother was part violet witch and plotting with a High Priestess to overthrow the realm?" Talhan snarled and took a step forward. "Exactly," Cole said with a bitter laugh. "I didn't want to be killed for even suggesting it. My ancestor wants to kill me for trying to stop her and the most powerful fae family in the realm would want to kill me for thinking I was on her side. I was wedged between two warring waves. I thought if I fled and tried to find Kira, it would save me from going under." He looked down at his soiled clothes. "Obviously, that was a mistake."

"Clearly." Talhan eyed Cole, his nose wrinkling. "How long since you've eaten? Hopefully less time than since you've bathed."

"I was kept imprisoned here for . . . Mother Moon, weeks? Months? I don't know." He shivered, his face wincing against an unknown pain. "There was a small retinue of guards. They beat me, starved me, forced me to work on her spells, continue deciphering her madness and honing her poisons . . . but a couple days ago, something spooked them." Talhan and Neelo exchanged knowing glances—the attack in the markets of Arboa. "They threw me in this box and left."

"Gods," Neelo muttered, feeling somehow responsible for worsening Cole's predicament. "I'm sorry, Cole."

"It won't end." He shook his head, his eyes flying wide and manic. "It won't end until you stop her."

"So how exactly do we stop Adisa Monroe?"

Cole lifted his bloodshot eyes to Neelo. "You kill her."

"She's immortal," Neelo countered. "*How* do we kill her?"

"With the weapon that gave her power: her dagger." Cole groaned and leaned forward, trying to clutch his head with his bound hands. "It's the only thing that can kill her," he whined.

"What's wrong?" Neelo bent down to touch his back.

Talhan took a step forward and hooked his finger into Neelo's belt, pulling them away from the distressed brown witch. "When will we ever be close enough to kill her?" they said instead. "We don't even know where she is."

"That opportunity is closer than you think, Your Highness," Cole said with a twisted smirk, not quite the person he'd been just seconds ago, his chest heaving as he groaned against a sudden pain. What was happening to him? "I believe her current shill, Augustus Norwood, will be attending the Summer Solstice in Saxbridge." He blinked and shouted as if coming up for air. "I'm sorry, I . . ." His eyes filled with a sheen similar to the dulled metal of the poisoned blade. "They're coming for you."

"Who?"

"You need to kill me," he whispered, his blue eyes filling with tears. "They'll leave me here, they'll . . ." His eyes rolled back and when they opened them again, his face was eerily calm. His lips twisted into a wicked smirk and Neelo knew that the person looking back at them was no longer Cole. "Hello, Neelo Emberspear."

The hatch door slammed shut above them.

CHAPTER TWENTY-NINE

Neelo leapt at the crash of wood from above.

"No!" Talhan whirled to the hatch, banging it with his fist, but the wood didn't budge.

The ship jolted to the side, throwing Neelo to the ground and extinguishing their torch. The cabin was thrown into darkness, Neelo's fae vision only making out the shapes of the shadows around them.

"What was that?" Talhan shouted, searching for the source of the sound as the ship rocked again.

A whooshing roar filled the hull as the ship began tilting. Talhan and Neelo fell to the back wall . . . which was now below their feet.

The ship rocked wildly again, throwing Talhan hard against the bunks, his dagger falling from his scabbard and into the black water pooling below them. Cole scrambled to an awkward stand as water began rushing up from below his feet.

"Shit," Talhan growled, climbing up the bunks like a ladder and banging on the hatch again. He turned back to Neelo, fear filling his eyes. "I think we'll have to swim down and out a porthole."

The haze in Cole's eyes was pure wrath, and Neelo knew it was Adisa Monroe staring back at them. Dark brown flames flickered in his eyes, casting the space in eerie light. "Eagles don't swim, Lord

Catullus. There's no way out, Heir of Saxbridge. Your reign has ended before it's even began."

"The South has done nothing to hurt the violet witches," Neelo snarled. "Why are you going after me?"

Cole—Adisa—cackled. "Because your court buys up all of our sacred flowers." An unsettling growl escaped Cole's mouth. "And you waste it on your revels without a care. And because the Emberspears never lifted a finger to help the witches, partying while my sisters to the north were enslaved and tortured. The rule of fae has ended. Witches will be the true power in Okrith once more.

"In short—because I *can*."

"We've stopped buying your flowers," Neelo pushed. Talhan's fists frantically banged on the wood behind them. "I put an end to it." Though, in truth, they hadn't—but they were going to when they got back to Saxbridge.

"You lie. And now it's too late," the witch hissed. "Our magic is too powerful for you Southerners and you are too weak to be my ally, Heir of Saxbridge. The only way forward is to end the reign of Emberspear and take the South for our own."

"Never," Neelo snarled. "I won't let you."

"It's good to see a spark still lives in you, little Emberspear. Adorable, really." The witch chortled. "But it is far too late to grow a backbone now. Even if your brute of a husband breaks down that hatch, there's five Eastern fae soldiers standing above your head, another dozen waiting on the shoreline." Cole cocked his head. "You think they didn't warn me you'd found the map in Arboa?" Another wicked cackle. "The wise humans and fae already bow to the power of the witches." Cole's eyes narrowed. "And when I heard, I couldn't pass up the opportunity. Destroying Saxbridge will be so much easier without you around, Heir of nothing."

"Why don't you come here yourself, coward?" Neelo hissed. "Why send Cole?"

"And what? Live in a cave on the off-chance you showed up? You really are a naive little recluse, aren't you? I don't have to step into the center of the room to pull all the strings, dear." The witch cackled. "And this useless, traitorous descendant of mine deserves what's coming to him. He is not the smallest seed. He is not the future king. He—like you—is nothing."

A scream rent from Neelo's lips as Cole picked up Talhan's fallen dagger with his bound hands and aimed it straight for his own throat.

The tip of the blade paused just above Cole's pale flesh, his arms shaking with restraint, battling his own hands. When he spoke, it was Cole's voice again. "Get out of here!"

"Gods." Talhan lurched forward, swatting the dagger out of Cole's hand. The dagger disappeared into the rising water. "Hang on, Cole," Talhan barked. "Fight her!"

The ship swayed and Talhan's boot slipped, falling back into the water that rapidly rose toward his waist. Neelo's arms shook from clinging to the bunk.

"We've got to swim down and out," Talhan panted.

Neelo shook their head. "And what about the soldiers on the shoreline?"

"One thing at a time! We'll swim out into the Crushwold, let the current take us downriver and then make our way to land."

"What . . . we . . ." Neelo searched all around them, desperate for another answer.

Talhan took a deep breath and ducked beneath the shadowed water. Neelo swallowed, waiting for his head to emerge. The seconds stretched by like hours. Talhan resurfaced, sweeping his short, wet hair off his face.

"The door's open now. There's three holes blown in the side. We'll swim out the largest . . ." Something about Talhan's pause tied Neelo's stomach in knots.

"What?" Neelo asked.

"My foot is tangled in rope," Talhan said. "Hold on."

He took another long suck of air and disappeared under the water. The darkness rushed higher, soaking Neelo in cold river water. When Talhan emerged again, his head barely broke the surface. He sucked in a sharp breath.

"I—"

"Shit." Neelo leapt from where they clung to the bunks and into the water. They dove down, pulling themself along Talhan's body and feeling for where the rope coiled around his ankle. They yanked his boot off, tugging with incredible force as their lungs burned. The boot finally was pulled free, but the rope's grip was impossibly tight. Their lungs seized, desperate for air and Neelo resurfaced. "I need to cut it."

"You need to get out of here, Neelo," Talhan shouted, his mouth already swallowing some water. "Before the cabin fills and you drown."

"I told you before: I'm not leaving you behind," Neelo seethed.

Talhan's arms sloshed across the jaw-deep water and grabbed Neelo by the cheeks, pulling them into a scorching kiss. "Please, love. Go."

"I'm cutting you free," Neelo snarled. "Kiss me on the other side."

They took another suck of air and dove again, battling against the darkness and the odd angle of the ship. When they collided with Cole's flailing body, their stomach roiled, but they kept moving, feeling past him.

Their fingers skimmed the hilt of the dagger twice before they were finally able to grab a hold of it. Their chest pulled, muscles straining as they denied their lungs a breath. Using Talhan's leg to pull themself deeper, they reached Talhan's ankle. Uncaring if they cut him in the process, they slid the blade between his trouser leg and the coiled rope, sawing back and forth. Their eyes spotted with bright stars as they labored. The rope frayed and they kept sawing, not stopping even as their body grew numb. Everything grew more distant. They couldn't feel their hands or face. No part of them felt real anymore and they wanted to sleep, wanted to breathe, wanted to drift away . . .

A hand found theirs, taking the hilt of the dagger from their grip, just as they yielded to the darkness.

CHAPTER THIRTY

A distant voice screamed their name. Lips covered their own, breathing life back into them. Neelo's eyes shot open and they rolled to their side, retching up river water as a hand pounded on their back.

"Thank the fucking Gods," Talhan's voice broke and he collapsed on the sodden earth.

Neelo's senses swarmed, the world rocking below them, the heavy pelt of rain, the caw of gulls. They glanced around at the marshland and rolled onto their back, taking deep gulps of air.

The earth squelched beneath Neelo as they collapsed backward and the summer rains showered them as the choppy river splashed through the reeds. Their body still felt like it was being tossed in the current and their stomach lurched with drops and sways until acid rose up their throat.

"Where are we?" they croaked as the fresh air and rain washed away their nausea.

"I don't know," Talhan rasped. "It felt like hours, but was probably only minutes. Catch your breath. We can't stay here."

They tried to obey, but it hurt to breathe. Still, they tried even as thunder cracked overhead and wind whipped strands of their wet hair across the mud. Memories swirled around and around and then with a flash of lightning it all came swarming back to them: the bones, the boat, Cole, the trap, Talhan's foot stuck . . . Neelo rolled to their side and yanked Talhan into a tight embrace as mud speckled their face.

His sodden clothes pressed into them as he dropped his head into their shoulder. "I thought I lost you." His voice broke. The rain was so heavy, Neelo couldn't tell if he was crying.

Their muscles strained as they silently held him, trying to fuse their bodies into one. Disbelief coursed through them as they grasped to remember what had happened. How did they survive?

"The last thing I remember, I was trying to cut you free . . ." They choked on their words and Talhan's fingers pressed in tighter to their back.

"You did," he whispered.

"And Cole?"

Talhan finally released Neelo and nodded over their shoulder. They lifted a hand over their face, shielding from the rain, and peeked out through the marshes to the first tree on the shoreline.

Cole sat unbound, hugging his knees to his chest. His eyes were closed, his mouth muttering words as if he were praying to the Rain Gods.

Neelo gaped at him. "Mother Moon. How?"

"Once you freed me, I cut loose his bindings." The waves and the steady thunk of thick droplets hitting the soil nearly drowned Talhan's voice out. "He was the first out of the ship."

"How did I survive?" Neelo tilted their face back up to the rain.

"You were semiconscious," Talhan said. "I tried to bring you round before that ship sunk, but I couldn't." He swallowed and cursed, clearly reliving the moment. "I tied you to me and swam as fast as I could. When I resurfaced, you were gone." His bottom lip wobbled and he cleared his throat. "I tried to swim with one arm and hold you aloft with the other, breathing for you, but . . . I thought that was it."

Tears trailed from the corner of Talhan's eyes and into his hair.

"I'm here," Neelo whispered, wiping away the tracks of his tears. "Hey." They rolled to their side and squinted at Talhan and tried to force a teasing tone into their voice. "When have you ever been more melancholy than me?"

Talhan rolled to face them, tucking his head into his arm. "Since I almost saw you die."

Neelo's eyes welled when Talhan didn't rise to their taunting bait. Neelo reached out to the tip of a pink scar trailing into the neckline of his tunic. "I'm not the only one who has challenged death and won." Talhan's eyes drifted closed at their gentle touch. "I thought I lost you too, not so long ago."

"You almost did," Talhan whispered.

"Where is the one that nearly cost you your life in Valtene?" they asked and Talhan pointed to his stomach and thigh.

Waves roared around them, sloshing river water across the marsh. The hot humid air was a relief against the cold onslaught. Talhan peeked his eyes open. Reaching behind his neck, he hauled his wet tunic over his head and chucked it against the nearest tree.

Neelo gasped at the new mottled bruises across his abdomen and visions of him crashing through debris in the pitch-black hull flashed through their mind. They had no memory of the escape but if they were semiconscious . . . had they kicked and flailed in his grip? Had they done this? It looked like he'd battled a sea monster to get them to shore. Neelo reached out and touched the blooming wounds. "Gods," they breathed. They blinked in surprise as their eyes began to well again.

"Neelo," Talhan whispered, reaching a hand out and cupping their cheek. "I'm alive."

"If you get to cry, I get to cry." Their tears hid amongst the raindrops. The only sign was the warmth of each droplet. Talhan smirked and swiped their tears with his thumb. "I swear I felt it that day." They sniffed. "I felt like someone had rammed me straight through with a sword all the way in Saxbridge. I was pacing like a wildcat all day long and didn't know why, and then Renwick contacted me."

"He did?" Talhan's eyebrows shot up. "What did he say?"

Neelo swallowed the hard lump in their throat. "He said he wanted to brief me on the battle and to prepare me for what was to come. He told me Augustus Norwood had plans to destroy the Southern Court and I've been trying to figure out how he meant to destroy us ever since." Neelo's gaze flitted to Talhan's amber eyes and back to the scar across his torso. "He told me you were gravely injured too, but that you had survived."

"I did," Talhan whispered, swiping the droplets from Neelo's cheek. "I had a lot of things to fight for. Renwick reminded me of that."

Neelo lifted their wet lashes and held Talhan's molten gaze. "Am I one of them?"

"You are all of them," he whispered, leaning forward and brushing his wet lips to Neelo's own.

Neelo tasted the salt of their tears on Talhan's mouth as he gently kissed them, his warm lips enveloping their own.

A rogue wave slid through the marshes, filling Neelo's boots with water again. Talhan wrapped Neelo tightly in his arms, as if that little wave might carry them away.

"I have more to tell you," Talhan said. "But if we don't want those Eastern soldiers to find us, we need to get further south."

"Agreed." Neelo squeezed him one more time and then rolled over and wobbled to their feet.

Talhan's arms shot out and grabbed them, holding them steady. Bending their legs, Neelo lunged as if trying to balance on a rocking ship.

"You look like you're going to spew."

"Please don't say 'spew,'" Neelo said as their stomach started to turn into a burning knot again.

"Deep breaths," Talhan commanded. Neelo swallowed the saliva pooling in their mouth with a groan. "We'll cut inland until we find the trail to Westdale."

Blinking against the onslaught of rain, Neelo found Cole sat in the same position still whispering to himself. "What are we going to do with him?"

This husk of a witch was not the same person Neelo had met in Silver Sands Harbor. The Cole they'd met then was filled with curiosity, slow, astute, methodical. He seemed like a talented healer and from what Neelo could tell of him, a good person too. Now he sat hunched and wet, staring at the ground. Horrifying thoughts must have been churning through his mind, even though his expression was blank, and they had to wonder if all of those thoughts were still his own.

"Cole?" Talhan took the lead. He stepped across the boggy marshes and up onto the bank. Talhan assessed the witch for a moment before he asked, "Is she still there? Is she in your mind?"

Cole didn't move for a beat before finally shaking his head, the movement nearly imperceptible.

"Will you talk with us?" Talhan asked and Cole shook his head again.

"He needs rest," Neelo cut in. "He needs to heal. Then we can ask our questions." To interrogate him when he'd nearly died seemed more than cruel, despite how much Neelo wanted more answers. They turned to Cole. "We'll take you with us to Westdale and find you transport south to Arboa when we arrive. Nothing a few Arboan steams and green witch meals can't fix." Talhan's lip curled when he glanced at Neelo. "We can trust Sy to care for him."

"You seem to trust Ersan with a lot," Talhan muttered. "Any more graves for him to dig up?"

"I knew you were upset about that! You seriously waited to do the jealousy thing *now*?" Neelo glared at him. "Really?"

"I guess not," Talhan said, giving them an apologetic glance. "If you trust him, then Arboa it is." He gave Cole a pat on the shoulder and then lifted him by the crook of his arms. Despite being taller than even Talhan, Cole was so lean it took no effort to hoist him to his feet. Cole seemed to understand and mindlessly ambled off into the jungle.

Neelo waited until he was a few paces ahead to speak. "We shouldn't tell anyone we've found him," they whispered, looking sideways at the forest as if someone might be listening. "Not until he's talking."

"Especially not Bri," Talhan said with a huff.

Neelo hummed in agreement. "I'm sure she's got many choice words for him."

"I think it's more likely to be fists than words," Talhan added. "The sooner we part ways with Cole, the better. Not when we don't fully understand how that violet witch controlled his mind. Can she do it again? Does it fade with distance and time or once the amethyst is out of his system?" Talhan's voice lowered into a growl. "I won't be able to sleep knowing our enemies could be in his mind."

"I don't think he wants to hurt me," Neelo countered.

"But his great-great-whatever grandmother does," Talhan said pointedly. "His grandmother, who can *control his mind*."

Something Cole said on the boat flashed to the front of Neelo's thoughts. "He said Augustus Norwood will be at the Summer Solstice."

"I can't believe he's not dead." Talhan shook his head. "He has more lives than a fucking cat."

Neelo glanced at the thick canopy, counting the days. "We need to be back in Saxbridge. If he attacks the palace like he did the Lyrei Basin in the North . . ."

"He had an army of cursed witches then," Talhan countered.

"If the amethyst works as I suspect," Neelo murmured, "he won't need to bring an army. He'll be able to make one when he gets there," they said, gesturing with their head toward Cole.

Neelo made to take another step and Talhan's hands reached out to circle around Neelo's waist, holding them against his firm body. "We will be back with plenty of time. It's only a few days' trek back to Saxbridge from Westdale."

"Do we have a few days?"

"We have what we have. Let's worry about one thing at a time—like getting away from here."

They nodded. "I'll try. But it's so hard—the picture Cole painted is bleaker than I thought."

"How much bleaker?"

"I assumed Adisa Monroe's plan was to distract the South with her potent brews while she took over the Eastern Court." Neelo rubbed their thumb across their sore shoulder. "But now I've realized she doesn't just want the East. She wants all of Okrith bowing to the violet witches."

"I heard her"—he pointed to Cole—"*him*, say that, but is it even possible?"

"It's definitely possible! Their sacred flower—the source of their powers—is everywhere. It's in their potions, their poisons, perfumes, lotions, candles, you name it. And nowadays it's in *our* things as well." They looked at Cole's mop of blond hair like a beacon cutting through the forest ahead of them. "And if she can use it as a conduit for her power, Adisa Monroe may soon have her claws in us all."

Talhan clenched his jaw. "How long until Saxbridge runs out of their current brew?"

"Not long if Sy kept to his word." Neelo and Talhan trailed after the lanky brown witch. "We get more deliveries from Arboa every week, but we should contact the others, warn everyone to get rid of everything that contains that purple flower, and find whoever supplies my mother's brew stores. There is no doubt in my mind that it too contains the amethyst flower now."

"Are we going to tell Remy and Hale about what Cole said?" Talhan hedged, his shoulders bunching higher as if readying to fight.

"We have to," Neelo said, feeling the same fear gripping their gut. If Adisa Monroe knew of a way to create more violet witches from her line . . . "When they come to Saxbridge for the Solstice, we'll tell them everything. They can't be in the dark about this."

Talhan nodded. "Better to do it face-to-face. Do you think Hale is the rightful heir that Cole was speaking of? The smallest seed or whatever?"

Neelo swallowed. "I don't know. Adisa Monroe seems to think so. And seems to be willing to burn down the world to see that seed grow." Neelo swatted through a swarm of mosquitoes and ducked under a low-hanging branch. They glanced over their shoulder at Talhan. "When we get home, promise me we won't have any more adventures for a long time."

"What if I promise they'll be fun adventures?" Neelo frowned at that and Talhan stepped forward, his sodden sock from his bootless foot squelching into the mud. He leaned forward to place a kiss on their neck—

A roar shook through the forest and they both leapt apart. Neelo turned toward the sound as trees cracked and the canopy swayed as something giant ran toward them.

"Fun like that?" Neelo shouted as Talhan grabbed them around the waist and pushed them behind him.

"Run!" he bellowed, unsheathing his sword just as a beast broke through the trees.

CHAPTER THIRTY-ONE

Neelo stumbled backward, their eyes flying wide at the sight of the creature. It was twice the size of an Eastern mountain lion with the tusks of a boar and curling horns of a ram. Feet frozen to the ground, Neelo gaped at the narrowing pupils in its giant yellow eyes.

Talhan collided into their chest, pushing them into a run with one hand as his other tightened on the hilt of his sword. They bolted through the forest and clambered up the volcanic black rocks. The lion beast roared, chasing after them and blasting through the trees as if they were wet reeds.

Neelo tripped over the craggy rock, their palms and knees biting into the sharp stone. Talhan jumped in front of them, brandishing his sword as the beast prowled closer.

"Get up. Get up. Get up," Talhan chanted, unsheathing his dagger with his other hand.

Spittle flew from the beast's maw as it growled. The whole forest vibrated with the sound of a thunderstorm rolling in. Neelo looked up to see the creature's narrowed snakelike eyes and its ears laid flat against its head.

The beast took another slow, predatory step as Neelo scrambled to their feet. Its lips pulled back in a snarl, exposing its giant tusks. Stumbling, Neelo's arms wheeled as their foot slipped on a crack in the earth. They peered down at the wide crevice behind them and back up to the beast stalking toward them.

Neelo clenched their side, panting deep belabored breaths. "Tal?"

"Yes?" Talhan asked without turning to them. He crouched lower into his fighting stance, both blades pointed toward the prowling creature as he waited for the beast to pounce.

"Do you trust me?"

"Yes." Talhan choked up the grip on his sword as the beast took another step closer. "But I don't know if now is really the time to be talking about—"

"Listen," Neelo snapped. "Do you hear it?"

Birdsong echoed through the caverns below their feet. Talhan twisted his head halfway to them, his eyebrows raised in recognition as they listened to the same song that reverberated through the hidden caves. Neelo's back foot tested the width of the crack in the earth. They could make it.

The beast roared toward the sky and Neelo seized the opportunity with the creatures eyes off its prey to grab Talhan by his belt and yank him backward.

"Jump!" Neelo shouted and Talhan leapt without turning. Neelo fell into the cracked rock, pulling Talhan into the cavern with them. Sharp stone scraped across their arms and legs as they dropped into a crouch, sheltering back against the lip of the cavern and peering up to the fissure they'd slipped through.

The beast lunged, mouth agape. With lethal precision, Talhan moved, shoving his sword upward through the creature's open mouth and out through its eye socket. The creature yowled, yanking backward and pulling Talhan's sword with it. Blood misted down upon them, dripping through the cracks above their head. Talhan pressed backward against Neelo so tightly they could barely see the little flashes of fur and teeth. The beast thrashed and scrambled, falling hard on its side.

Neelo held on to Talhan with a white-knuckled grip as they listened to the monster's death throes before its screeching wails finally subsided.

"Gods," Neelo panted.

Talhan whirled and cupped their cheeks with his bloodied hands. "Are you okay?"

His thumb tested a spot on the side of Neelo's head and only then did it sting. They must've scraped it falling through the crack. Neelo's stomach roiled but they nodded.

Shouts rang out all around them.

"Shit." Talhan stared up at the sunlight peeking through the cave.

"The Eastern soldiers," Neelo whispered. "I guess we didn't wash that far downriver."

"Where's Cole?" Talhan tilted his head toward the sky, listening.

"Hopefully halfway toward Westdale by now." Neelo's stomach tightened and they shook their head. "Those soldiers will kill Cole if they catch him, or worse."

"They're about to kill us," Talhan growled. "Let's worry about that first."

They couldn't disagree.

The shouts grew louder, accompanied by the sound of heavy stomping boots. The dead beast would be easy enough to find, having left a trail of snapped trees in its wake.

"Stay here." Talhan shucked his remaining boot and spun around to grab Neelo by the shoulders. He crouched lower so his eyes lined up with their own. "I will lead them off into the forest. You stay hidden until they chase after me."

"No!" Panic filled Neelo's voice. "We almost just died—twice. I'm not losing you again."

"Find Cole," Talhan said slowly, a smirk pulling across his face that made tears spring to Neelo's eyes. "Get to Westdale."

"No," they choked out, clenching a handful of his tunic in their grip.

"Yes." Talhan cursed and pulled Neelo into a burning kiss. "I love you," he murmured against their lips.

"Tal, please," they begged as Talhan planted a final kiss to their forehead. "Don't do this." Neelo reached for him again, but he pulled from their grip and scrambled back up the crevice.

"This is what I do," he said in farewell, and Neelo covered their mouth to muffle their sob as Talhan's low whistle cut through the air.

"Well if it isn't the Eastern traitors," Talhan called. "Come to kill some more innocents?"

The soldiers erupted into shouts, and Talhan took off running into the forest.

Neelo clenched their eyes shut as tears spilled down their cheeks. They retched, river water still roiling in their stomach, as they thought of Talhan's injured leg. He wasn't fully healed. They took a breath and then another, their body going numb as they felt Talhan's absence more keenly with every heartbeat.

Those soldiers were going to kill him. No, he was strong, he could fight them off. But he was hurt, and they outnumbered him—

Oh Gods. Neelo waited until the birds started singing again, the insects chirping back to life, as the skirmish drifted beyond earshot.

Minutes passed by as they struggled to find their breath. Finally, they stooped and placed their palms to the rocky soil below their feet, praying to the Earth Gods just as Talhan said he always did before battle. With the sudden attack, there'd been no time for Tal to pray, but Neelo could pray for him. They whispered the words over and over, that he may find calm, focus, and speed. Neelo murmured one last prayer that Tal would find his way back to them before gazing up at the cracked earth above their head.

With shaking hands they pulled themself out of the crevice, their chest and belly scraping against the sharp stones, but they didn't feel it. Their senses shot out in every direction as if they might be able to hear Talhan, *feel* him, somehow, but they only felt emptiness.

When they climbed out, they stared at the fallen beast and gagged until bile burned up their throat and splattered across the fallen leaves.

"I told you." A strange voice chuckled and Neelo whirled to find two Eastern soldiers leaning against a far tree. "I told you he was leading 'em off. You owe me three gold pieces," he said to the soldier next to him.

Neelo's heart leapt into their throat. They dropped into a crouch and yanked Talhan's sword free from the lion's head. Their chest seized as they realized Talhan had run off with only his dagger.

"Stay back!" Neelo boomed, pointing the bloodied sword at them.

"Or what, little book mouse?" The first soldier guffawed, swaggering closer. "You think you can land a strike on me, coward?"

Fury bloomed in Neelo's chest, fear replaced with something dark and menacing, and they took a step toward the soldiers. "Say it again."

The soldier faltered, his bravado slipping as Neelo took another step. All Neelo's life they felt prey to these people—their looks, and whispers, and judgment—so afraid of what would happen if people called them the names they feared.

Neelo chuckled and the soldiers lifted their swords higher, fear filling their eyes.

Now . . . now Neelo didn't feel like prey at all, they felt more predatory than the slayed lion behind them.

They advanced, lunging out and swiping at the first soldier as the second raised his sword. Neelo twisted, blocking the blade of one while they pivoted into the other and elbowed him in the nose.

"Fuck." He dropped, grabbing his shattered nose as blood poured down his chest plate.

Neelo felt the wind whipping and jumped backward just before the second soldier's sword collided with their knee.

"You bitch," he seethed, charging at them.

Neelo blocked his strike and sliced their sword down across his shoulder. They pivoted, trying to avoid another blow but the soldier's boot caught the back of their knee and they stumbled backward. His sword hit theirs as they struggled to keep their balance and they dropped the blade.

Shit.

The second soldier was about to strike when the first soldier screamed. They both snapped their attention in his direction and what they saw made Neelo want to vomit again.

Cole crouched over the soldier, holding the tip of the soldier's sword to the writhing fae's neck. The soldier's eyes wept black blood, the veins across his face spiderwebbing into black as the poisoned blade took his life.

Neelo took the opportunity with their opponent distracted and charged forward, tackling the soldier to the ground. He landed hard on the jagged rocks with an oomph as the air was knocked out of him. His sword clattered out of his grip and Neelo punched him square in the jaw. His eyes rolled back as Neelo smashed his face again, pummeling him with their fists, splitting his lips and brow.

"Call me mouse again," they screamed into his face, feeling the skin of their knuckles being ripped open with each blow. "Call me coward!"

Strong arms banded around Neelo's waist and hauled them backward. They kicked and scrambled, whirling on the third attacker. They were about to claw his face, blind with fury, when they saw two golden eyes staring back at them.

Talhan held them by the shoulders. His nose was bleeding, fresh bruises along his jaw, and his clothes were caked in gore, but he was there, he was okay.

Neelo's face cracked at the sight of him and Talhan yanked them into a fierce embrace. "You're alive."

"Did you ever doubt me?" he whispered into their hair.

"Gods." Neelo dropped their head into his shoulder. It was all they could think to say. They knew Talhan was a famed warrior, but to take on a whole crew of trained soldiers?

"When I saw two of them turn back, I knew I needed to end them quick," Talhan said, glancing over Neelo's shoulder. "But clearly you had everything well in hand." He let out a grunt of approval. "You're ferocious, love."

Neelo gave him one more tight squeeze and turned back to Cole. The brown witch stood like a statue over the soldier he'd killed with his own poisoned blade.

"Cole?"

The brown witch flinched at his own name.

"Come on," Talhan said, holding out a hand as if herding a skittish horse. "We need to get out of here."

Neelo's bloodied hands trembled as they passed Talhan's sword back to him. Fear began to seep in through the shock. Talhan had seen them snap, seen that inky black rage that rose up inside of them, and he didn't balk at it, didn't shame them for it. If anything, he seemed impressed.

Cole silently turned and headed back down the trail. A hollow shell once more, he drifted through the forest like a spirit halfway to the afterlife. Everything within him seemed empty while everything in Neelo felt full to bursting. They wended through the forest, making their way back toward the road to Westdale. Maybe they were in shock, maybe it was the echoes of battle, but something euphoric cut through their fear.

That look of confusion and fear in the soldiers' eyes as Neelo advanced on them—that wariness that perhaps he had miscalculated—Gods, that felt good. Maybe there were some sacred parts deep within Neelo that even a shy, grumpy bookworm was willing to defend.

CHAPTER THIRTY-TWO

The washwomen didn't have much on the line today, unfortunately," the green witch said, hefting a giant bundle of clothing into Neelo's arms. "But I think these will do."

"I can pay you when—"

The witch held up a placating hand. "One of them owes me a favor, it's fine." Her eyes flashed a sparkling green as she leaned in and whispered, "I didn't tell them who you were, Your Highness."

Neelo bowed their head to her. "Thank you."

Westdale commons was quiet at midday with the last morning ship departed and the first afternoon one yet to arrive. The sailors from the only merchant boat in port seemed to all have crammed into the tavern for a quick meal, leaving the grassy knolls and gardens of the commons empty.

Talhan had ventured off to get supplies from the shop across the way, while Neelo found clothes and safe passage for Cole. When they found a green witch passing through with a cart and donkey, Neelo flagged her down. She had a warm smile, dark hair braided to one side, and a young, round face. If the totem pouch weren't enough indication that she was a green witch, her flickering emerald eyes and mint cloak embroidered in silver petals gave her away.

Despite the quiet surrounds, the witch looked from side to side, checking for any eavesdroppers before saying, "Any friend of Rish's is a friend of mine."

"You know Rish?"

"My cousin."

Neelo considered her. "I can see the likeness." She had the same warmth as Rish—the same comfort and ease that infused her cooking.

The witch looked at Cole who sat on the back of her cart. He stared blankly at the river just as he'd done all day. "I'll take good care of him, I promise you."

"Thank you." Neelo nodded. "When you get to Arboa, Lord Ersan will pay you handsomely for your troubles. I have sent word to him and he has brown witches waiting to help."

The witch bowed and left to climb into the driver's seat, coaxing her donkey onward. Neelo thought about farewelling Cole, or at least thanking him for saving their life, but Cole was lost in the shadows of his mind again.

As the wagon creaked and rattled to life, Neelo searched across the gardens and found Talhan leaning against a tree in the shade, cornered by five old matrons.

"Curse the Gods," they muttered, watching as he inched away from an elderly redhead's flirtatious hand on his arm.

Neelo stalked across the gardens, blood burning in their veins at the tittering laughter so similar to the courtiers and high-class fae of the palace. Usually it was Talhan rescuing Neelo from a social situation, but where Talhan knew how to draw people in, Neelo knew how to make them go away.

When Talhan's eyes landed on Neelo, he seemed relieved. "Ah, there you are," he said with a grin.

But Neelo didn't stop moving, they pushed straight past the cluster of humans, shoving them apart. Talhan smirked as Neelo lifted on their tiptoes and planted a kiss on his lips.

"Here I am," they murmured against his mouth.

Talhan's hands circled around Neelo's back and he pulled them in closer as his mouth enveloped Neelo's own. The matrons behind Neelo let out indignant huffs and stormed off.

Neelo pulled away with a chuckle, lowering back to their feet and resting their forehead against Talhan's chest.

"Thank you for that." He snickered as he watched the harrumphing old ladies disappear around the corner.

"You seemed as if you were in need of rescuing," Neelo said, offering out half the bundle of clothing. "Change quickly. Did you get the rations?"

"Yep." Talhan stooped and patted the leather pack at his feet. "Mostly dried meat and hard cheeses, and enough water to last half of the journey. I've arranged with the stable master for two horses on the promise of payment once we reach Saxbridge."

"Good." Neelo nodded. "I suppose I could always commandeer them in the name of the Queen, but that would probably be a bad idea."

"Probably." Talhan snorted. "Though I'd love to see it." Talhan toyed with the button on the fresh tunic in his hands. "I've also arranged a quick meal in the tavern before we go."

Frowning, Neelo took a step back. "We need to deal with this threat before Augustus Norwood gets to Saxbridge."

"We also need to eat, Neelo." They glared, but Talhan's eyes twinkled. "That's why I said *quick*."

Neelo rolled their eyes. "Ten minutes," they said. "Or I'll head off without you."

"You wouldn't dare."

"I would," Neelo said with a mischievous grin. "But only because I know you'd drop everything and follow me."

"True." Talhan's hand swept up their arm to their neck and he pulled them into one final kiss before they headed to the tavern across the commons.

The tavern seemed to be the only busy place in Westdale. It was packed with the general rabble of sailors and merchants passing through the port town. Two plates sat waiting in the corner when they arrived. It didn't look like much compared to Rish's cooking, but it was warm and it would be another few days of travel on nothing but bread and cheese.

Talhan took the seat facing away from the crowd and immediately tucked into his meal.

Neelo speared a green bean with their fork. "Not feeling particularly social today?"

"There's too many Easterners around here," Talhan said, taking another bite of roasted chicken.

"And that is a bad thing?"

"Mostly not." Talhan shrugged. "But sometimes, it reminds me of being young, and all of the ways I failed my family back then."

Neelo paused their chewing, surprised he would admit it, but they'd been through so much that day, he was probably too exhausted to hold it back. Everything felt raw and real and just below the surface in that moment. "Do you blame Bri for not fighting more for herself?"

"Of course not." Talhan's eyes widened. "She was just a child."

"You're the same age," Neelo pointed out.

"I'm older by three minutes."

Neelo rolled their eyes. "Three minutes aside, you cannot blame yourself for what your parents did to her. You can wish that it was different, but it is not your fault, Tal. Bri knows that. We all know that."

His eyes stayed fixed to his plate for a long time. "We had a fight before she left for Swifthill. She almost died again because of my stubbornness."

"But she didn't. And you made amends."

"Still, she needed me and I should've been there," he muttered.

"Do you only count your failings?" Neelo asked, searching his distant expression. "Do you not weigh all of the people you've helped and lives you've saved as well?"

"The lives I save are at the cost of others," Talhan said. "Such is the life of a warrior, but it was my duty and obligation to serve Hale in that way, and I would do it all again to protect the people I care about."

"Exactly," they said, and at first Talhan looked confused until he realized what he had just said. Neelo took a slow sip of water, licking their lips before saying, "For a long time, I thought that you were here with me out of duty and obligation too."

Talhan snorted. "Please tell me you don't think that anymore?"

Neelo shrugged and Talhan reached across the table and grabbed their hand. "I admire your loyalty to those you love."

Talhan's thumb swept gently across the back of Neelo's hand. "The family I've made, I've chosen, all of them—Hale, Remy, Carys, Bri, Rua . . . I am loyal to each of them in my own way. I wish I could have done more for Bri then, but I know—in my mind, if nothing else—that it wasn't in my power. No, though, if any one of them needed me, I would always be there." Neelo's heart thundered and they tried to pull their hand away but Talhan threaded his fingers through Neelo's own. "But, when it comes to you—" He took a breath. "My loyalty to you is eternal and unfailing. I would battle death herself to get to you."

Neelo swallowed the knot in their throat, thinking of Talhan running off into the forest with a mob of Eastern soldiers chasing him. "You already have," they whispered.

"Talhan Catullus!" A drunken voice boomed above the din. Talhan cringed at the sound as the human stumbled up behind Talhan and clapped him on the shoulder. "I've always wanted to spar one day with the Golden Eagle."

The human had short blond hair, a weathered face, and a stubbled jawline. He probably would've seemed considerably more muscular if he wasn't standing beside Talhan.

Talhan rolled his shoulders back, and turned halfway, sizing up the man. "Today is not that day, friend."

"Friend." The man cackled and grabbed a tankard of ale off his table. He hooked his thumb at Talhan and looked at his three friends who seemed equally inebriated. "This one calls himself warrior. Come on, Eagle, let's see what you've got."

"No," Talhan growled with enough warning that any sober man would've run away, but the confidence of a drunk whose friends were watching could never be underestimated.

"Afraid?" The man heckled and his comrades cheered, pounding their fists on the table and raising their glasses. "You should be. I fought off five fae soldiers single-handedly on the bridge to Harrowsfeld last summer."

Neelo gaped at the man's bragging. They'd just seen Talhan slay a giant beast and fight off a whole crew of trained soldiers after nearly drowning and this man was trying to fight him? Neelo looked at Talhan, but he didn't seem the least bit surprised and their heart sunk for him. This couldn't be all people saw in Talhan: a famed warrior always keen for a fight? Someone these humans could goad into a drunken brawl?

And yet wasn't that how he'd been selected as their betrothed?

Rage built within them like rising sparks that flamed into an inferno. They'd just had their whole life cracked open and they would not allow this random stranger to reduce Talhan to no more than his battle skills—not like their mother had.

Talhan lifted his drink and the man slapped it out of his hand. The whole room let out a collective gasp as the glass shattered across the floor. Talhan's eyes darkened as he slowly turned his head, about to give this man the pummeling he was so desperately asking for, when Neelo shot up.

They held a hand out to Tal. "Let me handle this," they muttered, stepping in front of Talhan and knowing that they were probably saving this drunken man's life in the process. Neelo glowered at the human and he wisely reared back in momentary surprise before his beer-laden smugness returned again. "Your story is bullshit," Neelo said calmly.

The man swayed on his feet but his eyes flared with anger. "Excuse me?"

"It's Harrow*stern* not Harrows*feld*." Neelo stared him down as they spoke. "And the bridge that leads to Harrow*stern* is only crossable in the autumn and winter due to the monsoons. So unless you have gills, your story is bullshit."

Talhan chuckled and popped the last of his potatoes into his mouth. "Nicely done."

The whole tavern erupted into laughter and the blond man's face flushed an unseemly shade of scarlet. Neelo knew, however, their perfectly landed blow, had only provoked him further, so they made to end it.

"Go back to your meal. *Now*," Neelo ordered with all of the royal authority they could muster.

They shouldn't have been surprised when the man didn't listen and leaned around Neelo to glare at Talhan, but something in Neelo snapped as he shouted, "You're just afraid to fight me, stupid fucking oaf."

Before the man could finish his poisoned words, Neelo grabbed him by the neck and slammed his face into his plate. The crowd groaned with the sound of his face smacking into his meal. Peas and potatoes scattered across the floor. Neelo's hand pinned him to the spot, their fingernails digging into the flesh of his neck as they lowered their mouth to his ear. "Speak one more word and I will cut out your tongue." They lifted their eyes to find Talhan, slack-jawed, staring at them like they were the blistering sun. "It is only through my benevolence that I haven't let him kill you already, do you understand?"

The man nodded pathetically and Neelo shoved him away. He fell into a heap on the floor as Neelo turned back to Talhan.

"By all the Gods," he panted. "That was . . ."

"I've had more experience with drunken fools in my lifetime than any tavern barman." Neelo straightened their jacket. "And this idiot has made us late. Grab your things and your jaw off the floor. We're leaving. Now."

CHAPTER THIRTY-THREE

Neelo stumbled up the path, their sweat-crusted clothes clinging to their chest. The rain had eased as the tropical storm
blew past, the clouds pulling back to a beautiful summer's
day—a few hours of downpour and then brilliant blue skies and
scorching heat.

With everything that had happened, Neelo felt the mounting urgency to return to the palace, everything teetering on the precipice of
disaster. They needed to find the supplier of their mother's brew and
warn the guards of Augustus Norwood's possible arrival. Whatever
Adisa Monroe's puppet had planned for Saxbridge, it was clear now
that the violet witch was the one pulling the strings.

The eastern trail was terribly maintained. Creeping vines and large
cobwebs reclaimed the path and they had to lead their horses on foot
through the thickest parts. Neelo prayed the stomp of the horses'
hooves would scare off any lingering snakes and lizards. If one of them
got bit by a venomous snake this far from a village, no brown witch
would be able to save them.

One more thing my mother has neglected.

They passed the distinctive etchings on the tall *amasa* tree that
shot up from the forked path like a beacon marking the trail.

"Thank the Gods," Talhan panted, smiling at the three waving lines carved onto the trunk. "We've reached a waterfall."

Neelo doubled over, placing their hands on their knees and taking deep breaths. The exertion of their near-death swim the day before had exhausted them, even though Neelo had been unconscious and it had been Talhan doing all the swimming. With the barest of rations and a single skin of water left, the heat drained Neelo to the point of sickness. They wanted to urge Talhan onward, to get to the palace as quickly as possible, but knew they'd kill them both if they didn't stop and rest.

"Let's go," Neelo said, reaching back and taking Talhan's hand as they dragged him up the trail. The horses were more than happy to stop and graze in the shade, snorting contentedly as they chomped on the grasses. "Water first, then we rest."

Talhan's fingers constricted around Neelo's as they led him through the jungle and up the hillside covered in gnarled tree roots. The sound of the rushing water grew until the clearing appeared. Water rushed down smooth brown stones in cascading steps toward a plunge pool. Talhan stumbled to the edge and cupped his hands. He groaned as he drank the pristine water.

Neelo shucked off their boots, instantly cooling as the air reached their swollen, sweaty feet. They wandered over to Talhan and crouched beside him, taking a long drink from the swirling turquoise water. They wanted to drink more but their stomach began cramping and they sat back on their elbows instead. Talhan turned back to Neelo and they could see the horror of that morning written all over his face.

"We almost died." Neelo stared up into Talhan's sun-filled eyes. "Twice. You saved my life."

How many times would Neelo relive that moment before it started to sink in? It still felt like a terrible dream.

"We took turns." Talhan's eyes dipped down to Neelo's lips and back up to their eyes. "You've saved me more times than you know." Neelo's eyebrows pinched together. "You don't believe me?"

"I'm not a warrior—"

"And yet you fought two soldiers by yourself."

"Cole was there—"

"But you didn't know that. Not to mention you risked yourself to cut me free."

They wanted to protest, but he put a gentle finger under their chin, forcing them to meet his eyes. "It's okay for us to share something. To take care of each other."

Neelo stared into those golden eyes, the contact of that single finger making their whole body tremble—

But Talhan just sighed and took his finger away, scrubbing his hands down his stubbled jawline. His hair had grown scraggly over the past few days and in another week without shaving he'd have a full beard. "First, I want to hang these clothes to dry."

"Agreed," Neelo said, shaking back to reality. Their nose crinkled as they sniffed their shoulder. Despite getting fresh clothes in Westdale, Neelo's skin still had the faint acid scent of bile from retching up the river water and they were reminded once more of how close they'd come to death.

Talhan's cheeks dimpled. He didn't waste any time reaching back and yanking his sweat-stained tunic off over his head. He hung the garment on a low-hanging branch and then kicked off his boots and went for his belt buckle.

Glancing over his shoulder, Talhan arched his brow at Neelo. "Aren't you joining me?"

"I'm taking my time." Neelo pressed their lips together as they watched Talhan slide his trousers down his muscled backside.

"Look at you." Talhan winked. "A few brushes with death and you're practically a ruffian."

Neelo ignored his gibe, admiring instead the lines of corded muscle down Talhan's tanned flesh before he dove into the pool.

He swam with ease over toward the waterfall, giving Neelo a moment of privacy to quickly disrobe and Neelo was grateful for it. With those golden eyes trained upon them, they'd probably trip out of their trousers and faceplant butt naked in the dirt.

They hastily took their clothes off and tossed their sweaty garb onto a tree branch, thinking at any moment Talhan might turn back around to peek at them. But he didn't—once again confirming to Neelo that if they wanted him right then, they were going to need to make the first move.

Talhan waited until Neelo jumped in with a giant splash. When they emerged above the surface, they found him watching, smiling at them. Neelo crouched in the water, their feet sinking into the silty bottom of the pond. And, after nearly drowning, they were grateful they could touch. Their feet and knees found blissful relief in the weightlessness of the water.

Neelo peered up at the dappled sunlight from the canopy above. "It's nearly the Solstice," they said, glancing back at Talhan. "Your summer trip is almost over."

Talhan swirled his hands beside him as he stalked closer. "You still plan on sending me away?"

"Adisa Monroe brought her Eastern soldiers into the South. That means war—a war you don't have to fight, not yet." Neelo swallowed, thinking of how close they came to death, thinking of how close *Talhan* came to death. "This is your last chance, Tal. You cannot be here when this all burns down. You deserve better—"

"Are we really here again?" Talhan cut them off with a growl. "You think you don't deserve me? You actually believe that crap? Gods, Neelo—I thought you were smarter than that!" They were shocked by his vehemence, not quite clear if he was angry at them, but worried that was the case.

Yet—because he was Talhan, he said more gently, "That's what this is about isn't it?" He took another slow step through the water and Neelo took a step back at the intensity of his stare. "So let me make this perfectly clear: it is *I* who must strive to deserve *you*, Neelo Emberspear. You are the smartest most stunning, brave—"

"I am not brave," Neelo hissed.

"You *are*," Talhan snapped back, fire rising in his voice as if fighting for the honor Neelo couldn't find in themself. "Fiercely. Bravery isn't who has the bloodiest sword, Neelo. It's not who shouts the loudest or draws the most attention at a party. Bravery is the person who is afraid and tries anyway. Who holds their family together, who steps up when their people need them, who leads when it frightens them, who loves even when it terrifies them . . . You are brave, Neelo." Talhan took another step until he loomed over them, his voice a whisper. "Be brave for me, please.

"Be brave *with* me."

Neelo shook their head, tears pinpricking their eyes. "I . . . can't. I'm not. I—" They'd almost just died and all they could think about was the fact that they'd nearly let Talhan die too.

"Whatever the South faces, you don't have to face it alone," Talhan promised. "Not anymore."

"Yes I do." Neelo's voice dropped. "I have to."

"Why?" Talhan pushed, his chest rising further from the water and Neelo felt the rage rising within themself—not at Talhan, but at the bloody Fates and their mother and the evil forces of the world that made everything feel impossible.

Neelo lifted their chin, forcing themself to meet Talhan's gaze. "Because you can't be here with me."

"Why?"

"Because I'm not going to drag you under with me!" they shouted, their control snapping as their arms shook with unfettered wrath. "This court will poison you! It will strip all of the light and goodness from your soul, and I'd rather suffer every day of my life alone than watch that spark flicker out of your eyes."

Talhan rocked back at their words, his face hard, his eyes guarded. Then he took a step forward, carefully placing his finger under Neelo's chin again and lifting their eyes to meet his own. "Why?" he breathed, the question barely a rumble in his throat.

They stared up into his eyes for what felt like an eternity, knowing he'd wait forever to make them say it. "Because I love you."

The muscle in his cheek flickered as his eyes dropped to their mouth. "You think you will poison me?" he whispered. "You think you're sparing me?"

"Yes." The word hissed out through their teeth.

Talhan's lips fell to Neelo's ear. "I am stronger than you think I am," he whispered. "I burn brighter than all of your doubts."

Neelo's lips parted. "I—"

"You are not the poison, Neelo, you are the antidote," he murmured, tilting his head slightly as his eyes fixed on their mouth. "I told you, you saved my life and I meant it."

"You said in Valtene you were reminded you have something to fight for," Neelo whispered. "Tell me what Renwick said to you."

Talhan slicked back his hair and the jungle seemed to quiet in anticipation. "When I was in Valtene, the battle was thick. I was certain we were going to lose, but I kept fighting. They broke our formation apart and . . ." Talhan's eyes guttered and Neelo was certain the battle still played behind his eyes. "I took on seven guards on my own. One got me right in the gut, another in the leg, and I knew, I *knew* that was it. My life was over."

Neelo shook their head, their eyes welling with tears, their fingers straining in the water, wanting to reach out to him but holding themself back.

"Fenrin tried to stop the bleeding, healing me with his elixirs, but I was fading fast and I . . ." His eyes dropped to the water between them. "I was about to let go." Neelo swallowed the solid rock in their throat as tears spilled down their cheeks. "But Renwick came to me, he whispered in my ear a vision he had Seen. He told me if I held on that all I had hoped for would come true; that if I just held on, the person I saw every time I closed my eyes would be mine."

"And who did you see?" Neelo asked, afraid of what he was about to say.

"You."

Devastation. They shattered and reformed and shattered again at that one word.

He closed his eyes, as if to see them again. "Us. Our life together." Talhan's gaze lifted and he grinned, emotions welling in that look. "You saved me."

Slowly, he leaned forward and brushed a soft kiss to Neelo's lips. Neelo shuddered, leaning into the soft warmth of his mouth. Talhan's hand swept from Neelo's chin up to bracket their jaw as his other hand circled around their back and pulled them closer.

"I saved you." Neelo's voice cracked. Their wet skin slid against Talhan's own as they lifted on their tiptoes to deepen the kiss.

"Thank you for holding on to me," Talhan murmured against their lips. "Even if you didn't know it. You save me every day just by allowing me to be next to you."

Neelo's knees trembled and Talhan held them tighter. "That whole day I felt like I was holding on to a sail that was trying to pull me out to sea." A tear trailed down their cheek. "That feeling. It was you. I was holding on to you."

"And you didn't get swept away. You were the anchor. No," he said, frowning for a second. "Not an anchor. You pulled yourself aboard and took the rudder. You steered me back. You guided me . . ."

His voice faltered, but they didn't need his words. Neelo's hands roved up Talhan's back as Talhan pushed them back toward the falls. His tongue dipped into Neelo's mouth and his fingertips pressed tighter into Neelo's flesh.

They'd said it. They'd told him that they loved him—a secret they thought they'd never have the courage to reveal.

Their kisses deepened, their hands becoming frenzied as Neelo's back touched the rocks behind them. Talhan lifted them up by their ass, sliding their bare body across the stones pounded smooth by the rushing waterfall. Neelo's legs circled around him, hooking their ankles at the small of his back and pulling him closer. The feel of Talhan's hot, wet skin against the flesh of their thighs made Neelo's whole body shiver.

Talhan rose up in the water, just enough to brush a kiss across Neelo's lips before his mouth trailed down their neck and over their collarbone, skipping over their chest and dropping down to plant a kiss on the inside of their thigh. One hand lifted, circling Neelo's collarbone and pushing them back, urging them to lie down.

Neelo hummed, slicking back Talhan's hair as his mouth swept closer to their center, before relenting to his command and lying down. Talhan's hot breath shot tingling trails of pleasure through them and tickled the hairs between their legs. Moaning in anticipation, Neelo arched their head back against the slick rock, already craving the sensation they'd imagined a thousand times but never felt before. If it had been anyone else . . . Neelo's stomach clenched. There *was* no one else.

Here, with Talhan, this was the only thing that made sense. That was *right*.

They spread their legs wider, granting him access to their aching core. Talhan's fingertips pressed into the soft flesh of their thighs, opening them wider as his mouth lowered.

A sharp gasp caught in Neelo's throat, the sensation of Talhan's hot tongue setting them ablaze. The water and air and sun evoked strange new senses within them, even more pleasurable than the first time Talhan had touched them. They let out a ragged breath as Talhan's tongue slid over their center, sweeping in slow, torturous circles. Neelo tried to catch their breath, but couldn't, the release already building in them from the first flick of Talhan's tongue.

They groaned, their hands frantically finding places to grip in the rock as Talhan pushed their knees wider and feasted on them. They knew, though, that even if they couldn't find purchase, he was never going to let them fall. He was never going to let them go.

His tongue swept faster, lashing them up and down as he moaned against them, making their eyes clench closed, amazed at how much pleasure he was getting when it was Talhan doing it all to them . . .

Mist coated their skin, distant birds sang overhead and the wind rattled through the trees, but it all faded to the roaring of Neelo's heartbeat.

"Yes." It was the only thing their brain could get out, the word ending on a shuddering breath, Neelo's fingers clenching so hard into the stone they thought they might break something—the stone or their fingers, they weren't sure.

Talhan continued his wanton strokes, circling and flicking until Neelo was bucking their hips.

"Add your fingers," they panted desperately.

Talhan obeyed, dipping one long finger into them and then adding a second. A sharp breath escaped their lips as he massaged his fingers in and out, starting slow and building pace to match the rhythm of his tongue. Neelo had never felt this way in all the times they'd touched themself before. They hadn't really understood the point of it, but this. *This* was a whole astonishing myriad of sensations that rushed through them with each stroke of Talhan's fingers.

Neelo's sounds grew louder, their voice utterly unfamiliar even to their own ears as Talhan worked them higher and higher.

"Faster," they breathed and his fingers thrust quicker, his tongue circling at a frenzy that made Neelo rumble out a groan.

They lifted entirely off the stone, riding Talhan's fingers and mouth. Grinding into him, they chased their release, knowing exactly where they were aiming like an arrow to a bullseye. They'd never been there, but then again, they'd never trusted even themself to try to find it. Talhan made the search natural, like something unlocked inside them and it was there all along.

With one final thrust of his fingers, they shattered, a broken moan pulling from their lungs as their climax roared through them. The highs of their orgasm soared greater than they'd ever felt, their eyes clouding over until they couldn't see. Over and over, they tumbled through their trembling waves of ecstasy.

When their breathing finally steadied, Talhan released them, guiding them backward and lifting out of the water to lie beside them. He circled his arms around Neelo, and they rested their forehead into his muscled shoulder, enjoying the rise and fall of their chests together.

They'd never get used to it—the feeling of being so whole, so grounded, and shattering apart at the same time.

Neelo reached down, feeling Talhan's hard length pressed against their thigh. They stroked him and he groaned, his cheek dropping atop their head.

"What do you want?" they whispered, stroking him slowly.

"Anything you want to do feels amazing to me," he replied. His fingers dug into the soft flesh of their ass, his hips rolling into their touch.

Their hand stilled and they bit the inside of their cheek. Neelo looked up, finding his eyes. "Do you want to be inside of me?"

His brow furrowed for a second, searching their gaze. "Is that something you'd want?"

"I think so. Maybe." They nervously pressed their lips together and Talhan reached up with his thumb and pulled their bottom lip free.

"Maybe," he whispered, swiping his fingers down their cheek. "Maybe there are thousands of ways to bring each other pleasure." His eyelids drooped as Neelo began stroking up and down his shaft again.

"I know," they said.

His eyebrows lifted. "You know?"

"I was raised in the Southern Court," they said with a grin. "We have a whole section of the library dedicated to such things. I know everything there ever could possibly be to know."

"Of course." Talhan's cheeks dimpled. "You might have to read some of these books to me."

Despite everything, they blushed at that thought. Still, they pressed on. "I've just never wanted it for myself before," Neelo said. "I didn't understand why it was so important to everyone, but with you . . ."

Talhan's face softened, that cheeky grin morphing into something warm and raw. "I understood it before," he confessed. "But Gods, it feels different with you. Everything is heightened, better, *right*, for the first time ever."

This was it. It was exactly what they just thought before he'd made their legs into jelly. The thing they had suspected their entire life, Neelo now understood with certainty. Emotions overcame them, their eyes welling at the thought.

Talhan stilled. "Are you okay?"

"Did you know?" A tear slid down their cheek, and he swiped it away.

"Know what?" he asked hesitantly in a way that made it clear he knew exactly what they were talking about. His eyes began to well too, unspoken words brimming to the surface.

"We're Fated," Neelo whispered.

"We're Fated," he echoed, a sense of wonder in his tone.

"Yes." They nodded, relieved he felt the same.

"Renwick asked me if I knew," Talhan said, his eyes glistening as he smiled. "And I only said, I had hoped."

"You don't have to hope anymore," they said, shocked—and yet, perhaps not as surprised as before—by their boldness. Neelo lifted their hand up, tracing their fingers across his swollen lips. Talhan pulled Neelo tighter, his lips crashing into theirs as if sealing their Fate.

Whatever cosmic force dragged the two of them together again and again finally had a name: Fated. Neelo had always thought they were better on their own, better separate from the world than a part of it . . . except when they were with Talhan. He was light and effervescent and Neelo was his opposite in almost every way and yet . . . yet something about the two of them threw such thoughts away. Neelo reined him in and Talhan pushed them out. They'd always counterbalanced each other, and now, Neelo understood why.

"I want to try everything with you. At least once." They chuckled as they threaded their fingers through Talhan's hair, feeling that boldness growing. For the first time, they felt confident to ask for what they wanted. "I want you inside me."

Talhan's lips parted at their words, rolling Neelo onto their back as he bracketed his corded arms on either side of them. He put one knee between their legs, then the other, sliding them backward to make space on the slick ledge. He slid himself over Neelo's wet body, rubbing against their most sensitive parts until that yearning ignited within them anew.

He guided himself to their entrance and paused, teasing a taunting bite to Neelo's fingertips lingering on his lips. He pushed himself in an inch and stilled, watching as Neelo's mouth opened on a gasp. Their hand slid around to the back of his neck, pulling his mouth to theirs as he slowly pushed in further. A growling groan vibrated against their lips as he kissed them, inching in further until his arms were shaking with restraint.

Neelo's breath hitched as he filled them, stretching them further than they'd ever been before. Wet heat pooled in their core, their muscles already fluttering around him in anticipation of release. The feeling was so overwhelming, so unlike anything they'd ever suspected. It transcended their body and echoed into the ether as if they could see each hook that pulled their soul and Talhan's into one.

He was their Fated. They pulled Talhan back into a scorching kiss, suddenly needing to feel those words through every inch of their body. Talhan's lips crashed onto their own, his tongue dipping into their mouth as his hips started rolling.

"Gods," Neelo moaned as he thrust deeper, each movement sliding them up across the wet rocks, massaging across their back. "You feel so good."

That proclamation unleashed Talhan and he began to pick up speed, thrusting into them faster and faster as the building need in their core turned into white-hot yearning. They tipped their hips until he hit a spot that made their eyes roll back, a desperate breath escaping from them as they clawed down his arms, holding on for dear life. It was too much, this overwhelming free fall, this life-changing knowledge. They were Fated.

Neelo scrambled to hold on to Talhan's slick form as their sounds became increasingly desperate. He hit that spot again and again and again. The veins in his arms and forehead bulged as he tried to hold on to control.

His head dropped into the crook of Neelo's neck as he nipped at their shoulder.

"I'm so close," they moaned, hooking their heels into Talhan's ass and pulling him in tighter until they were meeting each of his thrusts. Talhan lifted onto one arm, his other hand snaking between them to rub between their legs. Neelo bucked as his fingers circled them, a breathy cry escaping their mouth.

Talhan's lips skimmed up the shell of their pointed ear and said, "I love you. I always have."

At his words, Neelo tipped over the cliff, a cry of pleasure ringing out as Talhan followed them over the edge. He barked out a groan as his hips jerked, his climax tearing through him as he clutched his hand in Neelo's hair and held their head to his chest. In that moment, reaching that precipice within themselves together, they were one, in every way—body, mind, and soul.

With a final panting breath, Talhan rolled to the side and gathered Neelo into his broad chest.

"I love you," he whispered again into their hair. His breath slowly started to settle as his fingers swept gentle strokes up and down their spine. "I'm glad I can finally say it."

"I love you too," Neelo murmured against his skin. "I thought I was the only one."

"You might be the smartest person in Okrith, Neelo Emberspear, but you're a fool too. If only you'd listened to me you would've known," Talhan said with a grin. "I suspected for a long time that you were meant to be mine. Though my sister's prophecy overshadowed any proclamations of my own."

"My mother said she was told I had a Fated," Neelo said with a snicker. "But forgot who." They chuckled at the absurdity. Only Queen Emberspear could forget something so important—only to risk it on that silly duel. But maybe it hadn't been so spontaneous. Perhaps it was always meant to happen this way. Their chest rose and fell in unison with Talhan's own.

Talhan hummed. "That moment in Valtene is when I knew what that love was for certain—that even the Gods knew you were meant to be mine."

Neelo tipped their head up to him. "I'm glad you didn't let go."

"I'm glad *you* didn't," he said, brushing a soft kiss to their lips. "Whatever life you end up choosing, Neelo Emberspear, I want to be a part of your story."

Neelo settled their head against Talhan's shoulder, grinning, and said, "You know how much I love stories."

CHAPTER THIRTY-FOUR

There was a rising urgency in each step back toward Saxbridge, as Neelo found themself more and more eager to get home.

Home. The word had never been pleasant to Neelo before. It had been the feeling of unease, the smell of booze and smoke, the exhaustion of trying to wrangle a crowd of disobedient revelers.

But with Talhan beside them, it felt utterly different. It felt like the warmth and calmness of sunrise and the smell of Rish's cooking and weathered old books. They'd waited their whole life for it to feel that way, for it to just come to them, never taking ownership over their own life. All those passive moments that tumbled them like crashing waves . . . Neelo had never thought of the endless string of happenstance as decisions before. But now they saw each moment as a forked path. Maybe life could feel like Talhan's warmth and his steady joy if only they kept choosing it. They couldn't sit back and let life happen to them anymore. They'd need to fight to protect this feeling of home every day and that meant stopping whatever plans Adisa Monroe had to destroy their newfound happiness.

Rish was the first to spot Neelo and Talhan when they emerged from the stables. The green witch ran to them like the Goddess of Death was chasing her.

"I'm okay," Neelo reassured her before Rish could even reach them.

"You are *not* okay, *mea raga*. Are you trying to kill me?" Rish shouted, her eyes frantically scanning Neelo for injury. "I said have a *little* adventure, not take on dark witch magic by yourself! Sy contacted the Queen and told us what little he knows from what little you told him." She took a gasp of air and carried on. "And let me tell you, it was not that much at all, and I've just baked some *gloftas* in the hope that you would be back and—"

Neelo yanked Rish into a tight hug and the witch's rambling words died on her lips. "I'm here, *mhehamma*." Rish's fingers squeezed Neelo tighter at the Mhenbic word for "mother" and she let out a surprised laugh. "I'm home."

Tears filled Rish's eyes when she pulled away. She wiped at the kohl lines streaking down her cheeks. "Have you eaten?"

Neelo chuckled. To a green witch, the question meant more than saying "I love you." Neelo shook their head. "We're starving, but it will have to wait—"

"Mother Moon." Rish cursed, clutching her totem pouch, before finally glancing at Talhan. "That'll never do, come, come. I have flat-bread fresh off the skillet."

She ushered them toward the kitchens like a dog herding sheep. Talhan laughed and slung his arm around Neelo's shoulders, pulling them into his side and planting a kiss atop their head, but Neelo held firm, saying to Rish, "I need to speak with my mother. Now."

"There is always time to eat," Rish countered. "Come. I made one of everything."

Talhan's shoulders shook. "You are so very loved," he murmured into their hair.

"And it will be the death of me," Neelo muttered back. "Augustus Norwood might be barging through this palace any minute now. Eating will have to wait."

Rish paused and stared at them. "This," she waved at the two of them. "This is new."

"Is it?" Neelo asked. "Or has it been there for a long time?"

"Ha!" Rish smirked and clapped her hand on her thigh. "I knew it!"

Neelo rolled their eyes. "You should've been a blue witch for all the things you seem to know after they're told to you."

"And you should have been a bat, for all the things you missed even though they were right before your eyes," Rish countered then patted Talhan on the arm and said, "All of your things are back in your room."

"This again?" Neelo's eyes darted between the two of them. "What things?"

Talhan cleared his throat and shrugged, not bothering with whatever terrible lie he was thinking of. Instead, he changed tack. "How is the Queen?"

"Much the same." Rish's smile faltered. "If not slightly worse, unfortunately. That brown witch from the High Mountains has been trying everything but has quite the unwilling patient."

"Poor Fen." Talhan snickered. "He can never catch a break."

"I think we found a solution to our problems in Arboa," Neelo said. "But we've found more troubles along the way too." They steered toward the entryway. "Which is why we need to speak with the Queen."

"Ah yes." Rish frowned. "Sy relayed your orders to the guards too. Luckily Farros had the good sense to intercept that message before it reached your mother. You signed a ten-year trade agreement without your mother's knowledge?" Rish lifted the hem of her skirt to climb the stone steps toward the kitchens. "Are you trying to make the other provinces think you're favoring Arboa, *mea raga*? You know Southerners don't handle jealousy well. Our court color is green after all."

"I'm trying to stop a war with the violet witches," Neelo gritted out. "And trying to save this city from imploding under its own addictions. But more and more I'm thinking those battles are one and the same." They glanced out at the white-capped waves of the harbor far in the distance and along to the white stone walls surrounding the palace. "It is the High Priestess's way past our defenses. No choppy seas or high gates will stop her if she can get into our minds."

"Curse the Moon, child," Rish muttered, grabbing her totem pouch again. "I think I need to add more protection stones to this thing."

"The people won't like being cut off from the witching brew,"

Talhan said. "But if it saves their court, then they will understand. The Queen on the other hand . . ."

"You haven't been in the South long enough, Lord Eagle," Rish jeered, swatting his elbow. "You will be battling violet witches with one hand and the rioting Southerners with the other, stolen minds or not. People here won't take kindly to ending their fun."

"Speaking of ending fun—" Something brushed against their calf and they peered down to find Indi weaving between their legs.

"Look at you." Neelo plucked up their cat into their arms, briefly waylaid from their plans by their friend. Indi aggressively headbutted into Neelo's hand, purring wildly. "You've doubled in size since we left." Neelo gave Rish a look but the green witch merely shrugged.

"How can I say no to that face?"

"Did Sy say anything about . . . anything else?" Neelo asked, praying that Cole had arrived in Arboa already.

Rish leaned forward, her voice dropping to a whisper. "He's there. He's safe." She watched the doorway, searching for passersby before adding, "But he's not said a word. It may be a long road ahead before he does. I—" A group of green witch gardeners walked past, chattering loudly, and Rish immediately changed the conversation. "I was beginning to wonder if the Solstice celebrations would be canceled, what with you gone, and the Queen unable to make any arrangements herself in her ill health."

"A party will be the perfect distraction to keep the people happy while we sort out this brew mess," Neelo said. "We shall throw a celebration the likes of which Saxbridge has never seen."

Rish cackled. "I would've bet a million *druni* you'd never say that. Your mother will be so pleased."

A group of young humans stumbled past the doorway, carrying vases of flowers and tittering hushed gossip to one another.

"Decorating already?" Neelo asked, following the group's swishing skirts as they disappeared around the corner. "I thought mother was too unwell to plan for the Solstice."

"All the crowns of Okrith are coming to watch the sun set on the longest day," Rish said with a shrug. "Some will be arriving early."

Neelo's stomach dropped. "When?"

"Today."

"Shit." Neelo set Indi back on the ground and hasted toward the far doorway. "I need to brief my mother on everything that has happened," Neelo insisted. Talhan frowned, looking forlornly in the direction of the kitchens but not saying any more about it. "We need to make a plan. We were tipped off that a certain Norwood Prince plans to be in attendance. I want to find him and make him talk."

"I knew it would be less than an hour before you were back to your morose self," Rish tutted, breezing through the double doors of the kitchen and returning with a tray of frosted marmalade biscuits. "Fine," she groused. "I suppose it is a worthy reason." She passed the tray to Talhan. "Eat these on the way."

He grinned down at the plate. "Have I told you you're my favorite witch?"

"Yes, yes," Rish said, shooing them out the door with a wave of her towel. "Flatter me more at dinnertime." She rounded the table and pulled Neelo into one last hug. "I like these smiles, *mea raga*," she whispered. "I knew your Fated would be someone who likes my cooking."

Neelo rolled their eyes but chuckled, giving Rish one more hug before following Talhan down the hall. Their smile faltered as they headed toward the Queen's chambers. Talhan offered the tray of biscuits out to them and they shook their head. No amount of sweets would fix the dread pooling in their gut. They'd just unearthed something important, something incredible within themself, and they hated the feeling they needed to shove it back down, lock it away, to protect from their mother. Someone like Queen Emberspear couldn't be trusted with Neelo's delicate joy. She'd take it and twist it and turn it back on them. And all of the fears they thought they had overcome crept a little closer to the surface with each step toward their mother's chambers.

"Where are you going?" Talhan asked, grabbing Neelo by the crook of their arm. "The Queen's chambers are that way."

"I'm going to get changed out of these sweaty clothes," Neelo frowned down at the mud-stained garb. The clothing had barely survived the trek to Arboa.

"Leave it," Talhan said with a confident nod. "Maybe we'll get some of your mother's pity when she sees us."

Neelo snorted, turning to follow Talhan back down the hall. "We'll need all the help we can get."

"WELL?" THE QUEEN sprawled across her throne, her kohl-lined eyes peering at the vaulted ceiling as Neelo's shoes clicked across the tiled floor. "Have you uncovered Norwood's plot in Arboa? Has some God whispered in your ear of the secret remedies to my current predicament? Or are you going to be Regent soon?"

"I am getting closer," Neelo gritted out. They nodded to the pipe held in their mother's slender fingers. "If you'd just put that out, I wouldn't have to find another way."

"Not going to happen." Their mother's rasping laugh ended on a cough. "I'd rather live briefly but happily than a lifetime of nothingness."

"You knew I wouldn't find answers to your brew problem in Arboa, didn't you, Mother?" Neelo cocked their head as they scanned the room of colorfully veiled courtiers sitting by the open window, forcing themself to scrutinize the group for the first time. Someone in this room knew more than they were letting on about the origins of her brew. "Where exactly does your stash come from and *how* exactly do you have more of it?"

The Queen waved her hand toward the scantily clad bodies behind her. "Was it Gus or Gala? I can't remember their names, they change like the wind," she tittered.

Neelo's heart sank. The Queen's words were more slurred, her eyes more vacant than they'd ever seen her before. Neelo turned to find Farros, leaning against the wall beside the throne. "What does that mean? Who are these people?"

"I don't know where it comes from, Your Highness." Farros shrugged and toyed with the bundle of white flowers tucked into his breast pocket. "It just shows up. More whenever we want it."

Hands clenched by their sides, Neelo asked, "And that never concerned you?"

Farros tongued the corner of his mouth thoughtfully. His gaze strayed to the Queen. "My only concern is when it stops."

Neelo froze. Their eyes narrowed on the flowers in Farros's pocket: snowflowers—a small posy of them just like the ones hanging from the shelf where the Queen's secret stash was hidden. They forced their eyes away, not wanting to let on that they might've found their rat. But Farros? Of all people, he was one of their mother's most trusted courtiers. It wasn't enough to outright condemn him. They needed to have him followed—watched—his every move cataloged until they could confirm he had something to do with their mother's personal brew. Talhan seemed to sense Neelo's racing heart and wooden movements and shifted closer to their side.

Queen Emberspear tracked the movement. "You two seem . . ."

Neelo braced for it, erecting a shield of armor within themself. *Please don't mention it,* Neelo silently pleaded to all the Gods who listened. They were terrified if their mother cast light on this thing—this beautiful, raw thing between them—that it might shatter under her scrutiny.

"Perhaps the Fates were right." The Queen snickered and Neelo readied for her verbal attack but instead she switched subjects. "What have you been up to in Arboa? I sense things seem amiss."

"I'm surprised you can sense anything at all with that much witching brew clouding your mind," Talhan said.

A few courtiers gasped at his insolence but the Queen just threw her head back and laughed. When she lifted her gaze to Neelo, her eyes were filled with mischief and Neelo cringed.

Farros cleared his throat, pulling the Queen's attention off Neelo as he proffered up a goblet of wine to her. Farros had always been good at deflecting the Queen's scrutiny. The courtier had probably saved Neelo from many verbal thrashings over the years. Neelo silently mouthed the words "thank you" to him, before remembering that he might not be as much of their ally as they'd once believed. Was he lying about their mother's brew because he didn't want to stop smoking it? Or for more nefarious reasons? Maybe he wasn't lying at all and it was all a terrible coincidence . . . but it was far too much to ignore.

"Ah yes," the Queen said, as if Farros's arched brow was enough to remind her. "The last shipment of brew from Arboa has not yet arrived at the docks."

Neelo's gut clenched but they held firm. They slipped on a new mask, one they knew their mother would appreciate. They lifted their chin and pushed confidence into their voice. "Don't worry, I'm sure the ship is delayed by the summer storms."

The Queen tapped out her pipe and let the ash dance to the floor. "If you two are a part of this delay," she shot an accusatory finger at Neelo, "then sort it out. The citizens of Saxbridge will not be happy."

Neelo's eyes casually flitted around the room in the act of indifference their mother had perfected. "Focus on the Solstice. If it is truly your last year on the throne, I'd imagine you'd want this celebration to be unparalleled."

Queen Emberspear's lips twisted up in a devious smirk. "Now *that* sounds like a good plan."

Neelo didn't like how easily their mother seemed to be directed these days. Her stubbornness was waning and swayed through the conversations like a sapling bending to the wind. Where was her strength? Her resolute nature? That sharpness was now all blurred edges. Neelo hadn't been gone that long but she seemed so much worse. A witch as powerful as Adisa Monroe could probably claw her way into such a weakened mind with ease.

A messenger scurried into the room with a note and passed it to Farros with a curtsy. Neelo's eyes narrowed at Farros, scrutinizing his every movement with suspicion. Talhan nudged Neelo with his elbow and Neelo gave him a nearly imperceptible shake of their head. They'd tell him once they were out of this room.

Farros opened the note and grinned. "Your visitors' carriages were just spotted passing through the gates of Ruttmore, Your Majesty."

"They're here already?" Neelo scowled, turning toward the door. "Shit. I need to go change."

"Where are you going?" The Queen's voice echoed off the stone and Neelo wondered if their mother had even heard the message. "To hide in the library I presume?"

"No, Mother." Neelo glanced over their shoulder, their grin a mirror to their mother's own. "I'm going to do what Southerners do best. I'm going to throw a party."

They delighted in the brief second of surprise that crossed the Queen's face, a flicker of the ruler she once was, before they turned and strode out into the hall.

Talhan fell into step beside them. "What was that about?"

Neelo dropped their voice to a whisper. "I need you to do me a favor."

"Anything."

They raced down the corridor toward their chambers. "I need you to organize someone to tail Farros." Neelo held up their hand to silence the inevitable questions. They'd explain more after they changed. "I want to know his every step, his every breath. Pay a guard named Erick—handsomely—to be Farros's shadow until I say otherwise. He is trustworthy."

Talhan lifted his chin, seemingly impressed. "Consider it done," he said and peeled off from Neelo to do as they commanded. They thanked the Gods for all of his soldierly training in that moment. Maybe the answers to their mother's ailments had been hiding right under their nose all along. Farros would lead Erick right to their mother's supplier and then Neelo would finally be able to intercede. But first, they need to fill the role they dreaded more than any other: host.

CHAPTER THIRTY-FIVE

O ut of the carriage stepped two witches, one blue, one green—
easy to spot, judging by their sapphire and forest green
dresses. A hawk ruffled its feathers from Aneryn's shoulder
as she offered Neelo a warm smile and a half-bow. Neelo returned the
gesture even though royal protocol didn't technically include witches.

Neelo had known Aneryn for as long as they could remember . . .
though they had few occasions to actually speak to each other. The blue
witch had become softer over the past few months, less guarded than
she'd seemed on previous visits.

Aneryn had always held her chin high, despite the scrutiny of both fae
and witches alike. One of the few blue witches who remained physically
unscathed during Hennen Vostemur's reign, Aneryn seemed trapped between two worlds. The other blue witches distrusted Aneryn for being
Renwick Vostemur's personal Seer and the rest of the arrogant Northern
fae looked at her like she was nothing more than a symbol of their power.
Neelo knew that feeling all too well—being more of an image than an
actual living person. They knew what it felt like to exist on the periphery
too. They saw that loneliness in Aneryn for a long time, though it seemed
to have faded. It bonded them somehow, in the same way it did Aneryn
and Rua.

"Greetings," Neelo said, shifting on their feet as if they had suddenly forgotten how to stand. Even with people who were more than mere acquaintances, Neelo suddenly had a keen feeling of awkwardness: how they stood, how they spoke, where their eyes drifted to, whether their hands should be in their pockets or clasped in front of them. Just the very act of *being* felt so painful sometimes they wanted to fade into the shadows.

Then Talhan stepped forward.

"Aneryn!" he exclaimed in that easy, delightful way that made Neelo lower their shoulders an inch. Talhan was here. He would fill every silence with his pleasantries and Neelo could be as silent and as awkward as they liked and no one would even notice with someone like Talhan Catullus around.

"Ah, a Twin Eagle," Aneryn said with a smirk, sizing up Talhan. "The Southern sun suits you."

Talhan batted away the compliment with a mock wave of his hand. "I'm a sweaty pig."

Aneryn's dark eyes flared to a magical sapphire. "Well, it could suit you maybe one day, I should say."

Talhan leaned in and whispered conspiratorially, "Have you Seen it?"

"She wouldn't tell you even if she had," the green witch said in a bright, feminine voice. She had thick, straight black hair, pale skin, and hooded brown eyes.

"Your Highness, this is Laris Tane," Aneryn said, introducing her friend as she dropped into a deep bow.

Neelo bobbed their head to Laris, assessing her gentle smile and sparkle in her eye that made Neelo think she was probably kind and creative—likely a good painter or singer. "Did you grow up in the North, Laris? Or do you hail from the green witch coven in the Southern Court?"

"I was born in the North, Your Highness," the witch said in her sharp accent, though it was tempered by the softness of her pitch. "Though I still have many family members residing in Saxbridge. I'm excited to meet them."

It was then Neelo realized this green witch probably never had occasion to travel before. Northern witches weren't given the freedom, money, or time to travel and visit family. They thought of the witches of old who were powerful sovereigns of their own covens, not servants and slaves to the fae. Neelo could barely remember life before the Siege of Yexshire. It felt like it had always been that way. It probably did for Laris as well—like she'd always been the property of the Northern King.

"I hope you get to see your family during your visit," Neelo said. "If you need help contacting them, the court ambassador can assist you." They looked halfway to Aneryn, their eyes landing on her fawn boots but not lifting to meet her dark brown stare.

Something about eyes. Staring into them made Neelo's stomach drop, as if looking too long might give the blue witch a glimpse of their future, nothing like the warmth of looking into Talhan's eyes.

They cleared their throat, feeling more off kilter than usual. "No one should give you trouble. You are all here as guests of the royal family."

Aneryn's cheeks dimpled. "Thank you."

Fenrin hovered by Talhan's side, clasping his hands eagerly as if he wanted to reach out and hug Aneryn. Neelo pressed their lips together to hide their smirk. The lanky blond witch watched Aneryn like a lovesick puppy.

Another carriage rolled in behind the two witches and Fenrin craned his neck. "Mother Moon, how much luggage did you bring?"

Aneryn snickered. "That is not our carriage."

The carriage had barely halted before the door swung open, and out jumped Carys, quickly followed by Rua and Renwick Vostemur. Neelo's shoulders dropped when they spotted Carys, a smile breaking through their icy visage.

"Car! Ru!" Talhan rushed over to Rua and scooped her up into a giant hug.

Rua guffawed but relented and hugged him back. Talhan had that way with people, even Rua. Renwick shook Talhan's hand and gave him a look, not exactly warm, but knowing, before his eyes lifted to Neelo.

"We thought we'd come a bit earlier since Aneryn and Laris will be staying for the rest of the summer," Rua said. "We may have told the others too." She tucked a wavy brown lock behind her ear. "Apologies for the early intrusion."

"And to make sure Aneryn is well looked after while she's here," Renwick added tightly.

Rua nudged him and he shifted his weight. Renwick had been a guard dog for Aneryn for most of her life. How many times had he been forced to give a threatening speech to the fae Lords about Aneryn? How many places had Renwick been forced to leave her where he feared for her safety?

"We won't be here for all that long," Aneryn chastised, giving Renwick a cutting look.

Carys darted straight for Neelo and kissed them on both cheeks. "I wasn't about to send this lot South without me," Carys said with a laugh and then whispered, "Sorry, I wanted to warn you but we hit the road as soon as we heard about the witches coming South."

Neelo chuckled. "You know me too well."

"I know you don't like surprises," Carys said. "Especially in the form of early visitors, but I figured my attendance might temper the blow."

"It does," Neelo said with a grateful smile, watching stiffly as everyone hugged one another. "Definitely. Let's go inside," they offered, wringing their hands and selecting one of the many sentences they stored in their mind to end a conversation. "I'll have Rish set out some refreshments."

Talhan perked up at that and led the others inside.

As they turned and headed toward the arched palace entryway, Neelo glanced back over their shoulders at the far stone walls and open gates that led to the palace. Nerves filled them as they stared at the two guards who manned either side of the entryway. Did Neelo trust them enough to be checking each carriage and wagon that rolled into the grounds? Neelo felt like the only one perched on the edge of a razor's blade, waiting for Augustus Norwood to appear and the world to spring into chaos.

Rua stepped up beside Neelo. "Please tell me you're dreading the prospect of another ball as much as me," she muttered. "It feels like there's a new one every week."

"Don't worry," Neelo whispered, breaking off their stare at the far walls. They glanced down at the Immortal Blade on Rua's hip, grateful the magical sword was in the palace too. One more line of defense. "There's plenty of books for you to hide behind too."

"Thank the Moon," Rua said with a sigh. "If I have to pretend I care about palace decor for one more second, I think I'm going to stab someone."

Renwick's arm wrapped around her waist as he came to Rua's other side. "Wouldn't be the first time."

THE ROYALS OF each court bounced back and forth between the guest rooms, shouting and laughing like children at a slumber party. Bri and Lina showed up with a crate filled with wine bottles and Remy and Hale arrived soon after. Fortunately, the guest wing was ready and waiting for their arrival despite Queen Emberspear's lack of planning. Councilor Denton, to his credit, arranged for the rooms to be cleaned and fresh cut flowers to be placed in each of the royal guest chambers. Watching the antics of the fae crew, though, Neelo knew they could've been camping out in the woods and still been enjoying themselves just as much.

Neelo found a spot against the wall with a clean line of sight out the window. They tracked Erick through a sliver of garden far below and knew he must be trailing behind Farros. He walked in his normal, militaristic way as if patrolling the garden walls, but Neelo could tell his attention was keyed in on someone just beyond the window's line of sight. At least Erick seemed focused on the task at hand. Neelo's eyes shifted to the cloaked green witches planting a new garden bed, imagining that under each hood were the beady black eyes and white-blond hair of Augustus Norwood. How was he planning on arriving in Saxbridge? Surely he wouldn't be brash enough to walk straight through the front door? Neelo had known the Norwood urchin his whole life and it seemed more likely he'd stow away in the back of a wagon like the little rat he was.

Rua was one of the few not scampering about. She leaned against the wall beside Neelo, her arms crossed, a bemused expression on her face. The Immortal Blade hung on her belt and the rubies of the hilt glinted in the light.

Remy paused in the middle of the hallway and looked down at Rua's laced burgundy boots. "Are those mine?"

"No," Rua said too quickly.

"Yeah right." Remy snorted and folded her arms over her chest in twin action to her sister. Neelo wondered if the sisters realized how similar they really were. Remy opened her mouth to say something but instead lifted her hand to her forehead.

Rua frowned at the action. "What's wrong?"

"Nothing," Remy said, hiding the movement by wiping the sweat across her brow but Rua had clearly noted it.

Renwick strode out of a room behind where Rua leaned, his eyes flickering a shade of sapphire so briefly that Neelo wondered if they'd imagined it.

"You're wearing too many layers for the Southern heat," Renwick said in that tight, clipped voice of his. His eyes were sharp on Remy's as if he was telling her something, and she gave a subtle nod before turning and disappearing back into her room.

Rua whirled on Renwick. "What was that about?"

Renwick circled his arms around Rua's waist. "I'll tell you after dinner." He bent down to kiss her neck and she leaned into his embrace.

"Don't think you can distract me," Rua snapped, her hand drifting toward the hilt of the sword on her hip. Renwick pulled her tighter into his chest in silent reprimand and Rua rolled her eyes.

He smiled against her skin. "Never, *mhenissa*."

Carys darted across the hall carrying a white linen dress, and despite the fact she was in the farthest room and running the fastest, she paused and immediately spotted Neelo hiding in the shadows with Rua.

"Supervising the unpacking, Heir of Saxbridge?" she called loud enough that everyone's heads popped out of their rooms and called their thanks out to Neelo.

Neelo gritted their teeth, the feeling as irksome as when they were sung to on their birthday. The attention of one, maybe two, was tolerable, but never a crowd. Neelo knew Carys had done it on purpose just to ruffle their feathers. She was one of the only ones Neelo allowed to do it without reproach.

With a final kiss to Rua's neck, Renwick disappeared into his room and Rua leaned back against the stone wall beside them.

"I'm surprised to see you without a book," Rua said, eyes dropping to Neelo's empty hands. "It seems odder than me being without this blade."

Neelo blanched, realizing they hadn't grabbed one of their books off their shelf when they left their rooms after changing, so focused on keeping an eye on the palace grounds as if Augustus Norwood might be hiding in every shrub. But they did grab their black satin jacket, which meant . . . They reached into their jacket pocket and pulled out a book so small it could fit in the size of their palm.

"Ah." Rua grinned. "I stand corrected." Rua leaned closer to Neelo. "Please tell me there are *two* little books in your jacket? I don't think I can handle a night with this lot."

"We can stop by the library on the way." They bit the corner of their lip and added, "I'm glad you're here." Rua seemed taken aback by that, but she smiled and gave Neelo a nudge with her shoulder. "I'm glad the Immortal Blade is always with you too."

"That doesn't sound ominous at all." Rua's lips curved down. "Do you expect trouble this Solstice?"

"Possibly. Yes." Neelo peered down the hall, the joy of everyone's ministrations making their dread grow further. Even the crowns of Okrith, Neelo's most trusted allies, didn't seem to pick up on the tension in the air. Were they overreacting? No. Everyone should be feeling the same as them, but Saxbridge had a way of quieting unease. It corrupted even the smartest and bravest in Okrith—witching brew or no. Neelo trained their eyes back to the window and said, "I've been thinking a lot about that letter you sent me months ago."

Rua's voice dropped into a whisper as she eyed the jovial frenzy of their crew unpacking. "The violet witches?" Neelo nodded. "Augustus said they'd already tied their strings in the South, one pull and the whole place would crumble." She shivered as if reliving that moment. "Have you learned what that means?"

"It has to do with the brew." Neelo's gaze continued to rove, unable to stop searching. "I think that sickeningly sweet smoke that you were attacked with in the North isn't the only kind of smoke Adisa Monroe has in her arsenal."

"So get rid of the brew," Rua said flatly.

"That simple, huh?" Neelo shot her a sharp look and Rua's mouth twisted. "Why didn't I think of that?"

Rua was about to say more when Bern popped out from down the hall and walked over to them, leaning against the opposite wall. Neelo cocked their brow at him, guessing he rolled in with Remy and Hale, though in the flurry of unpacking they might have missed his arrival.

"It is impolite to eavesdrop," Rua said.

"And it is impolite to keep important news from your family," Bern countered. The scar down his neck was prominently displayed by the open collar of his silver shirt. His attire matched his silvery gray hair, so at odds with his young features. "Have you found Cole?"

Neelo tilted their head, studying him. That was Bern's first question? The trip to Silver Sands Harbor had only been a short visit, but Bern and Cole seemed to become fast friends over that time. Perhaps Bern didn't believe Cole to be the threat that the others did . . . though given his current state, he wasn't a threat to anyone.

"He's alive," Neelo said, watching Bern's eyebrows shoot up in surprise and then a wave of relief cross his face.

"Where is he?"

"He . . . is not here," Neelo hedged. "He is recovering elsewhere. But he is alive."

"Recovering?" Bern pushed off the wall. "What—"

"Hey," Rua cut in and Bern stalled. "If Neelo could share more, they would."

"Of course," Bern said with a sigh. "The past few weeks have been . . . difficult."

"It hasn't been that long since . . ." Rua stopped before saying it but they all knew who she was speaking of: Raffiel—Rua's older brother and Bern's Fated. His death was still so recent. Okrith celebrated the fact he lived and mourned the fact he died on the same day, and it reminded Neelo again that time was not promised. Joy could be found and taken away in a single breath, and it made them regret that they would have to steal everyone's joy away on this visit.

As if summoned from their storming thoughts, Talhan stumbled out of his sister's room, Bri, Lina, and Carys in tow.

His lighthearted footsteps faltered. "Everything okay?"

"Just trying to figure out the plans of a centuries' old witch before she destroys the realm," Neelo said with a shrug. "Nothing major."

The group let out a collective chuckle, but an unease still filled the air, and this time, they hoped the group would follow up on it. They'd all been through so much to get to this moment, together, and every time it felt like the world would slow long enough for them to celebrate, another devastating blow would land upon them.

"I think we need some wine," Bri called from the back of the gathering group. She cast her amber gaze upon Neelo. "And to relax a bit."

Carys snorted. "When have they ever been relaxed?"

Neelo's stomach still grumbled, missing the meal they declined from Rish, but like food, drinks would have to wait. "Listen, I am delighted to have you all here b—"

"Okay, okay," Hale said, pushing to the front of the group. "Drinks first. Compliments second."

Neelo opened their mouth to correct him and faltered. They cursed their quiet voice and suddenly trembling hands. They were equals to these people, crown or no, but their nerves got the better of them and they hated the way they just shut their mouth and leaned back to let the group pass. Like a mighty undertow beneath still waters, a voice inside them screamed that they should make the others listen, but not a single sound came out. Instead of screams, there was silence, and the group carried on as if a war wasn't raging inside Neelo, as if Neelo hadn't minded at all. They tried to gather their storming thoughts. Maybe these people would listen better with a bottle of wine in their hands anyway . . .

The group followed closely behind Bri, filtering out until Neelo and Talhan were left standing there.

He seemed to be the only one to pick up on the storm inside Neelo. Talhan's eyes filled with concern as he prowled closer to Neelo and leaned his hands against the wall on either side of their head.

"You seem troubled," he whispered, his eyes dipping to their lips, and between that look in his eyes and the sudden silence, the anger in Neelo's chest blossomed into heat.

"Should I not be?" Neelo countered, trying to cling to their concerns and ignore the thrill that ran through them. "We still don't know what Adisa Monroe has planned. Think of the previous attacks: even if we have Remy's amulet and Rua's blade, if they have that violet smoke, it could nullify their powers. What if they've poisoned the cutlery and—"

Talhan cupped Neelo's jaw and kissed them hard, silencing their words with his lips. His tongue brushed the seam of Neelo's mouth and they opened for him, a groan rumbling from Talhan as he pinned them to the wall.

"Tal!" Bri's shout echoed up the stone hallway. "Come on!"

"She has the worst timing." Talhan pulled away, resting his forehead against Neelo's with a sigh.

Neelo skirted past him and took a step before Talhan caught their elbow. His amber eyes pierced into Neelo's as he said, "We will check all the metal. We've doubled the guards. Erick is tracking Farros as we speak." His voice was deep and steady, a soothing lull to the nightmare of "what-ifs" that flashed in Neelo's mind. "Their forces are weakened. They would not launch an in-person assault. They will come for your people through the witching brew, just as we suspected, but there will be no blooming amethyst in the new Arboan shipment and your people will be safe from it. We will prepare for every other eventuality just in case."

He briefed Neelo like a military captain. Short. Succinct. Confident. That assurance bled into Neelo like warmth from a fire.

"I want you to direct the Captain of the Guard on this," Neelo declared. Talhan's eyes widened and his fingertips tensed on their arms. "If we are to rule this court together, I want you to be in charge of our military tactics. I trust you more than anyone."

Talhan's eyes heated again and he yanked Neelo back into a burning kiss. His lip skimmed up to Neelo's ear. "Do have any idea how badly I want to fuck you right now?"

Neelo shook under his tight grip, pulling him closer as their lips fused.

"Tal—" Bri turned the corner, her words halting along with her footsteps as she took in the sight of them. She guffawed and quickly spun around.

"Bri, seriously," Talhan growled.

"Oh, don't *seriously* me," Bri said in a mock snarl. She kept her back turned and stared up at the high arched ceiling. "You're standing in the middle of the fucking hallway! It's not like I stumbled into your bedroom. At least Lina and I have the decency to lock the door!"

Neelo snickered, biting their lip as they straightened their jacket. It was not so long ago they'd stumbled upon Bri and Lina in the library at Silver Sands. They hadn't understood it at all then—what would compel them to spring upon each other in such a public place—but now . . . now they were beginning to get it.

"I can make your excuses if you want some time," Bri said, taking a step back.

"No, it's all right." Neelo began walking down the hallway and pausing beside Bri. "We have guests to entertain and I have things I need to tell them."

Bri clapped Neelo on the shoulder as they walked past. "Welcome to the family," she said with a wink. "And may the Gods help you."

Neelo's cheeks burned but they smiled as they murmured, "Thanks." They glanced back at Talhan to see him beaming that blindingly beautiful smile.

Bri took a step toward him and his smile flickered out.

"I need a word with you," she said pointedly.

He leaned past his sister and gestured for Neelo to carry on. "See you at the wine cellars."

Neelo rubbed their fingers together and nodded. Heat still flooded their veins from their frenzied kiss and the look in Talhan's eyes promised that their need would be sated soon enough. Neelo's heart fluttered as they followed the sound of echoing voices steering toward the kitchens.

They heard the Twin Eagles' whispered bickering behind them and they felt Bri's words settling into their bones as if being claimed by her. Neelo had thought they were separate from the others for so long but now they realized they were a part of this group too, and that meant Neelo should be able to speak up and they should all listen. They pushed faster, determined to try again. They would listen. For the first time in perhaps forever, it felt good to be part of a family—*this* family—one they had chosen as much as it had chosen them.

CHAPTER THIRTY-SIX

The ever-growing crew couldn't fit in the wine cellar, and so, they ventured to the gazebo in the center of the gardens. They'd carried out enough wine to get half of Saxbridge drunk and as soon as Rish spotted them in the gardens, trays upon trays of food began appearing all around the cool stone edifice. Sheltering from the hot summer sun, they lounged in a circle, catching up on the latest news from each of their courts.

Neelo kept trying to jump in, trying to steer the conversation toward the news they needed to share, but it seemed like not a single sentence was finished before another began. Maybe after they ate there'd be more pauses in conversation? How exactly was someone meant to speak over a group of gabbing royals?

"Ha!" Rua shouted, slamming down a card onto the growing stack.

Bri groaned and threw in her hand.

Renwick slung his arm around Rua's shoulder and pulled her in to kiss her temple. "My Queen," he whispered in her ear.

"It's no fun playing with you two," Bri groused.

Lina elbowed her and chuckled. "Then don't play."

Bri grabbed the bottle of wine from Lina's hand and took a long swig.

"I'm out," Talhan said, throwing in his cards. He leaned back on the stone wall beside Neelo and glanced across the circle to Remy and Hale.

Remy laid with her head in Hale's lap, her dark curly hair spilling across his legs as he casually draped a hand over her side. She reached for a blackberry and fed him one with a smirk.

"So . . . um," Talhan began.

Neelo whipped their head to him. "We're doing this now?" They'd been trying to steer the conversation in this direction since the moment the group arrived but now the words escaped them. Gods, they were meant to be a ruler, comparable to each and every one of these people, but when the time came their mind went blank. Talhan, on the other hand, seemed to have no such qualms and Neelo was once again grateful he could be their mouthpiece.

"Do what?" Bri asked from Talhan's other side.

"It's about your mother, Kira," Talhan hedged.

Hale's gray eyes narrowed. "What about her?"

Talhan nervously picked at the creeping vine twisting through the stone railing. "You know how her favorite flower is blooming amethyst?"

"And?"

Talhan swallowed. "And you know how her middle name is Monroe?"

"Mother Moon, what are you trying to say, Tal?" Remy asked as she sat up.

"Adisa Monroe mothered a fae line."

They all froze, and Neelo clenched their fingers around their book.

Hale looked at Talhan and then Neelo, blinking as if trying to wake from a trance.

"It's true." Neelo gave Hale an apologetic glance. "Kira is a descendant of the violet witch."

"Wait . . . does that mean Hale is part violet witch?" Rua asked.

Bri scrubbed a hand down her face. "For fuck's sake, will you all stop being part witch! I cannot keep up: first Renwick, now Hale? I suppose you're going to tell me I'm part dragon next?"

"It seems your great-great-however-many-grandmother may have been whispering in the late king Gedwin Norwood's ear for some time," Neelo said. "I suspect, though I cannot confirm, it was her who convinced him to claim you as his son."

Remy threaded her fingers through Hale's, forcing him to unclench his hands.

"Gods," Hale snarled. "Why?"

"She's obsessed with her descendant, a boy that will be King," Neelo said. "It's scrawled all over her journal."

"Wait." Carys held up her hand, gesturing between Neelo and Hale. "So *his* grandmother is an ancient violet witch, who now wants to use her great-great-grandchildren to start a violet witch uprising?"

"More or less," Neelo muttered.

"Shit," Bern growled.

"*The smallest seed shall be king.*" Neelo's shoulders bunched around their ears. "That's what her journal said."

"But Hale already is a king," Renwick countered. "Maybe the prophecy was misinterpreted."

"Wouldn't be the first time," Bri muttered.

Lina grabbed the bottle of wine from Bri and took another long drink before saying, "Renwick broke the curse on her blue witch army. Bri stopped the coup against my crown. Whatever else Adisa Monroe has planned, we can handle it."

Hale sighed and stood up with a groan. "I need to talk to my mother. Now."

Remy stood and wrapped her hand around his wrist. "Do you think she knows?"

"I have no idea." Hale shook his head. "How could she keep that from me? More secrets?"

Neelo rubbed their thumb across the pages of their book. They suspected Kira knew more than she was letting on. She did, after all, have the amethyst dagger at one point. And, unless Adisa Monroe managed to steal back that dagger without her knowing, then there was no way Kira didn't have some idea what magic ran in her veins.

"In Valtene," Rua said, her eyes growing vacant. Renwick growled at just the mention of it and shifted closer to her. "Augustus Norwood said that the South was already set to fall, and you now think that has something to do with your witching brew?".

"I think she originally planned to kill us all off under the weight of the growing brew addiction," Neelo muttered. "I think that plan changed when we survived after she attempted to drown us."

Carys spat out her drink, red wine flying across the gazebo. "*What?*"

"It only just happened," Neelo muttered, brushing droplets of wine off their jacket sleeve.

"I don't care!" Carys shouted. "You didn't tell me?"

"I was trying to tell you before and you weren't listening," Neelo said. "I'm telling you now, if you'd be quiet long enough to hear me."

Carys's head whipped toward Talhan. "I blame *you* for these little comebacks," she spat. "Don't think I won't be taking this out on you in the practice rings tomorrow morning."

Talhan threw his head back and whined, "But tomorrow is the first night of the sun festivals!"

"And?" Bri leaned forward and propped her elbows on her knees. "A soldier is only as sharp as his dullest day."

"And we should be drinking and dancing," Talhan groused and Neelo's eyes flared at him. Was he really complaining about partying when the very court he might one day rule was in danger? This is what Saxbridge did to people—blinded them. Surrounded by his friends, had Talhan completely abandoned his good sense or was he just joking? Neelo couldn't tell and they hated that they couldn't read this situation, that it agitated them until they were balling their fists. Life was not one big party and Neelo's leash to their restraint was about to snap.

"After we train," Bri said.

Talhan pouted. "Ugh." Bri's hand snapped out and slapped him across the face. "Hey!" he snarled at her.

She winked at her twin. "And *that* is why we need to train."

Lina guffawed. "Gods, I love you," she said, pulling Bri in to her side.

"Do you think they're going to be okay?" Rua asked, leaning past the group to watch Remy and Hale walking back to the palace.

Renwick's hand squeezed her knee in silent comfort. "Who's in for another round?" he asked, raking in the cards. Rua seemed to perk up at that.

"I'm in," Lina said.

"Me too," Bern added.

They were going back to their card game? At that, Neelo could take no more.

Shooting to their feet, they stared down at the royals and the group instantly sobered. "You're laughing?" they growled. "Why?" Everyone froze, their eyes landing on Neelo like a thousand needle pricks, but they fought against their stares and the urge to step back into the shadows. They needed to be heard, they needed to lead with their gut, they needed to stop overthinking and act before it was too late.

"Neelo," Talhan said.

"No." Neelo whirled on him. "Is food and drink all you care about? Card games? Do you not care that the place for all your parties might be gone tomorrow if you don't do something? Do you not care about its people?" They stared around the group, watching the weight of their gaze land like a blow on each of them. "You are the most powerful fae in all of Okrith. You are the sworn protectors of this realm and yet you drink and play cards when it is *my* court that is about to implode?" Neelo didn't need to be good at reading faces to see the shame now on theirs. "Now I'm going to the council chamber to plan for an attack against someone who has taken the lives of people from every single one of your courts." They turned toward the steps. "Enjoy your revels. Your joy is horrifying."

Neelo didn't get a single step before the entire group was on their feet and following after them.

THE GROUP BROKE off into factions—Renwick and Rua heading to the armory, Bern and Lina to the library, and Carys, Bri, and Talhan followed Neelo through the halls toward the council chamber. They couldn't believe they'd done it—they'd shouted at them—they'd shouted at Kings and Queens of all people. And those Kings and Queens had listened just as they'd knew deep in their bones they would. Their entire body trembled at the confrontation, their heart still racing, but they'd done it. Maybe if they could wake these royals up, they could wake up their people as well.

They careened down the hall, passing through the dormitories on their way to the third level.

"We should grab Fenrin," Bri said, nodding to the door ahead. "He might have some insights into how to counteract the brew in case Norwood rolls in with his own stash."

"He's had my mother to test on the past weeks," Neelo agreed. "If anyone knows how to treat it by now, it's him. Whatever he's using to treat her, we might need to stockpile it soon."

"Are you certain he's well?" Carys asked as they neared Fenrin's door. "I haven't seen him all afternoon."

"He's probably still exhausted from dealing with my mother," Neelo quipped.

They rounded the hall and Carys threw open the door.

"Fen!" Carys's hand fell from the handle and she froze.

Neelo rose on their tiptoes to see what caused Carys to gasp.

"Gods," Bri chuckled, stepping into the room as the door swung wide.

Carys and Bri stepped aside to reveal Fenrin in bed with Laris, the raven-haired green witch. They both yanked the covers up to their chins, their ruddy cheeks red with embarrassment . . . and probably also from other things.

"Get out!" Fenrin shouted, looking like he wished the floor would swallow him whole.

"I thought you were with Aneryn?" Bri strode in, folding her arms over her chest and leaning against the wall.

The bathing chamber door opened and Aneryn stepped out, bare shouldered with nothing but a blanket wrapped around her.

"He is with me," Aneryn said, sauntering over and perching next to Laris on the bed. "They both are."

"Damn, Fen," Bri said with a look of appreciation.

"The *three* of you are together?" Carys's eyebrows shot up.

"Yes," Fenrin said, waving to the door. "And we were planning on keeping it quiet, but seeing as you've brought half the royalty of Okrith to our door—"

"We won't tell anyone," Carys said.

"Yes we will," Bri cut in with a snort. "I have to tell Lina at least."

"Mother Moon." Fenrin pinched the bridge of his nose and Aneryn reached over and swept a soothing hand up his arm.

"Ew, no, weird." Carys covered her eyes and turned toward the door.

"You'll get used to it," Aneryn said.

Carys peeked through her fingers. "Have you Seen that or are you just saying that?"

Aneryn shrugged. "Both."

Talhan made his way down the hall and let out a loud guffaw as he stumbled into the room. "Oh ho!" Laris looked like she was about to shrink beneath the covers, but Aneryn rolled her shoulders back and gave Talhan a look. "A brown witch, a green witch, and a blue witch in bed together." He nudged Neelo with his elbow and they couldn't help but smile. "I'm pretty sure I've heard that one before."

"Can we talk about this *after* we get dressed?" Fenrin asked, his knuckles turning white from gripping the bedsheets.

"Is it just the three of you?" Talhan asked, craning his neck toward the bathing chamber. "Or is this like one of those Saxbridge lovefests?"

"See, that would be a good thing to answer when we have clothes on!" Fenrin's whole face flushed an unseemly shade of red.

"It's just us," Aneryn said. "It's always been the three of us."

"How *long* has it been the three of you?" Carys's brow furrowed. "You only met Fen a few months ago."

"Yeah, you were dancing with someone else at Rua's party . . . ," Talhan snapped and pointed to Laris. "Oh right . . . that was you."

Laris's lips thinned as she glowered at him.

"Why don't you seem particularly surprised?" Talhan narrowed his eyes at Neelo. "You knew, didn't you?"

"What?" Carys whipped around to face Neelo. "You knew? How?"

Neelo shrugged. They'd seen the witches in Yexshire at Remy's wedding and Murreneir at Rua's Equinox festivities. Neelo deduced from the smiles and whispers and shared looks that they each held a candle for the other.

"Don't you do your shruggy thing with me!" Carys scolded.

"I suspected, but never confirmed," Neelo said. "I wasn't going to share suspicions. Besides, it wasn't my story to tell, anyways."

Carys straightened, blinking at them, and Neelo realized it was the wrong thing to say. Shit. They couldn't have picked a worse thing to say to her.

Neelo scrambled to find the right words. "Carys—"

But Carys was already pushing past them.

"She'll get over it," Talhan murmured, pulling Neelo against his side. "It's not the same. What Ersan did to her. It was her own family secret he was keeping from her. This is different."

Neelo swallowed and nodded but their heart was still racing.

"Could you please have this conversation outside of my room?" Fenrin asked, exasperated as he waved at the door again.

"Right, sorry, Fen. Get changed and come meet us in the council chamber. Neelo needs us." Bri gave Neelo a nod of approval and Neelo returned the gesture, grateful they didn't need to shout again to get their point across. Bri shoved Talhan out of the door frame, glancing one more time over her shoulder at them. She leaned into Talhan and whispered, "Look at our little Fen all grown up."

"There's nothing little about him," Aneryn shouted through the door.

Bri pretended to gag. "Ugh. I didn't need to know that."

"It's a good thing they have Aneryn," Talhan said. "No one is going to mess with her."

Bri nudged Neelo with her elbow. "It's always the quiet ones, isn't that right, Neelo?"

Neelo shot her a dark look.

Bri winked. "Too soon?"

"Cut it out." Talhan shoved his sister.

"Or what?"

"Or he'll tell Lina," Neelo cut in.

"Fine." Bri let out a surprised laugh. "Well played, Heir of Saxbridge. My apologies."

They made it halfway down the hall before Renwick turned the corner.

He pulled up short, looking at the three of them. "I was just looking for Aneryn. I thought she might want to help with . . ."

"We were looking for her too," Bri said, ushering Renwick away from Fenrin's door. "Let's go look for her together."

Neelo anxiously clasped their hands. Renwick would probably lose his mind if he saw Aneryn in bed with anyone, let alone *two* other ones.

Aneryn's hawk, Ehiris, squawked down the hallway and Renwick paused, looking back over his shoulder. He pulled his elbow out of Bri's grip. "What are you hiding from me?"

"Wait!" Bri called after him.

He stormed back to Fenrin's door and opened it without warning. At least the three of them were mostly dressed when the door opened again. Fenrin's eyes bugged out of his head when he saw Renwick, his fingers dropping away from the top button of his tunic to hold them out like an arrow was pointing directly at him.

In a flash, Aneryn was in front of Renwick, her dress still unbuttoned to the navel but at least she was mostly covered. Laris rushed off and disappeared into the bathing chamber.

"This is not the way I wanted to tell you," Aneryn said, putting her hands on Renwick's chest. "But I need you to take a breath."

"Tell me what?" Renwick growled, his eyes never leaving Fenrin. "I'm going to kill you."

"Renwick, stop, it's not—"

Renwick pushed past Aneryn, unsheathing the sword on his hip in one swift move. He was about to take another step when he froze midair.

"Enough!" Rua's voice boomed from the doorway.

She pushed past their gathering group, her eyes and hands flaming crimson, her red witch magic holding Renwick in place.

"Aneryn is *not* your property. She can be with whoever she likes," Rua snarled.

"She's not my property," Renwick gritted out, trying to fight against Rua's magic. "She's my *family*." His eyes darted back to Fenrin. "And if you ever hurt her, I will run you through with my sword."

"If he ever hurts me, I'll gladly let you," Aneryn said with a huff, making Fenrin's mouth drop open. "But the stars will fall from the sky before that happens."

Rua curled her fingers in and Renwick stumbled back a step. She grabbed him by the back of his tunic and said, "We need to talk. Let's go."

Bri pressed her lips together, watching the two of them mutter whispers at each other as they stalked off down the hall. "Lina's going to be so mad she missed this."

Neelo grabbed the bedroom door handle and looked Aneryn up and down. "Lock it next time," they said and yanked it closed. "This court makes fools out of the lot of you."

"You're right," Talhan said, taking Neelo by the hand. "I'm so sorry." His voice dropped an octave as he swept his thumb over the back of their hand. "I shouldn't have gotten carried away before. I won't be your fool. I'm sorry."

Neelo's eyes guttered and they fought the urge to take it all back just to make him feel better even though it would've been dishonest. Talhan probably thought he was supporting Neelo by doubling the guard, when he really needed to be supporting them by deeply hearing them and amplifying their voice. This was the line they danced with—wanting for someone else and wanting for themself. The part of them that cared for Talhan wanted him to always be of the side of joy, but the part of them that cared for themself knew they shouldn't absolve him of his guilt. Only his future actions could do that.

Bri clapped Neelo on the shoulder, pulling them from the long silence. "I was hoping to have another crack at that witch after what she did to Lina. But how do we make a plan when we don't know how they're going to attack?"

Neelo turned and led them toward the stairwell. "We prepare in every way we know how."

CHAPTER THIRTY-SEVEN

The crowded gardens were a riot of colors, each outfit brighter than the last. Crystal tea lights dotted the tables and benches throughout the summer gardens, giant torches already lighting up the space, though the sun was still high in the sky. Intoxicating smells of night-blooming flowers circled the air. Giant goblets of sickly sweet wine and pots of spiced cinnamon nuts were served on little platters to partygoers. Stationed all around the festivities were tables of candles and paper lanterns, waiting for midnight when they'd release them all into the sky and bid farewell to the sun and the coming longest day. Seven days of revels to celebrate the glory and power of the sun . . . seven days of wondering if every shadow was Augustus Norwood.

Despite the aid of the Okrith royals, Neelo didn't have any more answers. They'd ordered all of the regions surrounding Saxbridge to be on high alert for anyone fitting the description of Augustus Norwood. Every cart and ship was being inspected coming in and out of the city. Every single thing that might contain the blooming amethyst flower was ordered to be dumped into the harbor or buried—every candle, every perfume, every lovely scented item—just in case it might give Adisa Monroe some sort of power.

So far Erick's shadowing of Farros had turned up nothing—Farros's actions were lewd and predictable, but brought them no closer to the origins of their mother's stash. The Queen's own personal guards seemed to be intentionally hindering Neelo's investigations, probably from her fear that their precious drugs would be taken from them.

For Neelo, every shadow was an assassin ready to spring, every laugh they imagined was the start of a scream, every hand holding a goblet was a dagger. But as the hours ticked by without incident, they began to wonder if they were preparing for something that wasn't going to happen. Had Augustus Norwood abandoned his plans? Could Cole's ramblings even be trusted?

The crowd jigged to the horns and drums, the music more full and stirring than in the other courts. The pounding sounds vibrated through Neelo from the top of their head to the tip of their toes, as if summoning them into the dance, and they remembered the way the drums made them feel when they'd inhaled all that witching brew. They felt that lust rise in them again even now like an echo, but that lust was nothing compared to what they knew their body could now experience. When the song finished, the crowd cheered and hastened toward their glasses of wine circling the patch of grass that had become a dance floor.

Remy and Hale had left to go back to the High Mountain Court. Whatever conversation Hale had had with his mother was still a mystery to them, but it was enough to prompt their immediate departure. Neelo agreed with their decision to get Hale out of Saxbridge. If Augustus Norwood was planning to show up, then at least Hale would be long gone, disrupting whatever plan Adisa Monroe had for her *smallest seed*.

But the others had remained to help Neelo, their nerves seeming to temper the festivities, and they were thankful their friends trusted their gut instinct enough to finally take them seriously. They all seemed rattled by the way Neelo had shouted at them and Neelo knew they weren't going to let it come to that again before aiding them next time. And if there was a next time, Neelo now knew they possessed the faculties to actually speak up and that made doing it again—slightly—less terrifying.

The rest of the city seemed to go on unknowing, gathering at the festivities to watch the longest day from the southernmost tip of Okrith. No celebration matched the Summer Solstice in Saxbridge. It was brighter, bigger, more filled with vibrancy and life than any other . . . much like the fae warrior standing below a bough of summer flowers across the clearing from them.

Neelo's heart leapt into their throat at the sight of Talhan. Their eyes trailed up from his shined brown boots and fitted leather trousers to his gold and silver tunic and gold-lined eyes. If Neelo hadn't already decided he was the Sun God incarnate, they would certainly be convinced now.

He wore a similar look of awe as he studied Neelo's midnight outfit, trimmed in a matching gold that they picked because they knew the Eagle would be wearing his own patron color. Sun and stars were embroidered along the sleeves and golden studs along the collar. Neelo had considered painting their lips in the ceremonial gold but then decided against it, just in case the Eagle decided to kiss them. They couldn't help but notice Talhan hadn't painted his lips either.

Talhan made his way through the crowd toward them, and Neelo's pulse climbed up their throat, beating louder with each of his steps. Bowing, Talhan opened his mouth to inevitably say something complimentary but Neelo cut him off.

"Have you seen any sign of Norwood?" They rose up on their tiptoes and peered over the crowd. It was all the usual faces: the rich elite of the Southern Court and the wealthy fae families from all of Okrith. A few witches and humans dotted about the crowd as well. Upon towering stone pedestals were the performers Neelo had selected, entertaining the easily impressed crowd.

Their mother was nowhere to be seen, nor her gaggle of courtiers, but the night was young and she was probably still getting dressed . . . or still in a state of undress.

Denton emerged from the crowd and bowed to Neelo. "A beautiful evening, Your Highness," he said. He wore a short-sleeved lilac tunic and ivory linen pants, silver jewelry draped down his chest and circling his wrists and fingers. His lips and eyes were painted with brilliant gold and his cheeks decorated with silver stars. He'd outdone himself just as any good Southerner would.

"Mostly thanks to you, Councilor," Neelo said with an approving nod, eyeing the guards stationed all along the palace walls. "I like how many guards I'm seeing."

"If Augustus Norwood even steps foot through the palace grounds this evening, we will apprehend him at once." Denton's voice was filled with confidence—too confident—and Neelo frowned at the goblet of wine in his hands.

"Keep your wits about you, Denton," Neelo scolded. "It's only the first night of the Solstice celebrations, and we have a potential threat looming over our court."

"Of course, Your Highness," Denton said, sketching a quick flustered bow. He scurried off back into the crowd.

"Go easy on him," Talhan said with a laugh. "He's one of the few people keeping this whole place running."

"I know." Neelo sighed. "I just . . ."

"You just want to catch Norwood and protect your court." He smiled down at them. "Like any good ruler would." Talhan snatched a glass of lemonade off a passing tray and handed it to Neelo. "I'd wager Norwood's plans changed after we thwarted that attack," he said, giving voice once again to Neelo's doubts. "I don't think he's still planning on coming here at all. But if he was, he'd probably pick the last night of the Solstice, when everyone is exhausted from partying for a week straight."

"You're right," Neelo muttered, still searching every head in the crowd for a flash of white-blond hair. They were prepared. They were protected. All of Saxbridge was on the lookout for him . . . and yet that nagging feeling in their gut wouldn't abate.

Talhan swayed back and forth as the music changed, and Neelo knew he was eager to join the throng of dancers. Candlelight flickered from the lanterns hanging around the grove as more and more revelers were called by the lutes, horns, and drums.

"Go." Neelo nudged Talhan's shoulder. "Dance."

"I don't have to," Talhan said even as he hummed along.

"We don't have to do this every time." Neelo took a long sip of their mint and blackberry lemonade before shoving Talhan a little harder. They ignored that nagging feeling and listened to their logic instead: Norwood wouldn't attack tonight. "Go on."

They watched as Talhan stumbled into the circle of dancers, finding a spot amongst the line. His smile broadened as he spun and clapped and Neelo's heart seemed to skip along with him. He was glorious. Strong and kind, lethal and joyful . . . he was singular in every way that he claimed Neelo to be.

Neelo heard the gravel shift then pause beside them. At the first whiff of the sharp, sweet scent of calendula and orchids, they knew it was Carys.

"Enjoying the festivities?" Neelo asked, keeping their eyes fixed on Talhan.

"Clearly not as much as you," Carys teased, leaning her shoulder into Neelo's. "Thanks for clearing away my competition for the Eastern throne."

Neelo blew out a puff of air. "Yes, that is the only reason. I was doing it for you, so, you're welcome."

Carys grinned, scanning Neelo head to toe. "You look amazing by the way," she said, quirking her brow. "Confident. Powerful. But there's something off about . . . Ah! No book."

Neelo gave her a sidelong glance. "You don't think I've changed that much have you?" They pointed to the potted plant sitting on the pedestal behind them. "I'm still me."

They felt the words even more as they spoke. Neelo had always forced themself to try new things in order to be more like someone else. They'd never considered there'd be new habits, new styles, new routines that made them feel even *more* like themself. They were only beginning to realize they could take the parts that worked for them and leave the parts that didn't. In a court of excess, they finally realized they didn't have to be all or nothing anymore.

Carys lifted onto her tiptoes and stuck her hand into the dense foliage, pulling out a heavy leather-bound tome. "Unbelievable." She weighed the hefty book in her hand and chortled. "Do you have these stashed all over the place?"

"Let's just say the library only contains a small portion of my collection," Neelo said with a grin.

"How do you not lose track of them?"

"I have a system."

Carys snorted. "Of course, how foolish of me." She threaded her arm through Neelo's and gave them a quick squeeze. "I'm sorry I stormed off earlier."

Neelo's lips pulled up to one side. "I'm sorry too." The conversation paused and Neelo knew exactly why Carys was biting her lip. "He's doing well," Neelo said, beating her to the question and Carys's shoulders sagged with relief. "Though he clearly still misses you."

Carys bristled at that. She crossed one arm under her bust and took a long drink of her red wine before speaking again. "Everything about here reminds me of him," she murmured. "I keep thinking I see him from the corner of my eye. His shadow darkens every heartbeat in my once homeland."

"It's still your homeland," Neelo said tightly.

"It hasn't been since the day my father died." She let out a long sigh. "Sorry. I'm ruining all the fun."

"Would it help if I banished him?" Neelo grinned.

With a half-hearted laugh, Carys inclined her head to Neelo and said, "One day I just might take you up on that offer."

The music dwindled and the dancers all paused, turning to the musicians in the gazebo as they waited for the next song. The first slow resonant note had them breaking off into pairs, leaving Talhan standing in the center of the circle. He looked to his feet and gave a soft grin that only Neelo knew was disappointment and took a step as if to leave the dance floor. Something about that look on his face made Neelo ache.

Without another thought they passed their glass of lemonade to Carys, practically shoving it into her hands. She didn't have time to question Neelo before they were walking away. Their heart raced and two steps from the dance floor, they spotted two Arboan fae and quickly plucked the broad hat off one. They pulled it down onto their head, blocking out the twinkling lights and sounds on either side of them as their eyes locked with Talhan's.

The warrior's lips parted, his eyes filled with heat as Neelo lifted their chin and strode straight up to him.

"Dance with me?" they asked.

Talhan's cheeks dimpled and he breathlessly bobbed his head. Neelo pulled him closer, placing one hand in his, the other snaking around to his lower back as he did the same to them. Neelo was taking the lead tonight. The feeling of Talhan's proximity filled the air with static lightning, every place they touched tingling. The Arboan hat blocked out every spectator, every stare, until all they could see were those gold-painted eyes watching them like they were the sun in the sky.

They swayed around the dance floor, rocking to the sweet slow strings. The music, the fragrant gardens, the warmth of Talhan's touch—it cast a spell over Neelo more potent than any magic. They adjusted their stolen hat, thinking of the advice Ersan had given them. Maybe they could do all the things they desired in the depths of their soul. Maybe they just needed to find their own way of doing them.

Neelo peered up into Talhan's face, his eyes locked on their mouth. A devious smirk tugged at their lips. "What are you thinking about?"

His hand splayed across Neelo's back and he pulled them closer until their bodies were flush against each other. Neelo led him around the dance floor as his fingers drifted lower to the small of Neelo's back. His voice was a low rumble as he said, "You know exactly what I'm thinking about."

Neelo smirked. "Saxbridge is working its magic on you too, I see."

Talhan shook his head, his fingertips pressing into Neelo's flesh. "There is only one person who can wield this magic over me." His eyes pinned Neelo with a heated look. "You are a magic all your own, Neelo Emberspear. I've known it my whole life."

"I should've known," Neelo whispered, shaking their head at him in awe-filled disbelief. "I should've known sooner. Maybe I did in the deepest parts of myself but . . ."

"But?"

"I was afraid I was wrong," they said.

"You weren't. Didn't you notice the flickers?"

"Flickers?"

"Moments between us," Talhan said, cocking his head.

Neelo hummed and took a deep breath of Talhan's spiced warm scent. "I guess I didn't. But maybe I should have noticed them too."

"Oh?"

"Like the fact you were the first person to call me Neelo," they said.

Talhan paused. "What?"

"You had these little nicknames for everyone. Bri, Hales . . ." Their mind wandered off to the memory. "It was so long ago. I've forgotten most of those earliest years, but that moment I remember like it was yesterday. We were all in the botanical gardens in Wynreach. I, of course, was sat off to the side while you all played that lawn bowling game."

Talhan's grin was warm and loving. "Yes."

"And you called to me, asking if I wanted to play." Their throat constricted and their eyes pricked with tears. "You called me Neelo instead of my old name and . . . and it felt like I was *seen* for the first time in my life."

Tears spilled from Neelo's eyes and Talhan gently swept them away. "I told you," he whispered, lifting Neelo's hand and brushing a kiss to the back of their knuckles. "You are smart, handsome, brave, and kind. You are so incredible that it leaves me in awe. I see you, Neelo Emberspear, and I could never mistake you for anything else."

Neelo took a step back from him and for a brief second worry clouded Talhan's expression before Neelo threaded their fingers through his and gave him a tug off the dance floor. They kept their head down, their hat blocking out what was sure to be people watching. Talhan snagged a tray of bread and dips from a server, holding it above the height of the rest of the crowd, just like old times. Neelo chuckled as they stared at the gravel below their boots and the crowd parted for them as they led Talhan deeper through the gardens.

"Where are we going?" Talhan asked, his voice filled with amusement as Neelo wiped away the last of their tears.

Their fingers squeezed tighter around Talhan's. "Somewhere where we can just be us."

CHAPTER THIRTY-EIGHT

Neelo led Talhan threw the gardens, their pulse thrumming in their ears. The only communication between them was the subtle squeeze Talhan gave them and they knew he was just as eager to find a quiet location. It would take too long to double back through the palace let alone get to their chambers, and that soft sweep of Talhan's thumb over the back of their hand had them burning.

Finally, Neelo lifted their head and pulled their hat back. The balcony was empty. Candles dotted the balustrade and incense burned but the location was too removed from the revelry and too early for others to have strayed so far from the drinks and banquet.

Neelo sat with their back to the gardens, leaning against the stone pillars of the balustrade. Placing the tray of food between them, Talhan sat. He dipped a piece of flatbread into the bowl of olive oil and then dabbed it in the salty red spice mixture.

He hummed as he chewed. "Solstice bread is my favorite."

Neelo watched him with new eyes. This was who they'd always been to each other, and yet, it felt brand-new too. The ease and comfort of their companionship mixed with the excitement and thrill of their romance. The sense of *rightness* sitting together and listening to the party from their little corner of the world—this was what love felt like.

Neelo popped a roasted almond into their cheek, yearning building in them as they looked up at their best friend.

"What sort of mischief are you up to, troublemaker?" Talhan asked as his eyes hungrily roved over Neelo's form. If they had ever questioned his desire for them before, now they were certain.

"You know the exact brand of mischief," Neelo whispered, their voice thick with lust.

Talhan dropped the bread in his hands, easily forgotten as he traced his palm up their arm and shoulder, skimming up the side of their neck and curving around the back to pull their lips to his. He lifted the tray and put it on the ledge above them.

"Thank the Gods," Talhan murmured against Neelo's lips. "I would've combusted."

Neelo smirked, their hands sliding up and down Talhan's sides. A thrill ran through them as Talhan shuddered and they realized how much control they had of the fae warrior in that moment, how acutely attuned he was to each of their touches. Neelo's fingers skimmed the hem of Talhan's golden tunic and he lifted his arms in response. His eyes fixed on Neelo as they whipped the gold-dusted garment over his head, exposing his perfectly sculpted chest.

Talhan's hands scrambled to do the same until they were both bare from the waist up. They both stood and made quick work of their shoes and trousers, stripping naked as the evening breeze provided relief from the heavy heat both in the air and in their veins.

Neelo reached for Talhan but the warrior took a step back, desire swirling in his gaze as he slowly scanned Neelo from head to toe. Gooseflesh trailed over their skin, following in the wake of his yearning assessment. Maybe it was the moon, or the soft echo of music, or the breeze on their skin but instead of shrinking themself smaller, Neelo leaned back, arching against the balustrade.

Talhan bit down on a groan as Neelo dipped their fingers into the olive oil and trailed their slick hand down their soft belly. Their fingers drifted lower, brushing oil through the hair between their legs.

Talhan took a step forward.

"Don't," Neelo commanded and Talhan halted, clenching his fists at his side. "Not yet."

Confidence filled them as they widened their stance. They were going to take the lead on this too. Their fingers drifted lower, stroking oil down the center of themselves as their hips lifted to their own touch. Air hissed out from Talhan's clenched teeth.

"You're trying to kill me aren't you?" His whole body was so tense—a tightly wound coil ready to spring.

Neelo's fingers circled themself again and they moaned. Talhan snarled in response. Neelo's fingers dipped into the oil again and they swept the slick liquid between their legs and all the way up to their back entrance.

"I want to try something different," Neelo said, feeling high on the boldness of finally taking what they wanted, and they wanted to be filled again, but in a way that felt more right, more *them*.

"Oh?" Talhan's voice was feral, barely escaping his gritted teeth.

"I want you to take me." Neelo swirled the oil across their ample backside. "Here." Talhan's chest rose and fell, his eyelids drooping. "Is that something you'd want?"

"Yes." The word was a clipped groan.

Neelo nodded. "Then you may move."

Talhan sprung forward, his leash snapped at Neelo's command. He grabbed the sides of their neck and pulled them into a burning kiss. Neelo's slick hands smeared down his muscled chest and to his thick, hard cock. Oil slathered his throbbing length and down his thighs as they stroked him. Talhan's hips tilted, thrusting into Neelo's hold as his hands snaked down Neelo's front and slipped between their legs.

Each sweeping circle of his fingers made Neelo lift higher onto their tiptoes, chasing the sensation he so easily elicited. Neelo spun around to the stone railing and leaned forward, pinning Talhan's hand between the balustrade and their aching center, writhing against his touch.

With one more stroke, Neelo lined him up to their back entrance, placing the tip of him exactly where they wanted him to go.

"Slow," Talhan groaned, steadying Neelo's hip with his free hand as they tried to push back and claim him. "We go slow," he panted. "Tell me if you want me to stop." Neelo ground their hips against his fingers. Talhan grabbed them by the back of the neck and twisted their head until they looked him in the eyes. "You'll tell me if you want me to stop?"

Neelo's eyelids shuttered, their mouth parted in a perfect circle, and they knew Talhan would wait all night for their response until they gave it.

"Yes," they whispered, craning their neck back to place a kiss on his lips.

Talhan dipped his fingers in the bowl oil and trailed his finger over Neelo again, slicking them further as his cock pressed into them. He pushed in an inch and Neelo groaned, the strange feeling sending lightning bolts of pleasure straight through them. Talhan circled his fingers around them again, waiting until their muscles relaxed and they loosened to his touch.

He pushed in a little further and Neelo gasped. His lips found Neelo's ear and he nibbled across the delicate peaks as he pushed in further. Neelo's mouth dropped open, yielding to the fullness until Talhan buried deep inside of them.

Their breath was a panting moan as Talhan's lips whispered into their ear, "Every little sound you make sets me on fire."

Neelo's hips jerked against Talhan's fingers. Slowly, Talhan began sliding himself out and in with tortuously gentle rolls of his hips until every inch of Neelo was honed into his touch. Neelo pushed backward, their body demanding that he pick up the pace.

Talhan dropped his mouth to Neelo's shoulder, his teeth grazing their flesh as he growled, "You feel so good."

He relented to Neelo's testing movements and began rolling into them faster, his fingers matching the speed.

"Gods," Neelo gasped, squeezing the ledge of the balustrade with a white-knuckled grip as Talhan pumped into them faster.

The sensation was so overwhelming, so all-consuming that it danced along the line between pain and pleasure. Their knees bowed and they bent over, their belly flush with the cool stone as they took each thrust. His movements grew erratic, his groans ending in growls as his fingers continued their unrelenting torture to Neelo's front matching the pumps coming from behind. Their whole body strummed, trembling and tingling as they vibrated closer to the edge within themself. Higher and higher he pushed them, his fingertips clawing into the flesh of Neelo's hip as he chased his pleasure and theirs.

With one final thrust, Neelo saw stars, a hoarse cry of pleasure ripping through them as they clenched. Talhan struggled against their tightness once, twice, and then he was spilling into them, his sweat slick chest, falling onto Neelo's back, his fingers continuing to ring every last ounce of pleasure from them until they melted against the cool stone.

They stayed like that for a long moment, too spent to move, the echoes of euphoria tingling through Neelo's body and winking wicked spots in their vision. Every part of them trembled, every muscle twitching in response.

Talhan slowly pulled out of them and fell to his knees, gathering Neelo by the waist and pulling them down to lie beside him. The patio cooled their burning flesh.

Talhan's forehead fell to Neelo's shoulder. "That was . . ."

Neelo placed a kiss into his auburn hair. "I know."

Talhan traced his fingers down Neelo's spine, his lips resting against their collarbone. "I thank the Fates for every single breath we share," he whispered, his mouth curving against Neelo's skin. "But especially for that one."

Massaging their fingers through Talhan's hair, Neelo hummed. "That was just the beginning," Neelo murmured, delighting as Talhan twitched against them in response. "Do you not know how we celebrate the Solstice in the South?" Neelo's mouth dropped to Talhan's ear. "We fuck until the sun comes up."

Talhan growled at Neelo's whispered words. "I don't know if I'm going to make it back to your chambers before I need you again."

"We'll take it one room at a time." Neelo chuckled.

"I love that sound," Talhan whispered, his fingers idly stroking their warm flesh. "The laugh you make only for me."

The sounds of far-off revelry and music danced through the night, along with a familiar voice. They thought they heard Rish, but the levelheaded witch was not one for shouting across a celebration for them.

Neelo strained, trying to pinpoint the sound. Perhaps they had just imagined it.

"Was that . . . ?" Talhan pushed up on his elbow, seeming to hear the same voice.

"Neelo!" It was Rish's scream.

CHAPTER THIRTY-NINE

Neelo tore through the palace, Talhan at their heels and Rish trailing behind. They didn't care that their clothes were haphazardly buttoned or that they stunk of sex. They didn't notice a single glance as they dashed up the stairs to the Queen's chamber but it was empty.

"The throne room!" Rish wheezed, her voice echoing over the steps as she ran to keep up.

Neelo bolted down the corridor. Their lungs burned and legs ached as they raced faster than they ever had in their life. They threw open the heavy wooden doors to the throne room, filling the hall with a cracking boom as the handles hit the wall. What they saw as they stepped over the threshold doused their whole body in ice. Their mother was slumped over her throne as the weeping sounds of courtiers filled the chamber. Fenrin frantically buzzed around the Queen, his hands and eyes glowing a dark bronze as he pulled potions and balms from his leather satchel. Aneryn stood next to Laris, holding the witch's hand tightly as her eyes flickered blue. She put her free hand on Fenrin's arm and Fenrin's voice broke.

"No. It shouldn't have gotten this much worse this quickly." He kept hastily rifling through his bag as if there was some remedy he hadn't thought of. His voice was thick with emotion. "I can save her."

Neelo floated forward, feeling lifeless as they stared at their mother's pallid face and barely open eyes.

"Fen," Aneryn whispered softly. She didn't need to say any more. This was it.

The Queen's watery eyes lifted to Neelo and then behind them, barely giving Neelo a passing glance before landing on the panting green witch stumbling through the doors.

"Rish," the Queen beckoned. "It's time."

Aneryn's and Laris's eyes flared in horror at the Queen's command.

Rish bowed her head and stepped forward preparing for the *midon brik*. It was an ancient witch ritual, the most powerful of the witch magics, that could swap one life for another. Rish brushed past Neelo, trembling as Neelo realized what was about to happen.

Their hand shot out, grabbing Rish in the crook of the arm. "No," they whispered. They looked up at their mother and pushed Rish behind them, summoning their voice and the confidence to speak. "No."

The Queen's brow furrowed as she gasped for air like a fish on dry land.

Betrayal—that was what flickered in her eyes and Neelo felt it like a knife to the gut. After scrambling nearly their whole life to keep their mother alive, they would be the death of her. If ever there was a time to use their voice, their power, it was now. They would not lose Rish.

"You have used up the very last of your lifelines, Your Majesty," Neelo said, steeling themself for their mother's hateful look. She really thought she could ask someone to sacrifice their life for her? How many more witches would she drag under on the way out?

"I suppose she was more mother to you than I ever was." The Queen's voice wobbled as she took another heavy drag from her pipe. She peered around the room as if to find another witch and Fenrin pushed Aneryn and Laris behind him. Resignation crossed Queen Emberspear's weak expression before her glassy eyes rolled back. No pain crossed her face. Her lips barely formed the words as she said, "May history make my end more heroic than it truly was."

Her hand went limp, the pipe falling from her grip and clattering onto the floor. Keening wails broke out from the courtiers as they dropped onto bowed knees. Neelo stared across the group, their eyes falling from one of the courtiers shined black boots across to Farros's heartbroken face. Something was off about the formal attire, something about those boots felt wrong, but then everything felt wrong with their mother dead upon her throne. Maybe their mind had shattered with the sight of it. Gods, they wondered if the courtiers were truly even crying for the Queen or for the drastic change in their circumstances now that she was gone.

Neelo blinked. These shouldn't be their first thoughts after watching their mother die. It hit them then. As if on a delay, a burning spark of realization and blinding pain.

Neelo's chest seized, the air pulling from their lungs as Talhan wrapped his arms around them. No sound came from Neelo's trembling lips, a silent sob pulling through them. She was gone. She was truly gone. The life they had been clinging to from utter fear was now gone and Neelo was left to fill the vast hole she'd left.

Fenrin, Aneryn, and Laris huddled together in a tight embrace. Grief spread through the room, weaving into a single thread that pulled them all closer. One crown of Okrith had fallen and another was there to take her place.

"I killed her," Neelo whispered and Talhan's arms banded tighter around their rib cage as he dropped his chin to their shoulder.

His voice was low and soothing. "You did *not* kill her, love."

"I let her die though." Neelo sucked in a painful breath.

"You saved Rish's life," Talhan whispered.

It was too much. This feeling. This press of so many bodies. Too many sounds. The entirety of their world seemed to fracture from one breath to the next. They'd failed.

Neelo stepped out of Talhan's grip and he let them go.

Neelo turned to find Denton hovering in the corner, wringing his hands in concern. "Councilor, I need to speak with you in the hall." Neelo kept their trembling hands in fists as they marched out of the room, Talhan and Denton following behind. The two of them watched Neelo with apprehension as the throne room doors clicked shut. "Not a single courtier is to leave this room," Neelo whispered, pointing an accusatory finger at the door. "Not until I have more answers."

"Answers?"

Neelo glared at the councilor, trying to push against the feeling like they might fall apart before they could give him these directions. *Wait, wait. Hang on.* First they needed justice, then they could mourn. "I want to know who it was. Whose fingers filled my mother's pipe? Who brought her the brew that killed her? No one leaves this room until I know who abetted my mother's death."

"Your Highness, they will be most displeased," Councilor Denton spluttered.

"Do I look pleased right now? The party is over, Denton," Neelo growled. "Send everyone home. Now."

"But—but, Your Highness," he protested. "That's sacrilege. The celebrations, they—the Queen would've—"

"I am the ruler of the Southern Court now, Councilor Denton," Neelo gritted out, building a wall around their aching heart. "You will do well to obey me."

Denton's eyebrows lifted and his mouth fell open. When had Neelo ever been so direct with him? When had they ever been as assertive as they were in that moment? They couldn't have people cheering and singing while their mother's body was being anointed with oils and her final prayers whispered over her body. Everything blossoming within Neelo turned to ash as they morphed into the cold ruler they needed to be. One with claws and armor. One who could survive this implosion of their court . . . and perhaps the court would implode even faster with Neelo taking away both their brew and now their celebrations.

Neelo held up their hand, keeping Denton fixed in his place. "We shall not cancel the Solstice, but it will be tempered by the Queen's death." Neelo glanced from Denton to Talhan, who bobbed his chin in approval. "It will now be a celebration both of the sun and of the glory of my mother's reign." They shifted, straightening the hem of their tunic to keep their hands busy as the pressure mounted. "And if the courtiers want to join the celebrations of my mother's life, then they need to give up whoever this supplier was. I want a detailed account of her last day from each of them. Now."

"Yes, right away," Denton said, bowing deeply before scuttling toward the door.

Neelo turned their attention to the guards stationed outside the throne room, not looking a single one in the eye. "Call a brown witch. Prepare the body," they said tightly. "We will burn her in the harbor in two days' time."

Neelo strode down the hallway, lifting their chin as they bit down on the inside of their cheek until they tasted blood.

"Where are you going?" Talhan asked.

"To collect a dossier on every person in that room." The last of their words wobbled and the sound made Neelo take a sharp breath. "You conduct a detailed inspection of all the guards."

"I've already done it," Talhan assured.

"Then do it again."

"Neelo—"

"Or help Denton." They knew they didn't have many more sentences in them before the tears would be unbridled and spilling down their cheeks—before the mask they wore that was saving them from falling apart would slip.

"Let me help you," Talhan said gently—too gently—as he continued to follow after them.

"If you care for me at all," Neelo choked out, "you will leave me alone right now."

Talhan halted instantly and Neelo knew it would've been kinder to stab him through with a sword. Instead, they stormed off, tears burning down their cheeks.

THEIR FOOTSTEPS ECHOED like claps of thunder, too loud in the silent stone room. The Queen's body was wrapped in all white, only her head free from the shroud that swaddled her body. She stunk of the myrrh and sweet cinnamon oils her body was bathed in. Queen Emberspear's face was painted so that her features were more perfectly designed than they had ever been alive. She'd been too busy drinking and smoking to maintain the soft curls teased into her hair and perfect application of rouge on her cheeks.

A crushing weight pressed in on Neelo's temples. Bile rose up their throat and their limbs pricked with a thousand needles, fading into numbness. They floated to her side, their mind vacant apart from the acute awareness of the crushing pressure behind their eyes. Is this what grief felt like? It was nagging and blinding and relentless and hollow all at once . . . but the one emotion Neelo couldn't seem to summon was sorrow. Not for the loss of their mother at least.

Neelo stared down at the Queen's too serene face and something like spite burned up within them. "I knew this would happen." Their words were rough and broken. "I knew you'd do this to me." They swallowed the blistering lump in their throat. "The only question was when. You made me a fool, thinking I could save you."

When was the last time they'd been alone with their mother? A hot tear burned down their cheek. When was the last time they'd had her full attention? The Queen had always surrounded herself with a gaggle of simpering courtiers and her mind addled with drugs. Neelo's lip curled, hating that they had inherited the desire to be anywhere but in their own body and mind.

"Of course you'd have to be on your own funeral pyre before I got a moment of your time." Neelo spat and wiped the tears from under their eyes. "Now that I have your attention . . ." Neelo leaned over their mother's body, their bottom lip trembling as they stared down into her peaceful face. "I deserved better from you. The Gods know, I deserved a whole fucking lot better." They sniffed, bracketing their hands on the stone altar beside their mother's shoulders. "I knew I'd get your praise if I threw parties and stumbled home drunk every night and rutted with every person within arm's reach . . . and since I couldn't bring myself to do those things, I decided I deserved your loathing. Your absence. Worst, your indifference." They leaned in until they were inches from her face. "I was too much of a coward to demand more from you, but I know now." They took a steeling breath as more tears slid down their cheeks. "I was worthy of your love exactly as I am."

Tears blurred their vision, dripping off their chin and onto their mother's lifeless form. At the sight of their tears speckling the Queen's cheeks, Neelo crumpled, dropping to the floor with their back against the stone altar and their knees tucked up to their chest.

They let the silent sobs rack through them, waves of grief, not for their mother's life but for the value they'd never seen in themself, for the child they wished they could've defended. The only time they'd ever truly put their foot down with their mother was in her last moments, when they refused to let her take one last part of them and the witch who loved them. Rish's life was where Neelo finally drew that line.

CHAPTER FORTY

Tears stained the stack of pages strewn across Neelo's lap and armchair. Fat heavy droplets dripped off their chin until the ink bled together in rivers of midnight. Neelo hadn't read a single word anyway, unable to even escape their own thoughts long enough to read through the notes the guards delivered detailing the courtier's personal accounts of the past day.

Indi purred furiously in their lap. The stubborn cat hadn't left Neelo's side all day. The royal guests had remained to attend the Queen's funeral, but Neelo refused to see them, even when Carys was trying to bang down their door. They couldn't. They weren't ready to be everything they needed to be.

The royals sent notes of condolence when Neelo refused to see any of them, and Neelo threw the notes in the fire. They'd rather claw their eyes out than read the pitying words, even though they'd all been in Neelo's shoes before, each and every one of them. Every crown worn was a symbol of a dead predecessor. Every single royal had felt the sharp pang of death hooking into them and hoisting them upon their thrones. Now, Neelo felt that hook piercing through them and pulling them toward the crown they'd always feared one day wearing.

The door clicked and soft sandaled footsteps scuffled in.

"Go away," Neelo said without lifting their head.

They smelled the plate of chili bread long before Rish appeared and offered it out to them. Neelo shook their head and Rish switched hands, offering out one of Neelo's favorite books instead. Neelo shook their head again.

Rish's frown deepened and she placed her cool palm to Neelo's warm forehead. "It's that bad, then."

"I'll be fine." Neelo pulled their knees into their chest, hugging themself as they stared out the golden window.

"Little liar." Rish huffed, lowering onto the cushioned seat beside them. "I'm guessing you were expecting someone else." Each of her movements seemed slower, more deliberate, as if she was aware of how fragile this moment was between them. Neelo didn't respond. "I think he might be writing a letter to every citizen in the entire court based on the amount of ink he's going through."

"That can't be." They wouldn't share of Talhan's struggle with letters, but it seemed unlikely he would be doing that when he could use the magic of fae fires to communicate with whoever he needed.

Rish picked at the flour beneath her fingernails. "You pushed him away again, didn't you?" Rish chuckled at Neelo's scowl.

"We shouldn't be laughing."

"Shouldn't we?" Rish arched her brow. "Do you think your mother would've wanted to go into the afterlife with the sounds of lamentation?"

Neelo wiped their nose with their sleeve. "No." Moments passed with only the sounds of their breathing. "She's being sent off into the afterlife even as we speak."

"Hmm." Rish gave Neelo a quizzical look. "And you will hide in corners reading a book until she goes?"

"I have seen to all the arrangements," Neelo grumbled. "My presence won't be necessary."

Rish reached out and brushed a short strand of Neelo's hair off their face.

"You think I should go," they said with a sigh—a statement, not a question.

"I remember the first time I saw you," Rish murmured, leaning back into her seat. "You crawled straight into the kitchens, following the scent of my famous black bean stew." She winked at Neelo before her face grew more solemn. "No one was watching you, the nurses charged with caring for you were sleeping or partying and there you were with your chubby cheeks and sparkling brown eyes. I took off my shawl and wrapped you to my hip." She squeezed Neelo's hand. "And you've been mine ever since."

"Sometimes I wondered if I was born and placed directly in your arms," Neelo whispered. That's how long Rish had loved them.

"I chose you," Rish said with her motherly warmth. "As much as you chose me."

The haunted, hurt look on the Queen's face flashed behind Neelo's eyes and tears welled again. "I didn't want to lose you too."

"I know." Rish's expression softened. "But one day, however long into the future, when I am old and gray, I pray the Gods take me before you." She squeezed their hand tighter. "And when I do I hope you will wear every color when you send me into the afterlife. Throw flowers in the air and sing and dance. I pray you will celebrate the vibrancy of my life and remember me with joy."

"One day," Neelo whispered. "Long, *long* into the future. I will."

Rish leaned forward until Neelo lifted their eyes to meet hers. "And most of all I pray that you have someone else beside you to ease your pain then."

"Gods." Neelo dropped their head into their hands. "I don't know how to do this. My thoughts, my words, my feelings . . . aren't strong enough to bear the weight of a crown."

"You are not a problem to be fixed." Rish's hand swept long soothing strokes across Neelo's back. "Just because they can't always hear it in your words or see it on your face, it still all exists within you. You feel deeper than I could ever fathom, and everyone who matters knows that."

Neelo blew out a shuddering breath. All they knew how to do was push and hide, even when they wanted to pull someone in. They'd thought they were starting to get there, and then the Queen's death made them waver again. A new wave of grief bloomed in Neelo's chest as they thought of Talhan.

"Everything feels upside down," they murmured.

"That's because it is," Rish replied softly. "And I hate to say it, but it will never truly right itself. So instead we'll just find a way to move forward in this upside-down world."

Neelo smoothed down their satin jacket. "I'm not the person I thought I'd be," they said. "And . . . even though I like who I could become, it scares me to be anything else."

"Sometimes we cast ourselves in the roles we need at the time." Rish looked up at the moonlight filtering in through the high arched windows. "Maybe it was good and right to be that way once. Maybe it helped you survive." She let out a long breath. "But if we hold on too tight to who we were, we'll never know who we could become." Neelo dropped their head into their hands and Rish placed a gentle hand on their back. "And even though it hurts sometimes, I think you like who you are becoming too, and you are becoming the sort of person who would regret not going to your mother's funeral."

Neelo clenched their jaw as angry tears welled in their eyes again. Gods, they needed to stop crying. "I think you should go."

Rish only laughed, a hearty witch's cackle. She grabbed Neelo's cheeks and shoved a piece of chili bread into their mouth. "I'm going to make more *haasala* for the mourners." She kissed the top of Neelo's head. "I expect this plate to be empty when I return . . . or perhaps I will see you at the harbor." Neelo's hand reached out and they squeezed Rish's wrist, the only acknowledgment of their thanks. "I love you too, *mea raga*," Rish whispered as she crossed the room. "Thank you for saving my life."

Neelo's head shot up but the door was already closing. Tears spilled again and they were more angry at them than sad now. Everything mounded on top of them. The sickly scent of the funeral oils turned their stomach. Their hair still stank of their mother's anointed body. They leapt up, throwing Indi off their lap, and storming across the room to grab the shears from their desk. They'd cut all their hair off before being reminded of her. Queen Emberspear's presence couldn't linger on them for one more second. Something in them snapped. They grabbed the shears as anger filled them and, Gods, it felt better to feel angry than to feel hurt.

THEY STOOD STOCK-STILL on the cliffside as they watched the mountainous barge drift out on the calm predawn waters. White smoke tinged in violet billowed from the hull until Neelo could no longer see the shrouded body laid to rest atop the stacks and stacks of witching brew. The courtiers had given up the location of the last of their stores upon Neelo's command, though they suspected there was still more brew hidden in the palace somewhere.

Neelo had refused to let them leave the throne room, ordering food and blankets to be brought to them and chamber pots emptied and that be it—a makeshift dungeon beside an empty throne. Had the brew made their minds so hollow they couldn't come up with answers? Why hadn't a single one of them spoken out? All of their recounting of the day were eerily similar and absent of any useful information. What could've possibly possessed them to keep quiet? Neelo thought missing the Queen's funeral would've been threat enough, let alone missing the rest of the Solstice, but not one of them had protested since the Queen's death, as if their tongues had all been cut out. Maybe after another night sleeping on the stone floor, they'd realize Neelo wasn't bluffing.

Neelo couldn't bring themself to go down to the wharf, to stand amongst the throng of mourners, wondering if any single one of them was honest in their sorrow. They found a lookout on the cliff through the forest where they could feel the jumble of emotions swinging between agony and hatred.

The air blew across their freshly cropped hair. They hadn't bothered to look in a mirror and were certain their head was a patchy mess. But they didn't care. They couldn't smell the myrrh or sweet cinnamon oil anymore. They didn't feel their mother's presence pushing into them at all. Instead, they felt as listless as the burning ship bobbing in the bay.

Smoke billowed across the horizon, too distant to affect them. The trees rustled behind them and Neelo tensed at the fresh scent of bay leaves. Of course, he'd found them like a hound on their trail. They sighed, wishing Talhan had continued to heed their warning and leave them alone. But the Eagle must've realized Neelo didn't know how to return to him by now—that the longer they kept away from him, the harder it seemed to ever turn back to him again.

Talhan slung an arm over Neelo's shoulders and Neelo immediately stepped out of his touch. How long could they hold him at arm's length? They thought they could let him in, had summited that mountain within themself . . . but now, it felt like they turned a corner only to find another peak towering above them. They wanted to retreat into their old life but everything felt strange, *wrong*, like wearing a too-tight jacket. Stories didn't steal them away from their mind anymore. The quiet didn't feel as comforting.

"I like this," Talhan whispered, rubbing a hand across Neelo's scalp.

The short hairs bristled under his touch. "Don't," they finally said, stepping further from him and folding their arms around themself.

Talhan mirrored their posture, standing stoically beside them. Neelo watched the buttery morning light kiss the smoky horizon, their chest tightening with each beam that crested about the endless sea.

She was really gone. There would be no coming back this time. And yet, all they felt was pressure, the weight of the mantle that the Queen had placed upon their shoulders when she died. Ready or not, they couldn't cling to the shadows anymore. And they didn't know how to absorb all of these warring emotions in the face of anyone, let alone the person who stood beside them. Who were they to him now? How were they meant to act? Did anyone else even ask these questions of themselves?

"The council was outraged," Neelo said, instead of voicing all of the worries in their heart. They watched the crackling flames as the barge drifted further out to sea. "They said it was improper." A bitter laugh rang out between them. "*Improper.* That is exactly who my mother was. She'd have loved to be burned on a witching brew ship instead of a normal burial raft."

"It is one impressive send-off," Talhan murmured as the whorls of smoke grew bigger.

Neelo shifted, irritation making them scratch at their skin. "And it serves my purposes too."

"Which are?"

"It gets rid of the brew. Sends a message to all of Saxbridge." Neelo scanned the docked ships in the harbor. "Hopefully I can curb the Southern appetite for it, though I fear it will still find its way here on occasion." They stared out at the purple-hued mist—the eeriest sort of dawn. "But they cannot argue with me using it this way if I say it was the Queen's dying wish."

Talhan hummed in understanding. "But it wasn't."

They narrowed their eyes at the horizon. "And no one shall ever know that except you and I."

"Clever as always." Talhan looked out toward the docks across the bay where a modest gathering of citizens stood. "I thought more people would come."

"It is dawn," Neelo muttered. "The South is going to sleep now. It is the quietest time in Saxbridge and I thought it might incite a mob to see the ship burning in the evening. Now, at the brink of day, everyone is too exhausted to riot."

"I know how hard you fought to save her," Talhan whispered. "I'm sorry."

"I think I was fighting my whole life against this moment." Neelo braced for the sharp sense of loss but it didn't come. "I'd lost her so long ago I don't even remember who she truly was. But still, I needed her, if only to spare me from the burden of a crown, and the tighter I held on to her, the faster she seemed to slip through my fingers."

"You seemed the only one willing to hold on," Talhan said. "That's courageous."

"It's cowardice," Neelo snapped. Talhan's words made their skin sear and cheeks burn. "I was afraid of losing her for *me*. I was scared to become Regent . . . I'm still not ready. It wasn't courage or kindness or even love. It was fear that made me help her for so long."

Talhan took a step closer. "You were right to stop Rish."

"She would've done it," Neelo gritted out. "I know she would've. Rish would've taken her life to save my mother, and for what? So that my mother could drown herself another year in drink and witching brew until another witch's life was needed to save her?"

Neelo clenched their jaw so tightly it made their teeth throb. They had said it in front of their dying mother, they'd asked Rish not to save her—no, *commanded* Rish not to save her. Shame burned them endlessly like a splatter of boiled sugar that could never be peeled off.

Talhan stepped in front of Neelo, blocking the view of the ship now engulfed in flames. He waited to speak until Neelo looked up into his amber eyes. "You were right to stop Rish," he said again.

They shook their head as a white-hot pain radiated out of them, one they needed to feel alone. "I'm going to bed."

"You're not going to watch the ship go down?"

Neelo struggled to keep their voice steady as they spoke. "Why bother? She's already gone."

His hand reached for their elbow. "Neelo—"

They yanked their elbow away, marching up the terraced steps back toward the palace. "I don't need your comfort."

"But you deserve my comfort." Talhan fell into stride beside them, a pained look on his face. "You don't need to feel this alone."

Neelo threw their shoulders back and lifted their chin, pushing down on the swirling pain that tightened in their gut.

"Maybe you should leave," Neelo hissed.

"No," Talhan growled. He took a quick step, reaching for their arm again and Neelo snapped.

They spun backward, grabbing the dagger off Talhan's belt and pointing it at him.

His hands flew up, his eyes wide, as he stared at the tip of his blade. "I thought you didn't know how to do that?"

"I was lying," Neelo spat, thinking of the pathetic way they'd let

Talhan teach them so that they could feel his body close to theirs. It almost made them want to laugh now. Of course they were trained in the art of combat. Of course the Queen would never let even her pitiful bookish child go without training.

Talhan stared at the blade for a long moment before he spoke. "Stab me, then. But if you think I'm going away, think again. I wasn't there for Bri when she needed me most and I won't make that mistake twice." Finally, he lifted his eyes to Neelo. "If you need time and space, I will give it. I will hole up in my chambers for months should you ask it, but I am not leaving you, my Fated, unless you say it."

"Say what?"

"Tell me you don't want me," Talhan said, his voice thick and raw as tears swelled in his eyes. Talhan took a step forward and Neelo's breath caught in their throat. "Tell me the Fates are liars. Tell me I'm wrong. Tell me I don't belong by your side."

Never had Neelo seen him so undone and, as they watched the single tear slide down his cheek, it hit them all at once: this mighty fae warrior wasn't made of stone. They tried so hard to keep him from feeling pain that they hadn't considered they were the one inflicting it. And maybe they could push and push and he wouldn't break, but it would *hurt* him. And he didn't deserve that pain, not from anyone, and especially not from them.

Talhan might be a warrior, but his armor wasn't impenetrable, and Neelo's actions cut worse than any blade. Maybe they didn't know how to be as open and vulnerable as him, but they could fucking stop hurting him like this.

Tears clouded Neelo's vision as Talhan's chest brushed against their own. He clenched and unclenched his hands, shifting on his feet, more raw in that moment than they'd ever seen him before. "Tell me if you need my arms around you or if you need space and time." His voice cracked. "But I am not leaving you. Ever. Whatever you need from me, say it and it's yours."

Neelo choked on a cry as the dagger slipped from their grip. "Arms."

Talhan caught them before their knees buckled and they crumpled to the ground, sobbing, finally wringing out the sorrow that had been rising in them. His hands constricted tighter around them as if he could hold together all of the pieces shattering inside of them and Neelo finally let themself break apart in his arms.

CHAPTER FORTY-ONE

They held each other so long their bodies molded into one. Neelo's cheek smoothed against Talhan's chest, his tunic stained wet with their tears as they released years of emotions into one long flood. They drifted into a dreamlike state, the world seeming far off except for the safety of Talhan's arms. Nothing else existed but them. If Neelo ever had any doubt that they were Fated, it was this moment that convinced them, not their moments of passion, but this slow steady magic that pulled them together until they were one breath, one soul, their sorrows flowing through them and out into the ether, one letting go of what the other couldn't hold. Stronger.

Talhan was the first to be snapped from the buzzing moment between them. He lifted his chin off Neelo's head at the sound of a call. Neelo was certain their cheek would be lined with the impression of Talhan's wrinkled tunic as they looked out at a guard on the third-floor balcony. He was waving his handkerchief at them from the fae fire room.

Neelo sighed. "Who?" they mouthed to the guard, the morning too silent to shout.

"Arboa," the guard mouthed back, gesturing to the east.

Neelo groaned as they pushed up off the grass, their body stiff from holding the same position for so long. "He probably has heard the news and wishes to send his sympathies." They offered their hand down to Talhan and helped him to his feet. He smirked at their act of chivalry. "Let's go."

A warm smile spread across Talhan's face and Neelo knew he expected them to send him away and speak to Ersan alone. But Neelo was done fighting, done pushing, their body was boneless and tired and they just wanted their Fated to be by their side. Finally, they accepted that's what they always had wanted: to simply be together.

They trudged up the dark stairwell, the morning sun not quite reaching the palace walls.

Neelo braced themself for another condolence from Ersan, another apology about their mother and false compliments about her life. They braced to receive the lies people would tell them to make the Queen sound like a hero, respectable and great only in death.

But as they neared the door and heard Ersan's sharp voice talking to the fae guard through the fire, they knew it had nothing to do with their mother.

Neelo rushed the last steps into the room toward the giant bracer in the center. "Sy?"

"Neelo." Ersan's sigh of relief echoed out from the yellow green flames. "I need to talk to you."

"I figured," Neelo said, crossing their arms.

"Are you . . . alone?"

Neelo glanced at the two fae servants who watched the fae fires and kept them lit. The two of them disappeared into the hall at Neelo's brief nod.

"Just us," Neelo said. "And Talhan," they added hastily. "What's going on?"

"Cole started talking a few days ago," Ersan said, pausing between each word as if debating how he was going to deliver some terrible news. "But with everything happening with the Queen, I thought I'd wait to tell you." Talhan shifted closer to Neelo, the barest of movement making that pain shoot through them again as they remembered everything. "He said he needed to find someone. He kept calling him *the smallest seed of the rebellion.*"

Talhan's brow furrowed. "Hale?"

"It was coming out all muddled," Ersan lamented. "The healers and I were trying to work it out, but it exhausted him. He'd sleep days on end after one conversation and . . . We set him up in one of the towers looking out to the sea with enough food and amenities so he could be left to himself during those days of rest. We were trying to bring him back gently but—" Ersan paused. What wasn't he saying?

"Spit it out, Sy."

"Cole seemed to be coming more back into his mind when . . ."

Neelo's stomach dropped. "When?"

"We went to his chambers this morning and he was gone. Scaled down the window by tying the curtains together." Ersan cleared his throat as Talhan's hand drifted to the hilt of his sword. "It had been two days since last we visited . . . we don't know how long he's been gone."

"Shit," Talhan growled. "Do you know where he went?"

"No." Ersan sounded just as frustrated.

"Did he give you any names?"

"He kept muttering about Adisa Monroe," Ersan said and Neelo ground their teeth. The name of the violet witch wouldn't help them. "Oh and one other." Neelo narrowed their eyes at the green flames. "There was one other name he kept saying . . . What was it? Oh, um, Fenrin."

Talhan reared back as if the word burned him. "Fen," he whispered.

"Shit. Go!" Neelo barked and turned toward the door.

They raced out of the room without so much as a goodbye to Ersan. Why would Cole have Fenrin's name in his mind? What had Fenrin done? Was he Adisa Monroe's target or ally? Neelo ran faster, their sleepy joints now filled with urgency.

Ersan should have been monitoring the brown witch more closely. Neelo would deal with the Arboan Lord and his mistakes later. First, they needed to get to Fenrin before Cole did. There was no telling whether Cole was still in his right mind or what he might do if Adisa Monroe still had her claws in him.

Neelo's mind raced as they dashed after Talhan, hoping they wouldn't reach Fenrin's chambers too late. Talhan unsheathed his dagger from his belt and Neelo wasn't sure if it was to protect Fenrin or use against him. Everything about it felt wrong, but Neelo's brain would have to catch up later. Right now was a time to act on instinct, and so they ran, unknowing what they were running into.

THEY WERE ABOUT to burst through Fenrin's door when he opened it and they stumbled inside. Neelo's shoulders sagged in relief. He seemed fine and blissfully unaware of their sudden panic. He looked at Talhan's dagger with an arched brow, his face so open and easily readable. There wasn't a malignant bone in this witch's body. This wasn't the face of Neelo's enemy.

"What have I told you about knocking?" Fenrin said with a mocking huff. Neelo glanced at the table by the window upon which sat three plates mounded with pastries and eggs, and suddenly felt guilty for even suspecting Fenrin capable of allying with Adisa Monroe. "Luckily I heard you coming this time."

Talhan snorted, sheathing his dagger, seemingly also backing down from his kneejerk suspicions. "You were a little *distracted* last time."

Fenrin looked back at Neelo and Talhan's panting faces. "What's going on? Why the stampede?"

"We heard word from the fae fire," Neelo said, the scent of breakfast distracting them. "Where are the others?"

Fenrin looked at Neelo, confused. "We're leaving today," he said. "They went to the bathhouses for a wash before the long journey north. What's going on?" he pushed again.

Neelo had forgotten that they were leaving. Most had departed straight after the Queen's funeral, hastened by Neelo's childish refusal to speak with them. Guilt swarmed them. Their first act as ruler had been to push all their allies away.

Talhan stepped forward, seeming to understand he needed to take over. "It's about—"

"Cole," Fenrin gasped, looking over Neelo's shoulder.

They whirled, following Fenrin's line of sight to the figure emerging from the bathing chamber, the window latches flung open wide.

One minute Talhan was frozen, staring at the tall blond witch, and the next he vaulted over the bed, grabbed Cole by the collar, and slammed him against the wall.

"You," Talhan seethed, choking the brown witch with the fabric of his tunic.

A pitcher crashed to the floor, shattering, and Neelo turned to find Fenrin's bloodless face. He'd stumbled backward, knocking the ceramic off the table but he didn't seem to notice as he gaped at the brown witch. Neelo glanced between Fenrin and Cole, the likeness suddenly apparent. Same tall stature, lean frame, shock of straw-blond hair, and ocean-blue eyes.

"Cole?" Fenrin whispered again.

The older brown witch's eyes bugged as they landed on Fenrin. An unexpected sob tore from his lips. "Fen!"

Talhan arched his brow, loosening his grip as he glanced between them. "You know him?"

Fenrin took a step forward, crunching across the broken ceramic. "He's my uncle."

Talhan narrowed his eyes at Cole. "Why did you run away from Arboa?"

"Let him go," Neelo said, placing a hand on Talhan's shoulder. "Let him speak."

At their command, Talhan released Cole's collar. Cole darted for Fenrin and grabbed him in a crushing hug.

"Are you okay? Are you hurt?" Cole scanned Fenrin from head to toe. "When Rose disappeared, I thought she'd taken you to the grave with her and I . . ." Tears welled in his eyes. "You're all grown up. Look at you! Where have you been all these years?"

"I'm all right. I'm all right." Fenrin chuckled, holding on to Cole's elbows as he stepped back from the hug, trying to steady him. "I was taken in by a brown witch named Heather. She was the one who was hiding the High Mountain Queen, Remini, all these years."

Cole's face paled, a tear spilling down his cheek. "Heather's still alive?"

Fenrin's eyes saddened. "No."

"Copper-red hair? Freckled cheeks? About this tall?" Cole held out his hand.

Fenrin cocked his head in confusion. "Did you know her?"

"She's my sister." Tears streamed down Cole's cheeks. "She's your aunt."

"No, that can't be." Fenrin's brows knitted together as he searched Cole's face. "It can't—she—she would've told me."

Cole wiped under his eyes. "What was this Heather's last name?"

"We had many last names." Fenrin blinked at him. "We changed them every time we moved to a new town, I . . ."

Cole shook his head. "Gods, she must've been trying to hide you from her."

"Who?"

"Adisa Monroe . . . our ancestor." Cole brought a trembling hand to his brow. "I think it's you she wants, Fenrin."

"Not Hale?" Neelo asked.

"No. That's what I had thought too, but once I knew Fenrin was alive, it all made sense. Fenrin is younger. He is the smallest seed."

"What are you talking about? This is madness," Fenrin said, looking to the others in the room to agree with him.

"In Swifthill," Talhan said, giving Fenrin a wary look, "Adisa Monroe said to Hale 'tell the rest of my grandchildren to come find me in the East.'" He scrubbed a hand down his stubbled jaw. "Maybe she was searching for you?"

"But I grew up in the family shop until Mother died and Heather found me on the streets." Fenrin frowned. "How did I not know about Heather? Not one note or mention from the rest of the family?"

"You knew the others," Cole said. "It was Heather, Rose, me, Evelyn, and Oliver. Heather left when we were still young and I don't think your mother ever forgave her. She cut her out of our lives when my father died. I'm surprised she even managed to find you."

"Heather wasn't hiding me from anyone." Fenrin scowled, squeezing his hands into fists as he paced about the room. "She was hiding Remy from witch hunters and King Vostemur."

"Remy wasn't the only one she was hiding, Fenrin," Cole huffed. "She's been keeping you in the West, out of the grasp of the violet witch magic stirring in the East."

Talhan's eyebrows shot up. "Do you think that's why she didn't let you come with us to Wynreach last autumn?"

"I don't think you can credit her with our sudden illness," Fenrin scoffed.

Cole shook his head. "I wouldn't be so sure."

Fenrin paused his pacing and stared at his uncle. Gods, they looked so much alike now that they were in the same room together. "You think she made us sick?"

"You think Heather Doledir, daughter of one of the most powerful healers in all of Okrith, wouldn't have been able to cure you if she wanted to?"

"Gods," Fenrin muttered. "This can't be real. Did I not even know her at all?" He kicked back his chair.

"Fenrin . . ." Cole extended his hand out to his nephew, but Fenrin pulled away.

"I . . ." Fenrin's gaze dropped to Cole's feet. His uncle wore scuffed black leather boots, rounded toes in the Western style and similar to the ones Fenrin wore when he'd arrived in Saxbridge but in a different shade. Most people knew better than to wear black in Saxbridge . . .

Neelo's eyes flew wide. Black boots. They threw open the door without another word and raced down the hallway.

"Your Highness, wait!" Cole chased after them, Fenrin and Talhan hot on their heels.

"Where are you going?" Talhan barked.

"The throne room," Neelo shouted as they sped down the hall. "Gods, why hadn't I spotted it before. He's here. He's *been* here."

"Who?" Talhan called as he raced after them.

They raced through the quiet morning castle, their bootsteps thundering against the marble. Talhan threw open the heavy doors to the throne room, the two guards stationed at the doors exchanging bemused glances.

"Let us pass," Neelo commanded, racing into the room.

Two dozen heads snapped up, the courtiers all gathered on pillows around the floor in makeshift beds. Some were still asleep, others were just waking and having their first sips of coffee, others still looked like they hadn't yet gone to sleep, their hooded eyes and wide pupils telling Neelo there was still some witching brew left in their possession.

Neelo searched the group, quickly landing on a sleeping figure, body turned from the gathering. Their eyes snagged on the set of perfectly shined black boots still on the courtier's feet.

"Black boots," Neelo whispered to Talhan. Those were not the shoes any Southerner would wear. They were also the sort of shoes the other courtiers would balk at . . . if they had the presence of mind to do so.

Talhan tiptoed over to the sleeping body and nudged it. The figure sat up instantly, an insect veil still around their head. Talhan tugged it back to reveal beady black eyes, a cruel smirk, and white-blond hair.

Augustus Norwood.

"You," Neelo breathed.

CHAPTER FORTY-TWO

Talhan unsheathed his dagger, but before he could point it at Augustus, the entire group shot to their feet. Talhan stumbled back, pushing Cole and Fenrin into the corner behind him.

Augustus frowned up at Talhan's dagger. "I wouldn't," he said, pulling a cigarette from his pocket and lighting it on the candle beside him. A puff of purple smoke circled his head and his eyes dilated as he grinned.

The courtiers swayed like limp puppets, their eyes glassed over, the same dull sheen as the poisoned blades.

Neelo prayed Aneryn had Seen this and was summoning the guards for help. She and Laris must be returning from the bathhouses soon and would ask questions when they found Fenrin missing and that shattered vase on the floor.

"Give the violet witches to me, Catullus." Augustus's voice was bored, as if uncaring if his command was received or not. "I'll take them both. Though it's the youngest one she's obsessed with."

"Afraid you're losing her favor?" Talhan asked.

"Hardly." Augustus's shoulders shook though his expression remained hard. "I just killed the Southern Queen after all. One word was all it took: more." His eyes were sharp above his crooked smile. "Still, I will be grateful to deliver him and get her boot off my neck."

Neelo tentatively took a step forward. "What does that mean?"

"It means at one of the many royal parties as a boy, I thought I'd partake in a new blend of witching brew." Smoke curled into his light hair. "My mother was too vain to notice me anyway—I was nothing compared to her golden child Belenus. When she wasn't doting over him, she was blinded by her hatred of Hale."

"Spare us. You seemed pretty coddled from the gatherings I remember," Talhan jeered.

"I was indulged, certainly, but I got away with a lot more too," Augustus said, his lips curling up at one side. "And on this one particular night, I smoked enough brew to forget my own name, and a goddess herself spoke directly into my mind . . . or so I thought."

"Adisa was probably dug up before then," Neelo said. "She was out in the world."

"Indeed," Augustus said with a slow sigh. "She was there that night. She frequented many of my father's parties over the years, hidden in the shadows, watching. She thought Hale was her youngest heir." His gaze drifted to Fenrin. "But she was mistaken. So many years wasted, biding her time."

"Time for what?"

"For when she would destroy the fae courts and claim the Eastern throne," Augustus said with disdain and rolled the cigarette in his fingers. "I thought she was my patron goddess, my own personal type of luck. She'd appear and good things would happen for me. I felt tied to her from the first time I heard her whisper in my mind." He sighed again. "But it wasn't luck at all. She wasn't mine; I was hers. I was her spy, her eyes in the castle, and she in return, she promised she would give me my father's throne. Not Hale. Not Belenus. Me."

"You can't seriously still believe she'll keep her word," Talhan growled, taking another decisive step forward.

"Careful," Augustus warned. "I only want the witches. But I'll have these mindless drones," he said, indicating the blank-eyed courtiers, "tear through you to get to them if I have to. My loyalty to a fellow Eastern fae only goes so far. Now step aside, Catullus." The group of spelled courtiers tensed, making Augustus's meaning clear: if Talhan didn't step aside, the spelled courtiers would make him.

Talhan pushed Fenrin further behind him. "No," he growled, unsheathing his sword.

Augustus shrugged. "Suit yourself."

And in a blink the room spun into chaos.

Before Neelo could even gasp, blood misted into the air. The sound of metal clanging rang out through the darkened room. Neelo screamed as Talhan's sword cut through the air, killing people they had known their entire life.

They grabbed the hilt of the dagger on his hip and Talhan twisted so they could easily pull it free. Neelo turned to find Farros and Thiago charging at them and their chest seized. They dodged Thiago's flying fist and Farros's careless kick, quickly outmaneuvering the two cursed courtiers, but loathe to attack them.

Thiago whirled on them and Neelo cracked him in the nose with their forehead. Thiago went down hard, buying Neelo time to deal with the hazel-eyed courtier to their left.

Neelo booted Farros in the gut, hurtling him into the open wardrobe. They snatched the sash from the curtains and tied the door shut.

Talhan cut through the group like a scythe to wheat, his fighting prowess on full display and wrath in his eyes. But the cursed people he was killing . . .

Another courtier turned on Neelo—Gara, the blond-haired beauty and newest member to their mother's collection. Stumbling backward, Neelo held aloft their blade pointing it out to her in warning but Gara didn't seem to see anything. Her eyes remained fixed on Neelo, no anger in her gaze, only an eerie calm that made Neelo quiver.

Baba Monroe had done it—she'd figured out how to curse the minds of the fae. The blue witches' curse first seen in the Northern Court had come to the South with a vengeance.

"Gara," Neelo warned, knowing it was useless. The beautiful fae didn't hear them. Probably didn't even know her own name.

Neelo threw out a punch, which Gara dodged, leaping forward

to tackle Neelo to the ground. Indecision was Neelo's grave error. They didn't want to kill Gara and instead of keeping the tip of their blade trained to her, they pulled it to the side. When the two of them collided with the ground, the dagger slipped from Neelo's grip and skidded across the floor.

Gara straddled Neelo, clawing and scratching at their face as Neelo lifted their forearms up to defend themself. They bucked their hips, trying to throw Gara off, but the cursed fae attacked with a wild abandon, no sense of self-preservation slowing her relentless attack. Neelo writhed beneath her, trying to shift her as one hand scrambled for something, anything, to use as a weapon. Their fingers brushed against the soft satin of the curtain behind them and they grabbed it into a tight fist. Yanking forth the flowing fabric, they wrapped it around Gara's neck in a vise and pulled. Gara's watery bloodshot eyes bugged, her face turning crimson red as she continued her assault as if she had no realization that she was about to die.

When her eyes fluttered closed, Neelo released her. Gara's body collapsed on the floor, her head cracking against the tiles, but her chest still rose and fell, and Neelo thanked the Gods for small miracles.

Neelo turned to scramble for the dropped dagger and what they saw made them gasp.

Fenrin knelt before Augustus. The Eastern Prince held Neelo's dropped dagger to Fenrin's throat and his hands twisted in Fenrin's hair, pulling his head back and exposing his neck.

"Steady there, Heir of Saxbridge," Augustus said with a wink.

His cigarette was poised between his lips, purple smoke rising in circles and haloing the crown of his head.

Augustus tipped his chin to Talhan who was still battling through a melee of courtiers. "Call off your dog."

"Tal!" Neelo called, not breaking their stare with the Norwood Prince.

The sound of clanking weapons and screams silenced at their command.

"How did you even get in here?" Talhan growled, whirling to Augustus. "We've been watching every entrance."

"For what, the last few days?" Augustus's laugh was filled with violence. "Idiots. You don't really pay much attention to the Queen's courtiers do you?" His grin was pure wickedness, so odd on such a young face. "I've been popping in and out for weeks. Who do you think keeps your friends in such good supply of brew?"

Neelo frowned. "How . . .?"

"Clever little funeral you held for your mother." Augustus nodded, his eyes scanning the carnage around him. "If you hadn't cut off the supplies, we'd have a whole army right now. But no need." His gaze lifted to the still-standing courtiers, frozen like sculptures. "This will do for our purposes."

Talhan's chest rose and fell in heavy pants. "Which are?"

Augustus turned toward the blood-splattered warrior. "To kill Queen Emberspear and to bring the witch king home. Who do you think planted the idea in the Queen's head to summon him here in the first place?"

"The witch *king*?" Cole's voice trembled.

Yanking Fenrin's head back further, Augustus let the dagger dig into Fenrin's neck until a single trickle of blood trailed down his throat. "When the High Priestess called for the smallest seed of the rebellion, I didn't think it would be someone so tall."

"The smallest seed," Neelo whispered. Their eyes shifted from Cole's horrified face to Fenrin's welling eyes. "She wants him to be king of the witches?"

"The witches don't have royalty." Talhan's voice was a lethal rumble. He took a step forward and Augustus pressed the blade tighter to Fenrin's neck.

Fenrin's lips trembled as another trail of blood dripped from the blade.

"They do now," Augustus hissed. "This pathetic thing will be ruler of all witches, just as I will be King of all fae. With the violet witch magic, we will make it so."

"What you speak of is madness," Cole whispered.

Augustus snickered, turning his leering stare on the brown witch. "One king's madness is another king's reckoning. Now. Don't move."

He shook Fenrin's head a little to make sure he was listening, then Augustus released his hair to lift his free hand up to the cigarette held between his lips. "You will let the High Priestess into your mind—"

"No," Fenrin spat.

"You didn't let me finish." Augustus chuckled and took another long drag of purple smoke. "You will let the High Priestess into your mind *or . . .*"

It happened so fast—the movements blurring into one chaotic second. The frozen courtiers all sprang to life, disarming Talhan, one holding each arm as another held his sword tip against his chest. In the same frenzy, Gara jolted to life and wrapped the curtain around Neelo's neck, yanking them backward. Gara waited, squeezing the fabric just enough to warn and not to suffocate. Another courtier held Cole's arm twisted behind his back, all three of them incapacitated in the blink of an eye.

"Or," Augustus said again with quiet venom-laced words. "I kill your friends and then make you watch as I kill these two." Augustus let out a sharp whistle and the door was kicked open.

Two hooded figures were marched in, hands bound behind their backs. They were led in by two more courtiers wearing the colorful veils that protected from swarming insects, their faces obscured. The courtiers kicked out the back of their captives' legs and made them kneel. When their knees cracked to the ground, their hoods were whipped off and the faces of Aneryn and Laris stared back at them.

"No!" Fenrin shouted, thrashing and opening the wound on his neck deeper, his totem pouch bounced erratically off his chest. "Please! No!"

"If you don't want to spill the blood of your lovers"—Augustus pulled the cigarette from his mouth and dropped it to Fenrin's lips— "let her in."

"Fenrin, don't!" Aneryn screamed. Her words were cut short by a swift kick to her back and she fell forward, her cheek smashing into the bloody tile. Laris shrieked, tears streaming thick down her face.

"I'm sorry." Fenrin's sorrowful eyes looked back and forth between the two witches. "I can't exist in a world where you don't." He swallowed.

"I love you two more than you'll ever know." Then he leaned forward . . . and took a long drag on the cigarette.

Laris screamed again, struggling against her bindings to reach him. Fenrin's eyes rolled back and the room froze, Laris's screams silenced, as a soft smile pulled on his lips.

He let out a long sigh and when he looked down again, it wasn't him anymore. "Much better." His voice was solid, thick, and filled with confidence, so unlike his regular tone.

"Fen." Aneryn's whisper broke into a sob.

Fenrin gazed at her with cold indifference as he took the cigarette from Augustus and took another long puff. He rolled his neck as if adjusting to the new body, the new clarity in his mind.

"You're lucky I don't make him kill you," Fenrin said, though they all knew the person speaking was not him. "But I won't. One day you'll come to his side willingly. You'll bow before him as your King, little witchlings. I waited in that earthen tomb for hundreds of years, waiting to sense the true prince in my bloodline again, waiting until the cursed wombs that only bore girls to finally end and see the prophecy of a witch king fulfilled. When that shooting star crossed the bloodred moon, I knew it was time. Mother Moon sent me to find the smallest seed, my youngest descendant, who would be the one. I thought it was the bastard prince for too long, but as I scoured the minds across the realm, I found a boy called Oliver and learned the truth.

"Fenrin was still alive."

Fenrin cackled and gooseflesh rippled over Neelo's skin. "It took me years to hunt down my dagger, all the while sowing discord wherever I went. Scattered our sacred flower wherever it could reach, testing which minds would be open to receive me." Fenrin gazed back to Augustus and the muscle in the prince's jaw tensed under Fenrin's glassy gaze. "Finally, I got a foothold in the Eastern Court." Fenrin surveyed the room one last time, his eyes landing on each of them in turn before he said, "You *will* bow to us. Or the Eastern Kings—both fae and witch alike—will bring a war the likes of which Okrith has never seen." Fenrin tipped his head to Augustus and then bent between Aneryn and Laris to whisper, "Be ready to kneel the next time you see me."

Then, as if in a dream—or, more, a nightmare—Fenrin and Augustus strode out of the room together, two courtiers turning and following them, while the rest remained frozen. The room hung in heavy silence as the door closed. The final snick of the door handle seemed to snap the spell on the cursed courtiers and they all dropped like stones, hanging their heads in their hands, wailing as if being set on fire, the euphoric drug of the spell ripped away and leaving them bereft.

Talhan darted to Neelo, grabbing them and wrapping them in his tight embrace. "Are you hurt?" He held them out at arm's length, scanning for injuries as Neelo shook their head.

A gasp cut through the sounds of pain and they found Aneryn's eyes flashing a brilliant sapphire blue.

"What do you See?" Laris whispered as more tears fell from her eyes. "Can we change this?"

"I—I See Fenrin on a throne." Aneryn's voice cracked. "Mother Moon." She blinked and the vision was gone, her eyes returning to their deep brown. Her broken gaze met Laris's as she whispered, "I think we really lost him."

CHAPTER FORTY-THREE

Remy's sobs cut through the room, sharp as a knife. Neelo stared at the flickering green fae fire where her inconsolable cries carried from. Talhan shifted closer on the bench to Neelo's side. Aneryn and Laris held each other tightly from across the fire. They had gathered the royal families around their fae fires to deliver the news.

Remy's pained sounds of mourning filled the space. Fenrin was her best friend. And Neelo knew she mourned for Heather anew too. Heather, her guardian, who was Fenrin's aunt and protector—all this time and Remy had never known.

It was a long time before anyone could say anything. Ultimately, it was Carys who first spoke. "They still don't have Wynreach. I've talked to my contacts on the council there. We'll move the competition forward. We need to crown a new sovereign and rally against Norwood and Fenrin."

Aneryn tensed across the fire and Remy sobbed harder.

"Agreed," Rua said. Her voice was sharp and calculated. "We will make her pay for what she's done," she vowed and Neelo knew she said it mostly to comfort her sister. "We will bring Fenrin back, I promise you that."

Laris sniffed, hanging her head in her hands. He'd done it to save her and Aneryn, and the guilt of his decision hung over the two of them as clear as a storm cloud. Though the witches couldn't communicate through the fae fire, Neelo felt they should be there. They could glean enough from Talhan's words to understand the direction of the conversation anyway, and with Aneryn's Sight, she'd probably Seen the conversation unfolding already.

"I can't believe Augustus was there the whole time," Bri said. "How did no one notice him?"

"He was covered by the veil that many wear to protect against the biting insects," Talhan said. "Besides, he supplied the witching brew to the Queen and her courtiers too, so he had them under his control." He rubbed the back of his neck. "Even if one of them did recognize him, they would've found themselves without the voice to say so."

"Gods," Lina said. "So it's not only witches who can be cursed. Anyone who breathes in the blooming amethyst can be controlled by the violet witches?"

"Can we please go back to when they just made perfumes and incense?" Bri snarled.

"That was never their real power," Neelo said. "Just a watered-down version of the truth. They use smokes and scents to wield incredible magic. Adisa Monroe can conjure monsters and control minds. She has the same strength as the ancient witches who forged the Immortal Blade, amulet of Aelusien, and the *Shil-de* ring. If her amethyst dagger is equally powerful and she wields it against us . . ." Neelo shuddered.

If that happened, Okrith would be doomed.

They glanced at Cole who sat on the ground, his head resting against the stone wall. His eyes were vacant once more and Neelo prayed he'd still have the will to help them. He'd found the last remainders of his family, only to have his nephew cruelly ripped away again. Neelo couldn't begin to imagine how that must feel.

Aneryn stood and walked to the window, staring out at the calm, mist-cloaked waters of the bay. An unseasonal fog had blown in, hanging over Saxbridge like a burial shroud. Like brew smoke, Neelo thought. The group kept talking, kept planning, but Neelo's eyes were transfixed on Aneryn's quiet, stoic form silhouetted by the window.

The plans were half-hearted: find Adisa Monroe and kill her.

Neelo knew a more intricate plan would need to be worked up, but now wasn't the time. Now was the time for mourning. Dozens of courtiers had died and Fenrin had been taken. Saxbridge was in a horrible upheaval as their withdrawal from the potent brew coursed through the city like a fever. But with Norwood's attack, at least now there was no resistance. No one rebelled in the streets, only grieved and raged in the quiet of their homes. Now that the people knew the brew could control their minds, that the drug could force them to kill, they were willing to give it all up lest they be the puppets to an evil witch. Augustus Norwood's attack had saved many of their lives in that way.

Talhan squeezed Neelo's forearm and they blinked back at the fae fire. The flames had shrunk back down and the hue had ebbed back to its normal orange. The discussion had ended. Neelo knew Talhan would fill them in on whatever else was said.

"Let me talk to her," Neelo whispered, nodding their head to Aneryn.

Talhan gave a sad smile and stood, offering his hand out to Laris. "Come," he said to the green witch. "I think Rish has something for us in the kitchens."

Neelo waited until the two of them had left to stand. They paced over to Aneryn, finding the blue witch squinting out at the horizon. Her face was hard, not a single tear welling in her eyes.

"This world has taken everything from me." Aneryn's voice was distant and vengeful. Neelo didn't dare speak. "I will be entering the games with Carys." Aneryn balled her fists at her sides. "I don't care if witches are *allowed*, I'm entering. With my Sight I might be able to outmaneuver even the fae. Either way, I will be there when *Baba* Monroe makes Fenrin come for the Eastern crown." Her eyes flickered a sapphire blue and she cast her gaze to them. Neelo rocked back on their heels at the force of her stare. "If she wants a war, I will bring it to her."

Aneryn's eyes flickered back to their deep brown and she squeezed them shut, taking a deep steadying breath. Only when she blew all of the air out did she open her eyes again. She didn't speak another word, only dipped her chin to Neelo and strode off.

Neelo turned back to the window, having no doubt that Aneryn would make a formidable opponent in the Eastern games. If Carys didn't win, they hoped Aneryn would.

The flames of the fae fire flashed again, creeping skyward.

"I request to speak with Neelo Emberspear," a deep voice said through the fire.

"I'm already here, Sy," Neelo muttered. They were still furious at him for losing Cole, for not warning them sooner, but even if he had, who knows how long it would've been before they discovered Augustus hiding under their noses. It was unfair, but so what was happening in the world. What was happening to Fenrin.

"What do you want?"

Ersan took a long pause before he responded. "I need to tell you something."

CHAPTER FORTY-FOUR

Fractals of light beamed through the stained glass windows and danced around the council chamber. The cheers and calls of a gathering crowd echoed outside the window as Indi wove around Neelo's legs, coating their tan trousers in gray fur. Of all the images they'd seen through that golden window frame, the assembly of people waiting to greet them is one they'd never fathomed.

"They're early," Neelo muttered, adjusting their sleeves for the hundredth time.

Talhan let out a soft breath and rose out of the leather chair by the door. "They want to get a good view of their new ruler," he said, sauntering up to Neelo.

They stared at themself in the floor-length mirror—a silver crown sat atop their short hair. The emeralds circling the crown's base flickered in their reflection. They wore a dark green cape, trimmed in silver fur, a shined chest plate, and the royal ceremonial sword belted to their hip. Fitted tan trousers and knee high leather boots completed their regal outfit.

"Just looking at you makes me want to drop to my knees," Talhan murmured, circling his hands around Neelo's waist and pulling them back against his chest, careful not to step on their cape.

"That can be arranged later," Neelo said slyly. "First, though, I must present myself to my people." Neelo's head leaned back and rested the heavy edge of their crown against Talhan's shoulder. "Our people," they added with a soft smirk. The crowd cheered again and Neelo tensed. "Do I really need to do this?"

"It will only be a few minutes of waving," Talhan promised.

"Want to bet?"

"I thought you didn't bet."

Neelo shrugged. "Maybe I will sometimes."

Talhan chuckled and squeezed them tighter. "I'll be right behind you."

Neelo shot him a look through the mirror. "You'll be right *beside* me."

"Fine." Talhan raised a placating hand. "Would it help if I told you I have organized something for you?"

Interest piqued, Neelo watched Talhan through the reflection. "What is it?"

Talhan flashed a mischievous grin. "I've converted the western ballroom into a library."

"Really?"

"Who needs three ballrooms when you could have two libraries, right?" Talhan said. "I hope you don't mind I took the liberties; I wanted it to be a surprise but . . ." He glanced up. "What are you thinking about?"

"How I would categorize them," Neelo said sheepishly. They toyed with the tassels hanging from their sword. "By author, by color, by how frequently I reread them?"

The crowd cheered again and Neelo cringed.

"Just think of the library," Talhan reassured them. "I figured we could go there for a break between the balcony address and the reception."

"The reception will take ages," Neelo muttered. They'd settled into their position as Sovereign well enough, but it didn't mean the people side of things wasn't still irksome. Luckily Talhan would be there to do all of the talking and if they needed to follow up with any of the families they would do it through written correspondence. "All of the lieges of the Southern Court are in attendance."

"Apart from Lord Ersan," Talhan corrected.

"He's on his way to Wynreach," Neelo said with a shrug.

Talhan released them and wandered over to the large oak desk against the far wall. "He's really going to compete for the Eastern crown?"

"So it would seem."

Talhan snorted and shook his head. "Just to get his lover back?"

"She's not his lover," Neelo said, watching in the mirror's reflection as Talhan lifted his head with a puzzled expression. "She's his Fated."

Talhan's mouth fell open. "No fucking way."

"I thought you knew."

"How is that even possible?" Talhan's voice rose an octave. "How is he not running after her right now? How . . . Gods, what a mess."

"Indeed."

"I hate even thinking about it," Talhan muttered. "To be separated from your Fated like that."

"It won't happen to us." Neelo softened. "You're mine, Talhan Catullus."

Talhan's cheeks dimpled and he pulled open the desk drawer. "I have something for you."

"You mean besides a library."

"Yes." He lifted out a parcel wrapped in fabric painted with little stencils of the *amasa* tree. "A coronation present."

"You didn't have to."

"There are many things I don't have to do, but do them because I want to see that look on your face." And those words alone were enough to make Neelo happier than they'd been in a long, long time. Talhan paced over, bouncing on his toes more than usual and Neelo knew he was nervous. They quirked their brow and took the present from him. Pulling the satin ribbon, Neelo slowly opened the gift as Talhan anxiously rubbed his hands together.

"What is this?" Neelo whispered, taking a step toward him.

"I made you something," Talhan said.

Neelo's mouth fell open as the fabric fell away revealing a dark green book. They smoothed their hand over the cover, the texture sending tingles down their arms.

Their heart skipped a beat as their eyebrows shot up. "You *wrote* me a book?"

"What do you give someone who has read every book in their library?" Talhan's warm words whispered across Neelo's cheek. "A brand-new story to read. My story."

"This . . . this is . . ." Tears welled in Neelo's eyes. Never had they ever felt more understood, more loved. "How?"

"Rish helped me with the first few chapters," Talhan said. "It got a bit easier with practice. It's not finished yet, but, I thought we could finish it together."

A tear traced down Neelo's cheek, knowing how hard he probably worked to get these words out. Talhan wiped away their tear with his knuckle. "Is this what she brought back from Arboa for you?"

Talhan grinned. "Yes."

"You've been writing it this whole time? For me?"

"Yes." His voice dropped to a whisper. He took another tentative step and reached for their hand. "I'm hoping these tears mean you like it?"

Neelo let out a sound that was half laugh, half sob. "It's perfect."

"You haven't even read it."

"It from you. From your heart and mind. For *me*." They looked up at him. "It's perfect.

"Look at the dedication," Talhan urged.

Neelo flipped open the book to the first page, squinting through teary eyes to read the dedication:

Neelo Emberspear, Sovereign of the Southern Court and ruler of my heart. Will you marry me?

Neelo looked up as Talhan dropped down on one knee, holding aloft a band of giant emeralds and curving silver leaves.

"I picked this out when I was thirteen." He chuckled, his thumb stroking the silver *amasa* leaves. "The Fates must have known before I did." His eyes welled as his cheeks stained a dark shade of red. "It may be a little over the top."

"No," Neelo whispered. "I love it. I thought marriage was already a given since we are Fated . . ."

"I'm not asking the Fates, I'm asking you and your answer is the only one I want or need." Talhan swallowed and held the ring higher. "From the moment I met you, you stole my every waking thought and filled my dreams. You're the first person I want to speak with every morning and the last person I want to see before I go to sleep. You make me feel brave and real and vulnerable and smart and all the things that no one else sees in me." Talhan's eyes welled. "I think you're the only person who really sees all of me."

"I do," Neelo whispered. "I see you, your wit and cunning, your secret smile that hides beneath the charm and swagger. I know the depths of your heart. The Fates may have woven our lives together but it is I with a clear mind and heart that chooses you. You make *me* brave and confident and joyful. You shine your bright light into every shadowed part of my soul."

Talhan wiped his knuckle beneath his eyes. "Is that a yes then?"

"Yes." Neelo beamed as Talhan shot to his feet and wrapped them up in a tight embrace. They buried their head into his neck, holding him just as tightly. "I can't believe you wrote me a whole book."

Talhan kissed the side of their head. "If I could, I'd ink your name on my soul." He slid the ring on their finger, his other hand sliding up to the nape of their neck and pulling them into a slow kiss. His hand snaked around their waist and pulled them in flush against his chest.

The cheers of the crowd beyond the balcony swelled as if in unknowing chorus to the celebration within their heart.

"I think it's time," Talhan murmured against their lips.

"One chapter first," Neelo whispered, lifting up the book in their hands.

"One." Talhan twisted the ring on their finger so the emeralds faced up, his other hand idly stroking down their back. "Read it to me."

DRAMATIS PERSONAE

Remini (Remy) Dammacus, fae with red witch magic, Queen of the High Mountain Court, Fated to Hale Norwood, sister to Rua

Ruadora (Rua) Dammacus, fae with red witch magic, Queen Consort of the Northern Court, Fated to Renwick Vostemur, sister to Remy, wielder of the Immortal Blade

Hale Norwood, fae, King Consort of the High Mountain Court, illegitimate prince of the Eastern Court, believed to be son of Gedwin Norwood but disproven, raised as the step-brother to Augustus Norwood, mother Kira Ashby

Gedwin Norwood, fae, deceased King of the Eastern Court

Augustus Norwood, fae, prince of the Eastern Court, youngest son of Gedwin Norwood, ally to Adisa Monroe

Abalina (Lina) Thorne, fae, Queen of the Western Court, Fated to Bri

Briata (Bri) Catullus, fae, Queen Consort of the Western Court, Fated to Lina, twin sister to Talhan Catullus, nicknamed the Twin Eagles or Golden Eagle when alone, member of Hale's crew

Talhan Catullus, fae, twin of Bri, nicknamed the Twin Eagles or Golden Eagle when alone, member of Hale's crew

Carys Hilgaard, fae, one of Hale's crew, childhood friend of Neelo

Neelo Emberspear, fae, Heir of Saxbridge, only child to Vitra Emberspear

Vitra Emberspear, fae, Queen of the Southern Court, mother to Neelo

Renwick Vostemur, fae and part blue witch, King of the Northern Court, Fated to Rua, son of Hennen Vostemur

Hennen Vostemur, fae, deceased King of the Northern Court, father to Renwick, ordered the Siege of Yexshire and the annihilation of red witches

Cole Doledir, brown witch healer, former head healer to the Western Court Queen

Adisa Monroe, immortal ancient violet witch, searching for her youngest heir to take over Okrith as King of the witches

Heather, deceased brown witch healer, surrogate mother figure to Remy and Fenrin

Fenrin, brown witch healer, head healer to the High Moutain Court

Rish, green witch, personal witch attendant to Neelo Emberspear

Red Witches, power of animation

Blue Witches, power of Sight

Green Witches, power of growing plants and making delicious food

Brown Witches, healers

Violet Witches, power to control smoke, scents, and incenses

ACKNOWLEDGMENTS

First and foremost, I want to thank all my queer friends and mentors who have walked with me through this journey of self-discovery and encouraged me to share more of myself in my stories. This book is for all of us who wished we could be the main characters and never saw ourselves in fantasy before. I hope you feel seen too!

Thank you to my amazing family for supporting me during this last whirlwind year! It's certainly been an adventure moving countries and writing at the same time. Thank you to my amazing husband and gorgeous children for your patience, support, and encouragement during the writing of this book. I love the life we've built together and love you to the moon and back.

Thank you to my Mountaineers for celebrating my books both online and out in the world. You are the most amazing group of readers! The best mountains to climb are fictional ones xx

Thank you to my Patreon members for supporting me and pushing the direction of my writing in amazing ways. I love the novellas we create together! I deeply appreciate each and every one of you! A very special thank you to Linda D, Marissa A, Nicole D, Leslie D, Traci O, Amy P, Charlotte B, Ciara M, Drea D, Hannah N, Maggie J, Shanda E, Virginia P, Kelly, and Sarah!

ACKNOWLEDGMENTS

To my writer friends, thank you for lifting me up through the writing of this book. Thank you, Kate, for being my book wifey and for always having my back. Thank you to my Welly writing friends, Anne, Moisy, and Rachael, for filling my creative cup and making this writer life a joyful one.

Thank you to Sabrina and Kate for keeping Team A.K. going. I so appreciate all of the work you do!

Thank you to Sacha Black for encouraging this little book rebellion. I'm so grateful to have had your little encouragements in my ear telling me to publish the queer story of my heart.

Thank you to my amazing agent, Jessica Watterson at SDLA, for supporting my stories and publishing journey. I love working with you and look forward to many more bookish adventures in the future!

Thank you to the whole Harper Voyager team: US, UK, NZ, AUS, and all over the world. It has been a pleasure working with you all on this book. Thank you to my amazing team for championing this series and supporting diverse stories. A big thank you to my editor, David Pomerico, for believing in this book and helping make Neelo's story shine!

Thank you to the best dog in the world, Ziggy, for lying on top of me when I got stressed out writing this book. You are the cutest weighted blanket. And thank you to the Australian sunshine for pulling me through the dark days. If you've read this far into the acknowledgements, go cuddle your pet or stand in a sunbeam for a little while for me xx

Explore a new world from A.K. Mulford in . . .

A River of Golden Bones

Fall 2023

A RIVER OF GOLDEN BONES

We raced into the silent hall, shoving through a wall of darkness. Trails of smoke swirled from snuffed out candles. Heavy clouds obscured the windows, leaving only the eerie green glow haloing one figure.

Sawyn, sorceress and unlawful ruler of Olmdere.

She was surprisingly young, appearing to be even younger than me, even though the first stories of her were from when my parents first met many decades ago. She had a tall slender posture with smooth skin as pale as starlight and blood red hair. Her eyes glowed an unearthly green as flickering green magic seeped from her. Luminous tendrils of power reached out like tentacles toward the cowering crowd. Her obsidian robes floated on an invisible breeze as she slowly stepped toward a person at the far end of the hall.

Everyone crouched and shielded their eyes apart from the object of her attention, frozen in a trance in front of her.

Briar.

My sister's eyes filled with light, a shimmering vicious green. Briar's expression was utterly vacant as she lifted her hand out to Sawyn.

A scream tore through my chest and I unsheathed my dagger,

blindly running. Grae charged forward by my side. Sawyn looked over her shoulder, her thin brow arching into a peak. With a flick of her hand as if shooing a fly, we flew across the room. My stomach lurched. That iridescent magic circled my legs and wrists, slamming me into the unyielding stone wall and pinning me there. I thrashed against her bindings, but they did not budge.

Sawyn let out a throaty laugh. Her voice was elegant and deep, like the woody notes of a lute. "Your servants have more spine than you, Nero." She laughed, darting a glare to where the king hid behind his throne.

Servant. She didn't even know I was a Wolf, let alone the child of her sworn enemies. Her ghostly eyes scanned me from the muddied hem of my plain brown tunic to the amber stone hanging from my neck. "A protection stone." Her eyebrows lifted in amusement. "We shall see."

She turned her attention back to Briar, whose hand froze in midair, waiting for Sawyn to return. Desperately flailing, I tried to break my restraints as I bellowed my voiceless screams. Whatever magic held me to the wall had silenced me. The harder I strained, the more my eyes blackened.

I darted pleading glances around the room to the pack, but not a single one moved.

Cowards! I wanted to scream. If they all charged forward at once, they could overtake her. Her magic couldn't keep them all at bay. Would they have fought if it was their king standing before the sorceress? But Briar wasn't their leader, only a token, a symbol, and a symbol wasn't worth dying for. I thrashed against my magical bindings. Why wasn't the king giving orders? Why wasn't he even trying to save her?

In that moment, I wondered if my father had felt the same way before he died. It was like a strange familiarity of a memory that wasn't my own. We'd lived this moment before—Sawyn striking down the Gold Wolf line, and the other Wolf packs doing nothing to stop it. King Nero had been there the night of my birth. Had he cowered behind his throne then too? I was certain I knew the answer. It highlighted all the more the lies he told, the facade of a life he built. Welcoming his new Gold Wolf daughter was nothing more than show. Once again, the Silver Wolves would not lift a finger to help my pack.

Sawyn ignored my voiceless screams as she took Briar's hand and flipped her palm up. With one long, sharpened fingernail, she traced a symbol on Briar's palm.

"Tell me," Sawyn purred. "Who is your one true love?"

Without looking, Briar lifted her free hand and pointed into the darkness.

"Ha! Come." The sorceress laughed as Maez walked forward, eyes filled with that same hypnotic glow. "So not your prince, after all." She grinned up at the empty throne and the king behind it. "I suppose my magic was wrong, Nero. I thought a Marriel Princess was the mate of your son . . ." She sneered over her shoulder at Grae, who remained pinned to the stone beside me. She didn't even bother to look back at me—the Marriel Princess who was his Fated mate.

"All the better for me." Sawyn snickered. With a flick of her hand, the throne toppled over, revealing more of King Nero's hunched figure. "You will never have a claim on Olmdere, Nero. Your lust for gold has made you too brash, but you're nothing more than weak, pathetic. Who was the last Wolf king who actually deserved his throne? I bet we've lost his name to time. This little Gold Wolf will serve as a reminder of who the true power on the continent is. If you do not wish to befall the same fate as her, you will stay out of my kingdom."

With that promise, she pricked her fingernail into Briar's finger and held up a single droplet of blood. Casting her glowing eyes to Briar, she commanded, "Sleep" and Briar dropped like a stone.

My voice shredded as I watched my sister fall, blood vessels bursting in my eyes.

"I will be taking your niece with me," Sawyn declared, grabbing Maez by the upper arm. "Just in case you get any ideas about breaking this curse." Spots clouded my vision as the tendrils of magic retracted. "All that you have, Nero, is because I allowed it. Remember that."

Darkness pulled in on Sawyn, and, with a whoosh of air, she and Maez vanished.

The moment they disappeared, the magic pinning me to the wall snapped. I collided with the ground, my head cracking on the hard stone. I faintly heard Grae screaming my name over the roar of rushing blood in my ears. The scent of earth and smoke circled me as the darkness pulled me under.

ABOUT THE AUTHOR

A.K. Mulford is a bestselling fantasy author and former wildlife biologist who swapped rehabilitating monkeys for writing novels. She/they are inspired to create diverse stories that transport readers to new realms, making them fall in love with fantasy for the first time, or, all over again. She now lives in Australia with her husband and two young human primates, creating lovable fantasy characters and making ridiculous TikToks (@akmulfordauthor).

THE HIGH MOUNTAIN COURT
THE FIVE CROWNS OF OKRITH, BOOK 1

Full of romance, intrigue, magic, and passion, the first book of The Five Crowns of Okrith—the thrilling TikTok sensation from A.K. Mulford—*The High Mountain Court* begins the journey of the fugitive red witch Remy as she fights to reclaim her kingdom and discover what's inside her heart.

THE WITCHES' BLADE
THE FIVE CROWNS OF OKRITH, BOOK 2

The second powerful novel in the Five Crowns of Okrith fantasy series brings us into a new part of the world as the fae princess Rua joins forces with a truly unlikely ally—all with the same romance and adventure readers have come to expect from A.K. Mulford's viral sensation!

THE ROGUE CROWN
THE FIVE CROWNS OF OKRITH, BOOK 3

The action moves west in A.K. Mulford's romantic, action-packed epic fantasy series, The Five Crowns of Okrith, as young fae warrior Bri investigates the murder of her queen while protecting the beautiful princess she may be falling for.

HARPER Voyager
An Imprint of HarperCollins*Publishers*

Discover great authors, exclusive
offers, and more at HC.com.